CRUSH
DEPTH

wm

WILLIAM MORROW

An Imprint of HarperCollins*Publishers*

JOE BUFF

CRUSH
DEPTH

HarperCollins books may be purchased for educational, business, or sales promotional use. For information please write: Special Markets Department, HarperCollins Publishers Inc., 10 East 53rd Street, New York, NY 10022.

FIRST EDITION

Designed by Bernard Klein

Printed on acid-free paper

Library of Congress Cataloging-in-Publication Data

Buff, Joe.
Crush depth / by Joe Buff.—1st ed.
p. cm.
ISBN 0-06-000964-0
1. Nuclear warfare—Fiction. 2. Submarine warfare—Fiction. 3. Submarines
(Ships)—Fiction. 4. Nuclear submarines—Fiction. I. Title.
PS3552.U3738 C78 2002
813'.6—dc21   2002022821

02 03 04 05 06   QW   10 9 8 7 6 5 4 3 2 1

In honored memory of the crew of the Russian nuclear submarine Kursk. *They may once have been our enemies, and their country might or might not now be our friend, but they were submariners.*

Where unrecorded names and navies rust, and untold hopes and anchors rot; where in her murderous hold this frigate earth is ballasted with bones of millions of the drowned; there, in that awful water-land, there was thy most familiar home.

—Herman Melville, *Moby-Dick*

Acknowledgments

The research and professional assistance which form the nonfiction technical underpinnings of *Crush Depth* are a direct outgrowth and continuation of those for *Thunder in the Deep* and *Deep Sound Channel*. First, I want to thank my formal manuscript readers: Melville Lyman, commanding officer of several SSBN strategic missile submarines, and now director for special weapons safety and surety at the Johns Hopkins Applied Physics Laboratory; Commander Jonathan Powis, Royal Navy, who was navigator on the fast-attack submarine HMS *Conqueror* during the Falklands crisis; Lieutenant Commander Jules Steinhauer, USNR (Ret.), World War II diesel boat veteran, and carrier battle group submarine liaison in the early Cold War; retired senior chief Bill Begin, veteran of many "boomer" strategic deterrent patrols; and Peter Petersen, who served on the German navy's *U-518* in World War II. I also want to thank two navy SEALs, Warrant Officer Bill Pozzi and Commander Jim Ostach, for their feedback, support, and friendship.

A number of other navy people gave valuable guidance: George Graveson, Jim Hay, and Ray Woolrich, all retired U.S. Navy captains, former submarine skippers, and active in the Naval Submarine League; Ralph Slane, vice president of the New York Council of the Navy League of the United States, and docent of the *Intrepid* Museum; Ann Hassinger, research librarian at the U.S. Naval Institute; Richard Rosenblatt, M.D., formerly a medical consultant to the U.S. Navy; and Commander Rick Dau, USN (Ret.), Operations Director of the Naval Submarine League.

Additional submariners and military contractors deserve acknowledgment. They are too many to name here, but standing out in my mind are pivotal conversations with Commander Mike Connor, at the time C.O. of USS *Seawolf,* and with Captain Ned Beach, USN (Ret.), a brilliant writer and one of the greatest submariners of all time. I also want to thank, for the guided tours of their fine submarines, the officers and men of USS *Alexandria,* USS *Connecticut,* USS *Dallas,* USS *Hartford,* USS *Memphis,* USS *Salt Lake City,* USS *Seawolf,* USS *Springfield,* USS *Topeka,* and the modern German diesel submarine *U-15.* I owe "deep" appreciation to everyone aboard the USS *Miami,* SSN 755, for four wonderful days on and under the sea.

Similar thanks go to the instructors and students of the New London Submarine School and the Coronado BUD/SEAL training facilities, and to all the people who demonstrated their weapons, equipment, attack vessels, and aircraft at the amphibious warfare bases in Coronado and Norfolk. Appreciation also goes to the men and women of the aircraft carrier USS *Constellation,* the Aegis guided missile cruiser USS *Vella Gulf,* the fleet-replenishment oiler USNS *Pecos,* the deep-submergence rescue vehicle *Avalon,* and its chartered tender the *Kellie Chouest.*

First among the publishing professionals who influenced my work is my wife, Sheila Buff, a nonfiction author with more than two dozen titles in birdwatching and nature, wellness and nutrition. Then comes my literary agent, John Talbot, who lets me know exactly what he likes or doesn't like in no uncertain terms. Equally crucial is my editor at William Morrow, Jennifer Fisher, always very accessible and remarkably perceptive on how to improve my manuscript drafts. Lastly, appreciation goes to my friend and fellow author Captain David E. Meadows, USN; and to Lee Glick, second lieutenant in the Civil Air Patrol and volunteer firefighter.

Note from the Author

World events of the last century or more have proven one thing repeat-edly: It is very difficult to predict the nature of the next big war to em-broil America and our Allies. But from World War I to World War II to the Cold War and beyond, the tremendous importance of submarines has always been clear.

Since their inception, in every era, submarines rank among the most advanced weapons systems, and the most advanced benchmarks of technology and engineering achieved by the human race. Stunning feats of courage by their crews, of sacrifice and endurance, loom large on the pages of history.

The tools and techniques of undersea warfare are constantly evolv-ing. Development will continue, rendered more urgent by the Anti-Terrorist War. With the U.S. Navy's *Seawolf* class, new sonar systems, called wide-aperture arrays, have revolutionized target searching and fire control. Advanced SEAL Delivery System minisubs, to covertly de-ploy Special Warfare commandos in the forward battle area, are opera-tional. Remote controlled Unmanned Undersea Vehicles and Unmanned Aerial Vehicles, operated from parent nuclear subs, form an essential part of the Pentagon's acquisition plans.

Equipment for scuba diving in very deep water, for combat and salvage and espionage, is always pushing the envelope. Actual capabilities are closely guarded by the military, but it is known that people have walked on the bottom at three thousand feet.

Ever improved quieting, and highly secret ways to reduce a submarine's nonacoustic signature (thermal and chemical traces, wake turbulence, etc.), transform the meaning of stealth. All these forces of change drastically reshape how undersea warfare will be fought—and whoever controls the ocean's depths controls its surface, and thus controls much of the world.

Studies are underway on using exotic hull materials to increase submarine operating depth. Alumina casing, a ceramic composite much stronger than steel, was declassified by the Navy after the Cold War. Someday, when the need grows compelling enough, vast areas of the ocean's floor will become a high-tech battleground for front-line manned fast attack subs and boomers, and for their smaller robotic proxies.

To some questions about the future of national defense, obtaining correct answers will be crucial to the fate of democracy and freedom: Which gaps in our security posture could be exploited in years to come, by some shrewd, aggressive new Evil Empire or Axis? From what quarter might the next surprise attack fall? What sacrifices and feats of courage will America need, to prevail in the Next Big War? Perhaps the only certain thing is that submarines, and their heroic crews, will play a vital part.

Joe Buff
February 14, 2002
Dutchess County, New York

Prologue

In mid-2011, Boer-led reactionaries seized control in South Africa in the midst of social chaos and restored apartheid. In response to a U.N. trade embargo, the Boer regime began sinking U.S. and British merchant ships. Coalition forces mobilized, with only Germany holding back. Troops and tanks drained from the rest of Western Europe and North America, and a joint task force set sail for Africa—into a giant, coordinated trap.

There was another coup, in Berlin, and Kaiser Wilhelm's great-grandson was crowned, the Hohenzollern throne restored after almost a century. Ultranationalists, exploiting American unpreparedness for all-out war, would give Germany her "place in the sun" at last. A secret military-industrial conspiracy had planned it all for years, brutal opportunists who hated the mediocre silliness of the European Union as much as they resented America's smug self-infatuation. The kaiser was their figurehead, to legitimize the New Order. Coercion by the noose won over citizens not swayed by patriotism or the sheer onrush of events.

This Berlin-Boer Axis had covertly built small tactical atomic weapons, the great equalizers in what would otherwise have been a most uneven fight—and once again America's CIA was clueless. The Axis used these low-yield A-bombs to ambush the Allied naval task force under way, then destroyed Warsaw and Tripoli. France surrendered at once, and Continental Europe was overrun. Germany won a strong beachhead in North Africa, while the South African army drove hard toward them to link up.

Germany grabbed nuclear subs from the French, and advanced diesel submarines from other countries. Some were shared with the Boers. A financially supine Russia, supposedly neutral yet long a believer in the practicality of limited tactical nuclear war, sold weapons to the Axis for hard cash. Most of the rest of the world stayed on the sidelines, biding their time out of fear or greed or both.

American supply convoys to starving Great Britain are being decimated by the modern U-boat threat, in another bloody Battle of the Atlantic. Tens of thousands of merchant seamen died in the Second World War, and the casualty lists grow very long this time too.

America herself depends both militarily and economically on vulnerable shipping lanes across the vast Pacific Ocean, to neutral Asia and the Persian Gulf. If these shipping lanes are cut, the U.S. will have no choice but to recognize Axis gains and sue for an armistice: an Axis victory. America and Great Britain each own one state-of-the-art ceramic-hulled fast-attack sub—such as USS Challenger, capable of tremendous depths—but Germany and South Africa own such vessels too.

Now, in February 2012, high summer in the Southern Hemisphere, the U.S. is on the defensive everywhere, and democracy has never been more threatened. In this terrible new war, with the midocean's surface a killing zone, America's last, best hope for enduring freedom rests with a special breed of fearless undersea warriors. . . .

Ten years in the future

In the Indian Ocean, east of South Africa, aboard the Boer ceramic-hulled nuclear submarine *Voortrekker*

In the cramped and crowded control room, everyone was quiet. It was dark, to stay in sync with nighttime high above the ship, up on the monsoon-tossed surface. First Officer Gunther Van Gelder breathed. The air was stale—the fans were stopped for greater stealth. Jan ter

Horst sat just to his left, in the center of the compartment. Van Gelder could see well enough by the glow of instruments and console screens, but he did not have the nerve to look directly at his captain now. Ter Horst's physical presence overwhelmed him. Van Gelder knew ter Horst too well. He knew ter Horst would be gloating.

"Dead men afloat," ter Horst said. With a finger he delicately traced the data windowed on his command workstation display, the noise signature of the enemy submarine. The line on the sonar waterfall grew gradually brighter. "Coming right at us, Gunther. They don't even realize we're here."

"Yes, Captain," Van Gelder said. At times like this it was best to just agree with the man. "Range now twenty thousand meters." Just over ten nautical miles. *Voortrekker* was aimed directly at their victim, moving very slowly, to hide. "Seehecht unit in tube one is ready to fire, sir. Tube one prepared in all respects."

The Seehecht torpedoes used conventional high-explosive warheads, nothing fancy. They were made by South Africa's Axis partner in war, resurgent Imperial Germany. Ter Horst's target, a *Collins*-class diesel sub, hardly rated one of *Voortrekker*'s homegrown nuclear weapons, tipped with trusty Boer uranium-235; the Royal Australian Navy's *Collins* boats were homegrown too, built in the 1990s, and never quite lived up to the Aussies' hopes. Van Gelder knew they were noisy, even on batteries, and their sensor performance was poor. Losses from eight months of limited tactical nuclear fighting on half the world's oceans forced the Allies to put every available warship into the field.

Dead men floating, indeed, Van Gelder thought. Some of the *Collins* subs had coed crews. Van Gelder didn't know if this one did. It didn't matter.

"We'll let them get just a little closer," ter Horst said. "Less time for them to pull evasive maneuvers that way." He sounded smug, not cautious.

"Understood." Van Gelder waited. At action stations, as first officer—executive officer—his job was to oversee target tracking, done mostly by sonar, and weapons, including *Voortrekker*'s cruise missiles and mines. He told himself that given ter Horst's war record so far, this *Collins* boat was minor prey.

But today was just a shakedown cruise. *Voortrekker* was fresh from underground dry dock, from two months of hurried round-the-clock repairs and upgrades. This sortie was mostly intended to check that everything worked. It was typical of ter Horst to make his battleworthiness check by plunging straight into mortal combat, against an inferior foe.

"Range now sixteen thousand meters," Van Gelder recited.

"Very well," ter Horst said. "Wait."

Van Gelder went back to waiting, and to thinking. Van Gelder and ter Horst had a good relationship, as such things went. Ter Horst saw Van Gelder as his protégé, his number one in important ways. He'd been ter Horst's senior aide for the tribunal back in Durban, South Africa—the investigation, which ter Horst chaired, of the mysterious mushroom cloud north of the city in early December. The mushroom cloud that obliterated a secret Axis biological weapons lab. The mushroom cloud in which USS *Challenger* was implicated, somehow, along with traitors in the Boer command infrastructure . . . perhaps.

The military tribunal wasn't over yet. After this shakedown cruise, *Voortrekker* would return to the hardened sub pens cut into the bluff near downtown Durban. Safely inside, they'd resolve any mechanical problems remaining—there always were some, after a long stretch in the yard. Then Van Gelder's workload would redouble, as before: endless quality control inspections on the ship, and crew refresher training—plus the lengthy interrogations of the tribunal. The final findings would undoubtedly lead to executions, grisly hangings broadcast on national TV, one more burden on Van Gelder's troubled soul. Right now, this little stretch under way was, if anything, a respite. Van Gelder could focus on the real war effort alone, and leave the politics and infighting of the land temporarily behind. The land had never made Van Gelder happy. It was the sea, going down into the sea, being one with the sea, that he loved.

"Range to target?" ter Horst snapped.

"Er, range now ten thousand meters, Captain." Five nautical miles.

"Very well, Number One. Tube one, target unchanged, the *Collins* boat. Update firing solution, and *shoot*." The weapon dashed through the sea.

Van Gelder had programmed the unit to follow a dog-leg approach to the target, to sneak at the *Collins* from the side and disguise *Voortrekker*'s location. Seehechts could be used by any sub in the Axis inventory. No one would guess *Voortrekker* fired the shot. Van Gelder watched his data screens as the one-sided drama began to unfold.

At last the target reacted. The *Collins* altered course and picked up speed. She launched a decoy, and then noisemakers. Van Gelder's fire-control technicians, arrayed at consoles along the control room's port bulkhead, handled the wire-guided Seehecht. *Voortrekker*'s special passive sonars looked up through the ocean-temperature layers and pinned the real target against the monsoon's wave action and rain noise. The *Collins* had nowhere to hide.

"Contact on acoustic intercept!" the sonar chief shouted.

"Target has pinged on active sonar," Van Gelder said. "Echo suppressed by out-of-phase emissions." With *Voortrekker*'s advanced acoustic masking, she was effectively invisible to such a substandard opponent.

The *Collins* lived long enough to fire two torpedoes in retaliation, but they were shooting blind, tearing in the wrong direction. Van Gelder knew this battle amounted to cold-blooded murder.

"Enemy torpedoes pose no threat to *Voortrekker*," he stated, "even if they carry tactical nuclear warheads." Because seawater was so rigid and dense, torpedo A-bomb warheads had to be very small—a kiloton or less—or the boat that used them could be hoist by its own petard. These yields were a fraction of the weapons America dropped on Hiroshima and Nagasaki, and were a mere ten-thousandth of the multimegaton hydrogen bombs tested in the atmosphere in the worst days of the Cold War. Yet Axis tactical atom bombs were still a thousand times more powerful than any conventional high-explosive torpedo—which was why the Axis used them, and which forced the Allies in self-defense to use them too.

As if to reemphasize the *Collins* boat's impotence, ter Horst ordered the helmsman to come to all stop.

"Weapon from tube one has detonated!" a fire-control technician shouted—the data came back through the guidance wire at the speed of light.

"Sonar on speakers," ter Horst ordered.

A second later Van Gelder heard the sharp metallic *whang* of the torpedo hit. The blast echoed off the surface and the sea floor, mixing on the sonar speakers with a two-toned roar: air forced into the *Collins's* ballast tanks as her crew desperately tried an emergency blow, plus water rushed through the gash in her hull at ambient sea pressure.

The sea pressure won. The target lost all positive buoyancy, and soon fell through her crush depth. The hull imploded hard.

The eerie rebounding *pshoing* of crushed metal hitting crushed metal was louder than the torpedo hit. Van Gelder knew any crew still living would have been cremated as the atmosphere compressed and heated to the ignition point of clothing and flesh.

"Excellent," ter Horst said, almost as an anticlimax. "Helm, steer one eight zero." Due south. "Increase speed. Make revs for top quiet speed." Thirty knots.

The helmsman acknowledged.

Van Gelder stood and paced the line of sonarmen on his right, to make extra sure there were no threats as *Voortrekker* cleared the area.

"Number One," ter Horst said a few minutes later, "we stay at battle stations. You have the deck and the conn."

"Aye aye, sir. Maintain present course?"

"No, put us on one three five."

"Southeast?" That was *away* from Durban, home base, which was southwest.

"I want to line us up with the covert message hydrophone in the Agulhas Abyssal Plain. I'm retiring to my cabin to compose a message for higher command."

"Aye aye, Captain." *What was going on now?* Well, at least Van Gelder always liked having the deck and conn. He was in almost total control of the ship, as much as anyone could be without being the captain.

Ter Horst returned a short time later with a data disk in his hand. "This requires your electronic countersignature." He gave Van Gelder the disk.

Van Gelder placed it in the reader on his console. He eyed what came on the screen. Van Gelder was shocked, and then more shocked. Ter Horst was rendering his final verdicts as chair of the tribunal. The accused were being sentenced to death with no real regard for the evidence—or lack of evidence. The choices of guilty or not guilty seemed based more on whim or blood lust. Van Gelder noticed all of the female suspects were to be hanged. This confirmed Van Gelder's suspicion, that ter Horst actually *liked* watching such executions. Since the condemned were strung up naked, the implications of erotic perversion were obvious.

But there was more. Ter Horst reported his victory over the *Collins* boat, and declared *Voortrekker* combat ready. He waived his planned return to dry dock, and insisted on permission for immediate departure on his next top-secret combat mission.

"But sir," Van Gelder said, "we have dozens of mechanical gripes and work-order exceptions to resolve."

"Don't whine, Gunther. Just sign it, and have the message sent."

Van Gelder opened his mouth to object. Ter Horst cut him short.

"*Don't* spoil a good day for us both. You just countersign, and see that the message is sent."

Van Gelder relayed it to the secure communications room.

"Thank you," ter Horst said exaggeratedly. "I have the conn."

"You have the conn, aye aye." Ter Horst had taken his ship back. *Voortrekker* maintained course and speed, further into the Indian Ocean, and also toward Antarctica.

It took almost an hour for Van Gelder's intercom light to flash. The junior lieutenant in charge of communications had the response from headquarters. It surprised Van Gelder. Ter Horst's tribunal decisions were accepted as is. Obviously, within the Boer power structure, ter Horst was well connected. Van Gelder saw the entire inquest had been a travesty, a purely political show trial. And besides, the television producers in Johannesburg were always hungry for more human meat for the ever-popular gallows show.

But that wasn't all. Higher command had news for ter Horst. USS *Challenger* was conclusively identified as the Allied submarine involved in an attack before Christmas on a stronghold on the German coast. *Challenger* was still laid up for weeks more of battle-damage repairs. And Boer freedom fighter Ilse Reebeck had been spotted as a participant in the Germany raid.

Van Gelder realized ter Horst was also reading the message when ter Horst cursed.

"That *bitch*."

Van Gelder knew that for two years, up until the war, ter Horst and Ilse Reebeck had been lovers. Van Gelder had met her several times, at receptions and banquets. He thought she was sexy and smart, a suitable consort for his captain. Only now, she worked for the other side.

"I'd like to watch *her* squirm at the end of a rope."

Van Gelder blanched, and was glad the red glow of instruments hid his discomfort.

"Now *this* is interesting," ter Horst went on. He was calm again, so calm it scared Van Gelder. "It seems during our own running fight with *Challenger,* her executive officer was in command. Hmmm. Jeffrey Fuller. I don't know him." Ter Horst turned to face Van Gelder. "Ha! That's as if *you* had been fighting me, Gunther."

Van Gelder winced. "Why her XO?"

"Our first torpedoes gave her captain a bad concussion."

Obviously, Van Gelder thought, Axis espionage sources were extremely well informed.

"Good," ter Horst said as he finished reading. "They agree we can begin our next combat mission at once."

Van Gelder hesitated. "Sir, if we're heading into battle against main enemy forces, I do think we need more time for completing maintenance." They'd taken a lot of damage themselves in their duel with *Challenger* back in early December, and not everything was fixed.

"You'll find work-arounds, Gunther. Improvise. I have total faith in you, my friend." Ter Horst turned to the helmsman. "Steer zero nine zero." The helmsman acknowledged.

Ter Horst looked Van Gelder right in the eyes, and smiled his most predatory smile. "Global weather conditions are perfect at the moment. Coordinated timing, and surprise, are everything now."

Van Gelder had to clear his throat. Zero nine zero was due *east.* "Sir, may I inquire, what are our orders, our next destination?"

"No, you may not."

1

Later that day

**Bachelor Officers Quarters,
Naval Submarine Base, New London, Connecticut**

OUTSIDE THE WINDOW, in the post-midnight pitch-blackness, the freezing wind howled and moaned. The wind slashed at the leafless trees on the slope that led down to the river. Now and then, sleet pattered the pane, the tail end of a strong nor'easter that had dumped a foot of snow. Inside the room, a candle glowed in one corner. The ancient steam-heat radiator hissed and dripped. Ilse Reebeck looked down at Jeffrey Fuller. "Do you want me to get off now?"

He met her gaze, with that slightly out-of-focus look in his eyes he always got right after making love. Jeffrey nodded, too sated to speak. Ilse felt him watch her intently as she left the bed. He stayed fully under the covers—she'd noticed since they'd first become intimate on New Year's Eve that he was strangely shy with her about his body, well endowed as he was with muscles and dark curly hair and the scars of an honorable war wound. Ilse was proud of her figure—she gave Jeffrey a last quick profile view and blew out the candle.

She got back in bed in the dark and put one arm across his chest and tried to fall asleep. It was good to lose herself in sex with Jeffrey Fuller, and tune out the rest of the world, but as the immediate ardor subsided she felt sad. Her family was dead, for resisting the old-line Boer takeover, her whole country in enemy hands. She'd been in pitched battle twice behind enemy lines, during tactical nuclear war, and killed and watched teammates be killed. The war was far from over, quite possibly unwinnable. Even the escape of sleep was a mixed blessing, because sleep brought on the nightmares. Nightmares of combat flashbacks, of hurling grenades and bayonet charges and incoming main battle tank fire. Nightmares of relatives hanging. Nightmares of reunions with friends who were decomposed corpses.

If she hadn't been at a marine biology conference in the U.S. when the war broke out, Ilse might well be dead now too, strung up with the rest of them.

The radiator stopped hissing. Jeffrey reached over Ilse for the battery-powered alarm clock on his bedstand. His elbow rubbed her left nipple. "Sorry," he said, but she thought it an odd thing to apologize for, just after making love.

"Zero one hundred," he said. "Right on schedule."

Wartime energy conservation, Ilse thought. The heat was turned off in all base housing every night at one until five in the morning, along with hot water and power.

"Typical U.S. Navy," she said out loud. "If anything, always *prompt.*" Ilse wasn't sure herself whether she meant to be sarcastic. It just came out. Jeffrey didn't respond. He rolled on his side and she rolled on her side so he could press himself against her in a hug. . . .

"You should go back to your room now."

Ilse stirred. She realized she'd fallen asleep like this and a few minutes must have passed.

"No," she told Jeffrey. "I want to stay." The bed was designed for one person, but they were both so used to sleeping on narrow racks in a submarine, the mattress seemed spacious in contrast.

"We have classes in the morning."

Also typical Jeffrey, always thinking ahead, making his plans and his schedules. Must do this, mustn't do that . . . The naval officer in him never really shut down, or turned off or whatever, to simply let him be a person. Even six weeks after they'd both been permanently detached from USS *Challenger*—and were rested now from the rigors of their Germany raid, when Jeffrey was acting captain—he still ran himself with military precision out of sheer habit. He was taking the Prospective Commanding Officers course, and she was going through the Basic Submarine Officers course—though she was technically a civilian, a consultant to the U.S. Navy.

"I'll set the alarm for four-thirty," Ilse said. "Plenty of time to get back to my room before the hallways start to liven up."

"Someone might see you. It's indiscreet."

"It's indiscreet me being here at one in the morning. I have makeup and stuff in my bag. I'll use your bathroom, and I'll have my briefcase, right? Anyone who sees me can think I worked the midnight shift."

"Clever girl."

"I'm not a *girl*. I'm nearly thirty." The thought sometimes frightened her.

"I meant—"

"You don't need to apologize." Ilse knew Jeffrey was no sexist, and she really did care about him. It was just that, well . . . Jeffrey was a great lion in battle, but taken out of purely military functions—like here right now—he wasn't exactly always at his best, socially speaking. He was almost forty, but had spent his entire adult life in navy circles.

Ilse began to doze off again, with her head on Jeffrey's forearm. She felt him squeeze her buttocks gently with his other hand. "Enough is enough," she told him. "It's very late."

She sensed Jeffrey pausing, a pregnant pause in the dark. "Who's better?" he finally said.

"What?"

"Who's better? Him or me?"

"*What?*" Ilse bristled.

"Ter Horst. What's he like? Hung like a horse?" Jeffrey sounded amused at his own little joke, but the amusement was forced.

"Don't be silly." *And please don't spoil the evening for us both.*

"No, I'm serious."

"Really, Jeffrey, there's no comparison." He was definitely a Jeffrey, not a Jeff; Ilse felt no impulse to give him a special nickname. "I knew Jan for more than two years, and you and I have been dating, what? Less than two months. . . . It was before the war and everything. It's a completely different situation."

Jeffrey waited for her to go on. When she didn't, he said, "How long did you know him before, you know, you two started having sex?"

This really annoyed Ilse. He'd said "having sex," not "making love." Ilse had loved Jan once, so blind had she been.

"It's after one in the morning." She knew she sounded cross. She didn't want to hurt Jeffrey's feelings. He was sweet and sincere and giving and other things Ilse liked. But he was a bit reserved in bed compared to Jan. Ilse knew Jeffrey had been engaged once, years ago, and it ended badly. He was estranged from his parents too, though she hadn't yet learned why.

"Jeffrey, do you want me to stay or not?"

His body posture stiffened. He drew a deep breath to say something. Ilse knew they were about to have a fight. The phone on the little desk rang.

"Crap," Jeffrey said.

"Maybe you should answer it." It had rung at midnight, but Jeffrey ignored it then. They were occupied, and he said that at that hour it was surely a wrong number. Now it was ringing again.

Jeffrey got out of bed and felt for the phone in the dark. The room was already cold. A draft got under the blanket, and Ilse shivered and pulled the covers close. Outside the window the storm blustered, but not as strong as before.

"Lieutenant Commander Fuller." Jeffrey spoke firmly into the phone. He paused to listen. He listened for some time.

"Understood." There was a shorter pause. "No, I'll tell her. . . . Yes, I have her extension. I'll do it. Very well." He hung up.

"What was that all about?"

Jeffrey stayed standing, naked in the dark—as a SEAL in younger days, he was desensitized to cold that would make other people's teeth chatter. Jeffrey cleared his throat. "They want us on the first train in the morning to Washington."

Ilse almost groaned. "How come?"

"A debriefing at the Pentagon. More brass desire to hear of our recent adventures."

"*Again?*"

"It's an overnight trip this time. We'll need to pack."

"Why train? That'll be slow."

"No flights available on such short notice. Travel restrictions, Ilse, aviation-fuel shortages . . . There's a war on."

"Don't we deserve a priority?"

"Last-minute changes like that raise eyebrows, draw attention, compromise security. This time we blend with the crowd on mass transit."

"What time's the train?"

"Six-fifteen."

"How do you want to get over there? Shuttle van, or the water taxi?" The local railroad station was on the other side of the river.

"Water taxi. The aide said they'll hold spaces. A messenger'll meet us with our travel documents."

"It'll be *freezing* out on the Thames," Ilse said.

"Yup, but at least we won't miss the train. Have you *seen* the traffic on I-95? . . . I don't trust the bridge. They're still repairing the damage." From a German high-explosive cruise missile raid, before Christmas.

"Won't there be ice on the river, in this weather?"

"The tug can get through fine. The snow's supposed to clear by morning. Colder, but clearing and sunny. A good day for travel."

"Reset the alarm for four, will you? I need time to pack." Ilse heard Jeffrey handling the alarm clock.

"Come back to bed," Ilse said. "Gawd, less than three hours' sleep. Barring more interruptions, that is."

"Business as usual," Jeffrey said. "You can nap on the train." It was a five-hour trip, with the Acela electrified service. They'd be in the Pentagon by noon.

Jeffrey got under the blanket and held Ilse close, and this time didn't ask her awkward questions. Soon, by his deep, steady breathing, she could tell he was asleep.

Ilse thought of the last time she'd made love to Jan, wildly and with carnal abandon, when she still thought she could trust him, before her whole world came unglued. She stared into the dark for a very long time, hating all wars and all warriors.

Next day, on the way to Washington, D.C.

Jeffrey glanced at Ilse snoozing next to him in the window seat. Then he gazed out as the New York City skyline loomed gradually larger. Their train was running late. It was already well past noon, and they were only now approaching Manhattan. Jeffrey was starving—the snack bar car had run out of everything hours ago, in large part because of food shortages nationwide.

After Jeffrey's train entered the railroad tunnel under New York's East River, the lights went out and the engineer braked to a halt. The powerless electric locomotive had to be pulled the rest of the way into Penn Station by a noisy, smelly diesel switching engine. Jeffrey found it strange that in the station, though the trains sitting on every track were dark and empty, the platforms were well lit.

Jeffrey looked up as a conductor came through the car. He told everybody to get off the train. Jeffrey nudged Ilse gently. She stirred.

Like all the other passengers, Jeffrey and Ilse grabbed their coats and luggage and gas-mask satchels, and took the stairs to the waiting room. It was wall-to-wall people, passing rumors and complaining, a continuous babbling din. Every train on the schedule board read DELAYED INDEFINITELY.

The stationmaster came on the loudspeakers. He said the railroad's power and signals and switching systems in the entire northeast had suffered a massive Axis information-warfare attack. It would take hours to restore service. Computer programs had failed in a cascade, and it was complicated to find and then stamp out the viruses and test everything—and safety had to come first. He said that a USO club was in

Times Square, not far. All passengers should report back to the station by 9 P.M.

Jeffrey heard a collective groan from the crowds in the station. No rail disruption this extensive, especially one triggered by the enemy, had happened in the U.S. homeland since the outbreak of the war. It was headline news, and unwelcome news. Jeffrey expected ground travel everywhere—from the nation's capital, through Pittsburgh, Philadelphia, and all the way toward Boston—would be a mess well into tomorrow.

"We need to call in again," Jeffrey said to Ilse. He smiled and tried to sound stoic, to mask his irritation and concern. They should have been at the Pentagon by now.

Jeffrey considered the long lines at the pay phones. "We can probably do better if we find one on the street." They'd been specifically ordered not to bring cell phones, to avoid interception by enemy signals intelligence.

"Can we get something to eat first, Jeffrey? *Please?*"

Jeffrey heard Ilse's stomach rumble. They stood on line at a bagel stand, ate quickly, then agreed to walk to the USO. They were stranded in New York, by Axis hands—and Jeffrey couldn't shake a sense of foreboding.

He was dismayed when they got to Times Square. All the colorful wide-screen TV displays—usually flashy and running all day—were dark, except for a handful of civil defense messages: *Save energy. Watch out for spies. Is that e-mail really necessary?* The sidewalks were half deserted, even taking into account the cold. Many people wore gas masks, though the radiation count today was normal.

A number of people's overcoats were baggy, as if they'd lost a lot of weight since the previous, prewar winter. Now, like the rest of the population, they followed government urgings to wear what they had until it wore out. With imports squeezed to a trickle, and North American manufacturers cranking out uniforms and protective suits, civilian clothes had to take a backseat.

Jeffrey glanced around again at the dearth of people, the shops with closed doors. He turned to Ilse, and tried not to sound too glum. "This war has been death to restaurants and tourism."

But it hadn't dented the vehemence of the area's curbside preachers. Repent your sins before it's too late, the end of the world is nigh, they bellowed to whomever would listen.

"This time," Jeffrey said under his breath, "they may have it right."

He found an unused pay phone that actually worked. When he got off, he told Ilse they'd be expected in Washington tomorrow morning; he realized they'd have to sleep on the train.

They passed a construction site for an office tower. The site was completely quiet: no cement mixers running and no big cranes or hard hats working. The project had been abandoned months ago because of the war—materials and skilled labor were in very short supply. If things got bad enough, Jeffrey knew, the skeleton of the building would be dismantled, to reuse the valuable steel.

By the time they reached the USO club it was too crowded to possibly get in. There was also a long line of teenagers outside the Armed Forces Recruiting Center next door; the draft had been reinstated, but many were volunteering.

"Good material," Jeffrey said as he eyed the teenagers. "Better than we got in peacetime."

Jeffrey didn't tell Ilse what he really thought, that if these kids understood what they were in for—cannon and missile fodder in limited tactical nuclear war—they wouldn't be so eager to get to the fighting. He and Ilse had twice set off small atom bombs on enemy soil out of necessity, obeying severely restrictive rules of engagement it had been Jeffrey's job to enforce. The thought in retrospect horrified him, as did the ever-present risk that the Axis might escalate, even though the enemy had sworn not to be first to use more nuclear weapons in populated areas. Escalation was everyone's worst nightmare, and the damage to the environment in combat zones was dreadful already. Ilse had been sent on that first mission, to South Africa, because her unique mix of technical skills and local knowledge was badly needed there. She did such a good job, the navy sent her on *Challenger* the second time, to Germany.

An MP with a bullhorn brought Jeffrey's mind back to the present. The MP said there was another USO at the top of the Empire State

Building. Jeffrey and Ilse decided to go there. They took an indirect route, to stretch their legs and get some air, since they had plenty of time to kill.

American flags flew everywhere, but many storefronts were vacant and drab. Glancing up at the tall apartment buildings as they strolled by, Jeffrey saw a number of units lacked any curtains or furnishings. For Rent and For Sale signs hung everywhere, looking weather-beaten, forlorn.

One auto dealership Jeffrey and Ilse walked past was converted into an equipment distribution center for home-front survival gear. Through the big showroom windows Jeffrey saw stacks of burn-treatment kits, water-purification tablets, Geiger counters and dosimeters, and piles of freeze-dried food. The original signs on the dealership were gone, but Jeffrey could see their outline against the building. Porsche, Audi, BMW. Not popular brands anymore.

THE people on the streets seemed less aggressive and rude than Ilse imagined New Yorkers to be. Almost no one jaywalked. Taxi horns rarely blared, and very few drivers cursed—there were hardly any private cars around anyway, because of strict gas rationing and appalling prices per gallon.

Instead, there was a feeling of shared defiance against the Axis threat. But beneath this determined exterior Ilse sensed people were gnawed by doubt: *Was* it the right thing to do to stand up to this shocking new enemy, one the CIA as usual hadn't seen coming till much too late? Why *couldn't* America just turn inward, and look out for number one, and leave Europe and Africa festering on the far side of a wide ocean?

Jeffrey and Ilse passed a supermarket. Ilse was disturbed to see a large sign in the window announcing a special on horse meat. Ilse loved horses, and had ridden whenever she could in South Africa. Horses were beautiful creatures, sleek and affectionate and fast, and good ones were smarter than people gave them credit for. The thought of eating horses upset her.

Everything flooded back. Her dead family, the Boer putsch, Ilse's own survivor guilt. Her younger brother especially, whom she loved and whom she'd always felt protective of, left unprotected when he'd needed Ilse most—because she'd been abroad, safe at a *conference.*

Ilse fought hard not to cry, standing there on the sidewalk. Jeffrey tried to comfort her, but she shook him off. She said it was just the freezing wind making tears in her eyes.

THE officers' club of the USO was on the Empire State Building's eighty-fifth floor. Jeffrey led Ilse to the cocktail lounge, large and crowded and noisy. A live band played swing music from World War II.

But Ilse didn't seem in a mood to mingle. She worked her way to the windows. Jeffrey followed. The view was stunning. The setting sun was a cold red-orange blob, fading behind dusky clouds low over New Jersey. The city and the harbor were spread out before them. Looking southeast, toward the ocean, Jeffrey longed wistfully to be under way on a submarine. After his training course in New London, his next assignment would be some fancy-sounding land job—those who even passed the course didn't get a ship right away.

Gradually, the view and the music began to work on Jeffrey. They lifted his spirits and made him feel romantic. The sense of being at war, the excitement and danger of it, heightened this for him. He reached for Ilse's hand. She pulled away.

"I'm not here as your *date,*" she said between clenched teeth. "We're traveling on *business.*"

JEFFREY convinced Ilse to go to the open-air observation deck, one flight up. A yeoman near the elevator lent them parkas from a rack. Ilse saw armed guards by the stairway to a navy communications center on the topmost floors; she figured it used the big antenna on the building's roof.

The yeoman lent them binoculars, for sightseeing. Jeffrey and Ilse went outside. Visibility was excellent and it was freezing—they were over a thousand feet high. By now it was dark, and the observation deck was deserted. The wind howled so strongly they took shelter on the downwind side of the building. Ilse looked straight up. The antenna needle reached another twenty or thirty stories above her head. She watched the tip of the mast sway back and forth in the wind; she got dizzy, and needed to turn away. She saw the tall art-deco Chrysler Building nearby. Its silvery spire came right up to her eye level, a fifth of a mile in the air.

Ilse glanced downwind, toward lower Manhattan. The skyscrapers now had blackout curtains drawn in all the tiny office windows. So did the shorter buildings in the foreground, near Greenwich Village and other residential neighborhoods. All vehicles on the streets had headlights hooded to narrow slits, painted blue. Only every third streetlight was on, and the bulbs were dim red.

A sliver of moon was poised on the eastern horizon over Brooklyn; Jeffrey and Ilse looked at the moon through their binoculars. With all the white, reflective snow on the ground, the moon lit the cityscape nicely. Overhead, the sky was perfectly clear. As her eyes adjusted to the dark, Ilse saw the Milky Way.

She felt badly for snubbing Jeffrey in the cocktail lounge. She reached out for his hand. From all around them air-raid sirens went off.

2

THE MOURNFUL HOWL of the sirens pierced the wind. As Jeffrey watched from the observation deck, streetlights switched off borough by borough. Down below, vehicles stopped and their headlight glows vanished. From upwind, Jeffrey heard a deafening roar. On the runways of Newark Airport, bright blue-violet flames lit off. They moved, faster and faster and up into the sky-—the afterburners of scrambling interceptor jets. A whole squadron, a dozen planes, took to the air and headed out to sea.

The yeoman stuck his head out of the door. "It's real! Get down to shelter!"

"What is it?" Jeffrey shouted back.

"Cruise missiles inbound! Submarine launched! Coming this way! Mach eight!"

"Mach *eight?*" Ilse yelled.

"Come *on!*" the yeoman shouted.

"We're staying," Jeffrey declared.

The yeoman shook his head and disappeared.

"Mach *eight,* Jeffrey," Ilse said. "I thought—"

"They had a handful left, in the supply pipeline."

"Shouldn't we go to the basement? They'll get here very soon."

"And be buried alive in the rubble? Or roasted in the firestorm, or drowned in shit when the sewer mains break?"

"How do you know they'll be nuclear?"

"Ilse, they wouldn't waste those missiles on high explosives. They're Mach *eight*."

"But if one gets through . . ."

"I know. Let's get it up here, then. Quick and clean. Not slow and awful running down to the basement."

Ilse nodded reluctantly as everything sank in. "This is because of us, isn't it, Jeffrey?"

"Yes. The retaliation. The escalation. Now it comes, the Axis revenge. Because of what we did."

Jeffrey silently walked to the very edge of the observation deck, peering through the grilled-in railing for a better view. Ilse followed, not wanting to be alone. The wind battered at them and chilled their faces numb. Jeffrey and Ilse waited to die. Sirens continued to moan like tortured souls.

"They'll use a big one, won't they?" Ilse said.

"Twenty kilotons, at least. Up here I doubt we'll feel much."

"Except guilt," Ilse said.

"Yes," Jeffrey said. "Except guilt. This is happening because of *us*."

Ilse hesitated. "The train problems, that computer attack, this was all part of their plan?"

"Yes. A distraction, I think, and to strand more military people in New York, to add to the high-value body count. . . ." The U-boat must have snuck through under that nor'easter, Jeffrey thought, coordinated timing with the info warfare attack.

"Do you—do you think they know we're here? Is it all really *that* personal?"

Jeffrey sighed. "There's no way we'll ever know. It's possible. . . . It doesn't matter."

On the horizon, in the Atlantic, Jeffrey could see flashes and streaks of light. He knew this would be the outer defenses, ships and naval aircraft, trying to knock down the inbound missiles. But nothing the Allies had could intercept Mach 8 ground-hugging cruise missiles.

Damn it, we should have been at sea on Challenger. *We might have made a difference, stopped this U-boat from launching, by working defense from under the storm. But* Challenger's *laid up in dry dock, because of battle damage suffered on my watch.*

ILSE saw red-orange bursts pepper the dark sky low in the distance, out over the Atlantic. The bursts were frighteningly hard and sudden, military high-explosive blast and fragmentation warheads. Their eerie silence, because the sound needed many seconds to reach her, only heightened her feeling of dread. She tried to see the incoming Axis cruise missiles, but no one knew better than Ilse how stealthy they were, how hard to stop.

A long series of harsh, sharp flashes ranged from right to left, low out over the ocean, then more bursts ran from left to right, seeking targets. There was pulsing glare beyond the horizon, in three different places, then endless salvoes of defensive missiles thrust into the sky from surface ships. Each missile—dozens and dozens of them—rode a brilliant moving point of hot yellow light.

As Ilse watched and waited for the inevitable, more streaks of flame took to the air, this time land-based defensive missiles launched from Sandy Hook, at the outer roadstead of New York Harbor. Another salvo of missiles rose from a ship at sea. Continuous boiling flame marked the launch point, strobing flashes and smoke trails marking each launch. The hard, sharp detonations on the horizon continued. Noise of the explosions began to reach Ilse, a deep rumbling counterpoint to the crying of the wind. The enemy Mach 8 missiles must be drawing close by now.

Heavy antiaircraft guns began to fire from Staten Island and the Meadowlands and Brooklyn, red searing gases belching from their muzzles, their reports unforgiving thuds that pounded Ilse's gut. The shells exploded in midair, more hard and sudden bangs and flashes. More heavy-caliber guns opened fire. Their muzzle discharges stabbed and slashed at the sky. Each shot, then each shell's detonation, lit the scene like infernal flashbulbs. Ilse saw the whole sky fill with fluffy balls of smoke from the flak. Now she smelled the stinking, acrid fumes, brought by the wind. Her eardrums started to ache from the constant punishment.

Antiaircraft missiles launched from Newark and Kennedy airports, and these streaked into the sky. One malfunctioned immediately and crashed on Staten Island. It started a huge fire there, whipped by the unceasing wind. The fire was in an area of residential housing. It spread faster than a man could run.

Still Ilse didn't see the Axis cruise missiles themselves. Smaller automatic weapons opened up, cannon and heavy machine guns ringing the inner harbor. Their muzzles flickered steadily. Their tracers all spewed skyward, red and green, weaving back and forth, adding to the wall of steel and gauntlet of blast that tried to save New York. But it was all for show, Ilse knew, an act of desperation, hoping against hope for a lucky hit.

Did the people working those guns and launchers know what was really in store? How did families cowering in cellars feel as shrapnel and spent bullets hit their homes, piercing shingled roofs or breaking curtained windows, chunks of red-hot metal raining from the sky?

Ilse watched in helplessness and despair. There was nothing she could do. She and Jeffrey had already done what they could to destroy these Axis hell-weapons. They'd succeeded but not well enough. Now the unstoppable enemy cruise missiles came right at them. There was so little time to feel regret or shame, to plead to God, to do anything but anguish over the death of a great city.

The missiles had to be very close now. They moved so terribly fast, and every weapon in sight, from foreground to distant horizon, was firing into the air. Defensive missiles locked onto each other by mistake and collided in double eruptions. Tracer shells of every caliber constantly crisscrossed the sky. Shell and missile bursts of every size and intensity lit up the harbor, reflecting off the water and off the land all covered with snow, bursts so constant and bright that the Milky Way and stars were drowned out by the glare. The bangs and thumps and roars of the defensive fire were endless, painfully loud.

The inbound missiles' projected path was bombarded so thoroughly, a man-made overcast formed—a continuous blanket of smoke and fumes from all the weapons operating. This choking overcast swirled and grew thicker and thicker. It pulsated from within like strobing lightning through a thunderhead, as gun after gun kept plastering the sky. Defensive missiles would launch, disappear in the smoke layer, then break out higher and turn and look for something to destroy. By now missile trails entwined and twisted everywhere, like satanic confetti.

One defensive missile hit a friendly fighter by mistake, and the fireball of jet and missile fuel plunged earthward in New Jersey, starting a conflagration at the point of impact with the ground. That area began exploding, sending up heaving sheets of liquid flame and flying sparks and thick black smoke—a tank farm or oil refinery. The fire on Staten Island was bigger now too.

Something tore through the air above Ilse's head with a wave of heat and a soul-tearing sonic boom. She was *inside* the sonic boom, deafened by it, shattered by it. A Mach 8 missile had made it through, bound for midtown. In seconds she and Jeffrey would be killed. She'd never felt so alone, felt nothing now but self-revulsion and guilt. Her face twisted into an ugly mask of rage and bitter resentment, at this war, at what she'd done behind enemy lines, at all the things she wanted to do in her life but would never get to do. She didn't want to die feeling nothing but cold anger and such loneliness. She turned to Jeffrey, and he turned to her, and his face showed deep regret.

There was a blinding flash right over the Statue of Liberty. Ilse waited for unimaginable heat to broil her skin, to melt her eyeballs, to set her parka afire. She waited for the invisible burst of neutrons and hard gamma rays to kill every cell in her body. She waited for the blast wave to come and knock her charred corpse to dust.

Instead there was whistling and banging. Fireworks began to explode over the Statue of Liberty, and more back behind her over midtown. Decorative fireworks, pretty cloudbursts of blue and green and silver—like on the Fourth of July—as if to mock the Americans.

Things began to blow on the wind, small strips. Ilse thought they were antiradar chaff.

Jeffrey angrily tried to catch one of the floating strips. He jumped and reached, and on the third attempt he grabbed one. It was a piece of paper, one of thousands scattering everywhere now. Jeffrey looked at the strip, then handed it to Ilse.

"They'll never be able to hush this up. It's the end of civilian morale."

Ilse read the slip with difficulty. There were tears in her eyes and she shivered, from the cold and fear and now from *this*. She knew Jeffrey was right. In large, bold, black Germanic script were printed words in English, a psychological-warfare body blow:

"If this had a nuclear warhead been, you would now be dead. Think of it."

3

Next morning, at the Pentagon

EVENTUALLY, PASSENGER RAILROAD service was restored. Jeffrey and Ilse spent an uncomfortable night on the train as it crept toward Washington. They carefully folded Jeffrey's dress uniform jacket, and the jacket of Ilse's pantsuit, and put them neatly on the overhead rack. Then they used their coats as improvised blankets—the crowded train was chilly, to save energy, since it took power to heat the cars. Jeffrey slept fitfully; sometimes he heard Ilse moan in her sleep. He was tempted to squeeze her hand to try to comfort her, but held back; he remembered her comment in the Empire State Building cocktail lounge, that this was strictly a business trip.

At the Pentagon, at least, Jeffrey and Ilse were able to freshen up and eat breakfast: bacon, actual bacon, and omelets made from real—not powdered—eggs. Now they sat in a waiting area, on a plush leather couch outside the big floor-to-ceiling double doors of a meeting room. The door was guarded by two enlisted marines. Jeffrey eyed the marines' crisp appearance, their mirror-hard shoeshines and the razor-sharp creases of their fatigues. He surreptitiously tried to smooth the wrinkles on his uniform.

The marines suddenly snapped to attention. Jeffrey instinctively jumped to his feet. Ilse stood up too.

An air force four-star general entered the waiting area. He was built like a football linebacker, and the way he moved made Jeffrey think of a taxiing B-52. He strode into the meeting room without even noticing Jeffrey and Ilse. The man looked very angry.

For a while that was all, and Jeffrey let his mind wander.

"What's the matter?" Ilse said. "What were you thinking about?"

Jeffrey realized he'd been frowning. "My father . . . It's not something I'm proud of."

"Why? What did he do?"

"It's nothing he did."

"I'll bet it is," Ilse teased. "What did he do? Peeping Tom? Mafia hit man? Ran a bordello in St. Louis?" After the terrors of last night in New York, her humor sounded lame.

Jeffrey had told Ilse he was from a suburb of St. Louis. That much, he'd told her. "It's not what *he* did. The last time we tried to talk, it was awful."

"You had an argument?"

"No. It would be better if we had. It was more like hard, quiet, seething rage."

"You or your father?"

"Him. Directed at me. And sarcasm. Biting, subtle, with surgical precision. Enough to make me bleed inside."

"My God. Why?"

"When I was younger, growing up, I treated my family like crap."

"How so?"

"I thought they were boring as all hell, and I did nothing to hide it."

"Come on, Jeffrey. All kids go through that."

"Not the way I did. I was a real asshole about it."

"What does your father do for a living?"

"He's a utility regulator. A career bureaucrat, basically."

"That does sound pretty dull. Though I suppose it's become more important nowadays."

"Yeah. I kinda dumped my family and decided to join the navy. For college, I did Navy ROTC at Purdue. My dad, by then, didn't try to stop me. But he resented it a lot."

"How come? He ought to have been proud of you."

"It was too late for that, by then. When I was a kid, I loved to read about the navy. I was so into the stuff, you know, book reports and things like that at school even, the junior-high guidance counselor once had a talk with my parents."

"Oh."

"Of course, that just made me more obstinate. My bedroom was all full of models of ships. Battleships, carriers, sailing ships, landing craft, and every class of sub I could find in the toy stores."

"But that's all good, isn't it? It's nice to know what you want to be when you grow up."

"Isn't it, though? Except I turned my back on my family the whole time. I condescended, like I was better than them. Like I'd found my calling, and it was visionary, and it put me on a higher plane than these tedious middle-class drones. Me, a kid, eight, twelve, sixteen, whenever. *Then* there were arguments. Sometimes it got ugly."

"But I still don't understand, what's the problem now? Your father should be proud of what you've done. You made the right career choice, didn't you? That's bloody obvious. Can't he let bygones alone?"

"Sometimes you push someone so far you kill the love and the trust. Sometimes you gall them so much with silent insolence, there's no going back afterward."

"What happened the last time you tried to speak to him?"

"I called him on the phone, from the base, a couple of months ago. He practically blamed me personally for starting the war, for losing the war, because of that nuclear ambush off western Africa where the navy lost all those ships."

"That's crazy."

"No. He's a smart, clearheaded man. Much more than I gave him credit for, years back. But he's as disillusioned and scared as everybody else right now, with what's been happening since the Double Putsch." The coordinated takeovers in Johannesburg and Berlin. "I think it was his way of getting out his pain at me, with the thing he knew would hurt me most. He said it was like Pearl Harbor all over *again,* except at sea, and this time we *did* lose the carriers."

"But you weren't even there!"

"He knows that."

"Can't you try to talk to him again? The stuff you've done, since that phone call anyway, it should make a difference."

"Right. Except it's all highly classified. He has no idea what I've been up to, and he never will, will he?"

"I guess not. I don't know what to say."

"There's nothing *to* say. Just try to forget about it. It's not something I like to talk about."

Jeffrey looked away from Ilse. There was nothing she could do to help him anyway.

Simultaneously, on *Voortrekker,* in the Indian Ocean

In the control room Gunther Van Gelder gripped his armrests as *Voortrekker* wallowed sickeningly at periscope depth, moving very slowly, in a race against time. Minutes before, *Voortrekker* had launched three dozen Mach 2.5 cruise missiles at Diego Garcia, four hundred miles away, the vital Allied forward bastion in the Indian Ocean. The nuclear carrier USS *Ronald Reagan*'s aircraft were doggedly hunting *Voortrekker* now, because of the noisy launch datum Jan ter Horst made. The *Reagan* was much closer to *Voortrekker* than *Voortrekker* was to Diego Garcia, and *Reagan*'s planes were almost as fast as ter Horst's missiles.

Van Gelder watched his tactical screens warily and nervously. His sonarmen and fire-control technicians were also on edge. Van Gelder could smell their sweat, feel their inner tension, see their worried faces clearly in the control room's daytime lighting. Eight brilliant decoys had been running in different directions for half an hour or more. *Voortrekker* hoped to be lost amid the distraction of the decoys, but Van Gelder had serious doubts, for a simple reason.

Voortrekker had both periscope masts up. Her satellite-communications antenna dish was also raised. This was exceedingly dangerous, despite their low-observable radar-absorbing designs, but ter Horst insisted. Jan ter Horst wanted to watch his handiwork at Diego Garcia unfold live.

"Soon now," ter Horst said. "You can see the antiair defenses getting more intense." He leaned closer to the full-color video feed from the satellite, monitoring the target on his main console display. Van Gelder watched identical imagery, windowed on his own screens. Sometimes large waves, outside the hull, buried *Voortrekker*'s antenna dish, and the picture went blank, then resumed. Even submerged, the ship rolled heavily, recovered, rolled hard the other way.

"Watch your trim," ter Horst snapped at the helmsman and chief of the boat. "Don't let her broach!"

The satellite was in high earth orbit, passing overhead. It belonged to a neutral Third World country, but had been built in Germany before the war. When the bird was launched its owners had no idea it carried extra circuitry they didn't pay for, covertly embedded military data-relay links the Allies wouldn't try to shoot down or jam, because they wouldn't know to.

But these satellites had no spy cameras, which would have been too obvious. The uplink feed came instead from an unmanned aerial vehicle, a stealthy recon drone launched by a German class 214 modern diesel sub. The sub lurked north of ter Horst's target, in support of his mission. The drone kept a close eye on Diego Garcia, from a few thousand meters' altitude, sending pictures up to the satellite by a focused microwave beam. *Voortrekker* herself was well to the south of the enemy's island base, hiding from visual detection beneath thin overcast. She was observing radio silence, just receiving the downlink feed.

Van Gelder forced himself to stay outwardly calm, to keep his men calm. It wasn't easy. Visibility under the overcast was good. With little warning, low-flying aircraft armed with nuclear depth bombs might spot *Voortrekker*'s masts at any moment.

The Pentagon

Ilse heard voices from inside the meeting room. The voices were muffled, but Ilse knew people were arguing, shouting. She heard an especially deep, booming voice, which sounded accusing and irritated. Others answered harshly, including at least two women, as tough as the men. The marine guards stood there stoically.

Ilse turned to Jeffrey. "Not a good start to the day."

"Last night was not a good night in New York."

Ilse rolled her eyes and nodded when it hit her. The taunting humiliation of that Mach 8 cruise-missile raid would preempt anything else on the agenda. She glanced at the double doors. *How long have they been in there? Since 5 A.M.? Since last night?*

The discussion quieted down. A navy captain came out. He was shorter than Ilse, maybe five foot five, balding, aloof, and arrogant. He introduced himself and curtly shook hands with Ilse and Jeffrey. He was the senior aide to the vice chief of naval operations, the four-star admiral who chaired the meeting.

"Exactly what group are we addressing?" Ilse asked.

"That's classified, who's on what committee. We don't publish organization charts these days. They're ready for you."

Ilse took a deep breath and stood up as straight as she could. She followed Jeffrey and the captain into the meeting room. In spite of the inconvenience of the trip, she'd been looking forward to this chance to show off what she'd done. Now, still emotionally numb from those few horrible minutes atop the Empire State Building, she saw twenty very senior faces stare at her from around a huge mahogany conference table. There were more generals' stars on their shoulder boards and admirals' rings on their jacket cuffs than she could count.

An atmosphere of conflict lingered heavily in the room, and in the body language. Not one person smiled, and their eyes were hard and unreachable.

On *Voortrekker*

Voortrekker was jarred by thunder that came right through the hull, building to a harsh crescendo, dying off abruptly. Nasty vibrations sent pins and needles up Van Gelder's arms and legs. "Loud explosion," the sonar chief shouted, "bearing two seven zero!" West. "Range eighty thousand meters." Forty nautical miles. "Classify as an Allied nuclear depth charge, twenty-kiloton yield!"

"Ooh, they're using biggies." Ter Horst tut-tutted. "They're clueless where we really are. They'd need a lucky shot to even come close."

"Sir," Van Gelder said, "that must be enemy aircraft, searching for us, attacking one of the decoys." He was doing his job, giving ter Horst a tactical assessment.

"Yes, yes. Carrier planes from the *Reagan*. Relax, Gunther. We're *not* submerging now. We need this imagery."

Telling Van Gelder to relax only heightened the tension in the control room—younger crewmen squirmed in their seats.

"Aye aye, Captain," Van Gelder said. "It's a big ocean they have to search, and our antenna mast is stealthy." He said that for the men, sounding as cocky as he could, trying to believe it so that they would.

I knew ter Horst was aggressive, but this is cutting things really *close.*

The Pentagon

By the time Jeffrey's second briefing slide came on the screen, the generals and admirals started arguing again—it was as if he and Ilse weren't there. They argued about the missile raid on New York, and the lack of supplies to the dwindling but crucial Central Africa pocket. They argued about the whole course of the war. There were accusations thrown between the army and navy and air force, and counteraccusations. The marines and coast guard argued too. It got so ugly the vice chief of naval operations had to call a fifteen-minute break.

The VCNO's senior aide came up to Jeffrey and Ilse. "You didn't hear *any* of that. After the recess, you two go on like it never happened. *Understand me?*"

Ilse nodded. Jeffrey said, "Aye aye, sir." Ilse asked directions to the ladies' room.

Jeffrey decided to walk some distance from the conference room. He didn't want to stand at a urinal next to someone from this crazy, trouble-filled meeting.

Jeffrey found a rest room in a hallway that seemed quiet. He entered and got the shock of his life. Standing there in a business suit, taking a leak, was his father.

4

JEFFREY'S DAD TURNED and noticed him, and did a double take. "It *is* you," Michael Fuller said to his son. Jeffrey felt his chest tighten. The man began to wash his hands, half ignoring Jeffrey. *Testing me. Challenging me.* Jeffrey knew too well he and his father both had their egos, especially with each other.

"I, um," Jeffrey stammered. He blurted out the first thing that came to mind. "How come you're here?"

Michael Fuller used his reflection in the mirror to look at Jeffrey. "That's the best you can manage? 'How come I'm here?' Not 'Good to see you, Pop'? Not 'How are the nieces and nephews'?" Jeffrey had two older sisters, both married and with kids.

"Sorry. It's been a rough couple of days."

"Yeah." His dad was sour. "For all of us." He turned to face Jeffrey, and grudgingly made conversation. "You stationed in the Pentagon now?"

"No. Just came from out of town, for a meeting. You?" Conflicting emotions flooded through Jeffrey as his father grabbed some paper towels. Part of Jeffrey wanted to run, in shame. Part of him wanted to talk to his dad here forever, to beg forgiveness, to make up for lost time. Jeffrey realized he was regressing—meeting parents often does this to people. He made himself maintain his dignity.

"I work in the DOE now," Michael Fuller stated. "That's the Department of Energy. Well, *you'd* know what DOE means. You sailor boys do love your acronyms."

Jeffrey winced.

"Right here in Washington," his father said. "They made me a deputy assistant secretary. Energy conservation on the home front, that's my bailiwick. The DOE's on the cabinet, and needs to be, with this war."

"That's great, Dad. Sounds like a real big promotion."

"I'm one of the top twelve people in the department."

"It, uh, it must have happened fast." Like in the last eight weeks.

"Yeah. There've been a lot of shakeups since the war's been going so badly. Peacetime yes-men and timeservers who couldn't hack it, they're out on their butts."

Jeffrey nodded. "That's happened in the navy too." Which was why the job as executive officer in *Challenger* had been vacant back in October, when Jeffrey got his transfer to the ship from a fast-track planning job at the Naval War College, in Newport, Rhode Island. The war broke out in July, and *Challenger*'s previous XO did not meet Captain Wilson's high demands preparing for combat.

"They liked what I'd been doing in Missouri," Michael Fuller went on. "Somebody liked the cut of my jib, to use your lingo. Reached over there for me, and here I am."

Jeffrey's father finished drying his hands. He stuffed the paper towels in the trash bin harder than he needed to, almost resentfully.

"I'm supposed to be good at getting people to cut out the blame games, cut out the turf fights, get them to work together better. That's what the secretary told me, anyhow. . . . I did a lot of soul-searching after *you* left home, asking myself where I coulda gone wrong, you turning out the way you did, all those fights and games in the house, a stranger to your own family. . . . Maybe I married too young. . . . Maybe I shoulda stopped with *two* kids. I always seemed better at raising daughters. . . . I guess it paid off, sort of, all that thinkin' because of you, paid off at work anyhow. Me, the Great Compromiser. And here I am."

Jeffrey studied his father. The man's face was deeply creased with worry lines. His middle-age spread was gone. His suit looked expensive.

He wore a perfectly knotted silk tie, not the polyester clip-ons Jeffrey remembered from when he was a kid. His father exuded an air of active intensity and drive that Jeffrey had never seen before. But maybe it had always been there, and he'd been too self-absorbed and immature to notice.

Michael Fuller peered at his son as if to take in every inch of him. "You look older."

"War does that to people," Jeffrey said.

"Tell me about it. . . . You look good in that uniform."

"Thanks." This was the closest thing to a compliment Jeffrey's dad had ever paid his naval career. Jeffrey decided to take a chance and reciprocate. "I like your suit."

The man's face softened. "One has to look the part. I got a big staff now, spend time at the White House, testify before Congress. . . . I've been hearing rumors about *you*."

"Sir?"

"You don't have to call me sir. I'm your own goddamn father. I've heard things, whispers. Scuttlebutt, I suppose you navy types would call it. About stuff you've done. Recent stuff. Good, important stuff, to make a man feel proud."

"I can't talk about it, Dad."

"Yeah, yeah. The walls have ears. Loose lips sink ships. It isn't funny anymore. . . . But I hear you've been doing a fine job out there. You know, where it matters, the sharp tip of the spear?"

"I guess so."

His father looked at Jeffrey very appraisingly. "It's what you always wanted, isn't it? Since you were a kid? To be a big naval hero, in a big shooting war?"

"Dad, nobody *wants* to be in a war. Jesus, especially not like this one."

"So you *did* learn something, since reading all those books. Good for you. . . . How's your old wound doing?"

"It's okay."

"In other words, it still hurts."

"Sometimes, yeah."

His father seemed lost in thought for a minute, lost in the past. "I know those were tough times. Nancy dumping you and all." Nancy was

Jeffrey's ex-fiancée, from the mid-1990s—she'd walked out on him while he was in orthopedic rehab after being hit in the thigh by a bullet on a secret SEAL operation in Iraq. He got a Silver Star and a Purple Heart; then, while he fought the pain to learn to walk again, Nancy returned his ring. Once more on active duty, Jeffrey was rated unfit for Special Warfare missions because of that wound. He loved being underwater, in scuba gear or otherwise, so he chose to transfer to subs; he wanted to stay in a specialty where each individual could really make a difference.

"This war's forced me to think about a lot of things, son. I—I sometimes wish I'd been there for you better, back then."

"I didn't make it easy, Dad. I know a lot was my fault, from *way* back."

"Big killing wars make people *think*, son." Michael Fuller looked off into space again, as if he hadn't heard the last thing Jeffrey said. "You see neighbors get the telegrams . . . yes, they still use telegrams. . . . You see black ribbons in the windows. It makes you realize how much you have, how easy you can lose it, lose everything. It—it reminds you of mortality, this war does, of how very little time we really get."

"I know. I'm almost forty."

"Crap, *I* just turned sixty. Don't rub it in." Michael Fuller actually smiled at Jeffrey. Tears nearly came to Jeffrey's eyes, for this small moment of closeness with his father, and for the decades of closeness he could have had but threw away. He saw his dad's eyes moisten too, for just a second. "You got a land job now?"

Jeffrey nodded.

His father's face grew tough.

"You don't look happy," Michael Fuller said, almost accusingly. His dad had seen right through him.

"A lot's been happening. . . ."

"Don't lie to me. You want to get to sea again."

Jeffrey hesitated. "Yeah."

"Christ, haven't you learned *anything*? Haven't you done *enough*? Have you *been* to Arlington Cemetery lately?"

Jeffrey shook his head. He knew what was coming, and that only made it more painful.

His dad grew sarcastic. "It's practically around the corner from here, damn it. Like some kind of cause and effect, the pair of them, the Pentagon and Arlington . . . Have you *seen* the daily funerals, crowds of mourning relatives, all the fresh-dug graves? No, I thought not. Well, *I* see the statistics, the *real* ones. People out there on the ocean are getting *creamed!* What use is a dead hero to me? You wouldn't be my son anymore, you'd just be *dead,* fucking *dead . . . forever* dead."

"Dad—"

"Didn't you hear *anything* I told you when you were a kid? There ain't no glory in war! There ain't no honor in being a corpse! Warriors get paid to *die.* I lost my own brother to Vietnam, and it *still* hurts every day. In your line of work we'd be lucky if there was enough left of you to even bury! Think how *that* would make your mother feel."

Jeffrey wondered if this was his father's way of expressing love, this worry and anger, just like years and years before. Had it always been Michael Fuller's way of showing love to a rebellious son—a disrespectful son, one hell-bent on military service—and Jeffrey didn't see it?

How to explain to the man that some people needed to volunteer, that preparedness for a big war couldn't wait for the shooting to start? How to convey that there was just no substitute for experience at sea, and Jeffrey had the experience, and when your country needed it, your soul ached for you to go? How to convince his father that Jeffrey did miss his uncle too, a man he'd never known except from photographs, killed in the Tet Offensive seven years before Jeffrey was born?

"A guy your age should be settled down, raising a family already. Not gallivanting off to win *another* medal, and get roasted alive in some mushroom cloud." His father turned away. "There's enough death as it is. Way too much death . . . I—I just—"

Someone barged into the men's room. "*There* you are, sir," he said to Michael Fuller. The intruder—that's how Jeffrey thought of him—was in his late twenties, handsome, smooth, and smug, in a gray pinstripe suit. "They're ready to start again." He seemed impatient, and glanced at Jeffrey in his uniform as if he were some kind of alien creature.

Jeffrey's father frowned, and looked at Jeffrey, and looked at the younger man. "Tell them I'll be along in a minute." The younger man left.

His father sighed. "Look, I gotta go. Big meeting. I can't keep half the Joint Chiefs waiting."

Jeffrey glanced at his watch. "I'm late too."

They both left the rest room. "When's your meeting over, Dad?"

"I dunno. Runs all day. Late . . ." He shrugged.

Jeffrey felt awful disappointment. "I'll be gone by then." Michael Fuller grunted and turned away.

"How's—how's Mom?" Jeffrey called after him. "You bring her out from St. Louis yet?"

Michael Fuller turned. His face seemed to sag. His whole body sagged. "She's in New York. Sloan-Kettering. Breast cancer. They think it might have spread."

5

Simultaneously, on *Voortrekker,* well south of Diego Garcia

VAN GELDER FELT his armpits grow moist as *Voortrekker's* electronic-support-measures mast picked up more and more enemy search radars. Around him in the control room, his technicians called out each sweep. Though he'd drilled them often to always speak calmly and clearly in battle, he heard the men's voices grow higher pitched and start to get slurred from excitement or stress.

Each radar sweep Van Gelder's people reported was windowed on his screen, as a strobing flash in livid yellow, on a digital compass rose that showed the source's direction. With each pulsing strobe, Van Gelder's console also emitted a warning beep, a ragged, ugly, deep-toned sound. The strobes and beeps were growing brighter and louder, and more numerous. Soon the enemy radars would become a lethal threat, as the aircraft from USS *Reagan* drew close. Ter Horst didn't seem to even care.

Both periscopes busily scanned the ocean and the sky. Their imagery showed in high-definition full color on monitors in the control room. The most advanced nuclear submarines in every navy involved in this war used photonic sensors instead of lenses on their periscope heads. The pictures from outside came through the hull on fiber-optic wires—

there were no old-fashioned periscope tubes to be raised and lowered, no handles to grab, no one-eyed lady to dance with as an observer scanned the horizon. Instead, crewmen near Van Gelder used small joysticks to make the image sensors pan around.

On a main display at the front of the control room, Van Gelder watched what the periscopes showed, the surface wave crests stretching into the distance. On every side of the ship, large blue swells were topped with whitecaps. The overcast sky was brightest in the west, and slightly red there, because it was almost dusk. Van Gelder dreaded at any moment seeing an Allied aircraft dive out of the overcast in *Voortrekker*'s direction.

He heard and felt another depth charge go off somewhere near. Once more *Voortrekker* rocked. Once more the discomfort of the shock to the ship came right through the deck and hurt Van Gelder's feet, then came through his chair and banged at his body. Mike cords jiggled, and crewmen squirmed in their seats. Van Gelder's chiefs, most of them needing to stand in the crowded compartment, spoke to the younger men reassuringly but firmly.

Van Gelder glanced down at his uniform shirt. Despite the chill from the brisk air-conditioning required by all the electronics, the crescents of sweat in his armpits were larger and darker than before.

Van Gelder returned to the digital feed from the satellite, to study the picture from the recon drone hundreds of miles to the north. He watched Diego Garcia on his screen. At the target, the sky was crystal clear.

The seventeen-mile-long atoll was spread before him, shaped like a giant V, with a sheltered lagoon between its two arms and small wooded islands at its mouth. Inside the lagoon was the harbor. Cargo ships and frigates were anchored there. The structures on the island all showed clearly despite their blotchy camouflage paint schemes. Van Gelder could see the long concrete runways of the air base, plus the hangars and aircraft shelters, the barracks and administrative buildings and warehouses, and the big storage tanks for gas and oil and lubricants. As he watched this world in miniature, Van Gelder saw flaming streaks of red and yellow take off into the sky, leaving smoke trails, like shooting stars in the wrong direction. These were antimissile missiles, launching from the atoll and some of the ships. More aircraft took to the runways and took to the air, either to intercept the cruise missiles coming from the south or to flee.

The picture had no sound. Everything Van Gelder saw at Diego Garcia, and would see, happened silently. He didn't hear the air-raid sirens, the hoarse shouts of commands. Ter Horst's thirty-six nuclear-tipped cruise missiles were converging on the atoll, tearing in at a kilometer per second, and everyone on the base must know it by now.

A third big air-dropped depth charge went off near *Voortrekker*, probably hitting another decoy, almost deafening through the hull. *This is Russian roulette*, Van Gelder told himself. Jan ter Horst just smiled. Van Gelder wanted to scream. The enemy airborne radar sweeps were stronger.

Another atomic depth bomb exploded, louder and much harder—closer than the last ones, shaking Van Gelder to his core.

Please, God, let our missiles hit and then let's dive and get out of here. Crewmen gasped as the fireball from this latest undersea blast reared skyward from beyond the horizon, on the main screen. A periscope technician zoomed in, and everyone saw the crown of the mushroom cloud soar. It blew a hole in the overcast, then disappeared higher up.

Van Gelder had to clear his throat. "Captain, urgently recommend submerging now."

"Negative," ter Horst said sternly. "You know as well as I do we have no telemetry to the missiles. We *must* have real-time battle-damage assessment. *Now* is the time to attack, with the Pentagon befuddled by that psy-war air raid on New York, and the *Reagan* battle group too far from Diego Garcia to intervene. Once the Allies realize we're out of dry dock so much sooner than they expected, all our strategic surprise will be lost. If the first missile salvo does not succeed, we need to know it immediately, and you'll have to fire more missiles *now*."

"Inbound visual contact!" one of Van Gelder's fire-control technicians shouted as he monitored a periscope display. "Enemy aircraft closing fast!"

Van Gelder took over the display control and flipped to maximum magnification. "A jet, Captain. Too fast to use an antiaircraft missile." The Polyphem high-explosive missiles *Voortrekker* could launch from her torpedo tubes were meant only for slow propeller planes or helicopters.

"Target bearing?" ter Horst snapped.

"Two eight five!" Van Gelder watched the distant dot of the aircraft. It gradually got larger. Suddenly the control room felt much, much too small, and *Voortrekker*'s hull too thin.

"It's slowing!" the fire-control tech shouted. "It's going to drop a parachute-retarded torpedo!"

"Snap shot," ter Horst ordered, "tube one, maximum yield, on course two eight five! *Shoot.*" A snap shot was a desperation move, a quick launch with no proper firing solution to lead the target.

Van Gelder relayed commands. A nuclear torpedo raced from the tube. But the Boer torpedo was so much slower than the jet. The jet raced at *Voortrekker*'s conspicuous antenna, and the wire-guided torpedo churned through the water toward the jet.

"Detonate the snap shot *now.*"

"Too close to our own ship!" Van Gelder warned.

"Do you want him to *drop?* I said now!"

Van Gelder pressed the firing button. The undersea warhead blew. The water shielded *Voortrekker*'s masts from the instantaneous electromagnetic pulse, but the ocean could do nothing to quench the fireball and the blast force. Through the periscope image, Van Gelder saw the ocean near the aircraft heave. The full energy of the warhead broke the surface, and a tower of white water rose and spread with violent speed, higher and higher and wider and wider. The fireball thrust above the water column, blanking out the image. When the glare subsided, a mushroom cloud stood proudly and the enemy aircraft was gone.

Voortrekker whipped and shivered viciously from the force of its own underwater blast. A sonar screen imploded and caught fire; a crewman doused it with an extinguisher. Damage reports came to Van Gelder from other parts of the ship—nothing major *yet.*

Van Gelder watched on the periscope as the tsunami of the detonation approached *Voortrekker* quickly, even as the mushroom cloud grew taller in the air. The tsunami was a solid wall of foaming, boiling seawater. Spume and spray blew backward from its breaking crown, as a man-made wind was sucked in toward ground zero by the updraft of the mushroom cloud.

"Lower all masts and antennas!" ter Horst ordered.

All the imagery went blank. Van Gelder gripped his armrests, white-knuckled, waiting for what was to come.

The ship rolled and corkscrewed madly, and Van Gelder's stomach rose toward his throat. *Voortrekker* dipped and heaved as the tsunami passed right overhead with a terrifying watery roaring sound.

"Raise all masts and antennas!" ter Horst shouted above the diminishing noise.

The satellite imagery came back. On Van Gelder's display of Diego Garcia, the screen showed nothing but snow for a moment, then a lurid hot-violet glow flickered beyond the horizon on the picture.

"*That* blast should be them, not us," ter Horst said. "The island's outer defenses have gone nuclear after all." Probably a destroyer or cruiser, Van Gelder thought, trying to smack the inbound missiles down.

A string of blinding lavender-violet fireballs bloomed, just over the southern horizon from the recon camera's point of view.

"Oh dear. A whole wall of them, across our missiles' line of approach. This I *don't* like. I'm sure we lost some missiles there."

Ter Horst sounded worried; Van Gelder was torn between praying for failure or success. He felt pity for the people on the atoll. Then he looked at the local periscope picture, at the fresh mushroom cloud that smashed the incoming enemy jet, standing now like a beacon marking *Voortrekker*'s location—he felt pity for himself and his crew.

"*There.*" Ter Horst pointed at his screen. "Our weapons are still in the air, a few at least."

Conventional antiaircraft guns, shorter-range weapons, opened up from the atoll. Guns began to fire from ships stuck in the harbor too—some just couldn't get up steam or warm their big diesel engines fast enough to leave. Van Gelder saw the gun flashes, vivid in the evening twilight. The shells invisibly flew away from Van Gelder, toward the south, and burst low over the ocean, leaving black puffs of smoke but showing no hits on incoming missiles. Van Gelder saw Allied fighters jinking to avoid the friendly fire, making less effective their own strafing runs against surviving hostile missiles. Van Gelder saw the surface of the lagoon roil from the firing concussions of heavy ack-ack guns. The surface of the sea splashed and rippled from the ack-ack's falling shrapnel. Sometimes there were bigger splashes, when dud shells hit the water. There seemed to be a lot of duds. Ter Horst laughed.

More antimissile missiles took to the sky, or leaped from the wings of fighter jets as afterburners strained. Van Gelder followed the moving glows of the exhausts against the dusk. A few defensive missiles connected with *something*, in stabbing secondary blasts, and sheets of liquid fire rained to the sea.

"Shit," ter Horst said. "Well, it's out of our control. We may need another salvo after all." Van Gelder's gut tightened at the thought, with the *Reagan*'s planes so near. Fire-controlmen reported more airborne search radars, closing on *Voortrekker* fast. The warning strobes and beeps of his console seemed to set the pace for Van Gelder's rising heartbeat.

Tracers, bright red and green, began to stitch the heavens over Diego Garcia—in the tropics, dark came quickly. The defenders still had targets, which meant *Voortrekker*'s cruise missiles still flew.

"You know, Number One," ter Horst said, "it all makes a lovely light show."

Dutifully, Van Gelder watched his screens. The last rays of the sunset cast a pink pall on the island bastion. Detonations right at sundown were part of ter Horst's plan: it made *Voortrekker*'s egress easier, and medical care on the shattered atoll that much harder to provide.

Ter Horst tapped his chronometer. "The *real* fireworks are about to begin . . . *now*."

Things happened fast.

ALL of Diego Garcia's military assets were on the left arm of the atoll's V. In rapid succession there blossomed six prolonged blinding flashes.

"*Yes*," ter Horst exclaimed. "Some got through!"

Crewmen cheered.

"Quiet in control!" he snapped.

Van Gelder stared at his screen, transfixed.

As the glare died down, shock waves spread from four points on the atoll's arm and two in the lagoon. Van Gelder saw gigantic domes of mist, where the moist tropical air condensed behind the spreading shock fronts. The mist domes quickly dissipated, and there *they* were, the atomic fireballs, six of them glowing and churning, ascending into the sky. Each was a breathtaking golden yellow, expanding as it rose: living, fulminating globes of unimaginable fire.

Pillars formed beneath the fireballs, black for the ones that hit land, white for the ones that hit water. The fireballs provided their own illumination for the nighttime scene around them; each cast livid shadows of the other mushroom clouds. At ground level, smoke and dust and fog-spray spread in fluffy, lethal disks. The shock waves of the different warheads met, rupturing the air.

Still the fireballs rose, and expanded, and cooled slightly. They sucked in more air at their bases. The pillars of the mushroom clouds grew thick, and lightning sizzled. Nothing on the ground could be seen through all the smoke and dust and steam and flying debris, no ships or planes or people. The water of the lagoon, farther off, foamed where it was punished by the shock fronts, and huge waves spread away from the two water bursts. Tall trees on the far side of the lagoon exploded into flame from the searing radiant heat of the blasts. The entire atoll seemed to burn.

Now the fireballs were more than two miles high. They broiled less fiercely. Smoke rings formed atop their crowns. They were interlaced with ethereal purple glows, the air itself fluorescing from the intense radiation. More lightning flashed from the tremendous static charges.

Ter Horst switched to the infrared feed. On Van Gelder's screen, in this mode, the fireballs still seared frighteningly. But infrared could see through smoke and dust. At ground level, fires burned everywhere. The petroleum-products tank farm was now one huge inferno, and the inferno spread. More flaming fuel oil covered the surface of the lagoon, and in the lagoon, ships burned and broke apart. The four deep craters on the ground all glowed intensely hot; not one but *two* missiles had hit the runways of the airbase.

Van Gelder was awestruck in spite of himself. *I helped do this.* Some primitive part of his being rejoiced at the combat success. An unspeakable part of his soul soared with exhilarated joy at the sheer *pleasure* of such push-button mass destruction. In a sick way it was *fun* to unleash fission bombs, see mushroom clouds erect themselves, smash someone else's toys and get to watch.

Am I becoming a monster, like my captain?

"Atoll denial, Gunther," ter Horst said.

"Sir?"

"That's what this is about. Atoll denial."

Van Gelder nodded. He grasped ter Horst's point. The cruise missiles all had plunging warheads, designed to bore in deep and throw up terrible local fallout—soil, vaporized wreckage, and radioactive seawater steam. From these appallingly dirty blasts, Diego Garcia would be unusable for many months, maybe years. The image jumped, then steadied, as each shock front finally reached the unmanned recon drone, the force too weak by now to knock it down.

"They think an island is an unsinkable aircraft carrier," ter Horst said.

"I've heard the saying, Captain." Ter Horst distracted Van Gelder, who was trying to make better sense of what he'd seen, and how he felt about it. *I've helped kill thousands of people.*

But it's legal, they were military targets. This is war, and I'm doing my job.

"They need to think again," ter Horst said. "An island is just a carrier that can't move. We *sank* Diego Garcia in every way that matters."

We did *destroy the bastion. We've dealt the Allies a terrible blow. We're closer to winning the war, aren't we? We'll save countless other lives, on both sides, if we help bring this conflict to a more rapid close. . . . Yes, that's right. I should feel good about this.*

So how come I don't?

Three nuclear depth charges went off one right after the other, much too close to *Voortrekker* for comfort. Mike cords jiggled on the overhead again, and light fixtures squeaked in their shock-absorbing mounts.

"I think word of our success has reached the *Reagan*," ter Horst said. "First Officer, we've seen enough. The recorders got all that?"

Van Gelder checked his console. "Yes, Captain. Good imagery." One of the last frames, six fresh mushroom clouds towering in infrared, sat frozen on his screen.

"Visual targets!" someone screamed, pointing at the periscope pictures. "*Multiple inbound aircraft!*"

Van Gelder stared. The planes were converging on *Voortrekker* from every point of the compass, using the mushroom cloud nearby as their aiming point. The enemy was coordinating skillfully, and *Voortrekker* couldn't possibly knock them all down with torpedoes. Van Gelder saw sonobuoys rain from some of the planes.

"Lower all masts and antennas!" ter Horst ordered. "Helm, flank speed ahead! Take her deep!" The bow nosed steeply down.

"Captain," Van Gelder said, "that won't help." *Voortrekker* had been localized, to well within the kill radius of a big atomic depth charge. Enemy active sonobuoys began to ping from all around.

"Snap shots, tubes two, three, and four, onto courses due north, south, and west. Maximum yield, no depth ceiling, stand by to detonate at minimum safe range!"

Van Gelder relayed the commands. *Three torpedoes will not save us. Our ceramic composite hull, our crush depth of five thousand meters will not save us either.*

"Number One, run the torpedoes deep and then drive them for the surface. Detonate when they leap into the air."

Van Gelder studied his data readouts. At the right moment he fired all three torpedo warheads simultaneously. Set off low in the atmosphere, he realized, they'd together make a big electromagnetic pulse, and throw a powerful shock wave through the air. *Ter Horst is clever.*

The force of the detonations was more muted this time as *Voortrekker* dived—air bursts didn't pass much energy into the sea.

Everyone stared at the overhead, praying or swearing, as *Voortrekker* accelerated, still aiming steeply down. Her depth urgently mounted to hundreds, then thousands of meters. Ter Horst snapped out course changes to confuse the Allied aircrews, their avionics now scrambled and their weapon-arming circuits hopefully fried. But Allied aircraft were shielded against an atomic electromagnetic pulse. *How badly had the planes been hurt?*

An underwater detonation pounded Van Gelder fiendishly, shaking his skull against his spine; his teeth rattled and he almost bit through his tongue. Crewmen shouted in pain or fear. Light fixtures shattered and broken glass went flying, and another console screen caught fire. Everyone rushed to don their emergency air-breather masks.

Another nuclear depth charge blew. A compressed-air manifold cracked somewhere and high-pressure air blew paper around the control room like a tornado. A cooling-water pipe exploded and freezing freshwater sprayed from the overhead.

More air-dropped sonobuoys began to ping above the din.

"Snap shots, tubes five through eight, maximum warhead yields, courses due north, south, east, and west! *Shoot!*"

Van Gelder forced himself to concentrate, to keep his men under control, to get the weapons programmed and launched.

"Detonate all weapons at maximum depth, at minimum safe range!"

"Captain, recommend an additional safety distance, with four simultaneous blasts in every quadrant around the ship."

"Negative," ter Horst yelled through his breather mask. "There's no time!" The constant pinging outside seemed to emphasize his point.

Van Gelder waited for the moment to fire. When it came, he dreaded triggering the weapons, because of what he knew they'd do to *Voortrekker*.

The feedback through the torpedo guidance wires showed all four warheads detonated. Seconds later the shock waves pummeled *Voortrekker* from all sides. TV monitors mounted on the bulkheads tore loose, fell to the deck, and smashed. Standing crewmen were knocked from their feet. A stanchion in the forward passageway snapped off from the overhead, severing a power cable. Both ends of the cable danced on the deck, throwing hot blue sparks. One end touched a crewman and his body jerked and spasmed and his hair burned and his eyes burst and his face began to steam.

"Noisemakers, Gunther," ter Horst shouted above the ungodly

racket. "I just used my own torpedoes as gigantic noisemakers! Let's hope they hide us well enough!"

Van Gelder nodded numbly, then went back to his instruments.

Another enemy depth charge detonated somewhere close. Emergency battle-lantern lenses shattered and their lightbulbs smashed; the remaining overhead lighting dimmed as one auxiliary turbogenerator back in engineering shorted out; all intercom circuits failed. The control room phone talker said there was a bad electrical fire in engineering; he could barely pitch his voice above the reverb and the aftershocks.

"Helm," ter Horst shouted, "take her to the bottom smartly! Steer one eight zero!" Due south.

"Sir," Van Gelder yelled, "strongly advise caution! Bottom here is deeper than our test depth!"

"But not our crush depth! It's getting too dicey. *Do it.*"

The helmsman acknowledged. *Voortrekker* dove deeper and deeper. The echoing rumble outside continued and sonobuoys pinged. Smoke and dust swirled through the air outside Van Gelder's breather mask. Icy freshwater sloshed on the deck. Van Gelder began to shiver as his shoes and pants were drenched.

Everyone in the control room waited for the next atomic eruption. Would it be near or far? Would it be the one that killed them all? And *when?* When would it come? The nerve-ripping lull seemed to go on forever. A crewman whimpered, "What's taking so long?"

"Easy, now," Van Gelder ordered. *This helpless expecting, this tenterhooks of life and death, is mental torture.*

Van Gelder felt and heard another enemy depth charge blow much closer than the last one. His teeth hurt and his arms and legs flailed wildly from the shock. The lights went out completely.

6

Three hours later

JEFFREY AND ILSE sat on the couch again, in the anteroom of the meeting chamber at the Pentagon. The vice chief of naval operations was still inside with some of his key people, holding a crisis meeting on the Indian Ocean attack. Word had reached Washington quickly, cutting short Jeffrey's presentation. Now, aides, messengers, senior officers came and went through the double doors, all of them in a hurry. Their faces betrayed their emotions, ranging from grim determination to anger to grief. Jeffrey and Ilse were ignored.

Jeffrey's inner turmoil rolled around inside him. He didn't mention to Ilse seeing his father, or the news about his mom. He tried not to think about this latest bad news either: the destruction of Diego Garcia, the obvious fact *Voortrekker* was on the loose, Jan ter Horst on the warpath. He wondered what Ilse would be thinking, being reminded of Jan.

"How much longer till someone tells us what's going on?" Ilse said.

"I don't know."

"Will they want us to continue with the briefing?"

"I think so. They'll still need the big picture. I hope they don't get tunnel vision now."

"But that's what happened already, isn't it? They got blindsided repeatedly. Now they're reeling in shock. They just keep *reacting,* to things the Axis already did. You saw them in there too."

"That's what happens. Standard military tactics. Diversion and deception. Then strike hard and aim to overload the enemy, paralyze his brain. Both sides can play that gambit."

"But I'd think your vaunted big shots would *know* that. They were acting like a bunch of *children.*"

"Ilse, that was uncalled for." Jeffrey felt defensive now. He glanced at the two marines. They both blinked, staring straight ahead, carefully expressionless.

"Is this what it's always like here?" Ilse said.

"Is *what* like *what?*"

"The Pentagon. The dirty politics. Finger-pointing, backbiting, he-said-she-said games . . . *You* used to work here." Ilse made it sound like an accusation. "Then there's the VCNO's senior aide, that arrogant little bastard. I saw the way he talked to us."

"Ilse, don't take it so personally."

Ilse turned to look at Jeffrey. "Don't you talk to me about *personally.* What could you possibly know about *personally?* You don't know how I *feel.* You don't know what really matters to *me.* You hardly *know* me."

"I—"

The VCNO's aide came out of the double doors.

Why now *of all times?* Jeffrey thought.

The captain read their body language, and cleared his throat pointedly. "Is something the matter here?"

Jeffrey recovered fast. "No, sir."

"Good." The man turned to Ilse. "Miss Reebeck."

"Captain?"

"Decisions have been made. We're pulling you out of the course you're taking."

"But I'm not finished."

"We have something more important for you to do. It'll use your skills as combat oceanographer."

"On a submarine?"

"No." The captain looked at his watch. "There's no time to explain, and it's top secret. Something new, fresh, and different."

"Where?"

"I can't say."

"But what about *Challenger*?"

"*Forget* about *Challenger*."

Jeffrey tried to step in. "Sir—"

"*Later.*"

A young man in civilian clothes arrived. "Good," the captain said to Ilse. "Your transportation's here."

"Where am I going?"

"Ask me no questions, I'll tell you no lies."

"*What?*"

The captain gave her a dirty look. "Reebeck, haven't you learned *anything* about operational security by now?"

To Jeffrey, Ilse looked furious. He was afraid she'd make a scene, but she bit her feelings down.

"Go with this person," the captain said. "That's all I can tell you."

"What about me?" Jeffrey said.

The captain looked down his nose at Jeffrey—not an easy thing to do, since Jeffrey was inches taller. "Aren't *you* taking some kind of course?"

"Yes, sir." Jeffrey *knew* the man was well aware he was in the Prospective Commanding Officers course. The captain was putting Jeffrey in his place.

"You're missing class. Get back to school."

"How?"

"You have an open ticket to New London, don't you?"

"Yes."

"Your travel papers should get you on the next train. You might have to stand, but so it goes. There *is* a war on."

The captain turned to Ilse. "Move out. Time is of the essence." He went back into the meeting room.

Ilse looked at Jeffrey. "I guess this is how we part."

Jeffrey's heart was pounding. "I thought we'd have more time together."

"Ma'am," the young man insisted.

"I have to go," Ilse said to Jeffrey.

"But—"

"I hate good-byes. I've seen too many good-byes." Ilse hurried away.

Jeffrey stood there, alone and very lonely. He remembered he had a train to catch, and he'd missed two days of school already.

When he got to D.C.'s Union Station, he phoned Sloan-Kettering. The train passed through New York; maybe he could get off to see his mother at the hospital. They said she'd just gone into surgery, and would be in the recovery room—no visitors—for many hours after that.

Jeffrey stood in the station's packed waiting room, leaning dejectedly against the wall between an empty vending machine and a withered potted plant. While he waited for his train to be called, he kept wondering where the navy was sending Ilse, and where Jan ter Horst and *Voortrekker* would strike next.

ILSE was rushed to Dulles International Airport in the back of an unmarked, windowless van. The driver was a lieutenant from Naval Intelligence. He told Ilse there were indications the Germans knew she'd been on the SEAL raid in the Baltic in December, and good indications the Axis had already tasked assassins working in the U.S. to kill her to get even. The driver wore a Super-Kevlar undershirt and had an Uzi submachine gun under the dashboard, and the van was armored. Still, Ilse didn't feel safe.

At the airport, the van went into an underground garage. Ilse was led up through a maze of drab corridors and locked in a windowless room, for her own protection. After hours of sitting on a cracked plastic chair, at 7:30 P.M. Ilse finally heard someone outside. Keys jangled and a woman opened the door. The woman wore a military flight suit, including a pistol. She had on red-tinted goggles and carried a bulky satchel. The aviator, who was about Ilse's height and build but maybe a few years older, put the satchel on the floor.

"Strip to your underwear and put these on."

Ilse unzipped the satchel. It contained another flight suit. Boots, helmet, G-suit attachments, inflatable life vest, everything.

"They're all your size. Leave your other clothes here. You won't need them where we're going."

Ilse looked doubtfully at all the flight gear.

"Let me give you a hand."

Eventually the aviator was satisfied. Wearing this getup felt strange to Ilse, but it was also exciting.

"Put the helmet on," the woman said. "Put down the sun visor. . . . Don't worry, you'll see well enough. Follow me. From now on, no talking."

Ilse put on the helmet and the woman helped her position the earphone cups and buckle the chin strap properly. The sun visor was shiny silver, like a one-way mirror. They left the room and the aviator locked it behind them. After a long walk down anonymous hallways, Ilse and the aviator came to a heavy metal door with security warnings. The woman punched in a number code, then opened the door.

Ilse was hit by a blast of cold air. She followed the aviator out onto the tarmac. The door slammed shut with dramatic finality. Ilse realized they were in the military section of Dulles Airport. The only lighting was dim and red. The sky had grown cloudy. Ilse's eyes adjusted to the dark. She strained to see through her sun visor. Parked there in front of them was a two-seat fighter jet, sleek and futuristic—twin-tailed, with stealthy angles to the wings and fuselage, deadly looking.

"You ride in back," the woman said to Ilse. Ilse watched her walk straight to the jet with a confident, possessive swagger.

We're going to fly in this *thing?*

Ordnancemen finished loading wicked air-to-air missiles into side bays in the fighter's fuselage. They shut the side-bay doors. Ilse eyed the plane more carefully. All she could read, black against the blue-gray of the fuselage, was USAF.

The woman and the crew chief helped Ilse use the ladder to the rear seat of the cockpit. Up close, Ilse noticed things painted over. But she could make out what was there, because of the layering of the paint. The pilot's name matched the name on the woman aviator's flight suit: Lt. Col. Rachel Barrows. Under the name, also visible from this close, were five double-headed Imperial German eagles. Barrows was a combat ace.

7

On *Voortrekker,* in the Indian Ocean

"SCHNAPPS, GUNTHER?"

Jan ter Horst poured Van Gelder a glass before he could refuse. Van Gelder didn't feel like drinking. He was exhausted from hours of supervising damage-control repairs throughout the ship. The air was breathable now without respirator masks, but it smelled bad. Van Gelder heard men go by outside ter Horst's closed cabin door, carrying tools and spare parts. Van Gelder knew the crew was still recovering, mentally and physically, from their thorough atomic depth charging by planes from the USS *Reagan.*

Ter Horst had said it would take a lucky shot to sink *Voortrekker.* But Van Gelder thought it was only luck that let *Voortrekker* survive.

On second thought, maybe I could use a drink.

This was the first time in a great while that ter Horst had summoned Van Gelder to a special private meeting, and Van Gelder was nervous. They sat with ter Horst's fold-down desk between them.

Did he see my hesitation, my qualms, during the attack on Diego Garcia? . . . Or worse, did he sense my vicarious sadism, watching the warheads blow, and he wants to reclaim all such emotion as his exclusive right?

What ter Horst did say was completely unexpected.

"Thank you for backstopping me before, Number One, with the men, in the control room."

"Sir?"

"When I told you to *relax,* while our missiles were in the air and our antenna dish was up. It had the exact opposite effect from what I intended, of course. It just made the men more nervous, and it undermined your authority as first officer. But what you said then settled everyone down quite nicely. You handled it well."

Van Gelder thought it safest to just let ter Horst go on. *He could be leading me onto very dangerous ground. . . .*

"With all the work in dry dock, and the tribunal on the nuclear sabotage at Umhlanga Rocks, I feel you and I have grown apart, Gunther, outside our official duties."

Van Gelder hesitated. "I know you've been very busy, Captain."

"As have you. As have you. The best proof of that was our successful attack today. Our ship and crew are responding well, thanks to your efforts."

"Thank you, sir."

"Do you know why you're here?"

"Sir?" *That question can be taken several ways.*

"Do you know why you're my first officer?"

Oh . . . uh-oh. "I was proud to be selected." Which was safe to say, and true.

This time ter Horst let the silence linger, forcing Van Gelder to speak. Ter Horst sipped from his schnapps. He looked over the rim of the glass at Van Gelder expectantly.

"I don't know much about the process by which you made the choice, Captain. I could only speculate."

"A number of men wanted the job. Some pulled strings, lobbied hard, tried to curry my favor. *Those* men disappointed me. *You,* in contrast, stayed modest and discrete. Yet your record caught my eye. It told me things your own words never could. About *you,* your experience, your character, your abilities."

"Again, thank you, sir."

"There's another reason, Gunther. You and I are different in many ways. But this is good. We complement one another ideally. . . . Yes, I know I love the theatrical, the grand gesture if you will. It's my nature, these things, and I know that in some ways I'm less than perfect."

"Sir, your combat success speaks for itself."

"*Our* combat success, Gunther. *Our* combat success. It wasn't lost on me that during our battle with USS *Challenger,* you made important contributions."

"Sir, I—"

"No, please, let me finish. Once or twice then, you even saw something vital a split second before I did, at times when a split second meant the margin between life and death. You saved the ship, and I'll never forget that."

"I only did my duty, sir." *Yes, it was that plus a healthy, practical desire to not get killed.*

"All true heroes will say they only did their duty, Gunther. All true heroes will say they were only helping their shipmates survive. . . . That's why I want you to know, I put you in for a decoration, before we left dry dock."

"I—"

"No, please. You deserve it. I expect it will be approved."

"Thank you, sir."

"You're probably wondering by now why we're having this little chat?"

Van Gelder nodded.

"More schnapps?"

"A little more, please."

Ter Horst poured. He lifted his shot glass dramatically, then quaffed it in one gulp. Van Gelder felt he'd better do the same. The strong liquor felt good going down. It did help lift Van Gelder's mood.

"Where we're heading next, Gunther, and what we have to do there, may well have a decisive effect on the war."

Again Van Gelder let ter Horst continue.

"You and I must work as one, going forward. What we do will be very risky and dangerous. I can't afford to brook any misunderstandings between us, any frictions, even unconscious ones."

Suddenly Van Gelder felt wary. "I didn't think there was friction, Captain." *Was this the trap ter Horst had set and sprung?*

But ter Horst waved his hand dismissively. "No, no. That's not what I meant. We naval officers aren't paid to be poets or philosophers. But I sense there's more of the philosopher in you than in me. I sense you're sometimes troubled about the rightness of our cause, I mean the need for the brutality, the mass destruction, the execution of traitors and spies."

"Captain, I—"

"No, no. *Please* let me finish. This is not a criticism session. I'm not accusing you of any weakness, or—or of *backsliding*, God forbid." Backsliding—a euphemism, Van Gelder knew, for cowardice and ideological doubt—was punishable by the noose. "I'm just trying to be a realist, about you and about me and about this war."

Van Gelder was surprised now, and concerned. He'd never seen ter Horst this open and confiding, even at times in the past—at parties or dinners ashore—when he'd had plenty to drink. Could this be because ter Horst himself was worried about the difficulty of *Voortrekker*'s next task? Did he feel the need to talk, to have an audience, so as to reassure *himself*, because he now faced something overwhelming?

Ter Horst hiccupped, then said, "Excuse me.

"I'm not a man to know fear easily," ter Horst went on. "I sometimes think I have some kind of character disorder. A fear *deficit*, you know?"

"Sir, the crew admire your bravery."

"Well, some men come alive in battle and forget there's such a thing as fear. I suppose I'm one of *them*. Others feel the naked vulnerability in combat all too vividly. Yet they carry on, they do their duty. I think these latter men are the ones with the *true* courage. . . . I believe you're one of these latter type of men, Gunther. A man who feels his fear as a personal enemy from deep inside, and yet who slays that enemy time and again so he can go on and slay the true enemy, the external foe."

"Er, thank you, Captain." *How many times have I thanked him now? What's he trying to get me to do?*

"I try to know myself, Gunther. A captain must. But I think of you as the more self-aware, the more sensitive of the two of us."

"I think you're probably right, sir."

"I've never lied to you, have I?"

How am I supposed to answer that? "Not that I know of, Captain."

"I pride myself that I've never lied to anyone. Oh, I withhold information, for security, but that's a captain's privilege."

"I understand."

"I seek to dupe the enemy, of course, but that's valid strategy."

"Of course."

"Those lies aren't sins. Killing in battle isn't a sin. I like to think that I've never committed a serious sin. I say my prayers each night with a clear conscience."

"Er, yes, sir." Van Gelder knew that ter Horst, like many Boers, was religiously devout—Van Gelder himself believed in God, but wasn't big on organized worship.

"So as I was saying, Gunther, I want to address—allay—any concerns you may have, before the next steps in our journey together."

"How so?" Van Gelder felt intoxication coming on from the schnapps, and he tried to be very careful now.

"Discipline and training are your job. What I want you to do is meet with the officers and men in small groups, over the next day. But first, get some rest, a good eight hours' rest. The schnapps will help."

"Yes, sir. Thank you, sir." It *would* be nice to get a decent night's sleep for once.

"Keep each gathering brief. Speak no more than fifteen minutes, say, and allow time for questions and open discussion."

"On what subject, sir?"

"On why we're fighting, on why our cause is just, on how well the war is going, and on where we're voyaging next."

"Where *are* we going next, Captain?"

"In due time. Let me take these points in order. You'll remember what I say? You don't want to take some notes?"

"I have a good memory, Captain." A first officer needed one. "I'll write things down if it becomes necessary. . . ."

Ter Horst drew a deep breath. "We and the Germans are together fighting a police action, Gunther, against American imperialism, against outside interference in our proud national destinies, and against Anglo-American military-political atrocities of the last century or more."

"You mean the forced end to apartheid," Van Gelder stated. "The abuses of the Versailles Treaty after World War I."

Ter Horst nodded. "Stripping Germany bare. Destroying her economy, and her self-esteem. Doing it again after World War II, especially in the East, under Soviet occupation for fifty years. . . . The Boer War, putting our forefathers' wives and children in concentration camps, where thousands died of typhus."

"But we fired the first shots, *this* time, in *this* war, sir."

Ter Horst shook his head vehemently. "It's all one long connected war, Gunther, going back decades and decades. Don't you see? This is just the latest battle. The Americans, the British, *they* fired the first shots, long ago. Militarily, politically, *they're* culpable for all that followed, and for all that follows now. They're culpable morally too."

"But the Germans nuked Warsaw and Tripoli."

"And the U.S. nuked Hiroshima and Nagasaki. Don't you see the duality, the *justice* of it, the revenge here on a global scale? Many readings of international law say *all* nuclear weapons are illegal. *Who* invented them? Who *used them* first?"

"I see your point, Captain."

"And take the collapse of apartheid. That system *worked* for us, for *all* South Africa. The Bantus, the coloreds, they had a proper place in our society, and a proper, safe place in which to work and live. The communist so-called Front Line States to our north made trouble along the border, sure, but we fought them back. We held the line against the Reds as much as America ever did, with their botch-up in Vietnam. We held it *better*, until the Berlin Wall came down! Then the Americans hit us with trade embargoes, sanctions. They claim we're violating human rights. So apartheid falls, and starting in 1994 our country becomes a democracy. And what do we get, from this *democracy?*" Ter Horst said the word like it was obscene. "Open borders, and an inrush of AIDS decimating our black population. An open economy, freedom for all, and violent crime *skyrockets*. Internal terrorism, tribal strife, they explode all out of control! Look at the statistics, Gunther. Years and years of statistics. The statistics don't lie."

"No, sir, they don't." Van Gelder felt himself being won over. He felt himself relaxing, his inner concerns being salved.

Watch out, my friend. Is this burgeoning peace of mind because of ter Horst's hard logic, or because of your own fatigue and the schnapps? Is ter Horst an inspiring leader, or is he just a manipulative, seducing bastard?

"It's the enemy who lies, Number One. It's the enemy who practices hypocrisy on a monumental scale. What the Brits have done to the Irish. What the U.S. did to their Native Americans, what the North did to the South in their bloody War Between the States . . . The joint NATO task force we and the Germans attacked at the outset of this latest conflict was a legitimate military target, Gunther. Diego Garcia was a legitimate military target. The Americans and British and the others we killed are the fools, for not thinking of the risks when they joined up, when they donned the uniform in what they thought was peacetime. There *has* been no peacetime, Gunther, not in a hundred, two hundred years! Only lulls between battles, and the Anglo-Americans choose to call each battle a separate war. *Now* do you see?"

"I think so, sir." Ter Horst had made some very telling points.

"Good. Good. It's all very simple, really, when you look at it the right way. The world has a *new* policeman, fighting against corruption, decadence, social chaos, and pandemic disease. Fighting *for* national self-determination, order, truth. That new policeman is us, Gunther, the Berlin-Boer Axis."

Ter Horst offered Van Gelder more schnapps. This time Van Gelder declined, and ter Horst put away the bottle. It was from Germany, and tasted very good. Van Gelder decided to see if the schnapps had made ter Horst loosen up at all.

"The last part of the briefings I'm to conduct, Captain? Our next destination?"

"We're going to deal the Americans the knockout blow. . . . The Axis doesn't intend to occupy them. You know that's never been our goal. Containment, diminishment, reduction to a second-rate vassal nation, those are our plans for America. . . . At the rate they're going, German forces in the North Atlantic should have the British starved out soon. And Russia remains firm in her thinly disguised support for us, providing conventional arms, and raw materials and fuels, in exchange for gold and diamonds."

"Just where do *we* come in?"

Ter Horst cleared his throat. "*Voortrekker* is tasked to open up a whole new front. We're going to expose the United States as completely naked and vulnerable, to undermine their will and ability to continue the fight, and, especially, win Asia over to the Axis side. Secret diplomatic efforts, ones I cannot disclose a thing to you about, are under way on several continents, timed to mesh with our next strike."

Van Gelder hesitated, very impressed. "But sir. We're almost out of ammo."

Ter Horst waved dismissively again. "All that will be taken care of soon."

"*How,* Captain? . . . Excuse me, I know I must be patient."

Van Gelder was surprised at himself for saying that. He realized ter Horst had had his desired effect. Van Gelder couldn't help but let ter Horst continue his seduction, finish casting his spell. *And by the time I run through all this five or six times with the men—each time making sure I sound as if I believe every word—he'll have me totally brainwashed.*

Ter Horst looked Van Gelder right in the eyes, very hard.

"You and I, Gunther. Together, and our crew. We're the fulcrum, the pivot point. A supercapable nuclear-powered fast-attack submarine, fully armed with tactical atomic weapons you and I are eager to use . . . We're going to run the Australia–New Zealand–Antarctic Gap, break out into the Pacific Ocean, and open a whole new front against America."

8

Simultaneously, at Dulles International Airport, Washington, D.C.

STRAPPED INTO THE rear of the cockpit, Ilse heard the purring of the fighter jet's twin engines rise to a steady, insistent whine. The crew chief and Rachel Barrows saluted. Ilse waved, and the crew chief waved back. *Barrows must know she can trust the crew chief. I'd hate it if he were a spy, and sabotaged us.*

Barrows closed and sealed the cockpit canopy. Ilse breathed deeply, slightly frightened yet almost giddy in anticipation of what was to come. Her oxygen mask smelled rubbery. The oxygen tasted metallic and felt cool and dry. It helped Ilse feel more alert.

Barrows's voice came over Ilse's headphones. "I'll leave the intercom mikes on so we can talk. We'll maintain strict radio and radar silence, for obvious reasons."

The plane taxied some distance in the pitch-dark. The plane's suspension was stiff; Ilse felt every bump and crack and seam in the taxiway.

"How can you see? I thought the Axis was distorting the global positioning system signals."

"I have infrared and low-light-level TV pictures, with cues on my head-up display. The cameras are in the nose."

Barrows put on the brakes. "We're waiting for takeoff clearance."

Ilse glanced around and was surprised to find she had a small rearview mirror mounted inside the canopy. She saw another, identical jet waiting behind her and Barrows.

"What type of airplane is this?"

"Two-seat version of the F-22 Raptor. Best air-dominance and strike fighter in the world, in my not-so-humble opinion."

"How come my instruments are all blacked out?"

"So you don't see aircraft performance. Maximum speed, altitude ceiling, stuff like that's top secret."

Ilse, held firmly by her ejection seat harness, squirmed to try to relax in the seat—the bottom and back were firm and hard.

"These chairs aren't very comfortable."

"When you're in a dogfight with the kaiser's Luftwaffe, the last thing you want is comfortable."

Ilse hesitated, chilled. It sank in, all at once, that these jets were personal killing machines, and sometimes the pilots who flew them died. "If it isn't *too* secret, where did you score your five victories?"

"Over Denmark and the North Sea. All in one night too, right before Christmas. There was a huge air battle, you might have heard about it."

Ilse *had* heard about it. She'd been right *under* it, in *Challenger,* the whole time. *This woman helped save my life.*

"Who is that behind us?"

"My wingman." Ilse, her vision dark-adapted now, looked again in the rearview mirror. The other pilot was a woman.

"Who's in the other passenger seat?"

"Someone who looks like you . . . And that's the weapon systems officer's seat, officially."

"You don't need one tonight?"

"Not where we're going. We'll be vectored to the rendezvous by an AWACS plane."

"So what's this all about? Can't you tell me anything?"

"We need to get you somewhere special really quick, far away. A fighter jet's the fastest method. We also need to keep the Axis from knowing where you're going, on the assumption they're trying to monitor you. The air force has a few tricks up our sleeve tonight."

Red lights came on, in two long rows along the ground, marking the edges of a concrete runway that stretched in front of the jet for more than two miles.

"We are clear for takeoff." Barrows kept the brakes on while she pushed the throttles to full power. The engine noise built from a whine to a roar. The whole plane shook and bucked like it was alive. Barrows released the brakes and hit the afterburners. The noise redoubled. Ilse was kicked back hard against her seat. The F-22 rolled down the runway faster and faster. The red runway lights streaked past in a blur.

The aircraft leaped into the sky. Barrows made a tight left turn, and kept climbing fast.

Ilse glanced around to spot the wingman. She noticed tiny, dim lights trailing her, not far away. Barrows waggled her wings. The dim lights waggled back. Both planes rushed into the overcast, a foggy murk that made the dark seem darker.

In seconds the murk was pierced and fell behind: the F-22s broke through the cloud cover. The view above and all around took Ilse's breath away. The sky was perfectly clear and vast and black. A sliver of moon rose in the east. The stars were sharper and more brilliant than Ilse had ever seen. Mars glowed a solid red, and Jupiter pale yellow. The Milky Way stretched over her head across the entire sky. Using the moon and stars, Ilse could tell the Raptors were flying west.

It's hard to believe the last time I looked at the Milky Way was on top of the Empire State Building, barely twenty-four hours ago. It feels like so much longer. . . . I wonder what Jeffrey Fuller is doing now. Maybe I'll try to find him, after the war.

ILSE heard a man's voice over the radio. She thought he must be in the airborne warning-and-control plane Barrows mentioned. He was guiding other Raptors to meet with Barrows and her wingman.

After a while, Ilse spotted the Raptors. Two came in from the right, and two from the left. They closed up on Barrows and her wingman. They all tucked into a tight arrowhead formation, with Barrows and Ilse in the lead.

I wonder if all the pilots and passengers are women.

"Now for some high-speed aerobatics," Barrows said with obvious relish. "If it makes your head spin, imagine how the Axis satellites will feel. And yes, they're definitely watching us now."

Ilse's heart began to pound, in anticipation and dread. Already this was like no airplane ride she'd ever had in her life.

The F-22 went into a steep dive. Ilse seemed to float against her harness, weightless, with her stomach in her throat. The formation of six F-22s drove back into the overcast together, then down under the clouds. When they broke through, Ilse could see lights of towns and roads below. They were well in from the Atlantic, beyond the official Coast Defense Zone; here the blackout didn't apply so strictly.

The F-22s began to break and zigzag right and left, crossing over and under each other in a giant high-speed shell game. Raptors came so close to Ilse's wings and tail and canopy that she was terrified. Sometimes Barrows and the other pilots all flew upside down, and Ilse hung from her shoulder straps. Her F-22 buffeted viciously, from hitting the other fighters' vortex wakes. The lights on the ground were Ilse's only solid point of reference, and they barely prevented her from getting completely disoriented.

On a command from the man in the AWACS, all six aircraft pulled up hard. The g-force this time pressed Ilse firmly into her seat, more and more. She began to feel faint, and her vision narrowed and darkened, even as the G-suit bladders squeezed her lower body. The F-22s stood on their tails and took off vertically on afterburner. They thrust back through the overcast and up into the sky. They broke into the clear but still kept climbing. The acceleration wasn't as brutal now, and Ilse's vision returned. The stars got closer and closer; she saw a meteor streak past Orion's sword. Ilse panted inside her oxygen mask. Her ears were popping painfully, and she kept trying to clear them, but her throat was parched by the oxygen. She could hear Barrows breathing too, much more calmly. Ilse managed to form spit in her mouth, and swallowed.

The planes closed into a tighter formation, making a hollow circle as they climbed straight up, wingtips of each jet almost touching those of its neighbors, all still standing on their tails. They began to rotate slowly to the right in unison, as if to follow a giant helix spiraling into the heavens, as if they were playing ring-around-the-rosie. They began to spiral faster and faster. Ilse didn't believe the maneuver was possible, let alone that anyone in their right mind would try it.

"Having fun yet?" Barrows said. The planes kept climbing and climbing.

"No," Ilse said very nervously.

Their altitude was so high, Ilse saw another meteor streak actually *below* her. She knew some burned out at fifty or sixty thousand feet.

At last the fighters peeled off, and each plunged toward the ground in an almost vertical dive. Suddenly Ilse's F-22 seemed to shiver, then the ride got smoother and quieter.

"We just broke the sound barrier," Barrows said.

"How come I didn't hear the sonic boom?"

"You never do. It's the people on the ground who feel our shock wave passing over them."

"Right."

"*That* bit was showing off for the opposition," Barrows said. "Here comes my favorite part, now that we have their complete attention. It's a maneuver we call flipping them the bird." The planes pulled out of their dives, into level flight, and lost some speed. Ilse's Raptor shimmied again, and she realized they were subsonic.

Five of them lined up side by side, wingtip to wingtip again. Ilse was in the second Raptor from the left. Another plane took the lead, positioned in front of the middle Raptor in the line. Slowly that lead Raptor drew ahead of the others. Then all six aircraft kicked in afterburners, and held formation going supersonic in level flight.

Barrows laughed. Ilse got it. Any satellite watching, using radar or visual or infrared, would see a giant five-fingered hand, sticking out its middle finger, in a gesture impossible to miss.

The AWACS man—Ilse realized he was calling this whole dance—said something Ilse didn't catch. Suddenly the planes broke into a dive and went through the clouds. Lost in the mist once more, Ilse couldn't make out the dim anticollision lights of the planes around her; she did see their brilliant afterburner glows. Under the clouds the afterburners stopped.

"Last act of the play," Barrows said.

Ilse was glad. She was sweating inside her helmet and flight suit. It wasn't just the fear. The ride was so very rough, the maneuvers and g-forces so aggressive, it was tremendous physical labor to just stay in the seat and breathe and not black out.

The F-22s went back up through the clouds, gaining altitude again. Suddenly Ilse heard popping sounds, and felt thumps. She grew alarmed. She saw flames spewing all over, and thought her plane had hit another and they were exploding and they would die.

"Heat flares," Barrows said. "Infrared countermeasures." The aircraft made tight turns. They passed back under their own burning flares. There were more pops and thumps. By the light of the flares, Ilse saw thousands of thin metal streamers floating everywhere.

"Radar chaff."

The planes all did a tight turn once again. They flew under the flares and clouds of chaff, and started another mind-numbing three-card monte shuffle, passing over and under one another with barely inches to spare. The maneuvers were so violent, Ilse's arms were thrown around the cockpit. She almost hit one of her ejection loops.

"Just a little more of this," Barrows grunted, "and the bad guys will have no idea which plane you're on."

"Then what?" Ilse grunted back. It was hard to talk as the G suit squeezed her abdomen.

"We all break away." Grunt. "Each Raptor refuels in midair." Grunt. "Then heads to a different installation." Grunt. "Somewhere in the U.S."

"Where do we go?"

"Alaska." Grunt. "Aleutian Islands."

The maneuvers under the screen of infrared and radar countermeasures got even *more* aggressive. Now it was a totally wild melee. Another F-22 came right at Ilse. She got so scared she had to close her eyes.

9

Same evening, New London, Connecticut

JEFFREY'S TRAIN ARRIVED on time in New London, and he did get a seat, but that was the best he could say for the ride. His mood—his morale about life in general—was at a low. It was just one thing after another the past forty-eight hours: the New York raid; him and Ilse fighting, and then her being sent God knows where; running into his father, and arguing, and separating again; the slaughter on Diego Garcia.

The worst thing for Jeffrey personally was his mother. He'd taken it for granted that she'd be around forever. He'd always just assumed that one day he would patch things up with his folks, like maybe when he got married and had kids and gave his mom and dad some grandchildren. Now Jeffrey might be running out of time, fast, to even say good-bye to his mom.

The whole trip from Washington to New London, as the sun set outside the windows and people got on and off the train at different stops, all this had swirled in Jeffrey's mind, eating at him. The one thing he did sort out during the time on the train was that he'd put in for compassionate leave, if only for a day, to try to visit his mother in New York. If that meant missing more of the course he was taking, so be it—he'd realized at long last that his family was more important.

When the train pulled in at New London, he dismounted in the dark and started for the pier to wait for the tug back to the sub base. Someone behind him, on the platform, shouted a name. Jeffrey felt so distracted inside, it took several shouts for him to realize it was the false name on his travel papers. He turned, and was approached by a junior enlisted man.

"Sir, I'm supposed to meet you. I have a car, sir."

"Thanks. The tug'll be much faster, son. Look at that traffic on the bridge."

This is the first time in my life I called someone else in the military "son." It made Jeffrey feel very old.

"No, sir. My orders are to take you by car."

Jeffrey shrugged to himself, and handed the enlisted man his luggage. They walked around the side of the picturesque old red-brick station building, to the parking lot. By standard naval courtesy, the younger man held open the rear right passenger door. Jeffrey got in the unmarked late-model subcompact. They drove off.

Three minutes later he said to the kid, "You missed the turn for the bridge."

"No, sir. I'm to take you up to the pens."

"The pens?"

"Yes, sir."

They took a local road straight upriver. The driver dropped Jeffrey off. After a camouflaged checkpoint with heavy security, Jeffrey used the blast-door interlock. He went underground—down toward the hardened submarine pens, hurriedly cut into the rock of the bluffs after the start of the war. Just inside, he showed his real ID.

"Come with me, sir, please," a senior chief told him. The chief took Jeffrey's bags.

They went deeper, down a ramp to the crowded office and administration area. The chief led Jeffrey into one cubicle.

"Sir, Commander Fuller is here." Lieutenant commanders were called commander in public.

The man at the desk looked up. It was Jeffrey's old boss, Commander Wilson, a full commander, captain of USS *Challenger*.

"Sit down, Commander," Wilson said rather dryly.

Jeffrey obeyed. He thought Wilson looked very tired. But Wilson's chocolate-brown complexion wasn't as ashen as back on New Year's Eve. That was the last time Jeffrey had seen him, when Wilson was still getting over a serious concussion.

But there were other changes in the man. He wore reading glasses—that was new. And he hadn't shaved in a week—which was startling. Captain Wilson *always* presented a crisp appearance. Even sitting down, even now, his posture was erect, his shoulders squared. If anything, despite the stubble on his chin, the man exuded more authority, more power, than ever.

The beard was coming in gray, though Wilson was barely forty.

Wilson took off the glasses. "I still get bad headaches. These help. The doctors said I ought to wear bifocals all the time, but I suppose I'm vain."

Wilson hadn't even said hello. This was typical of the man, getting right to the point, *always*. At least he was opening the meeting with some small talk.

Wilson saw Jeffrey staring at his almost-beard. "I went into the hospital a couple of weeks ago, for a brain scan. The medical corps types said the headaches should've stopped by now, and they wanted to check. Not a damn thing wrong with me, but I picked up some kind of skin infection while I was there. There's a big word for that, iatrogenic." Wilson pronounced it slowly and sarcastically. "Means something new you catch in the hospital, while they're supposed to be curing you. Probably a fungus, from the Central African front . . . They gave me a cream, and said that cured it, but I'm not supposed to shave yet."

"You wanted to see me, sir?"

"Yes. I want you to hear this from me first. I'm leaving *Challenger,* and you've been reassigned to the ship."

Jeffrey was delighted and dismayed at the same time. He would be back in the naval front lines after all, and the thought gave him an immediate surge of adrenaline. But Wilson, as hard to please as he was, had been Jeffrey's teacher and mentor in combat when Jeffrey was Wilson's executive officer.

"I'll miss working for you, sir . . . Where are you going?"

"They gave me DevRon Twelve." That was *Challenger*'s parent squadron, Submarine Development Squadron 12.

"Sir, congratulations." This was a huge promotion . . . *too* huge. "With respect, sir, that's a senior four-striper's billet."

"I got my fourth stripe this afternoon. Been too damn busy to change my insignia." He pointed to his collar tabs, which still showed him as a commander.

"Congratulations again, Captain . . . May I ask, who's your relief?" Relief in this context meant Wilson's replacement, the new CO of *Challenger*. Jeffrey could think of several good men who'd qualify.

"You don't get it, do you?"

"Sir?"

"You still work for me."

"Sir?"

"*You* are my relief."

Jeffrey was stunned, then excited, then confused.

"But I'm a lieutenant commander."

"You've been promoted, retroactive to the day before Christmas. Consider it a battlefield promotion."

"Sir, I don't know what to say."

"Then don't say it. This is for you." Wilson handed Jeffrey a small velvet case.

Jeffrey opened it. The case held a Navy Cross, the highest decoration the navy could give, second only to the Medal of Honor, which had to be approved by Congress. There was a gold star with the medal. The gold star, Jeffrey knew, was in lieu of a second award—he'd gotten *two* Navy Crosses.

"Sir, I don't know what to say."

"You earned them. One for each mission in December. We'll do the whole change-of-command thing, and the awards ceremony, in the morning. Right now there are more important matters to discuss."

"Captain?"

"No. *You're* a captain. *I'm* a commodore."

Jeffrey nodded. "Right." This was a lot to absorb, especially after everything else going on. Part of Jeffrey wanted to jump up and down and grin like a little boy—he was never one to be arrogant or smug or grandiose. His promotion, like Wilson's, was early. It was the strongest possible sign of recognition from their superiors.

"You know *Voortrekker* hit Diego Garcia?"

"Yes, sir." That put a stop to any grin. Jeffrey remembered what his father had said at the Pentagon, about personnel shakeups for better results. Jeffrey suspected there'd just been another shakeup, and Jeffrey and Wilson were caught at the epicenter now.

"Look at this map." Wilson put on his reading glasses, and gestured for Jeffrey to come around to his side of the desk.

The map on Wilson's laptop showed the huge expanse of the Indian Ocean. Africa bordered the left, the Middle East and southern Asia lay at the top, Australia and New Zealand were way on the right, and Antarctica edged the bottom. In the middle of the ocean itself was a tiny dot, Diego Garcia. *What's left of it.*

The map also showed the sea-floor topography in detail.

Wilson looked Jeffrey squarely in the eyes. "Search forces have found no sign of *Voortrekker* since the attack, and believe me, they're trying."

"She's hiding in the undersea ridge terrain. That's what I'd do."

"Concur. What's good for the Boers is that the Mid-Indian Ocean Ridge is Y-shaped. See? It's because of the layout of the tectonic plates."

Jeffrey nodded.

"One branch of the Y leads back to Durban," Wilson said, "*Voortrekker*'s home base. One branch leads toward the Arabian Sea, the Persian Gulf, the oil and natural gas fields. The third branch leads down past Australia and New Zealand, to the Pacific Ocean. Your orders, Captain Fuller, are to get under way at once and proceed at best possible speed to a position east of New Zealand, to guard the most vulnerable part of the Australia–New Zealand–Antarctic Gap. It is the consensus of those in a position to know best about these things that *Voortrekker* is heading for the Pacific."

"The Diego Garcia strike was the preamble, wasn't it?" Jeffrey said. "It cleared a major obstacle in *Voortrekker*'s path. While we're reeling from the blow, and trying to rescue survivors, they keep heading east."

"Yes," Wilson said, "precisely. So you have to get under way, and cut *Voortrekker* off."

"But *Challenger* still needs weeks of dry-dock work."

"Forty-eight hours. I'm giving you forty-eight hours to square your ship away. Then anything that isn't ready gets left behind. Ter Horst will be moving slowly, for stealth, and you can make the whole trip there through mostly friendly waters."

"Sir, I don't know what to say. I'm not sure the ship could be ready to sail in forty-eight hours."

"*Voortrekker* did it somehow. The *Yorktown* did it before the Battle of Midway in World War II. . . . I've already talked to the contractors, the union shop stewards, and *Challenger*'s skeleton crew. Everyone's working round the clock."

Jeffrey could picture the frenzied activity. He intended to do his part. He knew people were busting a gut to make *his* ship ready for *him*. Not meaning to, Jeffrey exhaled from the depths of his being.

"What is it?" Wilson said.

"Sir, I just learned my mother has breast cancer. It may have metastasized. I was going to ask for compassionate leave."

"That's out of the question. All leaves are canceled. You have your hands full, getting *Challenger* battle-ready. As battle-ready as possible."

"I understand, Commodore. . . . Is Miss Reebeck available, given the change of plans?" Her proven skills as combat oceanographer would be valuable.

"No. She's been sent to the study group that helps make sure our boomers remain undetectable by the enemy. The *Ohio*-class Trident missile subs are getting old. . . . It's not like we can drop hydrogen bombs on the heart of Europe or Africa, and kill millions of innocent civilians and hostages, just because the Axis caught us with our pants down by using tactical atomic weapons at sea. But if the Axis can threaten our Trident boats, and we lose our strategic deterrent against Russia and China, on top of everything else . . ."

"I understand, sir. Of course." Jeffrey thought the Germans and Boers had been much too clever and calculating. They exploited the wide but neglected gap in weaponry effects between NATO's conventional arms and the Armageddon-like power of NATO's H-bombs. The Axis used small atom bombs to drive a wedge far into that gap, to weaken Allied naval forces and sever essential supply lines—and now the Axis all but owned two continents. Fortunately, French commandos had been able to evacuate or destroy their country's hydrogen-bomb stocks before France folded to Germany. The hostages Wilson referred to included tens of thousands of touring American families and traveling business-people and vacationing college kids, all trapped on Axis turf when the war broke out last summer—and now interned in camps beside major enemy industrial sites.

A messenger arrived and handed Wilson a message slip. Wilson read it. His lips tightened and his jaw set.

Wilson looked at Jeffrey. "I'm sorry."

"Sir?" Jeffrey felt a stab to the heart. He thought his mother had died on the operating table.

"Miss Reebeck has been killed."

"Killed?" The word came out of his mouth like someone else spoke it.

"The aircraft she was riding in had a mishap. They ejected, but her ejection seat malfunctioned. The parachute failed to open."

"Are they *sure?*"

"The body was recovered quickly. . . . I'm sorry. I know the two of you were close."

"I . . ." Jeffrey just trailed off. He reminded himself he was a warship's captain now. He had an image to maintain as commanding officer. He fought a sense of bitterness that his big move up professionally, and the massive responsibilities it brought, were keeping him from tending to his own emotional needs.

Wilson watched him, read his inner struggle, and sighed. "We all lose people we care about in war. I lost a cousin and a nephew in the initial ambush off West Africa."

Jeffrey hesitated. "I didn't know that, sir."

"I don't like to talk about it."

Jeffrey sat there, not knowing what to say or do or feel.

"You need to get down to your ship," Wilson said gently, "and make the preparations."

"Yes, Commodore. Of course."

Jeffrey stood up, still in a bit of a daze. *My own command, my own command, and it has to happen like this.*

"There's more," Wilson said.

"Sir?"

"I'm coming with you to the Pacific."

"On *Challenger*, Commodore?"

"Yes. I'm detaching from DevRon Twelve, leaving things here to my deputy, to lead an undersea battle group. With such a vast area to cover, we can't afford to take on *Voortrekker* alone."

That stung, and it made Jeffrey angry. "Sir, is this a reference to my failure to sink ter Horst last time?"

Wilson's face grew stern. "I know you're upset, about your mother and now Miss Reebeck. But this is the wrong time and place to start getting touchy. And to answer your question, no, it's not a reference to anything. You just got two goddamn Navy Crosses, a promotion in rank, and a ship."

"Yes, sir. . . . What other vessels are in the battle group?"

"Several Royal Australian Navy diesel submarines. I don't know how many yet. Maybe four."

"Not *Collins* boats?"

"I'm afraid so."

"But they're death traps! They're noisy, they can't stay down long, their crush depth is barely a tenth of ours, and they're slow!"

"This isn't my decision, Captain. If *Voortrekker* does reach the Pacific, and gets loose in those tens of millions of square miles of very deep water . . ."

"Can't we work with our own fast-attacks?"

"The ones that haven't been sunk or badly damaged are stretched much too thin as it is. They're busy escorting the remaining carriers and our boomers, protecting the North and South Atlantic convoys, conducting special ops or spying against the Axis or Russia or China, not to mention keeping an eye on Third World rogues that might act up. It takes time to rejuggle deployments and refits. You know how it is. We'll get support, but not right away."

"I get the picture, sir."

"*Challenger* is by far the best platform to prosecute *Voortrekker*. You can handle *Challenger* in combat better than anyone, including me. You've faced *Voortrekker* before, and you *did* complete your assigned mission then."

"Understood."

"This is your chance for a rematch with ter Horst. Do it in Ilse Reebeck's memory."

Jeffrey was too worn out and beat up to feel much emotion at this point. He knew the real pain would come later.

Wilson rubbed his temples. Jeffrey suspected he was having another headache, and tried to look sympathetic.

Wilson glared at him. "Go down to your ship. We have to get to the other side of the planet, pronto."

Jeffrey turned to leave the cubicle. He drew some comfort that Wilson was as much a hard-ass as ever. Wilson seemed to be reminding him, none too subtly, that life simply had to go on.

"Oh," Wilson called after him. "One other thing."

"Commodore?"

"If you expect to make rear admiral, you'd better come up with something more articulate than 'I don't know what to say' when someone hands you a medal or a promotion or a command."

10

JEFFREY WOKE UP early, after barely four hours' sleep. The cot in the dormitory zone of the underground pens was uncomfortable. But with all the noise inside *Challenger*, from the contractors working frantically there, sleep on the ship was impossible.

Jeffrey put both feet on the floor, stretched to get the kinks out of his back, and *it* hit him. The handshakes and smiles, the flashbulbs, all the grand but hurried ceremonies of change of command and the medals, counted for little compared to the sense of loss that assaulted Jeffrey's mind as he stood up. Ilse Reebeck was dead. All their shared experiences during battle, all their passionate times in more recent nights, were as nothing now, wiped away.

Where could the captain of a U.S. Navy warship find the time or privacy to mourn? His cabin on *Challenger* was being used as a blueprint room by repair crews. He slept instead on a cot in a big room full of cots, hearing other people snore.

Jeffrey dressed as quietly as he could in the dark, so as not to wake the strangers slumbering near him. Then the other thing hit him, and he felt his insides sink even more.

His mother had come through surgery all right. But there were spots on the whole-body scan they'd done at Sloan-Kettering. Abnormalities on his mother's pancreas and liver. The doctors said the spots might just be *artifacts* of the imaging process itself. They might not be tumors at all, don't worry yet, they needed to run more tests. Jeffrey pictured what his mother might become: a wraith lying in a hospice bed, tubes in her arms, skin gray, body shrunken, life force draining away. He felt more grief and gnawing concern.

He made himself bottle it up. He shook his head to clear his thoughts, to compose himself for his hectic first full day as a nuclear submarine's commanding officer.

Jeffrey looked at his watch. There was just enough time to take a leak and grab a simple breakfast. A shower would need to wait. He'd scheduled a meeting very soon with his navigator and sonar officer.

Jeffrey sighed. He had so, so much work to do.

At least work eased the pain. Jeffrey knew the next time he'd sleep wouldn't be till *Challenger* was under way at sea.

JEFFREY sat in the little cubicle that was his temporary office. He nursed his third cup of coffee of the morning. The first to arrive was his navigator, with a laptop under one arm.

Lieutenant Richard Sessions had started as *Challenger*'s sonar officer, under Captain Wilson, even before Jeffrey first joined the ship as XO. Because of other casualties at the same time Wilson was wounded, Jeffrey made Sessions the acting navigator. Later this move up, to department head, was formalized.

Sessions was in his mid-twenties, earnest and capable. He came from a small town in Nebraska. He was a tad overweight, the sort of person whose clothes and hair always seemed a little sloppy no matter what he did. That might not go over well in the military, but Jeffrey liked and respected Sessions. One thing the lieutenant's work never was was sloppy, and in combat he kept his cool well. At the awards ceremony yesterday, when Jeffrey got his double Navy Cross, Sessions received a Bronze Star.

Sessions put his laptop on Jeffrey's desk, plugged it in, and turned it on. Then *Challenger*'s sonar officer scurried into the cubicle, Lieutenant

Kathy Milgrom of the Royal Navy. She'd been transferred from the crew of the U.K.'s ceramic-hulled nuclear submarine, HMS *Dreadnought,* after *Challenger*'s mission to South Africa. Before the war, the Royal Navy had begun to experiment with women on fast-attack crews. Kathy came to *Challenger* as an exchange officer, highly recommended. To some—but not all—higher-ups her presence was controversial. She fit in very well on the ship, and Jeffrey found her outstanding at her job.

Kathy was born in Liverpool; her accent was distinctive. Her family had been providing men—and more recently women—to the Royal Navy for generations. Kathy wore special submariner eyeglasses, with narrow frames to fit under an emergency air-breather mask. When she'd first joined *Challenger,* before the mission to Germany, she'd been plump. Two months later the love handles were gone. She was as businesslike as ever.

Kathy and Sessions took seats. There was a moment of mutual awkwardness. This was the first time they were talking serious matters since Jeffrey had formally assumed command. Having Jeffrey as acting captain in a crisis was one thing, but reporting to him as their official, ongoing commanding officer was new for all three of them.

Jeffrey hadn't anticipated this, the need to reorient relationships and subtly alter mind-sets. He decided immediately he'd continue as before. His style with his officers was collegial and confiding. If it worked in the heat of action, it would work again now. Jeffrey maintained discipline by example, by conspicuous dedication to his work, and through his contagious love of navy tradition and pomp. He knew his combat record spoke for itself.

"I'm sorry about Miss Reebeck," Sessions said.

Jeffrey nodded. "Thank you."

Kathy nodded too, and had to wipe back a tear. Then Jeffrey put it together: Kathy and Ilse had been roommates, and fast friends, on the ship. Kathy must miss her terribly.

It all came roaring back to Jeffrey, the sense of loss that was still sinking in, and he couldn't keep his eyes from moistening. He muttered to himself and reached for his handkerchief. Kathy pulled out a tissue. Then tears started in earnest. Sessions couldn't hold back either. The three of them let themselves cry. Mourning was a team effort, Jeffrey knew. Families had to mourn as a unit, together.

My crew is a family too. So be it. Let us mourn.

In a little while everyone felt better, and also felt bound closer together.

"All right, folks," Jeffrey said. Sessions and Kathy drew their chairs closer to his desk. Jeffrey used the laptop to bring up a map of the world.

"We have a problem," Jeffrey said. "We need to get from the East Coast of the U.S. all the way to the South Pacific quickly. We also need to be entirely covert about it, to make the Axis keep thinking that *Challenger*'s still caught in dry dock. I only see two ways to head, and I don't like either one of 'em."

"Go north or go south for starts, sir," Sessions said. "That's the main question, isn't it?"

"North means transiting under the ice cap, in the dead of winter. Very few areas of thin ice, so we'd be out of touch and possibly trapped. Russian attack subs lurking, protecting some of their boomers. *Anything* could happen, including an incident that triggers all-out World War Three."

Kathy Milgrom pointed to the spot on the map where Alaska and Siberia almost touched. "If we went north we'd have no choice but to come out here, Captain. The Bering Strait. Quite a tight choke point, right past Russian hydrophone grids. The chance of our being undetected is nil, I should say, and then the Russians might alert the Boers."

"You think they'd do that?" Sessions said.

"I wouldn't put it past them," Jeffrey said. "It's a very short step from selling arms to passing intelligence."

"Concur with that, sir," Sessions said.

"The southern route isn't much better," Jeffrey said. "In *that* direction, the choke point that really worries me is the Drake Passage." That was the gap between the southern tip of Argentina—Tierra del Fuego—and the northern tip of the jutting Antarctic Peninsula. "Half the neutral countries in South America are teetering on the fence, and Argentina is heavily rumored to favor the Axis side."

"Agreed, Captain," Kathy said. "Their navy may be cooperating with the Germans or Boers already, for all we know."

"Which route does Commodore Wilson want us to take?" Sessions asked.

"He hasn't decided yet, so we need to sketch out navigation and sonar counterdetection plans for both routes."

"There are thousands and thousands of miles to cross, Captain, whichever route we take," Sessions said.

"It's going to be very difficult to move fast yet remain invisible ourselves," Kathy added.

"That's the bind we're in, folks. Exactly. There's nothing we can do about it. There's another factor too, which makes the bind much worse: we'll be sailing with half our torpedo tubes sealed off. It's one penalty we pay for getting under way so quickly."

"There's nothing the yard workers can manage?" Sessions asked. "Jury-rig something so we have our full rate of fire?"

Jeffrey shook his head. "The battle damage was too serious. Four tubes is all we get."

Kathy and Sessions looked grim.

"At least we'll have our full complement of weapons," Jeffrey told them. More than fifty in *Challenger's* huge torpedo room, plus twelve cruise missiles in her separate vertical launch array.

"Very well," Jeffrey said. "Thanks. Get back to me when you have some basics worked out."

The two lieutenants took their laptops and their notes, and went off to find an unoccupied worktable somewhere. Jeffrey rose to go down to his ship. He had to check on the progress of the priority repairs. He needed to verify a million details: of equipment tests, of safety checks, of loading weapons and spare parts and food, of interfacing with the inspectors from Naval Reactors, of starting the cleanup of all the construction work so the ship would be ready for sea. There was no hope at all of time for a proper shakedown cruise, and this made Jeffrey nervous. There was hardly time to put a charge into *Challenger's* refurbished battery banks, and this made Jeffrey very nervous indeed.

"Sir!" a familiar voice called.

Jeffrey turned. It was his executive officer, Lieutenant Jackson Jefferson Bell. He was back a bit earlier then expected, from leave with his in-laws in Milwaukee. The two men shook hands warmly.

"How's the baby?" Jeffrey said. Bell's wife had just given birth to their first, a son, and mother and child were staying with her parents.

"Terrific." Bell grinned. "I brought pictures."

Jeffrey couldn't help smiling. "You look good," he told Bell. "Fatherhood suits you."

Bell did a double take when he saw Jeffrey's collar tabs. He reached to shake Jeffrey's hand again. Then Jeffrey smiled.

"I should congratulate *you,* Lieutenant Commander Bell."

"What?"

"Yesterday was a big day." Jeffrey filled Bell in on all the news, including Bell's promotion in rank and award of two Silver Stars, Bell's formal assignment as XO of *Challenger,* and the loss of Ilse Reebeck. The whole thing was bittersweet, but at least Bell was back. The two men were very close; Bell had done well as acting XO in mortal combat, twice. More to the point, as was his proper job now as official executive officer, Bell could help his captain—Jeffrey—with some of those final details of getting *Challenger* fit for battle in record time.

Most important of all, Bell could size up the twenty-five new crewmen, just assigned—all fresh trainees, starting the months of hard work needed to qualify on the boat and earn their dolphins. They were meant to replace an equal number of seasoned hands who'd been transferred off the ship when she went into dry dock. Twenty-five was a lot; it made Jeffrey fret. One entire fifth of his crew, when *Challenger* sailed in harm's way, would be facing enemy fire for the first time in their lives. Some of them didn't know yet which way to turn a cutoff valve to stop bad flooding, or even which end of the boat was up.

11

JEFFREY STOOD IN the open bridge cockpit atop *Challenger*'s sail—the conning tower. He was crammed between the phone talker and the officer of the deck. In spite of his parka, Jeffrey shivered in the heavy, freezing sleet and freakish wintertime hail. At least the wind was from behind him and the ship, from upriver. It was in the wee hours of the night. The total dark and terrible visibility were exactly what he and Commodore Wilson wanted. They were already five hours behind schedule, just now getting out of the pens. Fortunately this unexpected squall, with the perfect concealment it gave, took some of the edge off Wilson's displeasure at Jeffrey's delay.

Challenger's reactor was shut down, to suppress her infrared signature. As a consequence, the ship had no propulsion power. She was being pulled behind a big oil barge, itself pulled by a powerful civilian tugboat. The lash-up began to hurry down the river in the blinding squall.

The unladen, high-riding barge was there to mask *Challenger*'s already-stealthy radar cross section from prying enemy eyes. The barge also shielded *Challenger* from making telltale echoes off the tugboat's busy navigation radar, echoes which a hostile passive radar receiver might hear. To further avoid any witnesses, the Interstate 95 bridge was closed by state police—supposedly because of icing due to the squall. The railroad drawbridge was up, but it was normally kept open until just before a train came.

Jeffrey knew the path ahead had been swept for enemy mines, but such sweeps were made regularly in any case. He hoped that *Challenger*'s departure would go totally unnoticed.

Because of the dangers of this untried maneuver, Jeffrey himself had the conn. Now and then the wind shifted, and caught the sail, and *Challenger* rolled. Jeffrey would give helm orders over the intercom—the phone talker was there as backup, in case the intercom failed. Even without propulsion power, Jeffrey needed the rudder constantly to keep the submarine lined up behind the barge.

Challenger's helmsman was not the ship's regular battle stations helmsman, Lieutenant (j.g.) David Meltzer. Meltzer was one of eight experienced men on leave who, because of travel delays nationwide and Wilson's emergency order to sail, hadn't made it back to the ship. Jeffrey was thus working even more shorthanded than he'd expected, and on any submarine eight missing fully qualified crewmen was a lot. Instead, *Challenger* brought a dozen civilian contractors along, needed to keep working away on critical repairs and upgrades. They'd all eagerly volunteered, in spite of their draft exemptions, even knowing they might never return from this cruise.

Jeffrey hoped his stand-in helmsman, a raw ensign, would do an effective job. Without her own propulsion power, *Challenger* had no way to stop quickly. She might ram the barge if something went wrong. If that happened, the bow cap and the sonar dome would be smashed, and the mission would end before it began. It was the railroad drawbridge that really worried Jeffrey. The gap there was infamously tight.

Jeffrey held his breath as the soaring I-95 bridge went by overhead, unseen in the pitch-dark and bad weather. Jeffrey knew that broken concrete and twisted rebars dangled somewhere up there high above, damage from the cruise missile raid before Christmas that was still undergoing repair. People feared the whole bridge might come down, because of the constant heavy trucking that used the only two of the original six lanes still open. I-95 was a vital logistics artery for the whole Northeast. If the bridge did collapse—maybe because of wind stress from this storm—that artery would be cut. The wreckage, in the shallow riverbed, would also block the only way from the New London base to the sea.

The I-95 bridge, or debris from it, didn't fall. Jeffrey wiped the lenses of his night-vision goggles again. The constant sleet buildup made them almost useless. Jeffrey realized he couldn't count on much help from his lookouts either. They stood behind him, in their safety harnesses, on the roof of the sail. They peered intently into the murk all around, but Jeffrey knew no night-vision gear could penetrate such thick weather.

The sleet turned into hail the size of lima beans. The hail beat against Jeffrey's shoulders and his parka hood. It made a drumming, spattering sound against *Challenger*'s hull and the barge dead ahead. Sharp, cold fragments of hail punished Jeffrey's face. He and the phone talker and the officer of the deck huddled closer together for warmth and protection. The hail went through the grating on which they stood, down through the open hatches of the bridge trunk, and into a corridor inside the hull. Hail or worse getting into the ship just had to be put up with: It was a navy safety regulation to always keep these two hatches open when the bridge was manned.

Jeffrey held his breath again as the low railroad drawbridge came up, barely outlined on his goggles, close in on both sides. *Challenger* was committed.

The wind veered unexpectedly, and *Challenger* started to yaw off track. Jeffrey snapped more helm orders. But the yaw increased and Jeffrey saw they were going to hit the bridge. He looked ahead, then looked behind him, cursing that he couldn't see his rudder or wake in the murk. Something was very wrong.

"Helm, Bridge," he snapped into his intercom mike. "I said *right* ten degrees rudder, not *left*."

Silence on the intercom. The phone talker also stayed mute.

Jeffrey's heart was in his throat. *We're going to hit the bridge.* It was much too late to signal the tug to stop. It was too late even to try to maneuver on what battery charge Jeffrey had.

"Helm, *hard* right rudder smartly, *now now now!*"

Challenger began to yaw the other way, but not fast enough.

"Collision alarm!" Jeffrey could hear it blaring down inside the ship.

Jeffrey leaned over the side of the sail cockpit. He stared aft, watching helplessly, dreading the grinding thud of impact and the screaming tearing of ceramic composite and steel. The lookouts knelt and braced themselves.

The wind veered again, and caught the broad side of the barge. The barge yawed. The side force came back through the tow cables. The cables made *Challenger* pivot. The pivoting barely steered the sub through the opening in the drawbridge.

Jeffrey let himself breathe again. They'd made it, but only by the grace of a puff of wind, pure random luck.

"Helm, Bridge," Jeffrey called on the intercom, "please try to remember your right from your left."

"Bridge, Helm, sorry, Captain," a scared young voice responded. "No excuse, sir."

Jeffrey bit down his fright and his temper. "Helm, Bridge, no harm done." Jeffrey knew now he and Bell had their work cut out, melding all the newcomers from a rabble into a genuine, smooth-running crew.

From here, at least, the river was more open. Jeffrey's main concern for the moment was the big barge looming in front of him. Empty of oil, riding so high, the barge continued to catch the wind. It kept drifting right and left in the navigable channel. The tug crew did what they could to compensate, but this threesome follow-the-leader, snaking down the river at high speed to keep up with the squall, was nerve-racking. *Challenger* had deep draft even while surfaced. To run aground would be as bad as a collision: a permanent blot on Jeffrey's record, never mind what it meant to *Challenger* and his intercepting ter Horst.

They passed the spot where off to starboard, on the land, sat the railroad station. So recently Jeffrey had stood there in the early morning sun, waiting for the train to Washington, wishing instead he was headed out to sea, dreading he'd get stuck in a rear-area land job after his training course.

I got my wish. I'd gladly give it all up in a minute, if it would restore my mother to health and bring Ilse Reebeck back.

At dawn

To get the ship concealed before morning, Commodore Wilson ordered Jeffrey to dive *Challenger* as soon as they reached a hundred feet of water. Jeffrey knew this was much shallower than the minimum considered safe in peacetime, but it was a very long way from New London to the edge of the continental shelf, where the water first got deep. The dive would be all the more tricky with an inexperienced man at the helm and no propulsion power—but after some sweat-filled moments they made it down all right. The tug and barge proceeded on their way, tow cables coiled, their duty to *Challenger* done.

Jeffrey sat in the control room uneasily. He rubbed his hands together for warmth. He was out of his sleet-covered parka, and he'd changed to a dry set of clothes, but now, underwater, it was very cold on the ship with no heat. It was also strangely quiet, and dark. Only dim emergency lighting was on. The air fans were turned off, and hardly any other equipment was running—all to conserve precious amps from the battery banks.

Jeffrey didn't like his present tactical situation one bit. *Challenger* sat in such shallow water, in windswept seas, that she rolled constantly from side to side, from wave action right overhead. She was much too vulnerable like this, motionless except for the caprice of waves and currents and tide. She had no way to move on her own yet, with the reactor still shut down. If proper trim was lost, they could easily hit the bottom, only several feet beneath the keel, and suffer serious damage— or they might broach, exposing the sail or even the hull, and thus destroy their stealth, because the sun was coming up.

Passive sonar conditions here were poor. If a deep-draft merchant ship suddenly rounded Montauk Point on a collision course . . . Jeffrey didn't want to *begin* to think about that.

Jeffrey watched the status displays on his console, one of the very few switched on. Around him, in the cramped space, stood or sat some twenty members of his crew. The tension was palpable, and no one spoke unless they needed to.

Challenger's chief of the boat, whom everyone called COB, sat beside the helmsman at the front of the compartment; on the newest subs, the helmsman was a junior officer who himself controlled the bowplanes and sternplanes and rudder. COB was very busy, adjusting the ballast and trim. For now, the newbie helmsman had nothing to do. The contrast as they sat there with their backs to Jeffrey seemed to say so much: COB, Latino, forty-something, salty and irreverent, came from Jersey City, and was short and squat like a bulldog. The helmsman, Ensign Tom Harrison from Orlando, was barely twenty. His voice was as reedy as his build, and he would seem nerdy even in a crowd at MIT—where he finished college in three years.

Lieutenant Commander Jackson Bell sat just to Jeffrey's right, at the two-man command workstation in the middle of the control room. He perched on the edge of his seat, sharing Jeffrey's screens to save power. Bell was literally on the edge of his seat: as executive officer he was in charge of damage control. With the rush to get out of port on a shoe-string—with hardly enough in the battery charge for one try to get the reactor restarted—no one knew when something might break, something fatal.

The compartment's phone talker, a young enlisted man wearing a bulky sound-powered rig, relayed status reports to Jeffrey and Bell from other parts of the ship. The phone talker's throat sounded tight and dry, reflecting how everyone felt. The *Thresher* had been lost with all hands because of defects at the start of what was supposed to be a routine shakedown cruise.

The weapons officer, a lieutenant who in combat reported to Bell, was working at a console on a lower deck, outside the torpedo room. With the war, Weps's station was shifted there, for positive control of special—atomic—weapons in a fast-attack submarine. At the moment, Weps, who was new to the ship, was supervising final assembly of the warheads.

Lieutenant Willey, *Challenger's* engineer, was overseeing the propulsion plant restart, back in the maneuvering room, aft of the reactor compartment. His two dozen people had begun this work before the ship left dry dock, but only now could they do the important steps, the ones which involved heat. This cold startup with no outside support was a difficult endeavor. It would never have been attempted at all if there weren't such a drastic need for secrecy and stealth. Thermal energy from the reactor had to be used in carefully measured spurts to gradually warm up every main steam plant component. If one step didn't go right, *Challenger* would need to surface and radio for a tow back to the pens.

Jeffrey liked the tall and straight-talking Willey, who'd been with the ship on *Challenger*'s previous missions. Jeffrey understood the immense pressure Willey was under now—Jeffrey had been the engineer on a *Los Angeles*–class boat during his own department-head tour four years previously. There was no point in asking Willey to hurry. He was as aware as anyone else on board of the imminent danger of being run down by some civilian cargo vessel that didn't even know *Challenger* was there.

After a lengthy and worry-filled wait that saw Jeffrey eye the chronometer often, the phone talker relayed briskly, "Maneuvering reports ready to answer all bells."

Jeffrey wasn't much of a churchgoer, but he said a heartfelt prayer. He was about to find out, all at once, if the steam pipes and the condensors, the main turbogenerators and the big electric motors attached to the shaft, and the repaired pump-jet propulsor at the back of the boat really worked. There'd been no time to test the power train the proper way, tied up at a pier.

This is one hell of a way to begin the patrol, waiting step by step for a part of the ship to fall off.

If our pump jet doesn't turn, we go right back into dry dock . . . and Voortrekker *goes wherever Jan ter Horst wants.*

Jeffrey's heart pounded, but he also felt a nice silvery tingling anticipation in his chest. He paused, savoring the moment. He was about to give his first engine order as USS *Challenger*'s official commanding officer.

"Helm, ahead one-third." *Challenger* started to move.

12

A few hours later, on *Challenger*, under way at sea

CHALLENGER WAS PAST the edge of the continental shelf, submerged in very deep water. The crew had been sent to a hearty breakfast of nourishing hot food, with several choices of entrées, and now was settling in to the watch-keeping routines of being under way at sea.

Jeffrey sat alone at the desk in his stateroom. As usual, he kept the door open while he worked. In the control room, only a few feet up the corridor, a talented junior officer from engineering had the conn. Bell, in Jeffrey's absence, was command duty officer, Jeffrey's surrogate there. In a few more minutes Bell would turn in for badly needed sleep.

Jeffrey was a bit exhausted himself. His eyes burned. He knew they were bloodshot. His whole body felt wired, from lack of rest combined with too much adrenaline now growing stale.

Jeffrey was finishing paperwork, since the basic engineering tests were mostly complete. The ship had held up well enough as they gradually descended to test depth, ten thousand feet—two-thirds of their crush depth, which nominally was fifteen thousand. The problems discovered along the way were mostly small. They were resolved by isolating minor equipment, or bypassing sections of pipe.

The one potentially serious glitch was in the torpedo room. Several thousand feet down, during trials with seawater in the tubes at ambient pressure of more than a ton for each square inch, firing mechanism components failed in all four available tubes. COB and the weapons officer, aided by some of the contractors, had men working to install replacement parts from *Challenger*'s spares. This would take a while, but Jeffrey wasn't overly worried. Though the weapons officer was inexperienced, COB was very good at getting things done. Besides, Jeffrey didn't expect to need to shoot torpedoes very soon.

A messenger knocked on the doorjamb. Jeffrey looked up. The awkward youngster asked Jeffrey to go to the commodore's office—Wilson had taken over the executive officer's stateroom. Jeffrey's navigator, Lieutenant Sessions, was with the messenger.

When Jeffrey and Sessions arrived, Wilson rose to greet them curtly. Jeffrey was still getting used to Wilson's reading glasses and stubble of beard. Jeffrey thought they made Wilson look professorial. *Yeah, that type of hard-hearted slave-driving prof who'd always get the best out of you, and break you if you disappointed him once.*

"Sit down, both of you."

Jeffrey took the guest chair. Sessions perched on a filing cabinet.

"Captain," Wilson said to Jeffrey, "as commodore of a battle group I require a staff."

"Sir?"

"I want you to double as my operations officer, and Sessions here as my executive assistant. . . . I don't need a separate communications officer, I'll borrow yours as necessary."

"Yes, Commodore." Jeffrey glanced at Sessions. Sessions nodded.

"I want your XO and Sessions to trade racks for the duration of this cruise. That way Sessions and I can work together in here more closely. I'll keep to Lieutenant Sessions's watch schedule for now, so he and I will sleep at the same time." The XO's stateroom had an extra rack—bunk—usually reserved for a VIP rider such as an admiral, or members of Congress.

"I'll inform Commander Bell," Jeffrey said. "I'm sure it won't be a problem."

"I'm *quite* sure it won't be a problem."

"Yes, sir." By long naval tradition, not even the president of the United States could displace a warship's captain from his stateroom. The captain, on his own ship, was supreme.

But I can see already having Wilson here as more than just an observer is going to be tricky, Jeffrey told himself. *Where exactly does my authority end, and his begin? Where will the dividing line fall when we meet the Australian diesels days from now, and Wilson's undersea battle group becomes an untested reality?*

"If I may ask, Commodore, which route do you want us to follow to the Pacific?"

"South."

Jeffrey glanced at Sessions, as a cue; Jeffrey let Sessions speak for himself.

"We propose to hide in the Gulf Stream, Commodore, at least until we're past the Bahamas. Lieutenant Milgrom feels the confused sonar conditions in the stream will help conceal us."

"Good. I leave the details to you to work out. . . . Captain, I want the ship to go faster."

"How fast, Commodore?"

"Make flank speed until I say otherwise."

"*Flank* speed, Commodore?" For *Challenger*, that was over fifty knots. *Challenger* was extremely quiet, but at flank speed any sub was noisy.

Wilson looked impatiently at Jeffrey. "*Flank speed,* Captain. I expect you to use local sonar conditions, and ship's depth versus bottom terrain, to prevent our signature from carrying into the deep sound channel."

"Understood." If *Challenger*'s noise did leak into that acoustic super-conducting layer in the deep ocean, it could be picked up on the far side of the Atlantic—the German side. Jeffrey didn't like this, but what was his alternative?

"That's all."

Jeffrey and Sessions got up.

"Lieutenant, you stay here. We have things to discuss. Have your assistant navigator take over in the control room."

Sessions acknowledged.

Jeffrey, in the doorway, turned back to Wilson. "Sir, Commodore, I have a concern."

"Let's hear it."

"At flank speed we're almost totally sonar-blind. We could get into trouble."

"The route south has been sanitized for us by other forces, and will continue to be. You need to remind yourself that undersea warfare is a *team* sport, Commander Fuller.... If we stick to the safe corridors, we're immune to attack by our own antisubmarine assets."

"We'll be picked up by the Sound Surveillance System hydrophone nets for sure."

"Of course. *So?*" Wilson glowered at him.

Jeffrey caught himself starting to ball his fists in irritation. He made himself relax. "Sir, I apologize if I'm not expressing myself clearly. My point is that it's risky to create a big datum on our *own* SOSUS, even if the East Coast is clear of enemy subs. If the Axis has a spy on the SOSUS staff, or they're tapping our data directly somehow, they'll know we're at sea, and which way we're heading." Jeffrey wasn't naturally paranoid, but in force-on-force submarine missions paranoia was a survival trait.

"You really think the higher-ups haven't thought of that?"

Wilson's annoyance was obvious, but Jeffrey thought his own objection was perfectly valid. Now he really felt pissed, but by a supreme effort kept it internal.

"Shut the door," Wilson said. "Sit down."

Jeffrey pulled the door closed and took the guest seat again. Sessions still perched on the filing cabinet. He looked uncomfortable, and not just physically.

"First of all," Wilson said, "the lines are monitored constantly for eavesdropping, and the hydrophones are inspected periodically as well. *That* much, you should have figured out for yourself. Secondly, Atlantic Fleet has performed certain naval maneuvers near Norfolk intended to surely pique the Germans' attention, assuming they did have a mole in the SOSUS shop. We have our own espionage resources in Europe, I'm informed, and said maneuvers were not reacted to at all.

Hence, the Germans were not aware of them, and therefore do not have a mole."

"But—" *Maybe the Germans did have a well-placed spy, and knew the maneuvers were a trick and just ignored them.*

"This is highly classified. You and Sessions are not to relate this to anyone else in the crew."

"But the men, I mean Lieutenant Milgrom too . . . especially her, as Sonar . . . they'll be very concerned to see us take such chances, going so fast. What am I supposed to tell them?"

"Tell them you're the captain," Wilson snapped, "and they're *supposed* to obey your orders."

Jeffrey hesitated. "Yes, sir."

Wilson shuffled papers on his desk. "I said before, that's all."

Jeffrey turned to leave.

"Commander Fuller," Wilson called after him.

"Commodore?"

"Have me informed when we draw level with the mouth of Chesapeake Bay."

"Aye aye, sir."

"And tell someone to bring me another guest chair. I can't have my flagship staff sitting on filing cabinets."

13

Night of the first day at sea,
one hundred miles east of the mouth of Chesapeake Bay

"COMMODORE IN CONTROL," the messenger of the watch announced.

"As you were." Wilson came over and stood next to Jeffrey. Jeffrey, after a pleasant catnap, was expecting him. *Challenger* made flank speed, as ordered, vibrating steadily as the propulsion plant worked hard. Consoles squeaked gently in their shock-absorbing mounts, and mike cords near the overhead swayed back and forth. A boyish part of Jeffrey really enjoyed seeing and hearing these little signs of how fast his ship was going.

"Status, Captain?" Wilson asked.

"We've been following the edge of the continental shelf, sir. The north side of the Gulf Stream throws off meanders and eddies here. Horizontally, vertically, they form temperature and salinity cells that distort and attenuate sound."

"Why did you pick eleven hundred feet as your depth?"

"In case someone does get a whiff of us, they'll think we're a steel-hulled sub."

"Bring the ship to these coordinates. Slow to ahead one-third when you're twenty minutes out." Wilson handed Jeffrey a piece of paper.

Jeffrey raised his eyebrows. Wilson wanted a spot farther south, off North Carolina's Cape Fear. But the location was miles more away from the land, in very deep water, since the coast here ran southwest. They'd have to cut diagonally through the whole width of the Gulf Stream.

"Why there, Commodore?"

"More eddies and meanders on the far edge of the stream. We have a rendezvous."

Jeffrey was surprised. This was the first he'd heard of it. "With what ship?"

"No ship. A minisub." *Challenger* was sailing with her in-hull hangar empty, since the Advanced SEAL Delivery System mini she'd taken with her to Germany had had to be jettisoned in combat.

"The mini's one of ours?"

"Yes, an ASDS."

"Purpose of rendezvous, sir?"

"Pick up the crewmen we left behind, and keep the mini."

Jeffrey read the coordinates to his assistant navigator, a senior chief at the digital plotting table near the back of the control room. The chief recommended a course. Jeffrey gave the helm orders.

The helmsman for this watch acknowledged—Tom Harrison again. *Challenger* banked into the turn, still making a noisy flank speed.

Then Jeffrey started to wonder. "Commodore, do we need an ASDS where we're going?" If the minisub was carrying eight of Jeffrey's crew, there'd be no room in it for SEALs.

"Got your torpedo tubes working yet?"

"Not yet."

THEY were nearing the rendezvous. Jeffrey gave the order to reduce speed. The vibrations died down, and the ride became very smooth. The ship felt oddly sedate, after hours of tearing through the ocean at more than fifty knots. With much reduced self-noise, it was time for a thorough sonar sweep. Jeffrey turned to Kathy Milgrom. She sat nearby with her back to him, at the head of a line of sonar consoles along the control room's port side; thanks to advances in miniaturization and fiber-optic data fusion, Sonar no longer had a separate room.

It took some time to perform the sweep and analyze the data. *Challenger* turned slowly in a wide circle, to expose her hydrophone arrays on every compass bearing.

When the gradual circle was almost complete, Jeffrey drew a breath to tell the helmsman to resume course.

Kathy tensed in her seat before Jeffrey could speak. She looked his way. "New broadband contact, Captain. Ahead of us."

"Classify it?"

"Difficult in these conditions, sir. The signal surges and fades. Designate it Master One."

"Submerged?" *Could be it's the minisub.*

"Wait one." Kathy talked with her sonar chief. He spoke with the enlisted technicians. They studied their screens and listened on headphones.

"Master One is submerged," the sonar chief said confidently.

"The minisub must be out of position," Jeffrey said. "Good thing we found it." *Maybe the mini had a navigation error that brought it here. Such things do happen.*

"Negative," Kathy said. "Master One is not a minisub."

"I got tonals!" a sonarman shouted. "No, wait, it's gone."

"Play it back," Kathy ordered. She and the chief put on headphones. She typed on her keyboard, and Jeffrey saw the frequency spectrum of the contact's noise. "Captain, it's nuclear powered."

Jeffrey nodded. "Must be the fast-attack that dropped off the mini, going back to Norfolk."

"I can't be positive, sir."

Jeffrey waited and waited for more information. Technicians intently worked their gear. Kathy and her senior chief murmured in consultation.

Jeffrey forced himself to be patient. He knew Kathy Milgrom had been in combat on HMS *Dreadnought* since the very start of the war. He knew firsthand, from *Challenger*'s mission to Germany, that she was a more than capable officer.

"*Got 'em again,*" the sonarman exclaimed—with relief, and professional pride.

Jeffrey opened his mouth to offer a compliment.

The young man jolted like he'd gotten an electric shock. His voice rose two octaves. "Master One is hostile! Confirmed! Classify as a definite *Amethyste II!*"

Jeffrey was wide awake. Everyone sat up much straighter. The *Amethyste II*s were German, captured from France. They were state-of-the-art, and deadly.

"Chief of the Watch," Jeffrey snapped, "sound silent general quarters. Man battle stations antisubmarine." COB acknowledged.

The word passed quickly, and more men ran to the control room. The compartment became a sea of hurrying figures in blue cotton jumpsuits, squeezing past each other purposefully. Some men grabbed seats and powered up their consoles. Others stood in the aisles. The phone talker took his position, put on his rig, and did a communications check.

"COB," Jeffrey said, "get me a torpedo tube, fast."

"I better go down there, Captain."

"Do it." A senior chief took over from COB in the left seat at the ship-control station. Harrison still had the right seat as helmsman. Jeffrey saw Harrison shift in his chair. He flexed his fingers as he gripped the control wheel. *Sure. He's nervous.*

I'm nervous too.

Jeffrey set his jaw in firm concentration.

Bell dashed in in his boxer shorts, barefoot and rubbing sleep from his eyes, and sat down next to Jeffrey. At battle stations, Bell was fire-control coordinator. Sonar and weapons reported to him.

Commodore Wilson came in, followed by Sessions. Wilson wore a bathrobe and slippers. Sessions stuffed his khaki shirttails into his pants by the navigation console.

"What is it?" Wilson snapped.

Jeffrey told him.

"Evade it."

"That's my intent." Jeffrey turned to Bell. "Fire Control, can you give me the enemy's course?"

Bell got an update from the fire-controlmen who sat to his right.

"Not yet, Captain. Sparse data. The contact seems to bounce around a lot because of the eddies. We're in bad water, sir, sound paths get twisted all over the place."

"Range? Speed? Anything?"

"Nothing yet."

"Evade it," Wilson repeated, coldly.

Jeffrey needed to make a decision, with very little to go on. He figured the *Amethyste II* was waiting for a juicy target—a big, noisy carrier—to come out of the Norfolk, Virginia, naval base, heading for the North Atlantic battle front. Jeffrey would distance himself from Norfolk and hence from the enemy sub.

"Helm, right ten degrees rudder. Make your course one three five." Southeast.

Harrison acknowledged. He sounded calm enough, but his rudder work was still clumsy under pressure.

The new course should give Kathy better sonar data. It pointed *Challenger*'s port wide-aperture array directly toward Master One. The wide arrays, attached along both sides of the hull, could do powerful things with advanced signal processing.

"Fire Control," Jeffrey urged, "get me a firing solution, just in case."

"Still working, sir," Bell said. It was strange to see him sitting in his underwear, taller than Jeffrey, fit but not as muscular. Bell might just as well have been wearing a formal dress-mess tuxedo, for all the difference it made to his manner and bearing.

"Fire Control, sir," Kathy broke in. "We've got more detailed tonal data. Advise this *Amethyste II* is the *von Tirpitz*."

Bell raised his eyebrows. "Captain, that's the one that launched those Mach eight missiles at New York."

Jeffrey had a flashback, him and Ilse atop the Empire State Building. He frowned. *This is personal now.*

"But what's it doing *here*?" he asked pointedly, disturbed. "Intelligence said it evaded our forces that counterattacked and snuck back to Europe badly damaged."

"No evidence of damage in the tonals, Captain," Kathy said. "We've a definite match to the New York event's datum on the *von Tirpitz*."

"So much for intelligence," Wilson said. "Why am I not surprised?"

"Phone talker," Jeffrey said, "ask COB how they're doing." Jeffrey *had* to have the ability to defend himself.

"Torpedo room reports they need another few minutes."

That's not what I wanted to hear. If Master One's captain was willing to carry liquid-hydrogen-fueled cruise missiles, then what other awful weapons does he have aboard?

Jeffrey could only wait: for his ship to put some distance between him and the *Tirpitz,* for Bell to figure out the *Tirpitz's* depth and course and speed, and for COB to get a tube in order for Jeffrey to fight if forced to. Unfortunately, the acute need for stealth meant that *Challenger* had to move slowly, and the men in the torpedo room dared not bang against the hull.

Jeffrey made a conscious effort to keep from fidgeting in front of his crew. He was inherently a man of action. He disliked unavoidable idleness, this inevitable part of undersea warfare that required he hold for better data and better position before having something specific to do.

Jeffrey pictured the *von Tirpitz* lurking out there somewhere near, her hull containing a hundred-plus well-trained German officers and men who'd do their damnedest to sink *Challenger* if given the slightest chance.

Each second felt like an hour.

A sonarman shattered the edgy silence. "Hydrophone effects!" he screamed.

"Classify," Kathy ordered, very coolly.

"Underwater missile booster engine firing!"

"Where?" Jeffrey demanded.

"Source is Master One," Bell said.

Crap. "Put it on speakers." A rumbling roar filled the air.

"Main missile engine firing!" The roar got deeper and louder.

"It's a Shkval, Captain," Kathy reported. "Constant bearing and depth, signal strength increasing. It's aimed at *Challenger!*"

The Tirpitz *found us. With these quirky sonar conditions, we just weren't quiet enough.*

"Helm, ahead flank."

"Ahead flank, aye!" Harrison turned the engine order telegraph, a four-inch dial on his console. "Maneuvering answers, ahead flank!" *Challenger* sped up.

Jeffrey fought to keep himself from cursing aloud. The Shkval undersea missile-torpedoes were Russian, sold to the Axis. They rode through the water in a vacuum bubble caused by their own speed. They could do three hundred knots, and nothing could escape them.

Jeffrey grabbed an intercom handset.

"Get me COB. . . . COB, we've got a Shkval on our tail. We have to get a tube working so we can launch counterfire."

"Any minute, Captain, I'll give you tube three."

"We don't have minutes, COB. We barely have seconds."

Jeffrey put down the mike. He could picture the harried activity, as men struggled with parts and tools inside the torpedo tube. The ship topped forty knots, fast on the way to fifty. The flank speed vibrations resumed. *Challenger* shivered and quaked, as if to somehow shake off the Shkval, as if the ship herself felt fear.

Jeffrey listened as the Shkval roared and roared on the speakers, a mindless machine that ate up the distance relentlessly. Jeffrey began to order countertactics he knew would probably fail. Shkvals were nuclear armed. It didn't need to get close to do *Challenger* terrible damage. Jeffrey thought of the fallout any atomic blast would create. *Thank God we're far from the East Coast now, and the winds are blowing farther out to sea.*

"Helm, make a knuckle." The ship banked hard to port and then to starboard. It left a turbulent spot in the water, which an enemy weapon just might think was *Challenger*. The deep roar of the Shkval kept getting louder.

"Helm, left fifteen degrees rudder. Make your course one one zero."

"Left fifteen degrees rudder, aye! Make my course one one zero, aye!" A turn left, east-southeast. Jeffrey would try to jink out of the weapon's path, to force it to lead the target. This might confuse its sensors, and buy him precious time. It also led the weapon farther away from the land.

"Fire Control, launch noisemakers and acoustic jammers."

"Noisemakers, jammers, aye!" Loud gurgling, and an undulating siren noise, were heard now on the speakers. There was also the roar of the Shkval, deeper in tone as it came up to maximum speed, plus a nasty hiss from flow noise as *Challenger* herself reached fifty knots. The gurgling and sirens subsided, as *Challenger*'s countermeasures were quickly left behind.

Jeffrey picked up the handset again. "Maneuvering, Captain. Push the reactor to one hundred fifteen percent."

Challenger sped up slightly, and the flank-speed vibrations grew much rougher. Jeffrey bounced in his seat. The ship kept racing through the ocean, heading east-southeast at over fifty knots. The Shkval was following them around through the turn, closing by more than the length of a football field every second. It ignored the knuckle and countermeasures.

The data for weapons status on Jeffrey's console showed torpedo tube three turn green.

"*Tube three is operational,*" Bell said.

"Tube three, load a nuclear Mark 48, set warhead to maximum yield." *Challenger*'s Improved Advanced Capability Mark 48 torpedoes were good, but the latest version's top speed was seventy knots—barely a quarter of the Shkval's.

Bell and Jeffrey did the procedures to arm the atomic warhead; *Challenger*'s torpedo-room hydraulic autoloader, repaired in New London dry dock, seemed to be working well. *It better keep working or we're dead.*

Jeffrey felt an iron determination to survive. To defeat this enemy ambush he had to strike back fast and hard. "Make tube three ready in all respects including opening outer doors!"

"Ship ready. Weapon ready. Solution ready," Bell said.

"Tube three, Master One, match sonar bearings and *shoot.*"

"Tube three fired electrically."

"Unit is running normally!" a sonarman said.

"What are you doing?" Wilson said. "You aimed at Master One, not the Shkval."

"The unit will first pass near the Shkval. The *Amethyste*'s captain'll think it's my defensive shot at his missile, and he'll be lulled. We have to return fire, to distract him and keep him from sending off a message. If he knows we're *Challenger* . . ."

Wilson stayed quiet.

Good, this is my *fight.* Jeffrey's ship kept driving through the sea. The enemy Shkval kept following.

"Range to incoming Shkval?"

"Ten thousand yards," Bell said. Five nautical miles. If its warhead yield was one kiloton, standard in Axis torpedoes, the blast would be in lethal range at four thousand yards.

With these speeds and distances we have less than a minute to live.

"Fire Control, more noisemakers and jammers."

"Noisemakers, jammers, aye."

"Tube three, load a brilliant decoy."

"Tube three, decoy, aye."

"Set decoy course due north, flank speed, running depth same as ours."

"Due north, flank speed, same depth, aye."

"Make tube three ready in all respects including opening outer doors. Tube three, brilliant decoy, *shoot.*"

"Tube three fired electrically."

"Decoy is operating properly!"

Challenger kept fleeing. The propulsion plant worked its heart out. The noise of the Shkval on the sonar speakers was almost deafening now. Jeffrey was taking an awful gamble, that the seeker head at the tip of the enemy rocket would home on the decoy and not his ship. He was taking another awful gamble, that his own atomic fish would force the *Tirpitz*'s captain to take defensive steps, and buy COB time to give Jeffrey another working tube.

The universe shattered in an unimaginable thunderclap, and *Challenger* was pummeled as if by the fists of an angry God. Mike cords, light fixtures, consoles, crewmen, everything rattled and jarred.

"Shkval has detonated!" Bell shouted. "Decoy destroyed!" The Shkval had gone for the brilliant decoy after all.

The Shkval's nuclear blast reflected off the surface and the bottom, pounding *Challenger* more and more. Kathy turned off the speakers. Endless reverb sounded right through the hull. There were brutal aftershocks, as the fireball of the nuclear blast thrust upward for the surface. The fireball fell in on itself against the undersea water pressure, rebounded outward hard, fell in again and rebounded, over and over. Each rebound threw another hammer blow.

"Give me damage-control reports," Jeffrey shouted.

"Torpedo room autoloader is out of action!"

"Load tube three manually, a nuclear Mark forty-eight."

"Torpedo in the water!" Kathy yelled. "Assess as a defensive shot by Master One against our unit from tube three." The *Tirpitz* was trying to intercept Jeffrey's first torpedo with a nuclear countershot.

There was a huge eruption in the distance.

"Unit from tube three destroyed," Bell said.

The enemy captain had succeeded. Jeffrey distracted his Shkval, but he smashed Jeffrey's Mark 48. The initial exchange of fire was a draw.

"Shkval in the water," Kathy shouted. "Master One has launched another Shkval!"

Jeffrey frowned. *My decoy fooled the first Shkval, but it didn't fool the enemy captain. He knows that we're still out here, and he wants to sink us once and for all.*

Jeffrey grabbed the handset. "COB, I need another tube, *now.*"

"We're doing everything we can, sir! We got wounded down here! We got men working block and tackle loading the weapons. . . ."

Jeffrey clicked off.

"Helm, right full rudder, make your course one five zero." South-southeast, directly away from the *Tirpitz.*

Harrison acknowledged, shouting, and his voice cracked. The ship turned, banking too hard. Harrison lost control, and *Challenger* went into a snap roll—she'd heeled so much from the turn, her rudder began to act like sternplanes, forcing her down in a flank-speed dive. She plunged below three thousand feet before Harrison could recover.

If we had a steel hull, Jeffrey knew, *we'd've gone right through our crush depth.*

COB called on the intercom to complain about the wild maneuvers. They made it that much harder for his men to do their work.

"Get that unit loaded, COB, and load another as soon as I shoot."

The second Shkval was louder and louder. At last tube three was reloaded. Jeffrey and Bell armed the nuclear fish. Jeffrey ordered it fired. The unit rushed at the incoming Shkval. The Shkval kept rushing at *Challenger.* This time the range to intercept was barely outside the Shkval warhead's kill radius against *Challenger.*

Bell detonated the wire-guided torpedo as a preemptive blast to smash the Shkval. The Mark 48's maximum yield was a tenth of the Shkval's. But the desperate interception was so close to *Challenger,* the shock force was almost unbearable. The ship was slammed from astern. *Challenger* bucked and heaved hard. Objects broke loose and flew around the control room. Sonarmen's headphones were knocked from their heads. The vibrations were so vicious Jeffrey's vision was blurred.

As the reverb cleared, Kathy shouted that *another* Shkval was already in the water. Jeffrey waited impatiently while another nuclear Mark 48 was loaded by hand in his only working torpedo tube. He ordered it fired at the incoming Shkval, and ordered another fish loaded.

Again Bell smashed the inbound Shkval, too close, and once more *Challenger* rocked. Once more things broke loose and crewmen were injured.

Again torpedomen rushed to load another Mark 48. Again the *Tirpitz* launched another Shkval. Jeffrey reached for the handset. "COB, we need to get that tube reloaded faster."

"We're trying, Captain!" COB panted from exertion. In the background, over the handset, Jeffrey could hear clanks and thunking as the men struggled with block and tackle; he heard the torpedomen grunt and curse as they worked.

At last the unit was ready in the tube. Bell fired. The interception range was getting closer and closer to *Challenger.*

Jeffrey realized this engagement was a battle of attrition: an endurance contest trading blow for blow. *But the enemy captain must see*

I've got a very slow rate of fire. How many Shkvals does the Tirpitz *still have? How long can my men keep loading and firing like this, with just one tube and by hand, before they all drop from exhaustion?*

How much more punishment like this can Challenger *take?*

Again Bell smashed the inbound Shkval, much too close to *Challenger*. Once again *Challenger* rocked, worse than before. Sweating, swearing men rushed to load another fish. Again the *Tirpitz* fired.

They're shooting their Shkvals faster than we can shoot back. We lose more ground with every salvo. Our margin to intercept each inbound weapon wears thinner and thinner—soon it will be lethally small.

"Tube three ready in all respects!" Bell shouted.

"Tube three shoot!"

Another atomic fish leapt from the tube, and turned, and charged the Shkval as *Challenger* tore in the opposite direction.

But the German captain was smart. This time he'd set his Shkval, with its much bigger warhead, to blow before Bell's fish could get in range.

The blast was so loud it went past Jeffrey's real ability to hear. There was just a terrible pressure in his head and a painful dissonant ringing. The sharp force of the blast caught *Challenger*'s hull and pounded Jeffrey's feet and bruised his ass. Crewmen were knocked to the deck, and some were knocked unconscious. Light fixtures shattered, console screens darkened, locked cabinets burst open. Manuals and clipboards and metal tools became projectiles. Chips of paint and particles of heat insulation, and leftover construction dirt, were thrown into the air. Jeffrey felt the grit in his eyes and he coughed as he breathed it in.

Jeffrey's hearing came back slowly. As the numbness in his battered brain subsided, he saw Bell waving urgently to get his attention. The phone talker also was yelling something, and Jeffrey's intercom light flashed.

"A Mark forty-eight has broken loose in the torpedo room!" Bell shouted in Jeffrey's ear.

The noise and shaking and aftershocks of the Shkval blast went on and on. Jeffrey answered the intercom. It was COB, repeating Bell's terrible news, telling Jeffrey there was no way they could load the one working tube. In the background, over the handset, Jeffrey heard desperate orders, and shouting, and agonized screams.

"Get more damage-control teams in there!" Jeffrey said to Bell. Jeffrey turned to the phone talker. "Medical corpsman to the torpedo room on the double!"

Jeffrey waited. He forced himself to sit and exude a sense of control and let his crew do their jobs.

Jeffrey squeezed his armrests involuntarily, and just rode the ship.

Challenger shimmied and rolled, fighting her way through troubled water, still making flank speed. Jeffrey knew each shimmy and roll would throw that errant fish in the torpedo room even more, as it darted and veered and banged around, literally like a loose cannon.

"Weapon in torpedo room is fractured!" Bell reported.

Then Jeffrey heard the thing he dreaded most. *"Weapon's fuel is leaking, Captain. Fuel leak in the torpedo room!"*

"Countermeasures tubes are inoperable," the chief at the ship-control station yelled, almost as an afterthought.

"We're defenseless," Wilson said. "One more Shkval and we've had it."

"This can't be happening," a fire controlman whined.

"Cut it out," Bell told him. "I'm too underdressed to die." Bell was still wearing his boxer shorts.

Crewmen laughed at Bell's remark, but Jeffrey knew the laughs verged on hysteria. The wait for the next incoming Shkval was driving everyone mad. "We've been in worse fixes than this," Jeffrey said in a loud voice to Bell. Jeffrey tried to sound much more blasé than he felt, pretending to make idle conversation, to reassure and steady his men.

Bell nodded, his neck muscles visibly tight. The control-room crew grew silent.

Jeffrey listened to the ocean around them boil and roar, from all the effects of the nuclear blasts that had already taken place.

Another aftershock from the most recent Shkval hit *Challenger*.

The phone talker looked up, very alarmed. "Fire, fire, fire in the torpedo room. Fuel spill in torpedo room has ignited."

Jeffrey turned to Bell, and the two men made eye contact. Bell's face said more than words could: there were fifty weapons on the holding racks around that fire, with tons of volatile fuel, and tons more of high explosives and a lot of fissile material.

"Get down there, XO. Take charge at fighting the fire." Jeffrey dearly wanted to rush to the torpedo room himself. But his job as captain required that he remain in the control room, to stay in overall charge of the ship and maintain the big tactical picture. He caught himself squeezing his armrests in a death grip as he sat there. He forced his fingers to lighten up by a supreme exercise of will.

Jeffrey deeply trusted Bell. But Jeffrey knew Bell's efforts would only prolong the inevitable—any moment *Tirpitz* would set loose another Shkval. There was nothing Jeffrey could do now about it but make *Challenger* continue to flee, and the Shkval, once launched, would gain on Jeffrey's ship at an inescapable 250 knots net closing speed. Everybody, including Commodore Wilson, knew this simple, cold-blooded fact.

At the first word of the fire, the crew had begun to grab their emergency air-breather masks. They plugged them into the air manifolds in pipes that lined the overhead. The control room filled with eerie hissing and whooshing, as people inhaled and exhaled through the valves of their masks—and waited to die. Jeffrey felt an icy emptiness in his chest—never one for denial of harsh realities around him, Jeffrey finally started to run out of hope. He caught a whiff of acrid, toxic fumes, spreading from the torpedo-room fire. Before he had his mask fully on, Jeffrey also smelled urine. Someone, in panic, had wet himself—Harrison, at the helm.

Bell doggedly fed Jeffrey progress reports through the intercom. He'd put on a flameproof suit and was supervising near the fire. Bell's voice was hoarse from bellowing orders over the noise and pandemonium. He sounded muffled through the breather mask of a portable respirator pack. From exertion and overexcitement, Bell panted raggedly.

Bell said men were rushing to rig hoses and set up the fire-fighting foam. Meanwhile others did what they could with carbon dioxide extinguishers, with chemical powder extinguishers, with anything they had. It was difficult to work in the huge but cramped torpedo room, with clearance between the rows of holding racks barely as wide as one man's shoulders. Down on their hands and knees, avoiding the hot spots of burning fuel, dodging the leaky Mark 48 that still ran loose, slowed the men down badly. Bell said the deck was slippery with blood. The heat was intense and the smoke was thick and a weapon would cook off soon.

Jeffrey was out of alternatives. Defeat tasted rancid and foul. It seemed to force its way down his throat, cutting like broken glass.

Jeffrey heard another roar outside the hull. *Here it comes.*

"Shkval in the water!" Kathy screamed.

This is it, Jeffrey told himself. *All we can do is keep running, and that thing is six times faster than we are. The only question is, will the Shkval kill us before our own torpedo room blows up?*

Jeffrey looked around him. Most of the crewmen were barely half his age. They were much too young for their lives to end like this. He saw some of them holding their heads in despair, others pounding their consoles in impotent rage, others piously crossing themselves. He wished he could think of a way to somehow offer them final comfort.

"Captain," Kathy shouted through her mask, "Shkval signal strength is not increasing! . . . *Captain,* assess Master One's Shkval is on a hot run in the tube! Assess the Shkval on *von Tirpitz* is malfunctioning!"

"On speakers!"

There was a rumbling explosion in the distance, then a louder, heaving blast, then a whole series of sharp detonations.

"Assess weapons in Master One's torpedo room have cooked off!"

Jeffrey listened to the horrible sounds as *Tirpitz* died. He heard a last dull *boom* as the enemy sub sank through her crush depth, when the unflooded parts at the back of the German submarine caved in.

"XO reports fire in our torpedo room is extinguished!" the phone talker yelled. "Fire relight watch is set! . . . Corpsman states no fatal injuries! No radiological leakage from damaged weapons!"

Jeffrey felt the weight of a thousand worlds lift from his shoulders. *Challenger* and her people would survive, at least until the next fight.

But he'd never felt so small, so inconsequential. Jeffrey hadn't won this battle. It was the enemy who'd lost. Over a hundred men on *Tirpitz* paid the ultimate price for playing with undersea fire, using such high-risk weapons as the Shkval. There could be little satisfaction in this sort of victory, only a humbling realization of the role of sheer luck in war, and a recognition of one's own personal insignificance.

Kathy, and Commodore Wilson, and the rest of Jeffrey's crew all felt it too. There was no jubilation at the destruction of Master One, no cheering, no celebrating the kill. Just the noise of twenty air-breather masks, overly rapid hiss-whooshing, as everyone hyperventilated from fear and now giddy relief. Everybody was very quiet, turned inward, as each person in their own way tried to deal with having faced their own mortality, having really thought, having *known,* that they would die.

14

Simultaneously, on *Voortrekker,* in the eastern Indian Ocean

GUNTHER VAN GELDER felt relaxation and inner joy, as much as this was possible for a sailor at sea in a war. He had the conn in *Voortrekker's* control room, and Jan ter Horst was asleep.

Voortrekker was doing what she did best, moving quietly near the ocean floor in water three kilometers deep—snaking through the massifs and fissures of the Mid–Indian Ocean Ridge. These endless undersea volcanic mountains and valleys formed the ideal landscape in which *Voortrekker* could hide. To Van Gelder, watching the stark, razor-sharp faults and escarpments go by on the ship's gravimeter display, it was the ideal place for him to sightsee.

The ship made only seven knots, for safety as well as for stealth. A remote-controlled off-board probe was deployed well ahead of *Voortrekker,* scouting for enemy mines and hydrophone grids. The probe used special cameras to study the bottom in *Voortrekker's* path, and Van Gelder watched the images raptly.

Starfish in large groupings waved their arms on the ground. Huge jellyfish rippled by in the slow and steady bottom current. Other deep-sea creatures, with hideous black faces or bodies too weird to describe, came to examine or challenge *Voortrekker*'s probe. Diffuse glows, bright swirling starbursts, stabbing flashes of sheet lightning, all lit up the scene, in shades of otherworldly blue and electric white and vivid yellow. This was bioluminescence, Van Gelder knew. The ocean all around him, even this deep, was alive.

Voortrekker passed another black-smoker hydrothermal vent field. Van Gelder heard it rumbling and gurgling on sonar, and sent the probe closer to look. Again, here was life. Primordial microbes fed a teeming community of albino crabs and giant clams and thick red-blooded tube worms.

Until recently, only a handful of scientists had visited places like this. Few men and women had ever seen firsthand what Van Gelder was seeing. To be here now, to witness such things with his own eyes, made Gunther Van Gelder feel himself a very privileged man.

On *Challenger,* after the rendezvous with the minisub

The ASDS minisub was safely stowed in *Challenger*'s in-hull hangar bay. The mini's passengers were shaken up by the nearby *Challenger*-versus-*Tirpitz* fight, but they were otherwise unharmed. Once again, *Challenger* rushed along at flank speed, heading south-southwest inside the Gulf Stream. Jeffrey sat in his stateroom, pecking away at his laptop—commanders who neglected admin and paperwork might not get their fourth stripe. Jeffrey paused, agonized, typed another sentence, shook his head, deleted it, and sat there. His heart sank. The more he thought about his tactics against the *von Tirpitz,* the more he thought he'd never get that fourth stripe in any case, because he didn't deserve it.

Maybe the higher-ups were right, sending Commodore Wilson along as a nursemaid. Idly, and forlornly, Jeffrey wondered how many more millions of innocent fish and whales and dolphins he'd helped kill in this latest battle. *Challenger*'s crew was shielded from radiation sickness by all the water between her and the bursting warheads, and by the thickness of her hull, and the ship could quickly leave the contaminated area. The local sea life was stuck, and the effect of the war on the seafood industry and beachside resorts was devastating already.

Someone knocked. It was Bell, there to present his regular evening report.

"Sorry, XO, I lost track of the time."

"No problem, Skipper."

"Come on in. Sit."

Bell made himself comfortable quickly; he seemed matured, more well-anchored internally, and more outwardly positive about life since becoming a father. Jeffrey envied him these things.

Bell filled Jeffrey in on the status of the cleanup and repairs in the torpedo room. It would take a lot of work to custom-machine replacement parts to get the torpedo autoloader functioning again. The countermeasures launchers—which took up half the space in the medical corpsman's cubicle back near the enlisted mess—also needed more time to be made serviceable after the battle damage.

Jeffrey got up and shut the door and sat down again. "How are the wounded doing?"

"Our one potential crisis, sir, is the man whose arm was crushed by that loose torpedo. Circulation past the shoulder is not good. With what little more the corpsman can do for him here, he might lose the arm."

"Amputate?"

Bell nodded.

"Then we need to get the guy to a proper hospital. . . . With a minisub in our hangar now, maybe we can drop him off, covertly. I'll talk to the commodore."

"It would be important for morale for you to do something, Captain. Nobody wants to see the guy get gangrene and get sent home to his family maimed."

Jeffrey hesitated. "XO, what's your read on morale in general?" Jeffrey knew morale in war was a very volatile thing. Submarine crews, living in such close quarters, felt a strong sense of community and reacted emotionally as a group. To be at their best, they needed steady support and constant input of encouragement and good news. Jeffrey already intended to tour the ship again this evening, for exactly that purpose.

"Actually, sir," Bell said, "morale went from somewhat bad to rather good in a hurry, because of the *Tirpitz*." Bell smiled. "The men think you're a lucky captain, Captain. They're happy to be sailing with you now."

Jeffrey frowned. "What's the emphasis on the 'now' part?"

Bell took a deep breath. "The guys were troubled to see us ordered to leave dry dock before we were ready, missing qualified men and stuck with two dozen clueless replacements. They thought we were taking too many chances, and we wouldn't come back."

Jeffrey grunted. He couldn't entirely disagree with their reasoning. "But you say morale is up?"

Bell nodded.

Jeffrey didn't want to come across to Bell as insecure, but he was puzzled. "Explain the mechanics of this to me."

"Our meeting the *Tirpitz* at all was a sheer coincidence, one-in-a-million odds. The fact the score came out *Challenger* one, *Tirpitz* nothing, when *Tirpitz* had us dead to rights, was also pure random chance."

"But that was the enemy's bad luck, not our good luck. I don't get it."

"If you put the whole thing together, Captain, we've *had* our shakedown cruise and our working-up period now, in that battle. Everybody feels much better there. Plus, it's like it was destiny or something, an act of God, us meeting the *Tirpitz*—"

Jeffrey held up one hand. "I'm not sure about that last part, XO. I want to talk to you more about that in a minute."

"Well, the final thing I wanted to say is that we got to score a kill, a big one. We got even for the New York raid. *Us,* sir, USS *Challenger,* on our very first day at sea. That makes us a lucky ship, and you a lucky captain."

Jeffrey worked his jaw pondering this. Then he grinned. "I did think your crack about being too underdressed to die was pretty good." Both men laughed. Then Jeffrey glanced at his laptop, and felt a sinking feeling again.

Bell read Jeffrey's face and was confused. He thought Jeffrey was signaling that the meeting was over.

"You wanted to talk to me more about meeting the *Tirpitz,* sir?"

Jeffrey debated whether to confide in Bell or keep it to himself. *My XO is supposed to be my sounding board. But a captain is a superior being, all-knowing and infallible. . . .*

Hell, if I try to stay arms-length from my key people all the time, I'll wind up with ulcers for sure.

"I'm writing my after-action report on the battle with *Tirpitz.* I'm thinking about my turn away when we first made contact. I think I blew it, and endangered the ship and our crew and our mission."

"Sir?" Bell looked flabbergasted. "From where I sit, the men worship you now, even more than after the Germany raid. You always stay clear-headed in battle, and kept us fighting until the bitter end. You've got the best sort of credibility that any sub skipper could ask for. You produce results in combat, time after time."

Jeffrey shook his head. "Turning beam-on to the *Tirpitz,* showing them our full side-profile noise signature, with erratic sound-propagation conditions at the time, was just too risky. *Tirpitz* got a datum off us, and it let them shoot. If they hadn't blown up from their own weapon failure, we'd've definitely been sunk."

"Hmmm . . . You *had* to evade, Captain. That was in the Commodore's standing orders from above. We couldn't get Master One's course or speed, exactly *because* of said bad sonar conditions. For all you knew, she was coming right at us fast. You *had* to turn well away."

"I'm not sure you're right."

"What were you going to do? Put the ship into *reverse?* We're unstable enough going backward with a *seasoned* guy at the helm. It seems to me your turn away, a simple maneuver for Harrison, was the safer decision, given all the circumstances."

Jeffrey absorbed that. "Thanks, XO. I suppose needing to think about it again, to write out a formal report, it's got me second-guessing myself."

Bell smiled. "Nobody said it was easy being CO. That's what they pay you the big money for."

Both men laughed again. Jeffrey was glad he'd confided in Bell. The man's perspective had cheered Jeffrey up.

But then Bell frowned, which was rare for him. "Maybe you've got me second-guessing too now, Captain, but something's starting to not smell right, about meeting the *Tirpitz* the way we did. . . . Either it really was just one humongous coincidence, or the *Tirpitz* knew we were coming."

This was someplace Jeffrey didn't want to go. "How could they know we were coming?"

"Compromised our sound surveillance system data, maybe?"

"The good commodore insists that's not the case."

"You believe him?"

"I *think* I believe him. The *Tirpitz* is—was—a lot slower than us. How could she have been vectored into position so soon? She was right there in front of us, a perfect setup."

"Maybe they didn't tap our hydrophone grids. Maybe they've planted their own along our coast, or have some new secret weapon we don't know about."

"I think you've been watching too many old Cold War movies, XO."

Bell pursed his lips. "They might still have known in advance that we were coming, from a spy."

"The commodore told me he didn't decide which way to go, north or south, until we submerged. So it's not like anyone off the ship knew. . . . We're probably okay, about there being a leak."

Bell didn't relax. "The Germans didn't need to know we were heading south, Captain. All they needed to know was that we were sailing. Anybody can look at a map of the globe. . . . Maybe they sent *Tirpitz* south, and they sent another submarine north, to hit us near Newfoundland, say, in case we took the Arctic route. *Tirpitz* was the one that got lucky, or unlucky."

Jeffrey nodded slowly, reluctantly. "Don't tell anyone else about this, XO. If we've been compromised, I want the crew to stay in blissful ignorance. . . . I'm going to talk to Commodore Wilson."

JEFFREY knocked on Wilson's stateroom door. Lieutenant Sessions's voice called from inside, "Who's there?"

Jeffrey was annoyed. "Captain Fuller."

Sessions unlocked the door, and Jeffrey went in.

Wilson glanced up at Jeffrey. Wilson's eyes were sunken and red. He didn't look good. Wilson waited for Jeffrey to speak. On top of the filing cabinet, a computer printer was running.

"Commodore, I have some matters we need to discuss."

"Lieutenant," Wilson said, "stay, but close and lock the door."

Sessions and Jeffrey sat in the two guest chairs. Again Wilson waited for Jeffrey to speak.

"Sir, you're aware one of the men has a serious injury."

Wilson nodded. "His arm."

"We need to get him to a hospital."

"How do you propose to accomplish that?"

"Drop him off in the ASDS."

"And just where would you drop him off in the ASDS?"

"When we pass through the Yucatán Strait, sir, we'll have Cuba to port and Mexico to starboard." Mexico was one of the Allies, and Cuba was rabidly anti-Axis.

"And what will you do? Leave him at somebody's beach cottage, or a fishing village pier in the dead of night? With a note in Spanish, 'Please get me to a hospital'?"

Jeffrey was taken aback. "Sessions and I could work out the details, but yes, something like that."

Sessions's face brightened, but Wilson's did not.

"I need you to think more as my operations officer, Commander Fuller, not just as captain of your ship. You have to put the mission of my battle group above the fate of one man's arm."

Jeffrey, thunderstruck, shook his head. "Sir, that's much too harsh."

"No, it's not. . . . What else? Sessions and I are busy."

"I've just had a discussion with my XO. We believe that, after all, the Axis may know that we've sailed."

"From circumstantial evidence, like meeting *Tirpitz*? From making a nuclear datum off Cape Fear that surely carried through the deep sound channel clear across to Europe?"

Wilson was obviously ahead of Jeffrey on this, and not pleased. He'd told Jeffrey to keep *Challenger*'s signature *out* of the deep sound channel.

"Exactly, sir. What also concerns me, both as ops officer and as captain, is that we can't be sure either way. It's a key parameter of our strategy and tactics, Commodore, knowing whether or not we'll really catch *Voortrekker* by surprise."

"One *always* seeks the element of surprise," Wilson said pedantically. "But one must never assume that one retains it."

"Yes, Commodore." Jeffrey's mind was racing now, about Wilson's mood and attitude and intent.

"Have you eaten?"

The sudden change of tack surprised Jeffrey. "No, sir. Not yet."

"Go grab some fruit or something in the wardroom, and make it snappy. My flag lieutenant and I need several hours of your time. I was about to send Sessions to get you when you came in."

Jeffrey turned to the door.

"Wait, Captain. This is for you. Give them to your assistant navigator." Wilson handed Jeffrey a piece of paper. They were coordinates in the Caribbean Sea.

Jeffrey glanced at Sessions.

"Southwest of Jamaica, Captain."

"Another way point, Commodore?"

"No. Another rendezvous."

15

The next day, midafternoon, in the Caribbean Sea

CHALLENGER HOVERED NEAR the bottom in four thousand feet of water. The ship was at battle stations, rigged for ultraquiet. Around Jeffrey in the control room, his people talked in hushed tones, conveying information on shipping and aircraft contacts overhead or in the distance. The general feeling was tense, with Commodore Wilson grimly leaning over crewmen's shoulders, peering at various console screens.

Wilson stood up straight and turned to Jeffrey. "They're late."

"I thought *we* were running late," Jeffrey said.

"We are. Hold your position, and hope they catch up. If they don't appear we're in a lot of trouble."

"Sir, with respect, would you please inform me whom *they* are?"

"I'll know it when they get here."

Jeffrey was exasperated. How was his crew supposed to watch for something with which to rendezvous, when none of them knew what that something was?

"Is this secrecy really needed, Commodore?"

"We can't afford to ruin their cover."

"But—"

"You'll understand when we meet them. . . . *Challenger* left dry dock too soon, and too large a part of her crew is inexperienced."

"I—"

"That wasn't meant as a criticism of you or your people. We've been lucky so far, Captain. The ship could still suffer a bad equipment casualty at any time. At any moment we might need to do an emergency blow. Bobbing like a cork to the surface, in distress, would be bad enough for *us*. We can't risk them too."

"Then—"

"We don't know who might come to our 'aid' if we're stricken. Whatever you and your crew don't know, you can't reveal by mistake or under torture. Russian spy trawlers work these waters, and most of Central America is riddled with German espionage operatives."

"But Commodore . . ."

Wilson shook his head vehemently. "I simply can't take the chance. Far too much is at stake here. Too much, in dollars and years, was invested getting ready for an emergency like this."

Two hours later

"Our friend is here," Wilson said.

"*Which* friend?"

Wilson tapped Jeffrey's screen. "This one. Master Seventy-seven. The *Prima Latina,* out of Havana, bound for Lima, Peru."

"Through the *Panama Canal?*" Jeffrey knew that according to international neutrality law, the canal would be banned to all warships of belligerents—and Panama was neutral.

"Affirmative," Wilson said sharply. "Through the canal."

Using it would shorten *Challenger's* trip by thousands of miles. *The Joint Chiefs of Staff must feel under awful pressure, to have us take this risky, illegal shortcut to save a few days. . . . But wait a minute.*

"Sir, we can't hide under a merchant ship through the *canal*. It's much too shallow for that sort of gimmick."

"Who said we're going *under* her?"

*   *   *

JEFFREY read the database summary on his screen. *Prima Latina* was just the latest of many names she'd worn over the years. She was almost five hundred feet long, big for a coastal steamer, and had deep draft. But her engine plant was so old, and her hull so worn by metal fatigue, that the company which ran her now dared not send her on the high seas.

"Her speed is nine knots, course due south," Bell reported. "Advise her closest point of approach will be four miles from our location."

"Good," Wilson said. "Meet her."

"Navigator," Jeffrey said, "give me an intercept course at eleven knots."

If Wilson had told Lieutenant Sessions in private what this was about, Sessions showed no sign of it.

Jeffrey studied the gravimeter display and the digital nautical charts. There were shallow areas—banks and shoals—in almost every direction. Jeffrey would have to be careful, conning *Challenger* in such restricted waters. At least—thanks to the rendezvous off Cape Fear with the minisub—Jeffrey's battle-seasoned helmsman, Lieutenant (j.g.) David Meltzer, was back aboard. Meltzer was a tough kid from the Bronx, and a Naval Academy graduate, and Jeffrey liked him.

"Captain," Wilson said, "before you move, secure all active sonars. Listen on passive systems only."

"Commodore, we *need* the mine-avoidance sonars." There was always the chance another U-boat had snuck into the Caribbean and planted more naval mines.

"Overruled. Mines are a lesser risk for now than breaking stealth with sonar noise."

Jeffrey opened his mouth to object, but Wilson gave him a dirty look. Jeffrey closed his mouth so fast his teeth clicked.

Sessions relayed the rendezvous information to Jeffrey's console. Jeffrey issued helm orders. Meltzer acknowledged; Meltzer's enjoyment of having something unusual to do vanished at the thought of hitting a mine. Ensign Harrison, sitting near Meltzer, leaned closer, watching carefully—Bell had chosen Harrison as the battle-stations relief pilot. Harrison was more nervous, too, since Wilson mentioned mines.

COB kept a keen eye on the buoyancy and trim. Sometimes he made adjustments, using the pumps and valves he controlled. One hand stayed near the emergency blow handles, just in case.

Meltzer sang out when *Challenger* was directly under the proper spot, which was a moving target since the *Prima Latina* was moving too. Jeffrey ordered Meltzer to reduce speed from eleven knots to nine, to keep station with the merchant ship.

"Captain," Wilson said, "bring the ship to periscope depth. Be careful. The waters are crystal clear here, and it's almost always sunny this time of year."

What next?

"Helm, five degrees up bubble. Make your depth one five zero feet." Jeffrey would do this in stages, for caution. Meltzer pulled his control wheel back, and *Challenger*'s nose came up. Her depth decreased gradually, as she and the *Prima Latina* steamed south. The merchant ship's noises could be heard right through the hull: throbbing and humming and swishing, plus the odd clank or rattle.

"Chief of the Watch," Jeffrey said, "raise the search periscope mast." COB flipped a switch.

A picture appeared on several screens—the digital feed from the periscope. Jeffrey looked around outside the ship with a small joystick, which controlled the sensor head on the periscope mast. With *Challenger*'s depth at 150 feet, the periscope head was still tens of feet underwater.

"Master Seventy-seven in sight," Jeffrey announced, even though the others, including Wilson, could easily see it on the screens. Wilson was right—it was very sunny topside.

The merchant steamer's hull was a long dark shape above *Challenger*. It plowed through the water steadily. Jeffrey, looking up from below, could see *Prima Latina*'s creaming white bow wave, and her wake. Her twin propeller shafts, and big screws and rudder, were hard to make out. Though Jeffrey could *hear* the screws well enough, he wanted to avoid them at all costs.

The surface of the sea was a rippling, sparkling, endless translucent curtain. The sun cast green-blue streaks down through the water. Sometimes Jeffrey saw schools of fish, clouds of them swimming and darting. Jeffrey looked for bobbing mines, but so far there were none.

"Come to periscope depth," Wilson repeated. "I need to take a good look at her. There will be subtle signs, like ropes on lifeboats coiled a particular way, to indicate if she's still in friendly hands."

"Sir, if you're so concerned over stealth, we can't afford to make a periscope feather on the surface."

"Do it for a split second, to snap a picture. I *must* know if she's still in friendly hands."

On his screen, as the periscope head broke the surface, Jeffrey caught a glimpse of a scruffy bearded seaman leaning on one of *Prima Latina*'s railings, smoking a fat cigar. The seaman noticed the periscope at once, tossed his cigar in the water, and started for a ladder to the *Prima Latina*'s bridge. The freighter was flying a Cuban flag. Jeffrey cursed and ordered Meltzer deep.

Simultaneously, aboard *Voortrekker,* southwest of Perth, Australia

The sheer audacity of what they were doing was what impressed Van Gelder the most. Far above them on the surface bobbed an old Sri Lankan freighter, the *Trincomalee Tiger.*

Everything that could go wrong for the freighter *had* gone wrong. First her rudder jammed, then her engines failed. At fifty degrees south latitude, the furious fifties, she rose and plunged sickeningly. The *Trincomalee Tiger* was already well inside the extreme limit of Antarctic icebergs for this time of year: February, high summer in the Southern Hemisphere.

The wind, from the north at twenty-five knots, was forcing the now-crippled freighter ever further into the iceberg zone, and the southeast-running surface current wasn't helping either. To make things even worse, a severe tropical storm was brewing off the west coast of Australia—in the hours to come the winds and seas around the freighter would strengthen. With no engines or steering control, the worn, tired *Trincomalee Tiger* might hit an iceberg and sink. Or she could simply crack her seams and founder, overstressed by gale-force winds and massive, breaking waves.

The freighter, a neutral, wallowed several hundred miles southwest of Perth, Australia. She'd already radioed a mayday on the international distress frequency. A Royal Australian Navy destroyer was kindly rushing to her aid, but with the distances involved it would be hours before the Aussies could reach the scene. An Australian long-range maritime patrol aircraft was orbiting overhead, but that was mostly for moral support; the plane was designed for antisubmarine work, not search and rescue.

It was dark, and the sun wouldn't rise for some time, but floodlights on the freighter's decks shone brightly. Crewmen from the freighter kept waving and gesturing for the plane to somehow land and help them, or lower a rope and lift them off, before it was too late—this was a sure sign of panic. On top of everything else, the freighter's radar failed. In the night they wouldn't even see an iceberg bearing down upon them in time to man the lifeboats, and the crew knew that in this rising weather the ancient lifeboats were a death trap.

It was one more part of Jan ter Horst's master plan.

16

WILSON, SATISFIED BY the periscope photo, ordered Jeffrey to continue with the rendezvous. As shown by live periscope imagery, *Challenger* was directly under the *Prima Latina* now.

Jeffrey watched in amazement and then horror as the merchant ship split apart at the keel. *A mine?* Kathy reported new sonar transients—machinery noise, not breaking-up sounds. Jeffrey saw that this was supposed to happen: the ship's bottom was a giant double door.

"Here's your ride through the canal, Captain," Wilson said. "This wasn't *my* idea. It goes way above a mere commodore's pay grade, I assure you. I'm just following orders, as well as giving them."

"Understood."

"Surface your ship into the covert hold."

I was afraid he was going to say that.

"Can't we have her go any slower?"

"No. If she slows or stops it'll look suspicious. She's being painted by dozens of radars we know about, and watched by God knows how many spy satellites we don't know about."

Jeffrey thought hard how to do this. *Challenger* would lose speed as she surfaced, because of the power wasted when her hull began to make waves and the pump-jet propulsor's loss of suction at very shallow depth. Meltzer would have to speed up to compensate, but by how much? An impact by the bow or stern, between *Challenger* and the *Prima Latina,* seemed unavoidable. Jeffrey felt his blood pressure shoot up fast. His first priority as captain was the welfare of his ship.

"Commodore, we need to make some practice approaches first."

"Don't worry overly much. There are large rubber bumpers up there in case the two ships touch."

"We've never performed an evolution like this."

"The computer simulations said it could be done."

"Simulations aren't real life, Commodore. A bad collision could sink *both* ships."

"Get yourself up in there quickly. We're passing the shoals already. Once through we'll be in open water again, and the seas will be much higher. This will get even more dangerous than it already is."

Jeffrey and Meltzer talked it over, discussing tactics. Jeffrey called Lieutenant Willey on the intercom, and they talked it over too. Then COB and Bell offered their advice.

Finally, as Jeffrey snapped out orders, Meltzer brought *Challenger* shallower. The first try was to get the hang of matching speeds as the two vessels closed, to get the feel of the buffeting and suction effects of trapped water coursing between the two hulls. The first try didn't go well.

On *Voortrekker*

"Very well, Number One," ter Horst said. "You have the conn. I'll backstop you. Bring us up, and prepare to put us into the *Trincomalee Tiger*'s belly."

The freighter in distress, ter Horst had told Van Gelder, was a clandestine submarine tender. Her engines and rudder were perfectly fine. She was faking the equipment casualties as an excuse to stop on the high seas, to make *Voortrekker*'s docking easier without arousing suspicion. The orbiting maritime patrol aircraft and the approaching Australian destroyer were all part of the double bluff.

Van Gelder had to admire ter Horst's cunning and his guts. Not every submarine captain would willfully call down upon himself front-line enemy forces while he rendezvoused with a covert milch cow hiding in plain sight.

Van Gelder issued orders to the helmsman and chief of the watch. *Voortrekker* rose from the depths, and Van Gelder raised the digital periscope mast. The picture appeared on screens in the control room, looking straight up. The underwater keel doors of the freighter were already open, and the well-lit secret hold beckoned invitingly. Blue-green lights flashed steadily, outlining the hold. These let Van Gelder judge the surface ship's roll and drift, giving him his aiming point. Van Gelder could make out the bulk of the vessel's massive buoyancy tanks, lining the inside of the hull, surrounding the secret hold. The *Trincomalee Tiger* was, in effect, a camouflaged floating dry dock.

"*Surface impacts, sir,*" the sonar chief warned.

"Sonobuoys?" Van Gelder demanded. *Are the Allies on to us so soon?*

"Uh . . . no, sir. Sounded like an air-dropped life raft package and survival gear."

Good, the enemy plane's still falling for the playacted desperation on the freighter. Van Gelder relaxed, but only slightly. *Voortrekker* was nearing the freighter's bottom.

A rogue wave's surge and suction threw *Voortrekker* bodily toward the freighter's hull. Van Gelder snapped out helm orders, fearful of a collision. The rogue wave passed. Van Gelder hesitated to close the distance further lest another rogue wave hit.

"Surface impacts! *Air-dropped torpedoes!*"

Van Gelder jolted. Jan ter Horst cursed.

"Torpedoes are inert! . . . Confirmed, torpedoes are sinking!"

"Ha!" ter Horst exclaimed. "You see, Gunther? They dumped their weapons to give themselves longer on-station time over the freighter. That aircraft's no danger to us at all now."

"Sir," the sonar chief said uncomfortably, "I only counted two torpedoes dropped. That type of aircraft holds four."

On *Challenger*

Jeffrey had Meltzer return to a depth of 150 feet, and then try again. This time as *Challenger* rose she lined up better with the hole in the *Prima Latina*. But when the ships drew closer, *Challenger* kept yawing from side to side, way too much.

"Captain," Meltzer said, "we need to use the auxiliary propulsors for better lateral control."

"Concur," COB said, "but I have my hands full. When we do a blow and surface for real, if you can call this business surfacing, I'll be even busier."

"All right. Relief Pilot, I want you to handle the auxiliary thrusters."

"Yes, Captain," Harrison said. He did it the only way he could—he knelt on the deck next to Meltzer's seat, and reached in past Meltzer for the joysticks that worked the thrusters. Meltzer was totally occupied using the main control surfaces—bowplanes and sternplanes and rudder—to manage *Challenger*'s basic depth and course. The use of junior enlisted men to separately work sternplanes and rudder went out with the *Virginia* class, the first of which had entered service in 2004.

"Let's try this again," Jeffrey said. "The key seems to be to anticipate the jostling as we get closer, but not overcompensate."

Jeffrey told COB to activate *Challenger*'s hull-mounted photonics sensors, so the ship-control team and Jeffrey could get better close-range visual cues than with just the periscope. COB punched buttons. More pictures were windowed onto the console screens, viewpoints from the bow and stern and looking downward too.

Jeffrey grabbed the mike for the maneuvering room. "Engineer, do whatever you have to do to keep us moving at exactly nine knots as COB does a main ballast blow."

"Understood, Skipper," Willey said. "But what happens when we're partway into the hold and the freighter pulls the surrounding water right along with her? Our speed logs will give false readings, saying we've slowed down. Then if we speed up, we'll crash."

"I know, that's the hard part."

"Sir," Harrison said, "we can judge real speed over the bottom based on our inertial navigation system."

Jeffrey nodded. "Hey, that's using your head, shipmate!" Meltzer, impressed, slapped the ensign on the back, rather roughly, congratulating him but working in a little hazing too.

Jeffrey repeated the ensign's idea over the intercom to Willey.

"Sounds great," Willey said. "Only problem is, if you'll recall, Captain, we don't have navigation readouts back here."

A disappointed Jeffrey repeated what Willey said to the control room at large.

"Sir," Harrison said, "feed him data through the ship's local area network, and Lieutenant Willey can read it off his laptop. They can manage ship's speed under local control that way, reacting instantly, from back in the maneuvering room."

Geez, Jeffrey thought, *this kid's smarter than I thought.*

The arrangements were quickly made. This was an all-or-nothing effort now.

On *Voortrekker*

Van Gelder went back to the docking attempt.

"We must do this quickly," ter Horst urged. "The enemy destroyer that's coming may get nosy when the *Tiger's* engines and rudder miraculously repair themselves. . . . They may board the freighter for a close inspection, as is their right by international law."

"Understood, sir." Van Gelder tried not to be distracted as he studied his screens and issued more helm orders.

"The Aussies may dig their way through her dummy cargo, discover her false bottom, and find the hidden catwalk down to the submarine hold."

"I understand, Captain. I understand."

"We need to have been and gone by the time the destroyer gets here, and we have a lot of work to do before then."

On *Challenger*

Once more *Challenger* approached the *Prima Latina* from below. Jeffrey had Meltzer use the control surfaces and propulsion power to hold the ship as shallow as was safe until he felt satisfied the two vessels were lined up properly.

It was time to commit. On the live periscope image, Jeffrey saw Wilson was right—the surface swells outside were already stronger, as the nearby shallow banks and shoals fell astern. *Prima Latina* was rolling side to side noticeably now, making the docking maneuver even harder.

"Blow all main ballast!" Jeffrey shouted. COB's fingers danced on his panels. There was a roaring sound, as compressed air forced water out through the bottom of the ballast tanks. Meltzer and Harrison handled their controls in grim concentration.

But as *Challenger* rose into the *Prima Latina*'s hold, *Challenger*'s bulk interfered with the freighter's propellers biting the water. The freighter began to slow. Relative to the surface ship, *Challenger* seemed to speed up. Willey's laptop was useless now—Jeffrey would have to do it by eye. Meltzer reported that *Challenger* was surfaced.

"Helm back one-third!"

Meltzer acknowledged at once, but *Challenger* still surged forward in the hold. They were going to hit, and smash the bow dome and the sonar sphere, and maybe rupture the ballast tanks and detonate the missiles in the forward vertical launch array.

This was getting too tough. Jeffrey seriously considered diving and giving it up, in spite of Wilson's order.

"Contact on acoustic intercept!" Kathy shouted. This broke Jeffrey's focus badly—*Challenger* and the *Prima Latina* were being pinged by another sub. "Contact has an active towed array! Contact is a surface ship. Contact's sonar is Russian!" Not a submarine, a spy trawler, just as Wilson had warned.

Challenger was trapped: If Jeffrey dived, the trawler would surely catch her as a separate sonar contact. He simply had to make this docking work.

"Helm back two-*thirds!"*

Meltzer and Harrison walked a tightrope now—reversing on the pump-jet made *Challenger*'s stern slew sideways unpredictably. A bow collision was barely avoided, but then *Challenger* started drifting backward in the pool of water in the hold. They were going to hit at the stern, and smash their delicate pump-jet—and Russians were snooping somewhere near.

"Helm, ahead two-thirds!" Jeffrey could see the water around him churning and swirling wildly as he checked the sternway. He ordered, "Helm, ahead one-third," so as not to gain too much headway.

Kathy announced more Russian pinging, getting closer.

Jeffrey saw the bottom doors start to swing closed underneath him; *Challenger* shivered from violent new buffeting and turbulence, which also affected the *Prima Latina*'s speed. Jeffrey kept having to throw the pump-jet into forward and then reverse. He and Meltzer and Harrison juggled like madmen.

The Russians pinged again. *Do they know we're here? Are they getting suspicious? Will they try to ram the* Prima Latina, *the way the Soviets played chicken with our navy in the old days?*

The hold doors closed securely. "Helm, all stop. We're in."

Jeffrey had to sit down, then was surprised he'd been standing—he must have jumped up without realizing it as he issued his engine commands.

"Chief of the Watch, rig for reduced electrical." COB acknowledged, and everyone switched things off. Jeffrey called Lieutenant Willey, and told him to shut down the reactor.

Jeffrey used the periscope to explore their cramped and secret hiding place, which looked more high tech on the inside than the tramp steamer did from the outside.

But Jeffrey dreaded what he might see at any moment. If the freighter hit a mine, her hull would burst inward with sudden flame and blasting water. Her flotation tanks would be ruptured and she'd take *Challenger* with her to the grave. If the Russian trawler rammed them, the freighter's hull would burst inward with slicing steel and gushing water.

Challenger would die. The Russians could always claim it was an accident, just another maritime collision.

Strange, urgent vibrations began, though *Challenger*'s pump-jet wasn't moving. The periscope image showed the water in the hold was slapping around.

"*Prima Latina* engine noise increasing, Captain," Kathy said.

Jeffrey turned to Wilson. "Is this supposed to happen?"

Wilson, frowning, responded, "I don't know."

Jeffrey felt the deck heeling under his feet. *Challenger* creaked against the rubber blocks holding her firmly in the hold. The heeling grew much steeper, to port—the *Prima Latina* was turning hard to starboard.

The vibrations and heeling grew stronger; the water in the hold all rushed to *Challenger*'s port side, slopping over the submarine's hull, gurgling and roaring.

"She's making an emergency turn," Wilson said.

Above the other racket, Jeffrey could hear a warning bong begin to sound somewhere in the *Prima Latina*. He put two and two together fast.

"Chief of the Watch," Jeffrey snapped. "Collision alarm." The raucous siren blared. Crewmen tried to brace themselves.

The Russians are going to ram. Now Jeffrey heard a deep mechanical moan from outside the hull. Kathy said the freighter was sounding its horn, a lengthy, insistent blast.

The collision alarm kept blaring inside *Challenger*. Jeffrey watched through the periscopes, helpless, waiting to see the *Prima Latina* cut in half.

The *Prima Latina* turned sharply the other way. The heeling reversed. The maddened shaking and sloshing continued. Jeffrey gripped his armrests, hating having nothing to do. *She's trying to evade the trawler's charging bow.* All eyes were glued to the periscope pictures now, each person dreading to see what Jeffrey dreaded—an insider's view of a freighter being skewered on the high seas.

The freighter sounded her horn again, an endless series of angry staccato blasts. She turned sharply back toward starboard. The shaking went on and on.

Then the vibrations died down. *Challenger*'s deck righted itself. By gyrocompass, Jeffrey saw the freighter was resuming her course south.

In a little while, a crane on a catwalk in the hold lowered a gangplank onto *Challenger*'s hull. Jeffrey watched a man swagger down the ramp and knock on *Challenger*'s forward hatch with a pipe wrench. Jeffrey recognized the scruffy seaman who'd been smoking the cigar.

17

On *Voortrekker*, inside the *Trincomalee Tiger*

GUNTHER VAN GELDER sweated and his heart was pounding, both from exertion and from fear. He was truly caught between a rock and a hard place. *Hurry up. But be quiet. Work faster. Not so loud.*

Van Gelder and his men needed to maintain absolute silence, because the enemy was so near. But they also had to work quickly. The cruise missile vertical launch array was already reloaded, but there was so much still to be done. Van Gelder stood on *Voortrekker*'s hull behind the sail, next to the open weapons-loading hatch which led down to the torpedo room. He paused for just a moment, to wipe his dripping brow. He eyed his wristwatch and frowned. He glanced up from his labors and looked about the secret hold to take stock of the situation. The feeling of being on tenterhooks wouldn't subside.

The *Trincomalee Tiger* was well equipped—with the special cranes needed to transfer weapons to a nuclear submarine, and with the nuclear weapons themselves. The German Kampfschwimmer commando team that ter Horst had told Van Gelder to expect was already below with their gear.

But the loading of torpedoes—Van Gelder's major remaining task to supervise—was taking much longer than planned, in part because the seas around the *Tiger* had gotten so rough. Van Gelder thought the tropical storm off Australia must be stronger than forecast. Or maybe a different storm had formed unexpectedly off Antarctica; Antarctic weather often changed suddenly, violently.

The worse the weather outside, the longer the last of the loading would take. The longer the loading took, the worse the weather. Van Gelder just couldn't win.

The biggest problem was that, because of these delays, the Australian destroyer arrived. With typical British Commonwealth seamanship and flair, the Aussies sent over a motorized launch with a well-equipped repair party. They were aboard the *Trincomalee Tiger* right now. Sometimes Van Gelder could hear banging beyond the aft end of the submarine hold, where Royal Australian Navy sailors were trying to help fix machinery that wasn't really broken. *Voortrekker*'s weapons reloading was supposed to have been completed, and the fake mechanical problems on *Tiger* solved, well before the destroyer ever got there.

Outwardly, Van Gelder maintained the appearance of calm and confidence. He didn't allow crew discipline to slacken in the least. Inwardly, the thought of enemy forces so close, with *Voortrekker* so defenseless, sent chills right up his spine. Van Gelder's hands felt like ice cubes, yet he sweated all the more. He listened to his men whispering urgently while they worked.

Van Gelder glanced aft apprehensively. *How much longer will our luck hold out?* The maritime patrol plane was still orbiting overhead, and the destroyer would be well armed with nuclear antisubmarine weapons. This meant that *Voortrekker* dared not leave until the destroyer was gone—to even have the freighter open the secret hold's bottom doors, with the destroyer's sonars listening nearby, was an appalling risk.

Worst thought of all, if the enemy realized what the *Trincomalee Tiger* really was, her neutrality would be forfeit. She could be sunk quite legally, with *Voortrekker* still inside. There might be no advance warning down here in the hold, and a stream of five-inch armor-piercing shells might come through the *Tiger*'s sides at any time.

Van Gelder wiped his dripping forehead on his uniform sleeve yet again. Yet again he urged his loading crew to work faster, without making noise. Any strange thuds or clanking forward of the *Tiger*'s engine room might easily trigger suspicion, and cause an investigation by an armed Australian boarding party. If the freighter's crew were lax in their acting skills, or seemed nervous in the wrong way face to face with Royal Australian Navy officers and chiefs, the game would be up that much sooner. The Australians might even disable the tender's bottom doors, and capture the *Tiger* with *Voortrekker* trapped inside.

A crewman dropped a wrench. It made a dull thunk against the soft anechoic tiles that covered *Voortrekker*'s hull. Van Gelder almost jumped at the sound. He turned to the man and scolded him under his breath. The loading work went on.

A few minutes later Jan ter Horst climbed up on deck through the open forward escape trunk. Van Gelder was surprised to see he wore a pistol belt. Two Kampfschwimmer followed, the commander and the chief, lugging scratched-up, old Russian AK-47 rifles. *Ter Horst must be as worried at this point as I am.*

On *Challenger,* inside the *Prima Latina*

"*Buenos días, Señor Capitán.*"

Jeffrey, standing outside the open weapons-loading hatch of *Challenger,* shook hands with the bearded seaman. Up close, now, the man looked not so much scruffy as authoritative and shrewd. He smelled strongly of cigar smoke and stale sweat.

"Yes, *buenos días,*" Jeffrey replied. That much Spanish he knew.

"I am sorry for the rough ride before, *Capitán.* The Russians, since the war, they do not like Cuba so much, you know. Sometimes they try to scare us with the hazardous maneuvers. Their trawlers make our freighters get out of the way, and we file protests. Sometimes they even throw garbage, and we throw garbage back." The man laughed from deep in his belly, like it was all some great sailor's joke.

"Exactly who *are* you?"

The man touched the side of his nose. "My real name does not matter. The important thing is that I am a friend. You may, I suppose, call me Rodrigo if you wish."

Jeffrey looked him square in the eyes. "Who do you work for?"

"Can't you guess?"

"I couldn't begin to."

"But *surely* you can guess. Don't you enjoy guessing games, *Señor Capitán?*"

"You're not American," Jeffrey stated.

"But I am, or should I say, I *was*. I was born in Miami. My family returned to Habana, our ancestral home, after the Great Reconciliation, when our former enemy Castro retired. As Fidel himself was able to foresee, socialism and democracy are not so contradictory after all. Now I only use my Cuban passport."

That was all well and good, but Commodore Wilson expected Jeffrey to trust his command to this guy, and to whomever he represented. "So who do you work for?"

"Why, the CIA of course! . . . Please, *Capitán,* please, come with me."

Jeffrey followed the man up the catwalk inside the *Prima Latina*'s clandestine hold. They came to a small hatch.

"I apologize that we must go now on our hands and knees. The secret passages must be small, you understand, so as not to be discovered by an adversary."

Jeffrey nodded. Wilson had told him to go with the man, but told him nothing more.

"And please do not mind the rats."

"Rats?"

"Every aged tramp steamer must have rats, no? They discourage customs inspectors from inspecting us too closely." Rodrigo laughed again, a hearty, confiding laugh. "But do not worry, they are our pets."

"You keep rats as *pets?*"

"*Sí.* These are all former laboratory rats. How do you say? *Pedigreed.* Please, *Capitán,* after you." Rodrigo gestured at the entry into the crawl space.

Jeffrey hesitated.

"The rats are tame, and had their shots. I assure you they do not bite."

Jeffrey climbed into the tight companionway, followed a bend, then took the ladder up. He didn't see any rats. On Rodrigo's urging, he undogged the hatch at the other end of the crawl space.

He came out in a dark and dingy cargo hold, filled with stacks of large cardboard cartons on pallets. The deck he walked on was a solid floor of wooden packing crates. The hold reeked of stinking bilgewater. Jeffrey jumped when something on the deck, brownish and ugly, hissed and scurried out of his way.

"My apologies," Rodrigo rushed to say. "I forgot to mention we also have the spiders."

"That *thing* was a spider?" It was the size of a dinner plate.

"*Sí.* From the swamps of Venezuela. They are called bird-eating spiders, because they sometimes eat birds."

Oh God. Jeffrey almost vomited. "Don't tell me," he said sarcastically. "They've been defanged, and they're *also* pets, to keep your pet rats company."

Rodrigo smiled. "You understand almost perfectly, *Capitán!* But these are not defanged. Their venom is not poisonous to humans. They keep down the cockroaches nicely. . . . Many customs officials detest big spiders, you know."

Bright lights snapped on and seven deep male voices yelled, "Surprise!"

Jeffrey almost jumped out of his shoes. All around him, standing in tight corridors between the tall stacks of cargo, stood eight heavily armed men. Jeffrey recognized U.S. Navy SEAL Lieutenant Shajo Clayton, and his second in command, Chief Montgomery. The enlisted SEALs with them were all new to Jeffrey, but Shajo and Montgomery were old friends.

Hands were shaken with bone-crushing strength, backs were pounded hard enough to knock the wind from a large man's chest. Shajo Clayton had been with Jeffrey on *Challenger*'s South African raid, and then Montgomery joined them for the mission to northern Germany. They'd braved Axis fire together, seen comrades mortally wounded and die, and set off nuclear devices in the enemy's lap. Jeffrey was *very* glad to see them, given where *Challenger* was going next.

"Gentlemen, please," Rodrigo offered. "This is no place for a proper reunion. Come with me. Come, we have some delightful refreshments prepared."

But Jeffrey's face grew grim. "Shajo, Chief, don't toy with me."

"Sir?" Shajo Clayton was in his late twenties, from Atlanta; he possessed a trim build and a perfect swimmer's body. He had a good sense of humor, was even-tempered and easy to talk to. Chief Montgomery, in his thirties, was built like a football linebacker: over six feet tall, immensely broad and strong. His humor was very biting at times, especially in the stress of combat. If he had a first name other than "Chief," Jeffrey didn't know yet what it was.

Like many SEALs, both men loved practical jokes.

"No more *surprises*," Jeffrey said. "I have to ask. Is Ilse Reebeck here?"

Shajo Clayton looked confused and glanced at Chief Montgomery. The chief was just as confused.

"We thought she'd be with *you*," Clayton said.

Jeffrey's heart sank. He realized he finally had to give up hope. All this time, in his heart of hearts, he'd been daydreaming that Ilse's death was faked, a subterfuge to fool the Axis. "She was killed," Jeffrey said.

Clayton's and Montgomery's faces fell.

"What the hell happened?" Montgomery said. He sounded angry. "An enemy hit? Her ex-boyfriend's goons get even?"

"No, nothing like that. An accident. A freak accident."

"I'm really sorry," Clayton said. "You two were dating, last I heard through the grapevine, weren't you? . . . I'm—I'm sorry. How recent was it?"

"Just before we sailed."

"She was a good person, and a good fighter," Montgomery said. "We'll miss her where we're going. Wherever *that* might be?"

Jeffrey shrugged. "Commodore Wilson fills me in one step at a time."

"*Commodore* Wilson?" Clayton said.

Jeffrey nodded. "I made full commander. *Challenger*'s mine now." He'd removed his rank insignia, for security.

Clayton and Montgomery, all too experienced at coping with the loss of friends in war, congratulated Jeffrey with obvious relish. Jeffrey donned his mask of command, forgot about Ilse, and accepted their congratulations with warmest thanks.

Jeffrey turned to the Cuban, who'd been standing there stroking his beard. "Rodrigo, with all gratitude for your kind hospitality, I think we should just get to work."

Shajo and Montgomery and the enlisted SEALs agreed. They had a lot of equipment to load aboard *Challenger,* and all of it had to go through the crawl space.

"I understand," Rodrigo said. "Work first, refreshments perhaps later. There is no hurry, gentlemen. We will be several hours to reach and then go through the canal. . . . And *Capitán,* my sincerest condolences for your tragic loss."

18

On *Voortrekker*

"How many more torpedoes still to be loaded, Number One?"

"Six, Captain, not counting the one on the loading chute."

"Make it quick," ter Horst said. "The enemy's so close I can almost smell that destroyer through *Tiger's* hull."

"I know, sir." Van Gelder glanced again to the rear of the hold, where there'd just been more Australian clanking and hammering.

On *Voortrekker's* deck, someone shouted.

Van Gelder turned to censure the man. Instead he watched his worst nightmare of all unfold.

The *Tiger's* overworked loading crane failed. A big two-metric-ton nuclear torpedo, a German Sea Lion, teetered on a single length of fraying metal cable. The cable snapped and the Sea Lion landed nosefirst on *Voortrekker's* deck, then fell over. It instantly crushed one crewman to bloody pulp, maimed another, and knocked two more off the deck and into the water. The torpedo rolled into the water with a heavy splash. It began to hit *Voortrekker* in the side, as the *Tiger* rolled and the water inside the hold sloshed.

The maimed crewman on deck was screaming in agony, both legs from the knees down flattened like pancakes. The crewmen in the water also screamed, as the loose torpedo chased them in the demonic swimming pool the *Tiger*'s hold had become. One of the swimmers was caught and crushed against *Voortrekker*'s side. He screamed loudly before he went under in a cloud of blood, and didn't come up. The other man in the water splashed his arms desperately—he wasn't wearing a life jacket.

Van Gelder was first to react. He dived into the water, and both Kampfschwimmer followed immediately. Van Gelder dimly heard ter Horst shout orders, to silence the screaming crewman on deck and get him first aid, to rig lines to try to snag and hold the floating errant torpedo, and to rig more lines to pull Van Gelder and the others from the enclosed but vicious water.

Van Gelder plunged headfirst, rose to the surface, and gasped for breath. The salt water filled his ears and went up his nose. It tasted sharply brackish and made his eyes sting. He blinked and looked up and saw *Voortrekker* from an angle he'd dearly hoped never to see—the view by a man fallen overboard. Van Gelder reached the surviving crewman in the water, who grimaced and said he'd injured his thigh. Both Kampfschwimmer helped hold the man's head above the water.

The *Tiger* took a nasty roll to starboard, then righted herself. The Sea Lion was thrown against the side of the hold, and caromed off the *Tiger*'s hull with a deafening crash. The *Tiger* rolled to port.

The Kampfschwimmer shouted and Van Gelder turned, seeing the Sea Lion coming right at them. They had nowhere to go. It was impossible to climb the smooth, curved, slimy side of the submarine, and the crewmen on deck, caught by surprise and exhausted from hours of loading, were too slow with their man-overboard drill.

Both Kampfschwimmer gestured frantically. Van Gelder realized they only had one choice. They held their breaths and grabbed the injured man and swam *down*. The Sea Lion rushed right over their heads and slammed into *Voortrekker*'s side. At this rate, even her thick ceramic-composite hull might be damaged fatally. With the endless banging and screaming, the Australians were bound to investigate.

Finally ter Horst directed men to corral the torpedo and hold it firmly against *Voortrekker*'s side using a hastily rigged rubber bumper. Others helped Van Gelder and the crewman and Kampfschwimmer back on deck. The deck was covered in blood, thick and gumming up the antiskid coating.

Then *Voortrekker* jolted hard against the rubber blocks that held her, and Van Gelder was almost knocked from his feet. The *Trincomalee Tiger* was getting under way—the faked mechanical problems to engines and rudder must have been solved, and her crew couldn't delay the Australians any further.

Soon someone came through the hatch that led from the rest of the ship to the catwalk. He was dark-skinned and wore a turban. He said in heavily accented German that he was the master of the *Tiger*. He wanted to know what was going on, then took in the scene on *Voortrekker*'s deck and gasped.

Ter Horst and Van Gelder turned to speak to him. Behind the ship's master, smiling and obviously pleased with themselves, suddenly appeared two Australian navy chiefs. They'd followed the master without him realizing it, drawn by all the noise, and now they were obviously expecting another mechanical problem to fix.

They took in the clandestine hold, the nuclear submarine sitting there, and their jaws dropped. Ter Horst drew his pistol and aimed at them and fired. He missed. Each report echoed harshly, and pistol bullets zinged as they ricocheted. Everyone on *Voortrekker*'s deck ducked for what cover there was. The Australians ducked, realized they had no cover at all, and dashed for the hatch from the hold.

Ter Horst shouted to the Kampfschwimmer. They grabbed their AK-47s. Both fired well-aimed shots on semiautomatic fire. The muzzles flashed hot gases; the staccato reports were deafening. The Australians flopped on the catwalk, dead, and spent brass flew and clinked. Gunsmoke filled the air; crewmen coughed. More bright blood dripped to stain the water in the hold.

Ter Horst stared at the bodies. "Now that's just great."

Van Gelder considered their options. It was hard to think straight soaking wet, shivering from the coldness of the seawater and from the closeness of his brush with death.

The ship's master still stood on the catwalk, unharmed.

"Come down here, you," Van Gelder shouted in his best German. "Quickly!"

The master obeyed. He seemed an unsavory sort, someone you wouldn't want to meet in a dark alley, and this gave Van Gelder a desperate idea.

"Your crew," Van Gelder demanded. "What are their nationalities?"

"Most are Malaysians. They work cheap, and know how to keep their mouths shut."

"We have to do something to explain two dead Australians to the others on that destroyer."

"I know," the master said. He stroked his thick beard, thinking.

"Pirates," Van Gelder said.

"*What?*" ter Horst said.

"Some of your crew," Van Gelder said to the master. "They were pirates."

"Pirates?"

"Yes. That's what you must say. . . . Say that it was hard for you to hire experienced hands willing to sail through the war zone. Say you hired men you didn't know were criminals with weapons smuggled in their seabags. Say they must have reverted to their old ways—"

"Maddened when they thought my ship was sinking?"

"Yes, precisely. They ambushed the Australians in the cargo hold, intending to rob them."

"Yes, yes," ter Horst said. "You sensed something was wrong, you took your pistol, and went to investigate. You saw the crewmen, saw what they'd done, and had to shoot them in self-defense."

"But I don't have a pistol."

"Take mine," ter Horst said. "It's already been fired."

The master examined the pistol. "It's Czech."

"Yes, not German or Boer."

The master looked from ter Horst to Van Gelder. His eyes narrowed to mean slits. "I'll need to trick two of my men into coming down to the cargo hold."

"Kill them with the pistol," Van Gelder said. "Then put the AK-47s in their hands. If you have liquor, put some in their mouths and on their clothes. Try to force some down into their stomachs."

The master's eyes grew very hard. Slowly, he nodded. He understood what had to be done. The master took one AK-47 in each hand and started up the gantryway. The Kampfschwimmer went to help the master handle the enemy corpses on the catwalk.

"The spent brass!" Van Gelder yelled after them. "This has to look good. It has to look *perfect!*"

Crewmen on *Voortrekker*'s deck began to pick up the expended shell casings from the two automatic rifles; some brass had fallen in the water, but the collection off the deck was large enough to be convincing.

The Kampfschwimmer chief returned, dirtied with gore from dragging the dead Australians through the crawl space leading to the real cargo hold. Someone gave him a bucket of water and towels, to clean the blood trails. He put the spent shell casings in his pocket, and went back into the crawl space.

Crewmen, under Van Gelder's direction, hoisted the damaged, dripping Sea Lion back aboard and positioned it on the loading chute. A chief with a radiometer verified there was no leakage from the fissionable core inside. They sent the weapon down to the torpedo room. It was useless with its nose sensors smashed and its tail fins cracked and twisted, but it had to be put *somewhere,* somewhere safe and out of the way.

Van Gelder thought he heard distant pops, like pistol fire somewhere above.

Soon the two Kampfschwimmer and the *Tiger*'s master returned.

"It is done," the master said. "You must depart at once."

"But the destroyer's sonar," Van Gelder objected. "They'll hear the hold doors opening."

"Not with us moving like this. Our engine noise and pounding hull should cover your escape. . . . It was cold-blooded murder, sacrificing two of my own men to disguise *your* presence. Allah forgive me, we had no choice."

19

On *Challenger*

IN PRIVATE, IN THE commodore's office, Wilson looked at Jeffrey harshly. "That's exactly what I intended you to do all along. Did you really think I'd let one of your crewmen lose an arm or die?"

"Sorry, Commodore," Jeffrey said. "It *is* an obvious thing to do, now that I know that you knew we'd be going through Panama."

Challenger, inside the *Prima Latina,* was nearing the entrance to the canal. *Challenger* was just a huge passenger for now—a strange kind of cargo, as unusual as the sunken Russian *Golf*-class sub that Howard Hughes's *Glomar Explorer* had tried to salvage from the ocean floor back in the 1960s. Jeffrey had ordered *Challenger*'s reactor be shut down, partly for stealth and partly because there was no supply of cooling water. *Challenger* was therefore rigged for reduced electrical, and also for a modified form of ultraquiet.

"So talk to your CIA liaison," Wilson said. "This Rodrigo person. Work up some kind of story, that the injured man was part of the *Prima Latina*'s crew and was hurt in an accident. Cargo shifted, whatever."

"We can drop him off in a harbor boat at Cristobal, as we enter the canal. They must have decent hospital facilities there, or maybe even they'll fly him to Panama City."

"Yes, yes. You're going to have a problem with his lack of proper papers. If they find out he's American, he'll be interned for the duration of the war."

"Maybe Rodrigo can say the documents were soaked in blood and destroyed."

"You don't have to feed me *all* the details, Captain. A commodore rarely appreciates his operations officer thinking out loud in front of him when said commodore has more important work to do." Wilson gestured to all the notes and diagrams and computer disks on his desk, where he was developing battle doctrine for working with the *Collins* boats in the South Pacific.

Jeffrey excused himself, and left Wilson alone. Jeffrey was grateful they'd be able to get the torpedoman with the mangled arm proper medical attention soon, after all. He went into the control room, to have the officer of the deck talk to the corpsman and then make preparations to transport the injured man. This was dealt with quickly, and word passed, and the mood of the crew lifted visibly.

With Jeffrey's ship so inert, cocooned inside the *Prima Latina*, he had relatively little to do to keep himself occupied—except worry about all the things that might go wrong. He decided to stop in the wardroom for a coffee, to try to forget about naval mines and aggressive Russian trawlers for a minute.

Jeffrey shook his head to himself as he walked down the passageway, thinking. He didn't like Wilson's constant irritability.

But is it really irritability? He's always been hard and demanding. Even when he was captain of Challenger *and I was executive officer, he wouldn't hesitate to roast me in front of the crew. . . . Maybe he thinks he's building my character.*

And maybe he's right. If I flinch or lose my cool in front of him, *what showing am I going to make against* Voortrekker?

In the wardroom, Ensign Harrison sat hunched at the table, under the dimmed lighting. He was using some spare time to study for his submarine qualification. Jeffrey complimented Harrison again on his help while they docked with the *Prima Latina*. Then Jeffrey looked over his shoulder, kibitzing as Harrison memorized charts of *Challenger's* hydraulic systems. It brought back memories of Jeffrey's own early days in subs, cramming to earn his gold dolphins in every free moment.

That's really what the Silent Service community is all about. Everybody needs to keep on qualifying at a higher and higher professional level. Everyone needs to help their shipmates get better and better at their jobs. The difference between me and Commodore Wilson is in our approach, our personal styles. What he does works for him, and what I do works for me.

Jeffrey poured himself a mug of coffee and took a sip. It was cold, since the coffeemaker was off to help save power. It was nice to drink it cold—the air in the ship was already warm with no air conditioning, given the tropical weather outside. Jeffrey let the caffeine flow through his system. He took a deep breath, to unwind.

Then Jeffrey had second thoughts about the commodore.

Wilson didn't talk to Lieutenant Sessions at all the way he talked to Jeffrey. Actually, Jeffrey wasn't sure if Wilson talked to *anybody* the way he talked to Jeffrey. Jeffrey wondered if it was himself, then, and not Wilson. Something about *himself* that made Wilson be this rough.

Jeffrey thought of his father, Michael Fuller, and the relationship he had with his dad, the way his father talked to him. *Rough.*

Jeffrey almost blushed. Was it something Jeffrey was doing in front of *both* men, something in his own attitude toward authority figures? It certainly was his way to question everything and second-guess, and bristle if he felt he was being pushed around. He'd done it to Wilson already over working with the Australians, over making flank speed through the Gulf Stream, over the secrecy of the *Prima Latina*, and now about the crewman's arm. *What drives this in me? Pridefulness? Rebelliousness? Resentment, even?*

"Is something the matter, Captain?" Harrison asked.

That tore Jeffrey from his preoccupation fast. "I think I just made a useful connection, between two separate problems. They're not as separate as I thought."

"Is that good, sir?"

Jeffrey smiled at Harrison's earnest innocence. "I think it might be."

Jeffrey finished his coffee in one gulp, and departed the wardroom. He walked down the corridor with a lighter step. He'd gained an important insight about his own personality. He wasn't sure what to do about it, or where it might lead, but at least his approach to authority figures was something he could try to control. Jeffrey was always biased toward action over inaction. Now he had a clue about where there was room in himself to take positive action.

He decided next to visit the enlisted mess. Between mealtimes, some men off watch would be viewing a movie, or playing checkers or cards. Jeffrey knew he ought to put in another brief appearance, and thank them once more for all their hard work getting *Challenger* ready for sea and repaired again after battle. It always gave Jeffrey a special pleasure to show his face and mingle with the crew—within proper bounds of hierarchy and discipline, of course.

On his way to the mess he passed outside a packed and narrow enlisted berthing compartment. Jeffrey thought of the men who'd be sleeping in there, or trying to—each man stood watches six hours on, twelve off. With constant maintenance and training duties after standing watch, they were lucky to get four or five hours sleep in a day. Some men in the berthing space would be awake now, Jeffrey knew, studying for their silver dolphins, or writing letters home that might never be delivered, or simply enjoying privacy in the only place they could: their curtained-off, coffin-size racks.

Jeffrey smiled to himself to think what wonderful people his crewmen were, so carefully selected. He smiled again, more soberly, reminding himself with pride that now—as their captain—it was his ultimate, inescapable task to oversee their welfare, ensure their morale, and protect their very lives. This relentless and immense responsibility was, to Jeffrey, deeply gratifying. It was what he had sought for, fought for, craved, for his entire naval career.

His warm inner glow was eclipsed by a troubling realization. Thinking of his crew made Jeffrey think of the man with the injured arm.

A wounded American submariner kicking around in a neutral foreign country, sedated and on painkillers... How well can my torpedoman keep up the act of being someone he's not, and for how long? What if the Axis gets wind? Dropping him off is like us making a datum, a ticking time bomb, leaving a sign that Challenger *was here. . . .*

Simultaneously, on *Voortrekker*

Van Gelder thought *Voortrekker* must be the luckiest ship in the world. Right after the *Trincomalee Tiger* opened the submarine hold's bottom doors—while traveling at a dicey eleven knots—the Australian destroyer ordered her to stop because of the shootings. This gave ter Horst the best of both worlds: undetected access to the sea with the destroyer right there, and a *Tiger* that was stationary except for rolling and pitching. The bulk of the *Tiger's* hull around them masked the noise as ter Horst gently flooded his ballast tanks. *Voortrekker* dived away carefully, just as another motor launch started from the destroyer to the freighter.

An hour later both launches returned to the destroyer; the destroyer and the freighter got under way; *Voortrekker's* sonar showed the two surface ships were on diverging courses. The destroyer was heading back toward Perth, Australia, while the freighter was continuing with her real cargo to South America.

The Aussies must have believed the *Tiger's* story, that her master's two dead crewmen had reverted to piracy—muggers at sea might be a better term. Real pirates were a serious problem up in the South China Sea. Tragic, and senseless, though minor against the ongoing backdrop of tactical nuclear war.

But the more Van Gelder thought about the shooting incident, the less he liked it.

When forensic experts in Perth examined all the corpses and physical evidence carefully—as they surely would—flaws might well be found in the cover story. Ships or aircraft would then be sent to intercept the *Trincomalee Tiger.* A thorough search would reveal the submarine hold with its loading crane.

Those Australian corpses are like us making a datum, a ticking time bomb, leaving a sign that Voortrekker *was here.*

20

On *Challenger*

JEFFREY'S INJURED TORPEDOMAN was gone to a hospital. The *Prima Latina* was slowly being towed through the entry locks, at the beginning of the Panama Canal, by electric locomotives running on tracks along the bank. Sitting at his console in the control room, Jeffrey had to take this mostly on faith. He couldn't exactly go up on the freighter's bridge to greet the canal pilot and customs officials at Cristobal. All *Challenger*'s periscope showed him was the inside of the submarine hold. He had to take Rodrigo's word for what was going on.

The feeling in the control room was stuffy and tense. There was nowhere to go, trapped inside the tramp steamer, herself imprisoned inside the shallow canal locks. Jeffrey had set *Challenger* at battle stations hours ago, as a precaution, but the crew had no real way to defend themselves—except for last-ditch small arms.

Silence was their best, their *only* protection. Even though the decks all rode on sound-isolation gear, Jeffrey's crew walked gingerly on tiptoe. They spoke in whispers and sign language, if they spoke at all. Now and then someone would grab a wad of toilet paper, kept handy to clean the console touch screens. Instead they'd mop their brow.

With the fans stopped the air was warm, and getting warmer all the time.

Doubts and worries kept running through Jeffrey's mind. From the looks on the faces around him, he wasn't alone. Jeffrey hated this feeling of loss of control. The helpless wait was excruciating—and the trip of half a day through the canal had barely begun.

What if the *Prima Latina* had engine failure? What if she collided with another ship crossing big Gatun Lake in the middle of the canal? What if one of the locks got jammed, or the submarine-hold doors malfunctioned and dropped wide open and snagged the canal bottom? What if there was an earthquake here, or a landslide in the narrow Gaillard Cut through the high southern mountains? A dozen things could go horribly wrong.

COB and Meltzer manned the ship controls gamely, though there was nothing at all for them to do. COB, exhausted from days of nonstop repair work, began to nod off. He started to snore, and Meltzer immediately nudged him. COB roused, and Harrison offered a cup of stale coffee. COB gulped it gratefully.

Jeffrey himself had to stifle a yawn. He'd already had so much coffee he was getting acid stomach, so he resisted asking for another cup. He was sure he wouldn't sleep until his command was through the canal, and out of the freighter and out of this waking nightmare, safely submerged and free in the Pacific Ocean at last.

A nervous fire-controlman began to cough—he'd choked on his own saliva, his throat was so tight. He desperately covered his mouth with both hands to suppress the hacking noises. A friend pounded his back, firmly but quietly. The fire-controlman eventually stopped choking.

For the moment, it was so quiet Jeffrey could hear the sound of his own circulating blood, an unnerving rush in his ears. Jeffrey drew a deep breath. The ship's chronometer seemed to move so slowly, he thought it must be broken. But the chronometer and his wristwatch agreed, as did Bell's.

The same awful thoughts plagued Jeffrey again and again. Trapped within the *Prima Latina,* cornered in the canal, *Challenger* was a clay pigeon. Panama's armed forces, bitter since America's anti-Noriega sanctions wrecked the local economy years ago, would act violently. *Challenger*'s too-thin cloak, this secret hold, could easily become a secret execution chamber.

Worst thing of all, if found out—USS *Challenger*, a belligerent's nuclear submarine bearing many nuclear arms—she'd provoke a diplomatic incident of monumental proportions. The scandal and outrage as word spread fast might well push teetering Latin American countries to spurn the U.S. altogether and join the Axis cause. The impact on the outcome of the war would be disastrous.

Jeffrey felt this burden every second of the way, more suffocating than the stale air in the control room.

A messenger came from aft, so silent Jeffrey didn't notice until he felt a tap on his arm. The messenger mumbled in Jeffrey's ear. Wilson wanted to see him.

TRANSITING the canal, Jeffrey spent several hours with Commodore Wilson and Lieutenant Sessions in private, working further on their tactics for when they reached the South Pacific.

Then, back in the control room, Jeffrey saw on the periscope screens that Rodrigo was coming down the gangway to *Challenger*'s hull. Rodrigo's posture was casual, and he didn't look concerned, so Jeffrey tried to relax.

Rodrigo waved at the periscope head for Jeffrey to come up. Glad for any change of scenery, Jeffrey climbed the forward escape trunk.

"Greetings, *Capitán*."

"How are we doing?" Jeffrey asked.

"All is well so far. Your crewman is at a good hospital. My employer has agents in-country, who will keep an eye and make sure he is not bothered by enemy operatives."

"Good, terrific. Thank you, Rodrigo. . . . Was that everything?"

"By no means. I thought you might enjoy fresh air. How would you like to come on deck for a moment?"

"Is that wise?"

"You will have to be disguised, of course, lest the wrong person see you. But the crew of the *Prima Latina* are all picked men. They are very trustworthy."

"Okay."

Jeffrey followed Rodrigo through the crawl space. In the cargo hold, Jeffrey heard scurrying and pattering sounds. He was glad he didn't meet the local wildlife. Rodrigo pointed to a pile of clothes: dirty rubber boots, worn dungarees, and an oil-stained tank-top shirt.

Jeffrey gingerly inspected the outfit for spiders or rats. He changed. The clothes were baggy. Rodrigo led him out of the hold and along a passageway. Jeffrey clumped in the rubber boots. They came to a storeroom. Rodrigo gave Jeffrey dark sunglasses, a large straw hat, and a paste-on beard.

"We must avoid the bridge. The canal pilot is there."

Rodrigo and Jeffrey went out on deck.

The change from down inside the hold was stunning.

The bright sun, low in the east, was a beautiful extra-yellow. The early morning sky was cloudless, a brilliant cobalt blue. It was hot, but not too hot if Jeffrey didn't stand in the direct sun. The air was humid, but pleasantly so.

The *Prima Latina* was going around a broad curve, between steep hills that towered hundreds of feet on either side.

"This is the Gaillard Cut," Rodrigo said.

"I've heard of it."

"It was the most difficult part of building the canal. Thousands died, you know, of many nationalities and races, from malaria and yellow fever and worse."

"I know," Jeffrey said.

"Yet now it is so beautiful here."

Rodrigo was right. The jungle growth on the mountainsides was exuberantly dense and vibrantly green. The different colors of tropical flowers and bushes and vines were breathtakingly rich. Stands of bamboo seemed to shimmer dazzlingly in the sunlight. Strange trees with smooth gray trunks towered a hundred feet in the air.

Then Jeffrey remembered these mountainsides were artificial, here in the cut. Millions of cubic yards of earth and rock had had to be removed laboriously, much of it by pickax and shovel, by wheelbarrow or mule. More than once, huge mudslides had ruined the work and killed dozens or hundreds of men. That was all a century ago or more; in modern times, the cut had been widened and stabilized.

"Cigar?" Rodrigo offered.

"Yes, thank you."

"Cuban, of course." Rodrigo grinned.

"Of course."

Jeffrey rarely smoked. He drew a puff—it was delicious, and the smoke smelled very good. The tobacco made him lightheaded, so he took it slow. Slow was the best way to enjoy a fine cigar.

Rodrigo went to lean on the railing as the *Prima Latina* chugged along through the cut. The ship's deck vibrated steadily, reassuringly. Jeffrey came to stand next to Rodrigo, and turned his face to the sun. He let its warm rays bathe his cheeks and forehead, his arms and neck, relaxing the tightness he felt inside. Then Jeffrey leaned against the dented, rusty railing beside Rodrigo.

For a long while, neither man spoke. Jeffrey just enjoyed the ride and the cigar, and savored the air and the sun and the view. It was remarkable how totally refreshed he felt.

Then Jeffrey saw the bow of a freighter up ahead, coming around the curve in the cut from the opposite direction.

"I think perhaps, *Capitán,* that soon you should go below."

Jeffrey nodded.

Rodrigo sighed, and raised his cigar to the mountains. "To the fallen, to all those who made this great canal possible."

"Yes," Jeffrey said, raising his cigar, "to the fallen."

"And to the fallen who fought to make my Cuba free."

"Cuba Libre," Jeffrey said, then hoped it wasn't in bad taste.

Rodrigo looked at Jeffrey and his eyes were moist with joy and sorrow. "Thank you, my friend." Rodrigo raised his cigar once more. "To success in your journey, wherever you are bound."

"Thank you, Rodrigo," Jeffrey said from the heart. "Thank you."

Rodrigo paused. "And to the most recent fallen, *Capitán,* now in this latest fight we share to make the whole world free."

"Yes," Jeffrey said, thinking of Ilse. "To the fallen."

21

On *Voortrekker*

VAN GELDER HAD the conn. *Voortrekker* was back in the all-concealing bottom terrain of the Mid–Indian Ocean Ridge. She continued on her journey toward the Australia–New Zealand–Antarctic Gap and the wide Pacific beyond. As before, *Voortrekker* moved slowly, scouting ahead with an off-board probe. Van Gelder looked up from the imagery feed when a messenger came to his console.

"The captain's compliments, sir, and he requests your presence in his cabin."

"Very well . . . Navigator, take the conn."

Van Gelder stepped aft to ter Horst's cabin.

"Come in, Gunther, come in." Ter Horst switched from Afrikaans—the Boer tongue—to German. "I believe you already know Commander Bauer."

Van Gelder nodded. Bauer was the head of the Kampfschwimmer team. He was tall and blond and handsome, slim-waisted, and seemed like a real tight-ass. Van Gelder disliked him on sight.

"I enjoyed our little swim together, First Officer," Bauer said. "It is good we rescued your crewman from the water, *ja*? It is not so good about the killed Australians." Bauer shot ter Horst an almost dirty look, as if to say, Be glad my marksmanship is better than yours, *mein Kapitan*. Van Gelder was taken aback. Although Bauer outranked Van Gelder—a mere lieutenant commander—and was equal in rank to ter Horst—a full commander—it still was customary to show respect for a warship's senior officers.

Seated beside Bauer was one of the enlisted Kampfschwimmer, who didn't say anything.

Ter Horst waved dismissively. "We can't worry about that now." Van Gelder thought ter Horst still looked sad, shaken, aged a bit, by the intelligence Bauer had brought with him, that Ilse Reebeck had died in an accident in America. Van Gelder was surprised to see this human side of his captain. He realized ter Horst's relationship with Ilse Reebeck had been complex.

"Gunther, pull your chair over here, and let's look at a chart."

Van Gelder and Bauer sat where ter Horst showed them. Ter Horst typed on his laptop. A nautical chart appeared on the flat-screen TV on the wall of ter Horst's cabin. It showed the South Pacific.

"This is the problem we face," ter Horst said. "Australia, New Zealand, Antarctica. The so-called ANZA Gap . . . The waters north of Australia are much too shallow and constricted, butting up against Indonesia and New Guinea. That leaves us the Tasman Sea, between Australia and New Zealand, as one choice. The alternative is the part of the Southern Ocean between New Zealand and Antarctica."

This much was obvious, and Van Gelder had already been thinking about which route *Voortrekker* might take. He knew ter Horst was leading up to something . . . and maybe testing him. "Captain, I think the Tasman Sea is the poorer choice. The sea-floor terrain is nicely broken, but the Tasman route is much narrower than the Southern Ocean portion of the gap."

"*Ja*," Bauer said. "Besides, the Tasman is flanked by hundreds of miles of enemy coast on both sides. Australia and New Zealand are strong with surface and airborne antisubmarine defenses."

"Now we come to the Southern Ocean route," ter Horst said. "Antarctica is nonmilitarized, by international treaty. That's good for *us*. The weather there will be more severe than the Tasman Sea, which is *bad* for Allied antisubmarine ships and aircraft. The bottom terrain there also is good for us. Lots of fracture zones in which to hide."

Ter Horst obviously wasn't finished, so Van Gelder nodded. Van Gelder was starting to think, by the barely repressed smug grin on Bauer's face, that Bauer knew more than Van Gelder did.

Ter Horst stood and touched the nautical chart. "One thing to bear in mind is that the waters south of New Zealand are protected by this chain of islands running northeast, the same direction *we* want to go." Ter Horst reeled them off on his fingers. "Macquarie Island, Campbell Island, Antipodes Island, Bounty Island. The last of them is the little Chatham Island group, some five hundred nautical miles due east of New Zealand. . . . Now, south of them here on the chart, in the Southwest Pacific Basin, the water is close to six thousand meters deep."

"That's deeper than our crush depth," Van Gelder said.

"It is," ter Horst said. Bauer smirked.

"The Allies aren't dumb," ter Horst went on. "See these red arcs marked on the map? These are their bottom-moored hydrophone lines, part of their vaunted worldwide SOSUS system. The Southwest Pacific Basin is wired for sound, and most of the hydrophones are down in water much too deep for *Voortrekker* to get at them."

"And in such deep water," Van Gelder said, "the deep sound channel will function perfectly."

"Yes," ter Horst said. "We'd need to pass right over three of the hydrophone lines to get fully through the gap."

Van Gelder glanced at Bauer, then said, "I suppose we can't just nuke a segment of the SOSUS here, like the Germans did in the North Atlantic right at the start of the war." Bauer blinked.

"That's quite true, Gunther. With such ideal sound propagation, quiet as we are, they'd hear us coming before one of our torpedoes could be in range of the hydrophones. The detonation of the warhead would reveal *Voortrekker*'s presence, within a circle much too tight for comfort."

Van Gelder remembered the plastering the *Ronald Reagan* gave *Voortrekker* after Diego Garcia—running repairs were still going on in many parts of the ship. "So what do we do, Captain?"

Ter Horst turned to Bauer. Bauer turned to his enlisted man. "Stand up. Take off your shirt. Turn around."

Van Gelder was surprised to see two white plugs embedded in the skin in the small of the Kampfschwimmer's back. Each had a small valve, now sealed off.

"What are they?" Van Gelder said. "*Gills?*" He was half joking.

"Look more closely, please," Bauer said.

Van Gelder realized the plugs were intravenous ports—the things used in hospitals for chronically ill patients who needed repeated blood transfusions or constant chemotherapy drips.

"What are they for?"

"With these," Bauer said, "a man may dive to six thousand meters or more." Twenty thousand feet.

"You can't be serious. Not even mixed gases work below about six *hundred* meters. Six *thousand?* The pressure alone so deep . . ."

"We are not speaking of gases. We are speaking of breathing oxygenated saline solution, directly into the lungs, a fluid which self-equalizes to the metric tons of outside pressure."

"I've heard of that idea," Van Gelder said. "It's an old idea. Getting the oxygen *in* was never the problem. The problem was getting the carbon dioxide *out*. Once the carbon dioxide level in the blood builds up, the person dies!"

"Yes, they die. They die if the carbon dioxide level builds up in the diver's blood. *We* do not let the carbon dioxide build up."

Van Gelder hesitated. "That's what these implants are for?"

"*Ja.* The diver wears a backpack, which hooks up to the ports. Instead of tanks of gas, the backpack contains dialysis apparatus. There is, of course, also a form of rebreather oxygen supply. But the key, the great breakthrough by German science, is the perfection of the carbon dioxide dialysis process."

Van Gelder turned to the enlisted man. "Have you really done this? In actual field trials, at such great depths?"

"Yes, Commander."

"And how many others have died so far, doing this?"

The enlisted man looked at the floor.

"Decompression takes many, many hours," Bauer continued firmly. "That is why we brought our portable one-man pressure chambers."

"Those coffin-shaped crates?"

"*Ja*. A good disguise for the chambers, don't you agree? To ship them through Sri Lanka, and load them on the *Trincomalee Tiger*, crated to look like coffins?"

Coffins is right, Van Gelder thought.

Ter Horst smiled. "Now you see our plan, Gunther."

Van Gelder thought for a moment. "I do, and I don't, Captain. If one of these divers goes down and cuts the SOSUS fiber optic with a pair of scissors instead of an atom bomb, the Allies will still know right away there's a break in the line. Their equipment will tell them where. They'll investigate. We'll be found out."

"Who said anything about a break?" Bauer interrupted. "A diver is useless unless he performs useful work. Four of my men, in total, bear these port implants. They work in teams of two."

"They work in teams doing *what?*"

Ter Horst leaned over and touched Van Gelder on the knee. "This is the beautiful part."

"We have a device which taps into the fiber-optic line," Bauer said.

"I thought fiber optics can't be tapped without detection."

"No, they can. Even the Allies have been doing this for several years. But what good would it do your ship to listen on the Allied sound surveillance grid?"

"None! We don't want the SOSUS to listen to *us*."

"Ha!" Bauer was obviously very pleased with himself. "Our device does not listen. It *replaces*. It penetrates and intercepts the optic signals, and cancels them and substitutes signals *we* supply, from the device, using microlasers and a built-in high-speed computer. All without breaking the cable or interrupting the signal for even one moment."

"But—"

"Yes, it involves extremely fine work, which is why men must be down there on site and use their hands. . . . And in case you're concerned about the cold at six thousand meters, the men wear special dry suits lined with shielded plutonium. This gives a diver the manual dexterity of a brain surgeon, even spending hours in seawater near the freezing point."

"You're not serious. *Plutonium?*"

"The idea was tried by the Americans in the 1950s, you should know. Plutonium gives off constant heat, and keeps the divers toasty warm without an external power source that might be drained prematurely. The Americans abandoned the idea because they were afraid of nuclear-waste *pollution*." Bauer laughed sarcastically. "We're giving them plenty of such pollution every day, now, are we not?"

Van Gelder sensed that even ter Horst found Bauer overbearing.

Ter Horst cleared his throat. "So, Gunther, that's how we'll get through. . . . Terrific, don't you think?"

"It's amazing, Captain."

"We send the Kampfschwimmer team ahead of us in our minisub. It's small enough and quiet enough to escape detection, and also has plenty of range. In fact, Gunther, I would like you to go as copilot on the minisub, to monitor their efforts."

That sounded interesting, and frightening. "Yes, Captain."

"The divers leave the steel-hulled mini, with its shallow crush depth," ter Horst said. "They descend on a lengthy cable, bringing with them a low-light camera with feed up to the minisub, so you can watch as the divers work. The device they attach to the hydrophone line overlays a false signal, background ocean noise and such, while we sneak past."

"For years," Bauer said, "the Americans have depended too much on the SOSUS to track other submarines. When we defeat their system this way, it will deal them quite a shock."

"But eventually the enemy will suspect their incoming data is bad, Captain."

"By then we'll be long gone, sinking their tankers and carriers right and left. . . . Isn't science a wonderful thing?"

22

On *Challenger*

THE *PRIMA LATINA* was supposed to stop in Balboa harbor, at the Pacific Ocean end of the Panama Canal, to let the canal pilot off. By strange coincidence, just then, the *Prima Latina*'s throttles jammed at full power. Rodrigo, sent below by the master to shut the main fuel-cutoff valves, took forever as he pretended to fumble all around the engine room in search of the proper controls. While harbor-traffic authorities warned other shipping by radio to stay clear, *Prima Latina* ran at full speed the whole length of the Gulf of Panama. The launch meant to pick up the harbor pilot had no choice but to chase in the freighter's wake.

At last, at the very outlet of the gulf, the throttles were forced shut. The *Prima Latina* came to a halt. The pilot departed, cursing, swearing he would have the ship's canal toll doubled for wasting so much of his valuable time.

All this Jeffrey knew because Rodrigo told him about it with a chuckle once the canal pilot was gone. The mechanical failure was faked, all part of the CIA's plan—to get *Challenger* through the shallow gulf much faster, and then let the *Prima Latina* stop at sea without suspicion. Conveniently, the Gulf of Panama became the Pacific proper right at the edge of Central America's continental shelf.

Standing on *Challenger*'s hull, inside the *Prima Latina,* Rodrigo gave Jeffrey a farewell gift packed with fresh fruit, Havana cigars, and several up-to-the-minute intelligence data disks. The two men made their warm good-byes, and Rodrigo took the crawl space out of the submarine hold. Soon the secret bottom hold doors swung open.

The continental-shelf edge here was steep. *Challenger* immediately dived. She was on her way, following the bottom in water ten thousand feet deep. The *Prima Latina* started up again, on course for her destination in Peru, her throttles restored by her engine-room crew to proper working order.

Jeffrey wondered if he would ever meet Rodrigo again, during or after the war. He was a very likable man, and Jeffrey found his sincerity rather touching.

Several hours later

Jeffrey had the conn. The ship was at battle stations. The control room was hushed. Bell, as fire-control coordinator, sat right next to Jeffrey. Kathy Milgrom's technicians worked their sonar consoles, as she and her senior chief spoke. Lieutenant Sessions and Commodore Wilson stood at the navigation plot. COB and Meltzer manned the ship-control station; Harrison had the relief pilot's seat. Every position in the control room was occupied, and other men stood in the aisles, to help or to watch and learn.

Challenger made flank speed again. The deck vibrated, consoles squeaked, and spring-loaded light fixtures jiggled.

Deep underwater, the volcanic rise of the Coiba Ridge loomed just to *Challenger*'s starboard. The mass of the Malpelo Ridge lay just to port. *Challenger* was about to exit the valley between the two ridges, into the flat, wide-open depths of the Panama Basin. Crossing the basin would be risky—it was like a vast undersea plain, or a drowned plateau; there were no terrain features there to mask the ship. Even moving slowly for stealth, Jeffrey's vessel would be very exposed, almost naked.

But Jeffrey had no choice. The basin was the only possible route to the next long, rugged tectonic feature on the ocean floor, the Colon Ridge. The comfortably wide and jagged Colon Ridge ran southwest for a thousand miles, right into the all-concealing Galapagos Fracture Zone.

"Helm," Jeffrey ordered, "slow to ahead one-third, make turns for four knots."

Meltzer acknowledged. Jeffrey wanted to do a thorough sound search before they left the safe ridge valley to venture into the dangerous basin plain. Jeffrey's immediate tactical problem was crossing the Panama Basin unnoticed but quickly. Using the Panama Canal might have cut several crucial days from his trip to the South Pacific, but there still was a long way to go.

The passive sonar search began. More cargo shipping quickly appeared on the plot.

"New passive sonar contact," one of Kathy's people announced. "Contact is submerged."

A submarine. Is it one of ours? Is it hostile, and waiting for us?

"Contact classification?" Jeffrey demanded.

"A diesel running on batteries, Captain," Kathy said. "Multiple screws, heavy cavitation and blade-rate effects."

Jeffrey relaxed. He told Kathy to put the contact on the speakers. New sound filled the control room, a rhythmic churning with an underlying constant hiss.

Bell listened, then turned to Jeffrey. "It sure isn't trying to hide, sir. Not making *that* kind of noise."

This diesel boat was an old one. It was running so shallow that the suction of its screws created tiny vacuum bubbles which popped as they collapsed—cavitation hiss. The revolving screws were swishing distinctly as each blade cut through the wake turbulence from the diesel sub's rudder and sternplanes. This caused a steady, throbbing, syncopated beat—blade rate.

"Can you identify it?" Jeffrey said.

"Contact appears to be a Peruvian Foxtrot," Kathy said.

"No threat," Bell said. "A thirdhand, third-rate, Third World neutral vessel. Obsolete sonars and fire control."

"Obsolete is the word for it," Jeffrey said. Foxtrot was the old NATO code name for a class of Russian diesel sub. A handful still traded on the global arms market. "Maybe it's here on a training cruise."

"Sir," Kathy reported, "the Foxtrot is emitting now on superhigh-frequency active sonar."

"Curious," Jeffrey said. "They retrofitted something fancy." Only the latest equipment could handle the one-thousand-kilohertz band, forty times above the top range of human hearing.

"Sir, the signal reads as a frequency-agile encrypted communications burst." The digitized tones changed frequency thousands of times per second, to avoid detection by unwelcome guests.

"Who's he talking to?" Bell said. The fact that *Challenger* heard the message burst at all suggested the Foxtrot was using an Allied frequency-hopping format routine. Those protocols were highly classified.

Jeffrey's intercom light blinked. It was the lieutenant junior grade in charge of the secure communications room. The lieutenant asked for Commodore Wilson. Jeffrey was miffed.

"Commodore, it's for you."

Wilson took the handset and listened. "Very well." He hung up.

"Captain, bring your ship to one-five-hundred feet." Fifteen hundred feet. "Prepare to send your minisub to rendezvous underwater with the Foxtrot."

JEFFREY and Bell had decided to send SEAL Chief Montgomery to pilot the minisub, with Ensign Harrison along as copilot-under-instruction. This would get Harrison started on qualifying as a minisub pilot that much sooner. David Meltzer was already a combat veteran in the ASDS mini, but he couldn't be in two places at once, and Jeffrey needed Meltzer at the helm on *Challenger.*

Wilson had ordered that no one else go in the minisub, to allow for the weight of cargo being brought back from the Foxtrot. It appeared that Peru, like Cuba, was willing to quietly violate its own neutrality to aid the Allied cause.

Now, Jeffrey stood impatiently under the lockout trunk to *Challenger*'s streamlined in-hull minisub hangar. The mini had returned, and the docking procedures were almost complete.

Finally the lockout hatch swung open.

Jeffrey had a sudden awful feeling of hopeless longing and bitter regret. He realized he was dreaming, and was self-aware he was in the dream but couldn't make it stop.

It was a dream he'd had once before, a dream that left him drained and depressed. It was a wish-fulfillment dream, and he knew it, and the dream went on and he couldn't make it stop.

Standing in front of him, returned from the dead, was Ilse Reebeck. Not the real person, but a memory of her made real in his mind because of the weight of her loss.

Ilse Reebeck, in actuality cremated to ashes, was standing in front of him, whole, seeming alive. It was all a sick illusion, and Jeffrey knew it.

"What's the matter?" the false shade of Ilse Reebeck said. "I thought you'd be glad to see me."

Oh God, please make this stop. Jeffrey knew he'd wake up any moment in his stateroom, bathed in sweat.

"Jeffrey Fuller, what is *wrong* with you?"

This time, Chief Montgomery also appeared in the dream. He was smiling, as if to rub it in. Jeffrey resented this intrusion, even knowing Montgomery too wasn't real. Jeffrey wanted to be alone with the shade of Ilse Reebeck, and not have someone else there. He wanted the dream to go on forever, for Ilse to be there standing near him, alive and breathing and warm. He wanted this as badly as he wanted the nightmare to end.

"Captain," Montgomery said. "Captain!" The chief grabbed Jeffrey's shoulders and shook him, and Jeffrey realized it wasn't a dream.

Jeffrey opened and closed his mouth but words wouldn't form. He leaned back against the corridor wall, and punched the bulkhead with his knuckles to make sure the metal was real and the pain in his fingers was real.

Jeffrey stared at Ilse. "I . . . Jesus, I thought you were dead."

"What the hell are you talking about?"

"They told me you were *dead.*"

"That's ridiculous. Who's *they?*"

"Commodore Wilson."

"*Commodore* Wilson?"

"Ilse, I think you better come to my stateroom."

They walked down the passage together, leaving Montgomery to supervise unloading the cargo from the minisub. *It seems he decided to leave it to me to tell Ilse she was "dead." Montgomery's warped sense of humor hasn't mellowed any.*

They came to Jeffrey's cabin and went inside. Jeffrey was slightly embarrassed that he hadn't made the bed.

"Why are you in the captain's stateroom?"

Everything began to sink in. Jeffrey felt delight and affection and other emotions he couldn't name. He also felt anger—no, rage, real rage that he'd been lied to by Wilson.

"I'm captain of *Challenger* now."

"That's wonderful!" Ilse gave Jeffrey a hug, a friendly hug of congratulations. Jeffrey pressed Ilse close and soaked in her body heat and felt her softness and smelled her hair—he also noticed the unmistakable reek of diesel, lingering on her from being in the Foxtrot. Ilse broke away.

"Why would they say I was dead? Oh . . . I think I know why. Jeffrey, after you and I were split up at the Pentagon, someone from Naval Intelligence told me the Axis is after me."

"And your death was staged," Jeffrey stated, explaining it to himself out loud. "It was all an act, to get the enemy off your tail."

"Nobody told me a thing about it," Ilse said. "I sure hope it works."

"Lord, it's good to see you again."

Ilse gave Jeffrey a light kiss on the lips, but there was something too sisterly about it. There was nothing erotic, no inviting passion.

"How do you like my uniform?" she said.

"You're passing as a lieutenant?"

Ilse looked insulted. "I *am* a lieutenant. I have a commission in the Free South African Navy."

Jeffrey hesitated, pleased and happy for her, but also disturbed by her distance. "You always wanted something like this, didn't you, Ilse? Official recognition, being a genuine part of things in other people's eyes?"

"Obviously the admirals had a bunch of stuff in motion that they didn't tell us about."

"That puts it mildly."

"I'm sorry I was cross with you at the Pentagon. I had time to think things over while I was training in the Aleutians."

The Aleutians? Jeffrey didn't like Ilse's tone and the look on her face. His heart began to pound and he felt crestfallen.

"Jeffrey, I decided things between us weren't working."

"But—"

"No. Let me speak. I can't get serious with someone unless I think that I could love them permanently. Not now, not anymore, not with this war. I've had too much hurt already, and my own feelings need to come first."

"But I thought—"

"No. Just listen. You and I are from completely different worlds, on different continents. If we ever do win this war, I'll go home to South Africa, to help rebuild. You're a U.S. naval officer first and foremost. You'll want to continue your career, as an *American*. . . . You're good at what you do, Jeffrey. I've seen the way you come alive under fire, how there's a drive and purpose in you when the bullets and torpedoes fly, and it keeps you from inner peace in quieter times. . . . I want to have children someday. I want, I *need,* the father of my children to be some-one stable and sensible, not a man who loves the smell of gunsmoke and has something close to a death wish in him in battle."

Jeffrey stood there, living a different sort of waking nightmare. Ilse had come back, only to reject him. The worst of it was, everything she said made sense.

"Now I need to go. I need to hit the head and freshen up. We shouldn't even be in here alone together like this. People could talk. I'm a naval officer too now, for the duration of the war, and I'm a member of this crew, and you're my captain. . . . I'm sorry if I hurt your feelings."

23

WILSON GLARED AT Jeffrey. "How *dare* you come in here and speak to me like this?"

"Sir, you *lied* to me. You told me someone whom you knew I cared about was dead. You let me suffer for *days,* and you knew all along that Ilse Reebeck was alive."

"Yes, I knew. And no, I didn't tell you. Your behavior right now is perfect proof of why."

"What's *that* supposed to mean?"

"See that dressing mirror? Look at yourself."

Jeffrey's face was red and his fists were balled and his posture was antagonistic.

"What do you see?"

"I'm angry. I have every right to be. You violated the code of honor between naval officers, *sir.* You *lied* to me."

Wilson took off his reading glasses. "Do you want to know what I see when I look at you right now, Captain Fuller? I see someone who can't control his emotions when he needs to. I see someone who cannot grasp the larger picture. I see a commander who if he keeps this up is going to *stay* in that rank for however much longer he survives."

Jeffrey balled his fists tighter, and dug in his feet. Anger helped—it filled the hollow aching in his heart. He knew it wasn't smart, showing such anger to Commodore Wilson, and Jeffrey fought to calm down. He saw it was too late—he'd *really* set off Wilson this time.

Wilson lectured him sternly. "For once, will you *please* look at things from the whole navy's point of view? Do you think I'm some kind of *sadist?* Do you think I kept the truth from you for the *fun of it?* And goddamn it to hell, do you think it was easy for *me* to see your grief and have to keep quiet?"

"No, Commodore, I'm sorry. I just don't get it."

"Captain, Captain, Captain. The Axis *had* to believe that Ilse Reebeck was dead. We owe that much to her for what she's done for us already. We owe it to ourselves because her skills have become irreplaceable to this vessel, including her intimate knowledge of Jan ter Horst's mind."

This hurt Jeffrey a lot, hearing ter Horst's name, Ilse Reebeck's lover for two years. Jeffrey remembered that that love affair had ended only because of the war, when ter Horst betrayed Ilse's family. The same Ilse dumped Jeffrey, after barely two months, of her own accord. The worst of it was, Wilson had no idea what Ilse had just said to Jeffrey. "So you set me up."

"Yes, if you want to be that crude about it, I did. Commander Fuller, you have the world's worst poker face and you're an absolutely terrible liar. These traits make you an ideal leader in undersea combat, because the crew respects and trusts you implicitly, and inside our own hull the enemy cannot read your face. But if you had known while we were still in New London that Miss Reebeck was really alive, there is *no way* you could have behaved convincingly as if she were dead."

"But—"

"Be quiet. We have no idea how badly New London is penetrated by spies."

"Okay. Okay . . . Then why didn't you tell me after we'd sailed?"

"Christ, do I have to spell it out for you at every step? I already *told* you there was the constant danger we might suffer a mechanical casualty, or be damaged in combat, and need to do an emergency blow and abandon ship and be picked up by God knows what neutral ship or Russian spy trawler."

"I—"

"Miss Reebeck would still have been safe, and she could've done for another American submarine what she will do for us."

Jeffrey shook his head. "That doesn't make sense. What about *you*, sir? What if *you'd* been picked up by the Russians or Germans and tortured? You're most senior, they'd single you out."

"If I deemed the situation warranted it, I was to make sure I wasn't taken alive, because of *all* the things I know, not just about Miss Reebeck . . . Unlike you, Captain, I have a wife and three young children. So how do you think I felt about *that* part of my orders?"

Jeffrey took a deep breath, and let it out very slowly. "I feel pretty dumb, Commodore."

"You should. And that's the other reason I didn't tell you Ilse was okay. You needed to learn the hard way that you simply *must* get a better handle on your emotions. Just because an enemy like Jan ter Horst can't see your face underwater doesn't mean he cannot read your mind. He's met you in combat before, and I'll guarantee you he's read a full report on your action against the Germans."

"But how—"

"A few men got off in their minisub."

"I didn't realize that, Commodore."

"You didn't need to know, and now you do. In your very aggressiveness your battle tactics are becoming predictable. You're so predictable I knew before we left New London you'd storm in here the minute you found out Ilse Reebeck was alive."

Jeffrey felt himself blushing.

"Get predictable in battle and you're going to get yourself and me and this ship and your whole crew killed. Worse, such continued impulsiveness will keep you from being a proper team player. My flagship captain had better be a team player!"

Jeffrey stared at the overhead. *After I made the connection between my relationships with Wilson and my father, I swore I'd take the chip off my shoulder and stop second-guessing authority figures. I swore I'd be a good subordinate and show them proper deference.*

Now I've gone and made a total mess of it.

"I take it you have nothing further to say?"

"No, sir, except to apologize."

"Good. And if there is the slightest feeling in you that this is some kind of macho contest between you and ter Horst over Ilse Reebeck, push that far down in the back of your mind and put a huge mental boulder over it and leave it there forever, because otherwise such thoughts will cloud your judgment fatally."

"Understood, Commodore." *If Wilson only knew.*

Wilson looked Jeffrey right in the eyes. "I'm not sure you really do understand. . . . How do you think the Allies are going to win this war?"

Jeffrey was taken aback. "Sir, that's much too open-ended a question to respond to meaningfully."

"Commanders who think that way don't make full captain. How are we going to strike at the seat of German power, in the heart of Europe?"

"We need to send in ground troops. I suppose another landing eventually, like D-Day."

"With nuclear-powered U-boats exercising sea denial against us in the North Atlantic? With enemy tactical nukes poised to wipe out any amphibious force that tries to cross the English Channel?"

"It's a very difficult question to answer, sir."

"The *answer,* Captain, is that we do not go across the Atlantic, and do not attempt a force buildup in the U.K. that would be a sitting duck. Our only prayer of bringing the Germans to their knees without risking mutual nuclear annihilation is to come at Berlin from the opposite direction."

"Another eastern front? But Russia's pro-Axis, Commodore. They'd never come in on our side. We'll be lucky if they stick to the phony neutrality they're practicing so far."

"Did I say Russia? . . . Think about coming in *under* Russia, well *south* of Russia. The old Spice Trade route. Stage troops first to Australia, then send land armies through Malaysia, India, Pakistan, the Middle East, then Turkey. Advance with well-dispersed divisions, along a very broad front, with Allied navies protecting the flank on the Indian Ocean coast. Use tanks and personnel carriers equipped with bulldozer blades, so they can dig themselves giant foxholes quickly and escape the heat and blast of battlefield atom bombs. . . . Drive up into Imperial Germany *that* way."

"But most of those countries are neutral, or hate us, or are at each other's throats."

"Now you see what's really at stake here. Now you see what *Voortrekker*'s push really means. If she cuts America's shipping lines of communication to Asia, then the Hindu and Moslem nations along the Spice Trade route will not be very inclined to help us, and may well be tempted to join the Axis to share in the spoils of our defeat . . . and we'll have no way to ship our troops and vehicles over there anyway."

"But won't *Voortrekker* just run out of ammo? Ter Horst will be declawed."

"Once again Commander Fuller does not use his head. How did we cross the canal?"

"Okay. . . . If we can do it in *Prima Latina,* the Axis may have clandestine tenders too."

"If we had forever to work with, *Voortrekker*'s thrust wouldn't be such a decisive threat. But time, the initiative, the psychological edge, are all on the enemy side here. Building on their recent string of military successes, Axis attachés and sympathizers will press Asian countries to get off the fence very *soon,* before we can recover any strategic equilibrium. If they penetrate the SOSUS net in the ANZA Gap somehow, and then outflank my undersea battle group, all may be lost at the outset. Just one more grand gesture by ter Horst, say an attack on Pearl Harbor, might be all it takes. . . . *Now* do you see what I mean, Captain, that you need to do a better job of grasping the big picture and keeping your cool?"

"Yes, Commodore."

Wilson rubbed his eyes, then looked at Jeffrey very sternly. "Remember, I too have a boss, and he has a boss, and *he* has a boss, all the way up the ladder. You need to have more faith in the system. You ought to know by now that things always happen for reasons, as obscure as the reasons may seem." Wilson paused, then got nasty. "Have I gotten through to you this time?"

Jeffrey nodded.

"Good. Then kindly leave my office."

Jeffrey turned and opened the door.

"Oh, and Captain." Wilson's tone was suddenly perfectly normal, as if the whole conversation had never taken place.

I wish I had his self-control. . . . Aha. Again he's trying to teach me—by example—provided I'm willing to learn.

"Sir?" Jeffrey said in as even and polite a tone of voice as he could muster.

Wilson actually smiled, fleetingly, as if a grin from him were precious coin and he tightly held the purse strings.

"Captain, there are other things I know that now you also need to know. Arrange a mission briefing in your wardroom in one hour, please. Invite the SEAL team leaders Clayton and Montgomery, and your key officers, including Lieutenant Reebeck."

24

VAN GELDER WATCHED and listened, amazed that all this was happening and that he was here to see.

"I repeat," the Kampfschwimmer chief ordered into the mike with some impatience. "Confirm you are on the bottom."

The German chief, squashed in standing up, looked past Van Gelder's shoulder as Van Gelder sat in the minisub's copilot seat. Commander Bauer was the pilot, elbow to elbow on Van Gelder's left.

The chief read the display screens in the mini's cramped and dimly lit control compartment. They showed the data feed from his divers now fully six kilometers deep under the mini. The fiber-optic data line and the strong lift cable to which it was braided were the only links to the pair of men in the unimaginable depths below. The mini itself hovered submerged at only fifty meters. It was Van Gelder's job as copilot to hold it at that depth, rigged for ultraquiet.

Van Gelder saw an acknowledgment appear from the divers, typed letter by letter on one of the screens.

"As you notice," Bauer whispered to Van Gelder, "the normal initial reaction of someone on the bottom is a slowing of responses, both mental and physical. This is caused by the disorienting environment as much as by the seawater pressure. It passes quickly as the men adjust."

The divers could receive speech over the fiber-optic line. But because their helmets and lungs were filled with the oxygen-bearing fluid, they could only respond by typing on small keyboards among their equipment. The men seemed cocky enough to Van Gelder when they suited up in the mini, but Bauer's stiff, clipped manner betrayed his anxiety for their safety.

Van Gelder felt fear too, and not just for the human-fish divers. Divers and minisub both were literally on top of an enemy hydrophone sound-surveillance line.

Another screen activated in front of Van Gelder, but at first showed nothing from below. Then an eerie image appeared: glows and flashes reaching into the middle distance in the picture. Bioluminescence, even that far down.

"Confirmed your camera working in low-light-level mode," the German chief stated.

All the way down there, a bright floodlight suddenly lit a section of the sea floor.

"Still good feed from the camera," the chief said into the mike. Again a painstakingly typed acknowledgment came back.

"We require constant visual contact," Bauer said. "As their topside support, we must see to help resolve any problems they face." One of the mini's screens gave vital-sign telemetry from each diver's body. Bauer kept a careful eye on his men.

Van Gelder studied the picture. The water was clear out to only ten meters or so; anything beyond was obscured by murk and by back-glare from the floodlight. Particles of organic detritus from high above drifted past the camera slowly. The sea floor itself was uneven but mostly flat, covered with muddy ooze that looked gray-tan on the full-color image.

"Bottom anchor positioned" appeared on the screen. "Pressure capsules in place for return to minisub." The camera swiveled to show the special anchor at the far end of the strength cable. Clipped to the cable were the two one-man transfer capsules—they still reminded Van Gelder of coffins.

"Very well," the chief responded. "Remember, work quietly."

Van Gelder used his throttle and his joystick more frequently now, gingerly holding the minisub over the divers so the cable wouldn't be overstressed, or too slack, or worst of all get dragged along the bottom. The neutrally buoyant cable floated weightlessly through the water, but ocean currents tugged at it constantly. The currents were not very strong, but their speed and direction varied at different depths—Van Gelder had his hands full, even with help from the navigation computer. Given more than six thousand meters of cable played out, the moving water's drag force was considerable.

There are several crewmen on Voortrekker *who could do this as well as or better than I. Why did ter Horst send me? Am I here because he only trusts Bauer so far? Why do I keep feeling Bauer still hasn't told me everything yet?*

A new message came on the screen. "Deploying tools and equipment."

Van Gelder saw an arm move in front of the camera for a moment, as one of the divers did something. The arm was swathed in silvery material like a space-suit sleeve, and Van Gelder reminded himself the suit was lined with plutonium. The image shifted as the first diver repositioned the camera. The other diver walked by, into the distance, his back to the lens. The man moved slowly against the resistance of the water. Van Gelder saw the backpack which fed oxygen to the man's lungs, and which also removed waste gases by diverting and processing blood through the implanted surgical ports.

The diver carried heavy equipment cases with both hands. His backpack and his cases all trailed tethers back to the cable anchor, so nothing and no one could get lost in the mud or the murk. The man stepped very carefully, to keep silent and not spoil visibility. Each footprint stirred up ooze, making a small cloud. The mild bottom current carried the puffs of ooze away.

Van Gelder felt as if he were watching men walk on the moon. The world these divers had entered was so alien and dangerous, they might as well be on the far side of the moon. They worked in seawater under pressure at a staggering six hundred atmospheres—enough to crush *Voortrekker*'s hull in an instant. Tons and tons of icy ocean squeezed their bodies from every side, and squeezed their body tissues from inside too.

"Enemy SOSUS feed line located" came on the screen.

Simultaneously, on *Challenger*
East of New Zealand

Challenger made her mostly-flank-speed crossing of the Pacific unmolested. She hugged crags in the rugged bottom terrain along the way for stealth. For even better concealment, and in consultation with Ilse, Jeffrey had the ship stay under the complex thermal and salinity layers of the El Niño current as much as he could. During the days-long transit to reach the area of operations, Jeffrey made sure constant drills and training and maintenance kept the crew on their toes and prepared the ship for battle.

Then, based on specific directions from Wilson, *Challenger* made her rendezvous with the four Australian *Collins*-class diesel subs.

That rendezvous had taken place a few hours ago. Now, Jeffrey glanced around the wardroom—*his* wardroom, the wardroom of the squadron flagship, *Challenger*. Commodore Wilson was about to adjourn the formal commanding officers' conference.

The captains' conference at the start of a squadron's working together was a time-honored naval tradition. The only difference today was that the warships were all submarines, submerged for stealth, and the captains came to the flagship riding *Challenger*'s minisub.

The captains of the Australian boats seemed confident and determined. They'd just spent a good deal of time reviewing Wilson's basic combat doctrine. They critiqued his system of signals to control the undersea battle group, and went over his scheme for exploiting vital early warning data from the SOSUS grid. These were the topics Wilson, Lieutenant Sessions, and Jeffrey had sweated over for days.

Everything looked great on paper, and all the major questions by the diesel skippers were answered. They appeared to understand Wilson's intentions very clearly. The meeting began to break up.

But Jeffrey kept remembering the weaknesses of the *Collins* boats. He knew that in the impending clash with *Voortrekker* they were expendable. As Jeffrey looked around the room, he wondered how many of the visiting captains and their crews would still be alive at the end of the week. He liked them, these open, expressive, capable Australians, and he wondered if at the end of the week he would be alive to mourn their loss.

On *Voortrekker's* minisub

"Diver Two," the Kampfschwimmer chief said, "your reaction time is slowing. Increase your nutrient flow."

Van Gelder saw Diver Two turn toward the camera and make a quick hand signal for agreement. Then he touched the controls on the front of his suit.

"One great advantage of these dialysis backpacks," Bauer said, "is since we're already hooked up into their veins, we can feed the divers intravenously while they work. This gives them tremendous endurance." He looked Van Gelder arrogantly in the eyes. "Have you ever tried to *eat* underwater wearing scuba gear?"

"No. I've rarely skin-dived at all."

Bauer looked contemptuous . . . or displeased. Van Gelder thought best to ignore it—this was the worst possible time to rise to Bauer's baiting. Bauer seemed to read his mind, and seemed satisfied.

"Diver One," the chief said into the mike, "why have you stopped working?"

Diver One didn't respond. Van Gelder saw him adjusting his suit controls.

Bauer checked the diver's vital signs. He frowned. He grabbed the mike from the chief. "Diver One, your oxygen mix is too high. Reduce your oxygen mix."

Diver One awkwardly waved an acknowledgment. He kept bending forward, fiddling with his chest-mounted controls.

"Diver One, your oxygen mix is still rising. *Reduce your oxygen mix.*"

Van Gelder worried that something was going wrong. He knew that for any diver, however and whatever they breathed, too much oxygen under pressure caused convulsions. At six thousand meters, the margin between life and death was very thin.

"Diver Two," Bauer said, "assist Diver One. Check his backpack for him."

Diver Two moved closer to Diver One. They talked using hand signals Van Gelder didn't understand. Diver One's movements were getting jerky.

"Diver One, calm down," Bauer ordered.

Diver One's arms and legs started shaking.

"Two, get One calmed down. Lower his oxygen level, fast."

Two grabbed One and worked the controls on One's chest.

The chief leaned past Van Gelder and pointed at the biodata screen. "Level still rising, Commander."

Bauer took a deep breath. "We have an equipment problem."

Diver Two turned to the camera and shrugged.

"This is what I was afraid of," Bauer said to Van Gelder. "With backpacks we can't buddy-breathe, like sharing an air tank mouthpiece. Diver One is in trouble."

Diver One began to shake uncontrollably. He typed something on his keyboard but it was gibberish.

"Two," Bauer urged, "get One into his pressure capsule. We have to bring him up."

But Two began to fight with One, a weird wrestling match in slow motion shown starkly in the floodlights.

"He's become irrational, sir," the chief stated, belaboring the obvious.

Suddenly Diver One broke away from Two and unclipped his tether. He jettisoned his weight belt and started for the surface.

"One, One!" Bauer ordered. "Return to the bottom *now.*"

Diver One was out of the camera picture already, on his way up, propelled by too much positive buoyancy that would just get worse as he rose. Diver Two pointed upward and held out his hands in a gesture of helplessness.

"Two, stay on the bottom."

"He'll die," Two typed on his keyboard.

"Two, stay on the bottom." Bauer spoke soothingly now, but Van Gelder could tell his effort was forced. "Finish the job yourself. . . . You're almost done, you can do it," Bauer coaxed.

"But my buddy?" Two typed poignantly.

"Leave him to us."

Two shook his head. "No."

"I said leave him to us. There's nothing more you can do for him. Finish the job you both started."

Diver Two hesitated, then acknowledged reluctantly. He trudged away from the camera and went back to work, installing the equipment that fed false data into the Allied SOSUS net.

The chief made sure the mike to the bottom was off. "If One's body reaches the surface, sir," the chief said to Bauer, "we'll leave a sign for the enemy that we're here."

"I know," Bauer said. "You and your dive buddy get suited up." An enlisted Kampfschwimmer tended equipment in the back of the minisub. He and the chief donned their Draeger rebreather scuba rigs. They went into the mini's central swimmer lockout sphere and dogged the heavy hatches. Van Gelder did not envy them their task.

"Copilot," Bauer ordered, "come to ten meters depth."

"Ten meters, aye aye." Van Gelder was glad to have something to do, yet he dreaded what would happen next. As he went shallow, the minisub pitched and rolled heavily. The outside seas were rising as a major storm approached. The mini's motion was much rougher than usual, and the trim was unstable, because of the drag load against the stern-mounted winch reel caused by the long cable played out below. The cable yanked against the back of the minisub each time a passing wave surged and heaved. Van Gelder prayed the noise wouldn't give them away.

Holding as close to ten meters depth as he could, Van Gelder worked his control panel. He raised the air pressure in the lockout sphere to a mild two atmospheres, to equalize it with the outside water. Before the chief and his dive buddy could exit through the bottom hatch to search for Diver One, Van Gelder heard a desperate banging against the mini-sub's hull.

Bauer used the intercom into the lockout sphere. "For God's sake get him inside and get him quiet." If Diver Two hadn't completed the main part of his work, any noise One made would reveal their presence to enemy forces. "Copilot," Bauer snapped, "you have the conn." Van Gelder acknowledged. Bauer stood up.

When Diver One was in the sphere and the bottom hatch was shut, Van Gelder dropped the pressure back to one atmosphere. Bauer opened the hatch from the control compartment into the sphere. Van Gelder, both hands on the helm controls, glanced aft through the hatchway.

Diver One was lying on his back, twitching and jerking. His space suit had inflated like a balloon. It failed at the helmet joint, and saline solution sprayed explosively. Some of it squirted forward and drenched Van Gelder. He looked at himself and saw his clothes were tinged with mucus and blood—from Diver One's rupturing lungs. Diver One wheezed on the deck, struggling for breath like a drowning asthmatic. To Van Gelder the sound was oppressive, sickening.

"Get him into the spare capsule," Bauer snapped. "If we can re-equalize him to six thousand meters—"

"He'll die anyway," the chief snapped back. "His backpack's wrecked. He's had it." Diver One gave a strangled burbling moan. Van Gelder had no choice but to listen as he worked his helm controls. He glanced aft again, in spite of himself.

Diver One spit out more saline solution and blood. His eyes bulged and his face began to swell. At six kilometers down, water *was* compressible, by about three percent. Now all that water infused throughout One's body expanded back relentlessly. Even his nose and ears seemed much too big.

Van Gelder heard a crackling, crunching sound.

"Jesus," the chief said. "His bones. They're shattering from inside." One rolled onto his stomach, in agony, then rolled again, flat on his back. The crackling noise went on.

Diver One writhed and tried to scream, but only a choking gurgle came out now. His tongue became horribly swollen, protruding from his mouth. His jaw worked spastically, and he chewed right through his tongue. The end of it plopped to the deck—Van Gelder could no longer watch. He wished he could release the controls and cover his ears.

He heard One's joints begin to pop apart, with a ripping as tendons gave way; the water in One's tissue compartments continued to force its way out. One's limbs flailed more insanely. His gasping, hacking cough grew weak.

Soon there was stillness and quiet, except for the survivors' heavy breathing, and the sound of bloody water dripping from the bulkheads. The smell of it, and of body waste, made Van Gelder nauseous.

"Be careful with the backpack," Bauer said. "We'll need to take it apart and see what went wrong."

The chief and the enlisted Kampfschwimmer nodded.

"Put him in the spare pressure capsule," Bauer said very coldly. "We'll use it as a body bag. . . . His suit looks mostly intact, but check for plutonium leakage."

Simultaneously, on *Challenger*

Gentle snoring came from the topmost bunk in the little stateroom, but Ilse tried to ignore it. She was too busy cramming manuals and schematics at the small fold-down desk.

Yes, Kathy Milgrom snored—but she was Ilse's best friend and confidante, so it was hard to feel annoyed. Besides, Kathy said that Ilse often cried or moaned when *she* was sleeping. Ilse had a lot, maybe too much, on her mind.

Ilse paused to rub her tired eyes. She stood for a minute and stretched, to get the kinks out of her back. She glanced longingly at her neatly made bunk, the middle one, under Kathy's—the bottom one in the three-man stateroom was crammed with boxed supplies for the ship's office, since every cubic inch of spare space inside *Challenger*'s hull was needed for storage.

Ilse sat down again. She knew she really ought to turn in and get some rest. But late-night hard work disguised her chronic insomnia . . . and insomnia held back the awful dreams. Ilse tried to look on the bright side.

Only another day and I'm off. It'll be good to get away from Jeffrey and the ship. I never expected that being here would be so awkward for me now.

At least I get to do something interesting and fun, well behind friendly lines, in a supporting role for a change. I've had enough of being packed off with Jeffrey Fuller and the SEALs, to get shot at with bullets and nuclear torpedoes.

Chatham Island. A quaint English country village, lost on a tiny dot of land in the vast Pacific, in the middle of bloody nowhere. A thousand people, two hundred thousand sheep, and a minor link in the SOSUS system. Who'd ever launch atomic bombs at us?

On *Voortrekker*'s minisub

Van Gelder held the minisub at fifty meters depth, where the surface wave effects were gentler. By now he was drenched in sweat as well as the saline laced with another man's blood. Diver Two was finishing on the bottom, packing away equipment and erasing the last traces that Kampfschwimmer had ever been there. The black boxes that hacked the Allied SOSUS were well concealed in the ooze, buried under the feeder line to which they were attached. So far, the false data seemed to be working—Van Gelder saw no immediate sign on the mini's sonars that the enemy knew they were there.

Van Gelder watched Diver Two on the image from the bottom camera. Van Gelder was glad that Diver Two was unable to speak from below. He didn't want to hear the fear and grief in the man's voice, because it would remind him of his own. The loss of a diver always traumatized the whole team. Van Gelder knew this, but to be involved firsthand was a very hard blow. When Diver Two moved close enough to the camera, Van Gelder could see his facial features, obviously distraught. At least with his head in the helmet surrounded by fluid, it wouldn't show if he was shedding tears. It must be horribly lonely, to be so alone down there—to have no choice but keep working, following fixed procedures step by step, despite whatever emotions tore you apart inside.

Diver Two attached the last of his things to the lift cable. He switched off the floodlight, and the scene darkened with sudden finality.

Now the diver worked by feel. In a few moments the camera switched to active laser line-scan mode. The crisp black-and-white picture showed he'd entered the personnel-transfer pressure capsule, and brought the camera in with him. This way the minisub would maintain full communications as the lift cable brought up the man, with his equipment and the empty second capsule. The pressure capsule would keep Diver Two immersed at six hundred atmospheres, to avoid the horrible uncontrolled decompression effects that had killed his buddy. The capsule, still pressurized, would be loaded into the mini, and then brought back to *Voortrekker*. Once there, a proper decompression schedule would be used. Dialysis would remove metabolic wastes directly from Diver Two's blood, since it was impossible to urinate or defecate until he could leave the transfer capsule many long hours from now.

"Ready for lift," Diver Two typed.

"Lifting now," Bauer answered. He flicked a switch. Van Gelder fought his controls as the lengthy cable began to reel in. This process started new forces, which buffeted the mini.

"Don't resist it," Bauer told Van Gelder. "Let us drift when you can. Don't overstress the winch. Just watch out for our crush depth."

Van Gelder concentrated hard. He could tell the storm topside was strengthening, because the surface wave effects were getting worse.

The mini dipped unpredictably. Van Gelder shoved the throttle forward, using full speed ahead on the propeller to keep from being pulled too deep. He was sweating heavily now—this was the most difficult piloting job he'd ever faced. The steel mini had nowhere near *Voortrekker*'s depth capability. If he wasn't careful, they'd all pay the same price as Diver One but in the opposite manner: an implosion. The minisub's hull creaked.

The drag effects of the cable began to die down, as the bulk of the line was wound around the silent hydraulic winch reel. Van Gelder tried to relax. On sonar he heard the sound of a sperm whale feeding.

Unexpectedly, currents and drag once more took charge of the lift cable, with all the equipment and capsules—and Diver Two—dangling at its end. Van Gelder realized what must be happening. A deep-ocean storm front, an undersea current related to the surface tempest, was fast moving in.

From the increased resistance and shearing forces, the winch cable suddenly jammed. The mini was much too deep now for Draeger divers to go out and fix it. The mini began to be pulled down even more.

Van Gelder took drastic steps. Flank speed did no good. Pumping out the safety tank, to get more buoyancy, did no good. Van Gelder watched the depth meter as it ran into the warning zone, and then the danger zone. The mini's hull creaked again.

Bauer, tight-lipped, said, "Do something." An implosion would be so noisy it could be heard easily on the next line of the Allied SOSUS grid, which still received real data.

Van Gelder tilted the mini's nose steeply toward the surface, and used his propeller and all his side thrusters to get the greatest force possible aimed straight *up.* His own weight fell against the back of his seat. His legs were higher than his head, and blood rushed to his brain. He began to have a red-out.

The mini was pulled down more, by the slow but powerful storm current. The hull creaked even louder. Van Gelder reached for his last resort, the emergency blow handles. Even these might not be enough. Even if they were, the noise would be deafening, and the mini would bob to the surface like a cork, in plain view of enemy lookouts and radar. He began to think the unthinkable—that he would have to dump the cable winch and abandon Diver Two.

At the last second the propeller began to bite against the down-force, and the mini started to drive toward shallower depth. Van Gelder leveled off. But the winch reel still was jammed. The end of the line, with Diver Two in his capsule, was stuck down at a crushing one thousand meters.

"We have to get the cable freed," Bauer said. The chief and his man prepared to make another diving sortie. Van Gelder forced the minisub as shallow as he dared to go, without broaching in the heavy seas. The two Kampfschwimmer locked out through the sphere. They went to work on the winch towed behind the minisub. On sonar, the sperm whale was much closer now. The clicking noises the whale made sounded angry.

There was a hard jerk against the cable, jarring the minisub badly. Abruptly, the jerking stopped.

"You've got to hold us level and still," Bauer said.

"I know." If the chief and his assistant couldn't fix the winch, and they couldn't improvise a different way to lift Diver Two that last kilometer against the strong deep undertow, Two might yet need to be abandoned to his fate—a slow and horrible death.

"What's wrong?" Diver Two typed.

"Just a surface storm," Bauer said. "We'll have you up in a moment." He eyed the diver's vital signs—Van Gelder could see the man was alarmed. "Let me look at you," Bauer said into the mike.

Diver Two held the camera toward his face. Van Gelder watched him open and close his mouth, breathing fluid instead of air, more rapidly than he should.

The cable jerked again, and the camera was jostled from Diver Two's hands.

"Something out there," Diver Two typed. He retrieved the camera and aimed it out the viewport of his capsule, still in laser line-scan mode. Van Gelder saw a huge tentacle wave by, covered with suction pads larger than a man's head. Then Van Gelder caught a glimpse of a very large fin.

It's a giant squid, Van Gelder realized, attracted or confused by the commotion. *They live here, south of New Zealand, in very deep water. Sperm whales eat them. That fin was the sperm whale's fin.* The squid and the whale were fighting, and both were as long and heavy as the minisub itself. Diver Two was caught in the middle, defenseless.

Bauer signaled to the chief outside to hurry fixing the winch. The mini jerked again. Turbulence thrown by the squid and whale in mortal combat was jarring against the lift cable, and shaking all the gear at its end. Sometimes the squid or the whale crashed into the cable with their bodies.

"Two's panicking," Bauer said between clenched teeth. Van Gelder saw he was right. Two's vital signs, the tremoring as he held the camera, his garbled words on his keyboard, all made this clear. Bauer grabbed the mike and tried to calm Diver Two down.

A fragment of tentacle flew by the viewport, vivid on Van Gelder's picture—the whale was biting the squid. The huge whale flashed by the capsule with its lower jaw gaping wide open. Van Gelder saw an endless row of large teeth, and then a giant, intelligent eye. The whole bulk of the sperm whale drove past the capsule. The force of its tail flukes thrashing the water made the capsule spin in dizzying circles.

Diver Two switched on his floodlight and shined it out the viewport, to try to scare away the battling, maddened undersea creatures. This was a big mistake. Before Bauer could order him to stop, the squid and the whale both noticed the light, and attacked.

The last thing Van Gelder saw on the picture was a close-up blur of tentacles and hard, sharp, beaklike squid mouth parts, of gnashing whale teeth and smashing fins. On the sonar he heard a crunching noise, and the picture went totally blank. Bauer cursed.

The load on the cable was instantly lighter. On sonar, Van Gelder could hear the squid and the whale still fighting. The sperm whale won, and Van Gelder heard more crunching, tearing, chewing sounds that made him sick.

The winch at last unjammed. The cable reeled in quickly. But the end was a ragged stump. There was no sign of any pressure capsule, no sign of Diver Two. The chief and his man hurried back into the mini before the sperm whale could decide to come shallow and hunt for more rivals or prey. Bauer went aft to assist them. Van Gelder, hands trembling, steered the minisub back to *Voortrekker*.

25

The next day

JEFFREY SAT TENSE and worried at the command console in *Challenger's* control room. Outwardly, in order to do his duty and show good leadership to his crew, he made sure he exuded nothing but calm and confidence. The cost of this internal versus external conflict was a tight knot in Jeffrey's stomach, and gradually increasing fatigue. He hoped to grab another catnap soon.

But not right now. Commodore Wilson stood sternly in the aisle, supervising as the diesel boats reported in. The Royal Australian Navy submarines *Farncomb, Rankin, Sheean,* and *Waller* were holding for now to the east of Chatham Island, arrayed in a line.

Each vessel was thirty-five miles from the next. The four *Collins*-class subs created a scouting and search line a hundred miles across, under Wilson's control. Orders and reports would be passed up and down the line using covert acoustic communication bursts. At least that was the plan.

The Australians would listen on passive sonar, ping on active when needed, launch atomic torpedoes, and also serve as decoys and lures—all while *Challenger* lurked very deep, to catch ter Horst unawares and destroy *Voortrekker* in a pincers.

But the most iffy part of the plan was that the diesel boats couldn't cover great distances quickly. To cruise very far at all they had to snorkel and run their main engines, which would ruin strategic stealth. Specific targeting data—ter Horst's route of approach, *Voortrekker*'s course and speed—had to come well in advance, from the SOSUS network. The first of the three SOSUS lines guarding the ANZA Gap lay several hundred miles to the south, hopefully far enough away to give Wilson and his squadron adequate warning to get into proper position for the attack. A real-time downlink to the squadron from the main SOSUS land-based processing center, while *Challenger* stayed concealed and mobile, was Ilse Reebeck's job. This downlink was new, and experimental.

Diego Garcia had proved to the Pentagon that when facing Jan ter Horst, surface ships and planes and depth bombs simply weren't enough. Jeffrey knew full well that the best platforms to use against any sub were other submarines. But *Voortrekker* was so quiet that the SOSUS data would be vague and soft. There'd also be a lag between when the raw jumble of the ocean's innumerable sound waves hit the hydrophones and when the center's supercomputers could sniff out *Voortrekker*'s signature. Wilson's squadron would have to work very hard to hunt ter Horst once he was localized.

All this was why Jeffrey was inwardly tense. As self-disciplined as he was, he couldn't make himself forget how awfully dependent they were on the SOSUS. As always in naval combat, *everything* hinged on making the first detection of the adversary, on being able to fire effectively first.

On *Voortrekker*'s minisub

After the first line of the SOSUS grid was hacked, the minisub rendezvoused with *Voortrekker* and docked. Then *Voortrekker* spent hours sneaking farther north along the bottom. Van Gelder got some fitful sleep, his head filled with images of swelling, bursting men and gnashing sea monsters. Maintenance technicians looked over the mini, and topped off its tanks with more hydrogen peroxide air-independent fuel. Then ter Horst released the mini again, in range of the second SOSUS line.

That was yesterday and earlier today. Now, Van Gelder drove the minisub while Bauer relaxed in the pilot's seat. The second pair of dialysis divers had already done their jobs and were safely retrieved. They lay now, cocooned in their pressurized transfer capsules, in the passenger compartment aft of the mini's lockout chamber. The Kampfschwimmer chief and his assistant tended them there.

Van Gelder tried to unwind, and sought to make conversation with this inscrutable German, Bauer. Sitting practically in his lap, it was difficult to ignore the man. "Everything went well this time," Van Gelder said.

"Compared to yesterday, *ja*." Bauer laughed roughly.

"But you knew you might suffer losses, didn't you?"

"It comes with the work." Bauer seemed very pleased with himself.

"Then I don't understand something. If there are three SOSUS lines we need to disable, and we have to do all this one more time tomorrow, why didn't you bring *three* pairs of men fitted with ports for the backpacks?"

"The whole point of the pressure capsules is we can send the same men down to make repeated dives. We just hold them inside the capsules after the first excursion, and lower them to the sea floor when needed again, and avoid the whole decompression and recompression cycle."

"But what if something bad had happened today? We'd be really stuck, wouldn't we?"

Bauer cleared his throat in an ominous way. "We're taking a different approach for the last part of the SOSUS."

Van Gelder didn't like the tone of this. "What exactly?"

"It's just as well you brought it up. In the interest of time, Captain ter Horst had asked me to brief you here, while we make the trip back to *Voortrekker*."

"I'm listening."

"You're aware of the ostentatious rules of engagement for nuclear demolitions on land used by the so-called Allies?"

"Yes."

"A responsible naval officer not part of the commando team must accompany the team," Bauer recited, "to independently affirm that the blast will not cause undue collateral damage among enemy civilians."

"That's right. They make a big deal that their SEALs don't ever set off an atomic weapon without an objective second opinion rendered on site."

Bauer glanced at Van Gelder and smiled. "Now it's your turn."

"My turn for *what?*"

"We're taking out the third SOSUS line with a tactical nuclear device."

"I thought the whole point was stealth!"

"Mind your depth, Copilot," Bauer snapped.

Van Gelder was so distracted he'd let the mini's bow nose up. He corrected, and Bauer sneered.

"Stealth so far, yes, out of necessity. But the whole point is the last line is the *last* line. Once we cut it we're through the ANZA Gap, into the Pacific and free, where more clandestine tenders wait for *Voortrekker.*"

"More reloads, you mean, more missiles and torpedoes?"

Bauer nodded. "The problem of submarines is that when properly used they stay invisible. Yet High Command wants to send an unmistakable message to Asia and the rest of the globe. The Axis is winning, the Axis is on the march, look at our chain of mushroom clouds, the self-infatuated U.S. is puny and finished. . . . Thus, the last step tomorrow will be to make some noise."

"How? Where?" Van Gelder was horrified, and angry.

Bauer read his face and chuckled. "Ah. You figured it out. *You* come with us as the rules-of-engagement man. The Americans have sent a submarine's first officer more than once. We can't let ourselves be viewed by world opinion as lagging any in our humanitarian care and concern for native populations."

"You mean I have to go with you and help set off an atom bomb."

"That's exactly right."

Van Gelder knew he looked distressed. Bauer had cynically ambushed him with a terrible but unspoken moral dilemma: Up to now, every target *Voortrekker* attacked had been purely military. But Bauer kept referring to *civilian* casualties.

Bauer fingered the butt of the pistol he always wore on a belt holster.

Seated shoulder to shoulder, Van Gelder saw Bauer's pupils narrow—a physical sign of aggressive intent impossible to fake.

"I'm sure I needn't remind you, First Officer, that cowardice in the face of the enemy is punished by death."

Damn you to hell, you high-ranking German thug. "I didn't say I wouldn't do it."

"Good, good. You're *supposed* to be the contrite one. That's the whole idea. We Kampfschwimmer do all the real work, exploding things." Bauer eyed Van Gelder up and down. "I'd prefer a man of sterner stuff, but you'll do."

"Don't push me, Commander, *sir*. I've seen plenty of nuclear combat."

"Yes. I heard. And *Challenger* got away." Bauer tut-tutted sarcastically.

Now Van Gelder was truly livid. . . . He realized this was Bauer's goal: anger displaced Van Gelder's natural fear of the upcoming mission.

But Van Gelder still had serious doubts. "Is this thing really authorized? Or are you some kind of rogue?"

"A *rogue?* No. I'm working under written orders from Berlin, with enthusiastic concurrence from your government in Johannesburg. The whole thing's a joint operation. Your captain has seen the orders, I assure you."

"And I was kept in the dark."

"Now you're in the bright shining light with the rest of us. And don't think I'm dragging you along just to assure your skipper won't abandon us if something goes wrong."

"You seem to be too good at reading my mind."

Bauer gave a conciliatory shrug. "We're both naval officers, you and I, and professionals. Remember, this is all grand strategy, high planning to win the war. You'll be a hero, Van Gelder. You'll win medals, you'll personally help cement the bond between South Africa and Germany."

Van Gelder grunted. *This son of a bitch is using my own devotion to duty and love of country against me. The worst of it is, from a patriotic perspective he's right.*

"Besides," Bauer said, "Jan ter Horst won't command *Voortrekker* forever. He has his eyes on much bigger game, in the Boer regime in Johannesburg. Do a good job on this special mission tomorrow, and you're one step closer to getting promoted. You *do* want *Voortrekker* yourself, don't you, some day soon?"

Van Gelder nodded grudgingly. *Bauer sure knows how to push my buttons.*

"Timing is very important, to keep up the psychological pressure on the enemy and on neutrals after the New York and Diego Garcia raids. So don't shit yourself. Adjust to it fast. The device we'll use is tiny, less than half a kiloton. Just enough to destroy a hardened land node in the last leg of the SOSUS."

"All right. You've made your point. . . . Will we face much opposition?"

"No trained troops, just local militia, and a lot of them are aborigine coloreds. . . . A godforsaken place called Chatham Island. A pushover."

Twenty-four hours later, on *Challenger*

As Jeffrey watched in the control room, Commodore Wilson read the latest data assessment relayed to *Challenger* from the central SOSUS processing center via Ilse's land-to-sea communications downlink. The live feed from sound-surveillance lines went first to the processing center, for detailed interpretation. Reports from there were radioed to Ilse on Chatham Island. Then she worked an acoustic array that sent the reports on to *Challenger,* deeply submerged. Ilse's local sonar-based downlink was needed because no radio waves—not even extremely low-frequency ones—could penetrate thousands of feet of seawater and have any useful bandwidth or baud rate.

Not for the first time, Wilson frowned as he read the report. Jeffrey felt frustrated too. Jeffrey knew that a lot of this local SOSUS infrastructure had been cobbled together hastily since the outbreak of the war—maybe *too* hastily. Jeffrey ran the different steps of the process through his head, picturing what could go wrong at each stage.

The supercomputers outside Sydney, Australia, manned by U.S. Navy specialists, were busy digesting raw inputs from all the lines of SOSUS hydrophones. Jeffrey knew the inputs from the more distant lines were passed along to Sydney by satellite link, for redundancy in case of equipment failure or attack. Breaks in the undersea feed lines weren't unknown—sharks sometimes tried to bite right through them, so they had to be buried and armored.

One ground station for this satellite relay network was built at a point where the northernmost hydrophone line's main fiber-optic cable made landfall, on Chatham Island. The satellite loomed high overhead in geosynchronous orbit, a tenth of the way to the moon—which should be beyond the range of Axis antisatellite rockets and lasers. To try to tune out enemy jamming from off to the sides—based in Axis-held territory away from the ANZA Gap—the antennas that sent the radio beams back and forth through space were tightly focused.

Ilse was secretly using that same satellite link in reverse, to get key information covertly from Sydney. She passed the intelligence—radioed via the satellite—down through the ocean for Wilson's consumption, using a line of special microphones strung into the deep by Clayton's SEALs. But for good effective range and proper data reliability, Ilse had to constantly adjust for oceanographic conditions. Temperature and salinity at different depths, currents and tides and wind and waves and background noise, all varied over time. They'd degrade her signal badly if ignored. This was what she'd been trained for in the Aleutians off Alaska.

Jeffrey thought the whole thing sounded great, in theory. He wondered whether in practice it was functioning at all.

"We should have heard *something* by now," Wilson stated.

"Concur, sir," Jeffrey said. "Unless ter Horst is traveling a lot more slowly than we thought."

"No. Sessions and I went over all the routes he could have taken. You saw our calculations, our time-and-motion estimates."

"Maybe he wants to wait, so our side lets our guard down."

"Emphatically negative, Captain. Think about it. The longer he hangs back from the SOSUS gauntlet in the ANZA Gap, the more nuclear subs we could free up from other duty and vector in, and the more Australia and New Zealand can strengthen their minefields and other defenses. The more time ter Horst allows to pass before his next attack, the more our embassies abroad can reclaim the initiative against the diplomatic repercussions of the Diego Garcia catastrophe. As far as ter Horst's supposed to know, if he gives enough time, *we* could be here standing in his path."

"What do you think we should do?"

"Launch your minisub again. I want you to go to the island in person, and report to me over the link."

"Yes, sir." Jeffrey gestured to Ensign Harrison to get the mini ready— Harrison had already made two trips to Chatham Island and back, to ferry Ilse and the SEALs and all their gear.

"Conduct a close on-site inspection," Wilson said. "Make sure the equipment is set up properly, the locals are cooperating, and Lieutenant Reebeck knows her business."

26

Later, on *Challenger*'s minisub

To Jeffrey it was refreshing and pleasantly different, almost a tourist junket, to be going somewhere in the minisub outside a combat zone. It would also be the first time Jeffrey stepped ashore in a foreign country since becoming commanding officer, and he was looking forward to this small but momentous event.

Jeffrey manned the mini's copilot seat and Harrison, sitting next to him, had the conn. The trip from *Challenger*'s hiding place to Chatham Island took a while; they shared the driving. Back in the transport compartment, one of Lieutenant Clayton's logistics-support enlisted SEALs rested having a coffee—he alternated with Harrison as pilot every hour, so they all stayed sharp while cruising submerged to and from the island.

The battery-powered mini's control compartment, with its low headroom and red lighting and computer icons dancing on display screens, formed an intimate setting, and Jeffrey was feeling expansive. He'd taken a shining to the earnest and eager young Harrison by now. They'd already traded life stories, with the more painful parts left out. But Harrison did say his parents went through an ugly divorce when he was twelve—he'd viewed the navy as a way to afford a good college, and then find order and purpose in life and gain a substitute family. Though they'd come at doing Navy ROTC from different directions, Jeffrey saw something of himself in Harrison.

The conversation paused. Jeffrey's mind ran to his own folks, and he felt that sudden sinking feeling again: the recurrent gnawing concern for his mom. There'd been no news from Sloan-Kettering, but that was to be expected. Personal e-mail familygrams got very low priority these days.

Jeffrey had hoped that going to sea would clear his mind of such distractions. Usually when a sailor left the land beyond the horizon, and settled into the rhythm of the ship, shore-based cares fell away and he or she saw life with greater ease and clarity. This time, for Jeffrey, it hadn't helped.

He told himself he was selfish. With all the radioactive fallout in the air worldwide from this terrible war, many thousands of people would be coming down with cancer—most of them years from now—people who would otherwise have gotten to live a full and healthy life. But that viewpoint didn't help either—Jeffrey still felt very bad about his mother. Scenes from his early childhood with her, when life was simple and parents seemed perfect and he and his mom were on much better terms, kept flashing through his head. These images and impressions came unbidden and unwelcome, too vivid and unsettling and unreachably, painfully nostalgic, like a video recording running out of control. At times the sense of loss was almost unbearable.

Then there was Jeffrey's biggest worry of all, everyone's biggest worry: that the brutal fighting might escalate, that limited tactical nuclear war at sea might spread to all-out atomic devastation on land. Thank God the Axis didn't have hydrogen bombs, but Hiroshima-sized mushroom clouds over Allied cities would be bad enough. To Jeffrey, since his trip to New York and Washington, the threat felt very personal. No longer were his mom and dad safe in America's heartland, well away from the coast. Now his mother might still lie in a hospital bed in Manhattan, and his father worked in D.C.—prime ground zeroes for cruise missiles tipped with fission bombs. Since Diego Garcia the risk seemed so much higher. On *Challenger* no one talked about it. It was as if the entire subject, mass destruction on land, was taboo by a silent consensus; to bring it up would just destroy morale. The best thing, the *only* thing, that Jeffrey and his crew could do was to do their best to help bring the war to a close. . . .

Harrison, hands firmly on throttle and steering yoke, opened his mouth as if he had something to say, but he hesitated.

"What's on your mind?" Jeffrey asked, welcoming any change of subject. "Go ahead. No one has personal secrets for long on a submarine."

Harrison kept his eyes glued to his instruments. "I feel there's some unfinished business, Captain. . . . Basically I—I wanted to apologize, for pissing my pants in our action with the *Tirpitz.*"

"Oh, that." Jeffrey chuckled, feeling expansive once again. "I can't tell you how often I've seen guys do that in combat. Especially their first time." He turned to Harrison and gave him a confiding wink. "Don't tell anybody, but I peed my pants on our last mission, and I probably would've twice except the second time I was much too busy to think of it."

"What happened, sir? If it's not classified?"

"I had an unexpected meeting with some Kampfschwimmer."

"I heard those guys are pretty wicked and fierce."

"They are. Believe me."

Harrison grew introspective and serious. "But the thing is, sir, plenty of people *don't* wet themselves under fire. Right?"

"Have the guys been ribbing you?"

"No, nothing like that. It's just that it makes me wonder, why do some people panic and some people don't? We didn't expect to meet the *Tirpitz* either, and no one else lost control of their bladder."

Jeffrey saw that Harrison still blamed himself, and this wasn't healthy. Jeffrey's job was to do what he could to give Harrison perspective. That was one part of Jeffrey's workload he truly enjoyed, leading and counseling juniors on their careers and on life in general. He was just barely old enough to be Harrison's father, and people like Harrison were the closest thing that Jeffrey had to his own kids. Jeffrey, still unmarried and almost forty, had *that* worry on his mind as well—he'd begun to think his last chance had vanished when Ilse left him. He feared that he'd stay single the rest of his days and never get to raise a family, even assuming he survived and Armageddon didn't come. Jeffrey forced his mind back to Harrison's needs.

"I've had this private theory for years, Tom, that *everybody* panics, and it's completely random who shows it first. In a good, disciplined unit like ours, that first person's reaction, his visible reaction, triggers the others to focus on duty, and it helps them force back their fear. It just happened to be you who helped to tighten our unit cohesion. It could've been anyone."

Harrison pondered. "That's an interesting take on it, sir. The social effects of the group dynamic in battle. A sort of one for all and all for one when the first guy says, 'I'm scared.' It makes sense."

"You know, animals often instinctively piss or crap when they come against that urgent fight-or-flight decision. It ties in with another theory I have, that we all should get in better touch with our inner caveman selves."

Harrison laughed. "That's a good one, Captain."

"Thank you, but I mean it. I read about a study once, I think done by some anthropologists, they were looking at just this question. Why drop a load at such a critical time? Their answer was, that that was precisely the point. *You weigh less.*"

"Like, if you were a caveman you could run faster, or jump higher, or whatever?"

Jeffrey nodded. "Besides, it was your very first day at sea with us, and we *did* win the battle. You did great when we met with the *Prima Latina,* which has to be the craziest docking maneuver *I've* ever pulled. And I'm getting good reports on your attitude and learning curve from my XO." *Challenger* had only eleven officers, counting Jeffrey, so every person's role and progress mattered a great deal.

"Thank you for telling me, Captain."

The conversation paused again. This time it was Jeffrey who hesitated. "If you don't mind my asking, how come you're still an ensign?" Officers were supposed to be at least lieutenant j.g.'s by the time they'd finished nuclear power school and been assigned to a ship. "What did you do, dishonor some high admiral's comely daughter?"

Even in the red lighting, Jeffrey saw Harrison blush. Jeffrey put it together: Harrison did college in three years, at a pressure-cooker like MIT of all places. Maybe he was still a virgin.

Harrison had to clear his throat. "No, sir. Nothing like that . . ."

Yup, he's a virgin.

"I didn't want to push it, Captain, considering I'm just a tiny little cog and there's a war, but my detailer said the paperwork for the change in rank got lost, somewhere in the bowels of the bureaucracy in Washington."

"Well, talk about your *bowel* movements! . . . I'm gonna get this business deconstipated right now. I am, after all, commanding officer of USS *Challenger*, am I not? I'm giving you a battlefield promotion. Thomas Harrison, you are henceforth Lieutenant Junior Grade Harrison."

Harrison beamed. Jeffrey too was pleased. With the right nurturing, Jeffrey felt sure, Harrison would go far.

Jeffrey was self-aware enough to know his moods were on a seesaw today, up and down and up—exhaustion and overwork did that to him. So did the pins-and-needles anticipation of imminent combat. He resolved that once he sorted things out on the island and got back to *Challenger*, he'd make sure to get a solid block of uninterrupted sleep. *That way I'll be fresh and alert when the big matchup comes with ter Horst.*

And I better make the rounds of the ship before the fateful day. Talk to the men in small gatherings. Visit with the seasoned hands and help them steady the new guys. Bring out the group dynamic, as Harrison called it. Stiffen our unit cohesion in advance, 'cause we'll need it when the shooting starts.

Jeffrey glanced at the navigation display. He picked up the intercom mike. The enlisted SEAL in the transport compartment responded. "Come forward, please. We're closing fast on the minefield protecting the fishing piers."

27

Owenga fishing station, Chatham Island

JEFFREY GINGERLY OPENED the minisub's top hatch. It rose partway and hit the planks of the pier the mini was hiding under. Jeffrey peeked outside. It was barely dawn. Jeffrey caught his first whiff of natural air in almost a week. What struck him at once were the smells. Dead fish, diesel fuel and lubricants, and tarry creosote—the odors of a working waterfront. The minisub bobbed in the swell, which was noticeable even here on the downwind side of the island.

Jeffrey listened. The swell sloshed. Rope lines creaked. The minisub scraped gently against seaweed and barnacles growing on the pilings of the pier.

Next to the pier, as Jeffrey expected, was an old fishing boat, large but wooden hulled, resting on the bottom mud, derelict. By the red light coming from down in the mini's lockout chamber, Jeffrey spotted a stained and dirty canvas tarpaulin hanging over the side of the hulk, between the rotting fenders that still held the boat against the pier. He motioned for Harrison to follow him.

Harrison held the hatch open as far as he could, and Jeffrey clambered up. Then he helped Harrison. They dogged the hatch—the enlisted SEAL and the mini would wait for them here.

Jeffrey crawled along the cold, wet top deck of the mini. He timed the swells carefully, so he wouldn't be crushed. At the right moment he worked his way under the tarpaulin, climbed over the side of the fishing boat, and flopped onto its greasy deck in front of the half-collapsed wheelhouse. He moved aside, concealed beneath the canvas sheet, and Harrison followed. They were already filthy.

Jeffrey waited, listening carefully again. There was nothing but the wind and waves, and the normal clanking and swishing sounds of dormant, tied-up vessels. Jeffrey glanced from under the tarpaulin. Scattered lights along the shore showed him it was very misty. Jeffrey and Harrison climbed from the derelict boat to the pier. They walked onto the land as casually as they could. More mist blew by a lamppost. Gravel crunched beneath their feet.

"Who goes there?" someone called. The accent fell between Australian and British.

"Serenity," Jeffrey said. "Serenity One." "Serenity" was the code name Clayton had established for the submarine on which the SEALs had come. "One" was navy talk for the captain himself.

A figure stepped from behind a parked vehicle. He advanced and offered his hand.

"WELCOME to Chatham Island!" Constable Joshua Henga smiled. "Precisely halfway between the South Pole and the equator, right on the international date line. The first populated land to greet every new calendar day . . . That's one of our main claims to fame, Captain. We like to say we're quite easy to find on a map, though usually no one bothers looking."

Given word from SEAL lieutenant Clayton, already on the island, Henga had been expecting Jeffrey, including Jeffrey's sneaky approach to the land. Henga started up his ancient Land Rover truck and took a narrow road west. Jeffrey sat in the passenger seat, and Harrison sat behind Jeffrey—Jeffrey brought Harrison along as his aide, and also just for fun. They'd both removed their dirty coveralls and thrown them in back. Underneath they wore low-key civilian clothes.

"Thanks, Constable," Jeffrey said. "I hope we haven't inconvenienced you." Henga was tall and wiry, mid-thirties, and wore a revolver on his policeman's equipment belt. He seemed relaxed and patient in a manner almost alien to Jeffrey.

Henga laughed, a friendly, welcoming laugh. "I'm not inconvenienced in the least. Your team coming is the most interesting thing to happen here in some time." The Land Rover bounced along.

"That isolated, are you?"

Henga glanced at Jeffrey and made keen eye contact. "It's a big event when the supply ship puts in from New Zealand once a month. Tourism stopped right dead with the war."

"I imagine it would have." Just like New York. Jeffrey knew it would take a little while to get where they were going, so he made small talk. "You used to get many tourists?"

"Ecotourism. Lots of it. We're so far away from anywhere, we have dozens of species of birds and plants found no place else in the world. Birdwatchers came especially. Our famous endangered black robins."

That sounded interesting. "Can you point them out to us?"

"Not here, sorry. Only on some of the outlying islets. They need virgin forest, you see, and all the forest on Chatham Island itself was cleared for pasture land. That's why they're endangered."

Jeffrey paused, then gave in to curiosity. Henga looked like a West Indies black. "If you don't mind my asking, Constable, are you Maori, or Moriori?"

"Some of both, plus English blood. There's been intermarriage for many decades. We're a tight-knit community."

"Being a constable keep you busy?"

"No. That's why there's just one of me. In the old days I'd mostly keep an eye out for nature conservation problems, and make sure the kids at least were discreet if they smoked marijuana. Never any real crime here. A magistrate makes a day trip from the mainland every six months. In the interim, I dish out justice with a tongue lashing or my fist." Henga chuckled. "We don't even have a high school. For that the older children board over in New Zealand. They fly home for holidays, if they ever come back at all."

"They see this as a place to escape from?"

"Unless you want to fish or raise sheep or farm for the rest of your life . . ."

Henga made a left turn onto a rough dirt road. It was bright enough now that he could turn off his headlights. Jeffrey looked around. The land was rolling, covered by lime-green grasses or purplish moss. There was also low scrub brush, and patches of red and yellow wildflowers, and weathered volcanic rock. Jeffrey saw barbed-wire fences and low stone walls dividing grazing fields. The Land Rover went by scattered houses and outbuildings. All were one story, some ramshackle; some of them had tin roofs, like sheep-shearing sheds. Sometimes the truck passed local people on porches or in their farmyards, up with the dawn. The people waved at the constable and eyed his passengers with interest. Jeffrey saw young children playing.

"Another two or three kilometers," Henga said. The land began to rise. Chatham Island was shaped like a giant letter I, twenty-five miles from top to bottom. Just to the east of the shaft of the I, which ran north-south, a line of sandbars enclosed a big tidal lagoon. The hamlet of Owenga, where they'd started out, was nestled in the southeast corner of the I. Ilse's setup was near the middle of the southern edge of the island.

Jeffrey held on as the road got rougher and bumpy. In low spots, sheltered hollows, with the windows of the Land Rover open, Jeffrey smelled the manure-and-urine odor buildup of cattle. He saw many sheep and cows, and sometimes a horse or two. Trees stood in lonely isolation, all bending the same way, leaning permanently eastward toward the morning sun.

"That's from the wind?"

"The trade winds almost never stop. Hang onto your hat, Captain, or you'll have to send to Peru to find it." Henga laughed again. "That's, oh, five thousand miles from here."

The wind and rising sun had cleared the mist. The sky was a beautiful turquoise, flecked with high fluffy clouds. The road went past a stream, then took a culvert over a larger stream.

"Rained recently," Harrison said idly as he glanced back down the road—which by now was more like a rutted, rough-hewn trail. "We aren't kicking up dust."

"That's quite correct," Henga said. "One thing about Chatham Island, the weather is unpredictable and never stays the same for very long. This afternoon could be perfectly sunny, or cloudy and cold. By tomorrow a tropical storm could hit. There's a severe one passing New Zealand right now, you know. Drenched half of Australia on the way."

Jeffrey nodded, then thought ahead. They were nearing Ilse and the SEALs.

"You've worked out rules of engagement?" Jeffrey didn't want to take friendly fire.

"Oh yes, first thing. Your Lieutenant Clayton and I agreed, and I've informed my home-guard militia. Point one, no one shoots first. Point two, if you see strangers working in and around the water, leave them alone."

"Good, good . . . How big is your militia?"

"One hundred twenty men and women. I put them through regular drills with vigor. Mandatory firearms practice every Saturday. We even have an old armored car."

Harrison perked up. "What kind?"

"A Saracen. Ex–British Army. It usually stays by the airport. Fuel is short, you understand, and the thing's transmission is rather worn, as is the barrel of its gun."

"How large is your airport?" Harrison asked.

Henga smiled. "To call it an airport insults other airports. It's an asphalt strip, uneven and not very long, barely adequate to take small propeller airplanes. We have one aircraft, in fact, privately owned, for short hops to the other inhabited island in the Chatham group, Pitt Island. . . . Before the war there were more-or-less daily flights from Wellington and Christchurch."

Jeffrey knew those were cities on the New Zealand mainland, five hundred miles to the west. "Why do you say more-or-less?"

"The airplanes are what you Americans would call puddle jumpers. If they don't have good weather, they can't fly, as simple as that. As I mentioned, the weather here is very unpredictable."

The road took a turn to the left and topped a rise. In front of Jeffrey loomed a big satellite dish. Near it was an equipment bunker dug into jutting bedrock. The door of the bunker stood open, and cables ran in and out. By the downwind side of the rock outcropping, Jeffrey saw a pair of khaki tents.

Chief Montgomery stepped from behind a stunted tree, one that was barely wide enough to hide his bulk. He'd obviously been waiting for them. He didn't smile.

JEFFREY followed Ilse's lead and glanced carefully over the edge of the jagged cliff on the rugged headland. A hundred feet below, strong white surf creamed endlessly against the base of the tan-yellow stone. The wind howled, the air was filled with seabirds and their cries, and further out seals and dolphins fed and played.

Jeffrey saw the cable Ilse was pointing to, draped over the edge of the cliff, leading down into the water. The main part of the lengthy cable, the acoustic link to *Challenger,* had been strung along the sea floor using the minisub.

"You know as well as I do," Ilse said, "the microphone line has sensors that let me adjust for hydrographic conditions. I'm not doing this by the seat of my pants."

"You've made communications checks with Sydney?"

"Repeatedly. And also with . . . Serenity. You heard me loud and clear, didn't you? You didn't miss a single one of my reports. Or do you want to run through the entire list *again?*"

"But the whole thing's so theoretical."

Ilse bristled. "I've seen you use weird tactical tricks in combat based on theories far crazier than this downlink. And I didn't invent it, I just use it."

"But—"

"I *do* know how to use it. It worked fine in the Aleutians, which is a harsher environment than here. It's working just fine now."

"So what's wrong?"

"Maybe *nothing's* wrong. Maybe he isn't coming. Maybe he was sunk after all, or damaged and went back to Durban, and this whole thing is one giant fucking wild-goose chase."

"Ilse, you shouldn't use foul language."

"Honest to God, Jeffrey, sometimes you're too much."

"It's Captain to you, Lieutenant. Watch out, you're on the verge of insubordination."

"And you're way past the verge of pompousness. I'm an officer in a foreign navy, and we're on foreign soil. Off the ship you can't push me around like you tried to on the last mission."

"It doesn't work like that. I'm still your commanding officer. I deserve, I insist on, your respect."

"Well excuse me, *Captain* Fuller."

"Why are you so irritable?"

"Because you're irritating. You're second-guessing me, just like you used to. It's insulting. I'm an expert at this work and you know it."

"So like I said, what's wrong?"

"Like *I* said, maybe nothing's wrong."

"No, we know for sure he's coming."

"How? How do you know? He's the most unpredictable bastard you or I ever met."

"The Australians intercepted a neutral merchant ship. They got tipped off by some kind of shooting, during a rescue when the ship broke down. The ship was hollow inside, Ilse, like the one we took through the canal. The boarding party found a handful of Axis nuclear torpedoes in the secret hold."

"You mean he got fresh ammo?"

"Yes. But something happened. Maybe the Aussies surprised him, blundering into the hold, and they had to be killed. The merchant master tried to tell some cockamamie story about pirates. It didn't hold up. So ter Horst is definitely coming, and we definitely should have heard by now."

"Then I don't know what to tell you."

"Let's go back to the tent. You can get the SOSUS center for me live on voice?"

"Yes. I told you, didn't I? I've talked to them myself."

"Let's go. And in front of the others, Ilse, act with decorum. What happened between us is private."

"I had no idea we'd be assigned together again, on the ship. If I thought that would possibly happen, I'd never have let what went on between us get started to begin with."

"So you blew it, because it *did* get started, and here we are. At least be discreet. I cannot let you argue with me in front of Clayton and Montgomery."

Ilse balled her fists. "Stop lecturing me. This is exactly why I knew you and I would never work out. You've got some kind of complex. You don't treat women with respect."

"That's *it,* Lieutenant! *You're* the one with the complex. You don't know how to take orders and play on a team."

JEFFREY and Ilse trudged back the three hundred yards or so from the edge of the cliff to where the tents were set up. Out of the corner of his eye, Jeffrey spotted movement in the dense bushes, on the edge of a nature reserve that bordered the satellite ground-station site. *A wild pig, probably.*

When Jeffrey and Ilse got back to the others, Clayton and Montgomery and some of their men were standing or sitting and eating rations, and chatting with Harrison and Constable Henga. The SEALs were posing as rear-area security troops, sent along by the U.S. Navy with Ilse and Jeffrey and Harrison, who were supposed to be SOSUS maintenance workers. That was the cover story Henga fed to curious islanders who'd asked, and it would lull enemy recon sensors too.

Ilse entered her tent, to establish the voice link with Sydney using her portable console. Jeffrey left her alone so she could cool off.

Jeffrey stood there catching his breath, winded from climbing and walking in rough terrain. *I've been so busy with all the duties as* Challenger's *captain plus Wilson's operations officer, I neglected my need for exercise. I'm really out of shape.* Jeffrey idly took a closer look at the rock outcropping that held the equipment bunker for the local satellite ground station. The rock was volcanic, old, weathered, but strong and hard. The parts Jeffrey could see from where he stood were rough matte black, with veins of dark gray. The outcropping formed a big hump jutting out of the soil. The portion that held the bunker showed fresh marks from blasting and jackhammers, presumably done by U.S. Navy Seabees or New Zealand military engineers.

Jeffrey heard a strange *crack* as a hot angry bee rushed past his ear. One of the enlisted SEALs caved in on himself and fell forward. There was another *crack* and someone plucked Jeffrey's sleeve. He turned in confusion since nobody was next to him. Montgomery came running at Jeffrey as fast as he could.

"Wha—"

"Sniper!" Montgomery bellowed as he knocked Jeffrey off his feet.

28

JEFFREY LAY ON his back, bewildered, staring at the sky, in mental shock as his heart pounded. Around him he sensed a disordered swirl of frantic motion and raised voices. Montgomery was already some distance away. Everyone was scrambling for cover and grabbing their weapons. Jeffrey's former SEAL training came back from his younger days. He rolled onto his stomach and belly-crawled to a better position. *Where's the sniper? And who the hell is shooting at us?*

There was a *bang* in the distance, and a tearing sound.

"Incoming!" Clayton shouted. Everyone squashed flat.

Jeffrey caressed the damp soil with urgent intimacy, and tried to become one with the moss. The initial surprise of it all was wearing off, and now stark terror sank in. Jeffrey badly wished he had a helmet. A glowing ball was tearing toward him low over the ground, leaving a trail of dirty smoke. The rocket slammed into Ilse's tent and exploded inside. The canvas billowed outward and ripped, riddled with white-hot shrapnel. The tent burst into flame at once. It collapsed, roaring and crackling.

Ilse glanced from around the rock outcropping; she'd had the sense to abandon the tent at the first sign of trouble. The tent burned merrily, fanned by the wind—and that ended their only link with *Challenger*. There was no way to sound a warning, no way to call quickly for help.

Jeffrey fought hard to regain mental balance. They had to respond to this sudden emergency with speed and focused violence, or they'd be overwhelmed and defeated both individually and as a group—defeated emotionally and then physically. Jeffrey's mind registered scattered rifle shots from the enlisted SEALs. He could tell they were uncoordinated, shooting wild, to try to suppress the enemy fire. *But who was the enemy?*

Jeffrey heard Shajo Clayton's voice, tough and commanding amid the din. The SEAL lieutenant was calling orders to his team, to stop wasting ammo and organize a meaningful hasty defense. Jeffrey drew comfort from Clayton's leadership as Clayton rallied and prodded his men. Jeffrey's own combat instincts clicked in more and more, and some of his fear began to give way to excitement and rising purposefulness. The key was not to stay passive, but do something useful immediately. Yet tactically, in this situation, Clayton was in charge.

Clayton crawled up next to Jeffrey. His closeness made Jeffrey feel better. Jeffrey felt less lost and alone, no longer quite so isolated as everyone else near him sought concealment or dug themselves in.

Both men gained scant cover using a small dip in the ground. Clayton showed Jeffrey a grin. The two had been here several times before, this special, taxing, mystical place where courageous people braved death together with righteousness on their side.

Another bullet crazed the soil, too near Jeffrey's head. Clayton and Jeffrey were forced to move apart. Their separation made Jeffrey feel more anxious. He forced himself to get a grip.

"They're after you, Captain. They know you're senior."

"Yeah, but who's *they?*"

GUNTHER Van Gelder lay in the bushes beside Commander Bauer. Bauer studied their objective with his binoculars.

"It doesn't make sense," Bauer whispered. "They haven't broken and run."

"Maybe they're too scared to move."

Bauer made hand signals for his sniper to fire again.

*   *   *

"*I GOT targets*," Chief Montgomery shouted. "Two groups, three or four men each, heading right and left! They're trying to outflank us!"

"Hold your fire," Clayton ordered. "They might be friendly troops!"

"Constable," Jeffrey yelled. "Are they yours? Some kind of mix-up?"

"No!" Henga yelled back. "Nobody dresses like that."

"Like what?" Jeffrey couldn't get a clear view. He was pinned down as the enemy sniper learned the feel of the wind—his shots were closer and closer.

"Black body stockings," Henga yelled.

"Kampfschwimmer," Jeffrey said. There was a moment of shocked silence. Then the SEALs visibly braced themselves. Clayton licked his lips, as if he welcomed this one-on-one contest of champion teams. Jeffrey thought fast. "They're after the bunker."

"Return fire!" Clayton ordered. "*Weapons free!*"

The SEALs resumed firing the time-worn M-16s they'd brought with them, part of their disguise as rear-area troops. The outflanking Kampfschwimmer went to ground. M-16s crackled and spent brass flew as each SEAL took carefully aimed shots. They needed to make every round count: they hadn't brought heavy weapons, or much of an ammo supply.

The flanking Kampfschwimmer fired back. Their rifles made a deeper booming noise than the M-16s. Jeffrey knew those telltale reports from the old days: AK-47s, also aged, but lethal. Their bullets were much heavier than the ones from an M-16. Both Kampfschwimmer flanking teams advanced, using fire and movement skillfully. Jeffrey felt the pressure mount as the enemy pincers advanced.

Clayton raised his head, just long enough to squeeze off a round. Burnt powder went up Jeffrey's nose and stirred his adrenaline more, but he was unarmed and they were in serious danger of being surrounded. Jeffrey began to choke on thin but acrid smoke—the fire in Ilse's tent had spread and the second tent was burning.

"There's a radio in my truck!" Henga yelled.

Harrison was the only one close enough to stand a chance of reaching Henga's Land Rover alive. He broke cover without hesitation, and dashed behind the truck. The German sniper loosed a round that smashed the windshield to bits. Jeffrey judged the sniper had changed his firing position. *He's good.*

Jeffrey saw the Land Rover's far-side door swing open. Jeffrey knew that if Harrison failed, they might all be killed or captured where they lay. A sniper round pierced the sheet-metal side of the driver's door.

"Tom!" Jeffrey shouted in concern.

"I'm okay!" Harrison shouted.

Bullets flew in both directions viciously now. The Land Rover bounced and sagged as its tires were hit and exploded. All the different noises hurt Jeffrey's ears.

Henga fired his revolver twice at a distant clump of bushes. Jeffrey knew the weapon was useless at such range—and Kampfschwimmer wouldn't be slowed by ineffective fire. But then Jeffrey had an idea. He turned to Clayton. "We don't want the Kampfschwimmer knowing we're SEALs."

"Concur, Skipper. Let's show 'em some sloppy fire discipline." With difficulty, since the slightest movement drew more fire, Clayton tossed Jeffrey his pistol. It landed on the ground halfway between them. As Jeffrey reached, a sniper bullet almost took his hand off at the wrist.

Jeffrey grabbed the pistol and checked that the muzzle was clear of dirt. Like Henga, he fired two rounds. The AK-47s boomed, and the M-16s responded, but the outflanking enemy men advanced again. Soon the line of retreat would be cut off.

"Who do I call?" Harrison yelled from down inside the driver's compartment. His voice sounded deep and confident; Jeffrey was very glad they'd had that talk in the minisub.

"Waitangi!" Henga shouted. That was the only town, in the middle of the island. "Tell the council duty clerk to sound the invasion alarm."

Jeffrey waited impatiently—Harrison seemed to take forever. *If that radio is busted we're in very serious trouble.* This was an uninhabited part of the island. Anyone who heard the firing from farther off might just think Henga was holding an exercise.

"I've got him," Harrison yelled.

Henga shouted his orders. "Waitangi platoon to head here by the Tuku Road. Owenga platoon to come the way we came, and Saracen to follow the Naim River trail! Others to muster in place and hold the rest of the island!"

"Okay!"

Jeffrey and Clayton looked at each other. Henga sounded like he knew what he was doing. Reinforcements from Owenga would strengthen their hold on the satellite site. From Tuku, the militia could threaten the enemy from the rear. The Saracen, with its cannon and machine gun raking the Germans from off to the side, could tip the balance decisively.

But this would all take precious time, and the time factor favored the Germans. The SOSUS bunker itself would have made a beautiful defensive stronghold, but the path there was much too exposed for Clayton's men to get inside—the door faced right at the enemy's center.

Bullets continued to fly. One of Clayton's spent shell casings burned the back of Jeffrey's hand. There was a loud clang, then a screeching whine, as an incoming bullet ricocheted off the Land Rover's engine block. In the far distance, carried on the wind, Jeffrey could hear air-raid sirens now.

"Tom," Jeffrey yelled. "Get out of there before they hit the fuel tank!"

"Tom," Henga yelled, "take my shotgun, under the dashboard! Shells are in the glove box!"

Jeffrey saw Harrison roll out of the Land Rover. As enemy rounds chewed the dirt near his feet, Harrison bobbed and weaved and dashed behind the outcropping next to Ilse. He was smart enough to hold his fire—a shotgun was a close-in weapon. Jeffrey urged him to fire a couple of rounds—again, the deception plan that they were rear-area troops.

The shotgun blasts were deafening crashes. Another sniper bullet barely missed Jeffrey's head. He crawled and shifted position again. The firefight had been raging long enough for him to take stock of what was happening and why.

How did the Germans get here? Dropped from a secret compartment of a pseudoneutral airliner? High-altitude-low-opening parachute tactics at sea, then move inshore with the wind and tide, using rubber boats or even underwater scooters? Do they want to commandeer the SOSUS site to

eavesdrop on the data? Use it to locate Allied subs, and then use that to help
Voortrekker? . . .

So that's what ter Horst is waiting for, our undersea fleet dispositions,
before he tackles the Gap.

Yeah, that's what the Germans are after. Even with all this shooting
they're leaving the satellite bunker untouched.

They're clever, I'll give them that.

Clayton fired another round from his smoking rifle, then ejected the
empty magazine, his last. "Captain, we have to withdraw. We're outnumbered and outgunned."

"We can't," Jeffrey said. "We have to destroy the equipment bunker."
Jeffrey told Clayton why: the whole outcome of the battle between
Challenger and *Voortrekker* could hinge around this little bunker.

Clayton told his man nearest the bunker to throw in fragmentation
grenades.

As the man rose off the ground he screamed, hit in the neck by the
sniper. Bright red arterial blood arced into the air and soaked the grass.
Montgomery dashed to help the wounded man, dodging incoming
rounds, and the chief was quickly soaked by the blood. From behind a
boulder he looked at Clayton and shook his head.

That's two dead, Jeffrey told himself, counting the SEAL killed by the
sniper at the very start of the action.

Another enlisted SEAL made a try for the bunker. The distant sniper
fired but missed.

A German light machine gun, held in reserve, opened up immediately. The SEAL was almost cut in half. He dropped both live grenades.
They exploded next to his body. The double concussion through the
ground made Jeffrey hurt. Intestines and body parts flew, but the
bunker was undamaged. The corpse began to burn. The stink was unbearable. The dead SEAL's ammunition cooked off like strings of fire-
crackers.

That's three dead, one-fourth of our manpower, and it confirms they
really want the bunker intact. The Kampfschwimmer flanking units were
swinging wide now. Soon they'd surround Clayton's team and hit the
SEALs with fire from every direction at once.

Clayton lobbed a grenade, to try to cut Ilse's cable that ran to the sea. The concussion flashed and pounded the earth and more shrapnel whizzed through the air. Jeffrey aimed at the satellite dish, and kept firing rounds from his pistol to try to knock the dish out. At this distance, he couldn't tell if he'd done anything. He ran out of ammo, and Clayton threw him another clip for the pistol, his last.

"We have to withdraw!" Clayton repeated.

Jeffrey shook his head. "They'll pick us all off if we move." As if to emphasize, the German light machine gun fired again, peppering the SEALs and Jeffrey with dirt and fragments of rock. "We need a smokescreen or we're finished."

"We don't have that many smoke grenades. Not with this wind, it's too strong!"

"The truck's fuel tank. We can *use* that."

Clayton nodded. Jeffrey crawled flat on his stomach until he had a good line of fire. He shot at the underside of the truck. The bullet found its mark, and diesel fuel leaked in a widening puddle. Jeffrey fired again, at a stone under the vehicle, to make a spark. The diesel refused to ignite. Jeffrey signaled for Clayton to pass him his other grenade. Jeffrey set the timer to "Long," seven seconds.

"Grenade!" Jeffrey shouted. He rolled it beneath the truck and scrambled away.

A split second after the grenade went off, the whole fuel tank exploded with a gut-pounding *whump*. Parts of the Land Rover flew through the air. Jeffrey felt a wave of blistering heat that didn't diminish. The truck was giving off heavy gray-black smoke. It grew even thicker when all four punctured tires began to burn. The combined odors at this point were revolting.

"Pop what smoke you got," Montgomery ordered at the top of his lungs. The chief was hoarse from shouting and breathing the smoke, and Jeffrey's eardrums ached so badly it was hard for him to hear.

The surviving SEALs tossed the few smoke grenades they had. Clouds of chemical smoke puffed out in green and orange and purple. The different colors blended oddly with the oily, choking smoke from the burning truck.

Montgomery shouldered the nearest dead SEAL's body. Henga was closest to the enlisted SEAL who'd been killed first—Henga crawled and grabbed the body and started to drag it along. Ilse, with nothing to do up to now, darted through the smokescreen and snatched the corpses' intact M-16s. She threw one rifle to Jeffrey, then with the other began to send short bursts blindly through the smoke, toward the Germans.

The third SEAL, killed by the machine-gun fire, had to be left behind. The corpse had been shattered by the SEAL's own grenades, and was self-cremating anyway.

"*Back!*" Clayton shouted. "*Fall back!*"

Minutes later

Van Gelder looked away from the smoldering broken skeleton near the rock outcropping. The other two large pools of blood were congealed now, sticky and brown. The stench of burning rubber and flesh made Van Gelder nauseous, and the lingering smoke from the tents and the truck made him cough. The ground was littered with brass shell casings and empty smoke grenades. Sharp bits of shrapnel poked out from the grass. The wind blew scattered bits of paper and unwound streamers of white field-dressing gauze. To Van Gelder the small abandoned battlefield was depressing. The bright sunny sky and twittering birds made it worse.

The enemy was fleeing to a low stone wall a thousand meters away. Bauer had his sniper and his machine gunner hold their fire. He told them to let the defeated men run, to save ammo for the militia's counterattack—the Kampfschwimmer radioman had been monitoring communications on the island all along. Some of Bauer's men spread wide to form a defensive perimeter, and blended into terrain and disappeared.

At intervals one of the enemy fired a round from a pistol or shotgun. To show his contempt, Bauer paraded around in plain sight, forcing Van Gelder to do so as well. The Kampfschwimmer chief crept off north, inland toward the Naim River, lugging two antitank rockets to ambush the armored car when it came.

* * *

THE SEALs retreated over the long stone wall, then piled rocks and logs on top for better protection. Jeffrey flopped behind the wall and sat in the dirt with Clayton's pistol warm in his hand. He leaned back against the stones and fought to catch his breath. He tried not to look at the dead SEALs laid out neatly by the wall. He felt their unseeing eyes stare at him, and he blamed himself for their deaths.

I distracted Clayton's team by coming here when I did, to no good purpose. If it wasn't for me they might've been more alert.

Ilse knelt behind the wall, clutching a dead man's M-16. She glanced at Jeffrey; he thought she did it accusingly. Her face was streaked with sweat, and stained with black soot and green moss. Jeffrey knew he looked the same. He had a powerful thirst but lacked a canteen. He'd lost his sunglasses somewhere, and he squinted in the glaring sun. There was no shade here at all, but the endless wind prevented the sun from giving him any warmth.

Henga fired his revolver toward the enemy, then Harrison quickly fired another shotgun round. Each report made Jeffrey jump.

Apprehensive, he peered over the wall. The Kampfschwimmer weren't pursuing.

Way up there, next to the rock outcropping, Jeffrey spotted the whip antenna for a German tactical radio. He knew they'd also have longer range communications gear. *They want the bunker, not us.*

"IT'S coming," the radioman said. "There it is."

Van Gelder heard a puttering, droning sound in the sky. He saw a black dot approaching, growing larger fast, a small airplane. The island militia had sent it up for reconnaissance and spotting.

Bauer reached for an equipment pack and pulled out an antiaircraft missile. He waved for Van Gelder to get out of the way of the back blast.

Bauer crouched and hefted the missile launcher to his shoulder. He armed it, aimed, then pressed the trigger.

With a loud bang and a gush of flame the missile left the launcher; Bauer jolted, then regained his balance and put the empty launcher down. The missile rose into the sky, homing crabwise on the aircraft as its flight was caught by the crosswind.

The plane began to bank away. The missile impacted. There was a red-orange flash, followed seconds later by the sound of a sharp detonation. Pieces of aircraft, and burning fuel, fell to the ground in the distance. The earth shook slightly when the pieces hit. A pillar of smoke rose from the impact sight.

"So much for him," Bauer said.

The two demolition specialists left their concealment and brought up the atom bomb, a heavy box in a waterproof black outer casing. In shoulder satchels they carried their tools and supplies.

Van Gelder eyed the satellite-equipment bunker. It seemed such a flimsy thing.

"They left the door wide open," he said to Bauer.

"So?"

"I don't think you need to use an atom bomb."

Bauer walked to the bunker, kicked the severed ends of wires and cables out of the way, and swung the armored door closed. He snapped the padlock onto the hasp, and jiggled it pointedly to show the door was locked now. "Satisfied?"

"No, I'm not. If this bunker is hardened at all, it's against conventional bombs. Look at it. We do not need a fission weapon here." Van Gelder was doing his job, to enforce the rules of engagement for using a nuclear weapon near civilians.

"We need to destroy this bunker," Bauer said. "It's a military target. We didn't bring high-explosive charges. My hands are tied."

"But this is just a backup relay site. *Look at it.* They'll have spare links and nodes in other places, and cables underwater, too, for redundancy. Destroying this little bunker will hardly hurt the SOSUS at all!"

"We use the device."

Van Gelder felt his blood pressure rise. There was an uncomfortable silence, punctuated by the rushing of the wind. "Can I speak to you in private?"

Bauer made a face and led Van Gelder to the side.

"Just what do you think you're doing?" Van Gelder said.

"What do you think *you're* doing?"

"Following my orders." Van Gelder held up the thick binder Bauer had made him bring, detailing the ROEs at great length in German. "The rules of engagement aren't satisfied. You can't set off the atom bomb."

"You're so naive, Van Gelder."

"I'm doing what you told me to do. There're a dozen ways a nuclear blast here would break international law. The principle of just cause, proportionality of collateral damage, protection of the environment . . . No such conditions have been met."

"They were never meant to be, you idiot."

29

"THANKS." JEFFREY TOOK a swig from Clayton's canteen, and swished to rid the bitter taste of smoke and cordite. He spat, then took a few good swallows, and handed the canteen back.

Beside him, Clayton looked at his two dead enlisted SEALs and sighed. "Man, it never gets any easier."

"I told you first time we fought together, Shaj. When you're the guy in command, you have to give the orders. Sometimes people get hurt."

"Yeah . . . Right now we got bigger problems."

Jeffrey nodded. He peeked over the wall using Clayton's binoculars. "What the hell are they up to over there?" He passed the binocs to Clayton.

Clayton took another careful look, through the space between the top of the wall and a twisted log the SEALs had placed above the lichen-covered stones. "I dunno, Skipper. That big box is out of sight now. I think they put it on the far side of the outcropping. I can't tell what they're doing in the bunker. I can't see the door from here."

"You think the box is some kind of portable supercomputer?"

Clayton shrugged. "Nothing else makes sense. . . . Do you think it could tell them that *Challenger*'s here, by processing the SOSUS data? Maybe you should clear out, Skipper, now."

Jeffrey shook his head. "If they know what they're doing, they could even track the minisub if it tries to make a move. . . . No, you need every bit of manpower." *And with Wilson and Bell on* Challenger, *I'm hardly irreplaceable as captain.* "My best place to protect the ship is right here."

Jeffrey dearly wished the militia reinforcements would arrive. Any second the enemy might activate their listening post, and any moment after that something might be heard to let them draw a bead on *Challenger.* Jeffrey considered charging the bunker now, with what small force he and Clayton had—but that would be sheer suicide, a useless, hopeless gesture.

THE atom bomb was out of the waterproof cover. Its stainless-steel casing gleamed in the sun. Van Gelder looked at the bomb with revulsion, and looked at himself with calculated disgust.

He was a patsy, and his professional opinion counted for nought. His continued attempts to argue with Commander Bauer fell on deaf ears. Van Gelder was more the fool for not realizing sooner the game that Bauer was playing with him—the same game Jan ter Horst had played. *My captain used me, by sending me on this abominable mission, to implicate me further in the Boer cause.*

Van Gelder knew now he'd been brought just so the Axis could say he was here, simply to pander to world opinion with a bald-faced lie, to claim that the tactical nuclear blast was justified. As Bauer pointed out, the blast itself would remove the evidence either way about military necessity, so let the Allies make what counterclaims they liked. Once the mushroom cloud rose high, the message to neutral nations would be sent, demonstrating Axis power and projecting Axis will.

Plus, as Bauer had just taunted Van Gelder, if this bomb was a war crime, then Van Gelder was an accessory: guilt by association, by being involved. If he were arrested by the Allies he'd be tried and hanged; protestations after the fact would be jeered at by the judges, and sincere denials wouldn't save Van Gelder's neck. Bauer caressed his pistol meaningfully as he said this; he'd made sure that Van Gelder was unarmed. He reminded Van Gelder that cowardice in the face of the enemy—however Bauer chose to interpret cowardice on the spot—was punishable by summary execution. By the hard look in Bauer's eyes, Van Gelder knew that any attempt to interfere, to try to halt the emplacement of the atom bomb, would be sheer suicide, a useless, hopeless gesture.

This is outrageous extortion, and I walked right into the trap. . . . They're forcing me to be one of them, another amoral aggressor. Is this how ter Horst intends to guarantee my lasting loyalty?

Still, it isn't over yet. Morally torn, Van Gelder decided to bide his time. *If I pretend to go along for now, and Bauer lets his guard down . . .*

Bauer's radioman reported the militia reinforcements were getting closer.

"Hurry up," Bauer told his two bomb specialists.

"*Jawohl,*" one of the demolitions men responded. "We're rigging the booby traps and antitampers now."

"This is the tricky part, Commander," the other man said. "If we make one slip it could go off prematurely."

Van Gelder glanced at the bomb, and Bauer gave him a dirty look. "Don't worry, you wouldn't feel anything."

That made Van Gelder very angry. "I suppose you'll tell me a premature blast would still achieve our mission?"

"No, in fact it would not. Timing is very important. *Our* lives count for nothing, but timing is a vital part of the plan."

ILSE heard an eerie, wheezing, moaning sound from downslope, from the rear. The skirling tune sent a chill up her spine. She realized it was bagpipes. The militia platoon from Owenga was moving up in style.

The martial music stirred her blood, as it was meant to, as it had for fighting men and women for centuries. Ilse's fatigue and post-adrenaline drowsiness fell away. She was eager to avenge the SEALs she'd watched be killed as she cowered behind the rock outcropping helpless and unarmed—the rock outcropping now in enemy hands.

She wished the militia would get here already. She needed more loaded magazines for her borrowed M-16. She glanced at the corpse of its previous owner, and promised him she'd use his weapon well.

*   *   *

JEFFREY saw the Owenga platoon's point element approach the SEALs' position carefully through the underbrush and broken terrain. They wore ill-fitting khaki combat fatigues, British Commonwealth style, that looked as if they dated back to World War II. When they got closer he saw their weapons were beat-up FNC assault rifles, an obsolescent British/Belgian design. The FNCs used the same ammo as the M-16: the NATO 5.56mm round. They even took identical magazines.

Quickly the militia platoon and the SEALs linked up. Cursory introductions were made. Constable Henga and Clayton planned their counterattack on the Kampfschwimmer. Henga understood the need to press home the assault with dispatch. Any minute "Serenity's" presence might be betrayed to the Germans, by her own noise signature picked up on the SOSUS.

Jeffrey heard a sudden flurry of firing, far away on the right: at least one AK-47 and several FNCs. The shooting stopped just as abruptly. The platoon's radioman spoke to Henga.

"Our Saracen is almost in position," Henga told Jeffrey and Clayton.

"What was that shooting?" Jeffrey asked.

"A German tried to ambush the armored car."

"What happened?"

"My men captured him, with two antitank weapons he didn't get a chance to use. . . . They say he appears to be senior, probably a chief."

"Good work." Jeffrey was very impressed; he slapped Henga on the back.

"Thank you, Captain." Henga gave a ferocious grin. "The German was overconfident. Some of my men used that against him. They took him by surprise on foot. No friendly casualties, and he's wounded in the leg."

"Terrific."

Henga smiled, proud for himself and his followers. "You don't have to go to Sandhurst, Captain, or West Point, to know you don't send armor into battle without close infantry support."

Speaking of infantry tactics gave Jeffrey a thought. "Constable, can you dismount a machine gun from the Saracen? Use it for suppressing fire against the one the Germans brought? We don't want all our heavy weapons in one basket. They may have more antitank rockets."

Henga gave the order over the radio.

The radioman answered another call. The Waitangi platoon was coming into position, infiltrating the Tuku nature reserve, to catch the Kampfschwimmer from behind.

Soon everything was ready. Clayton and Jeffrey agreed that Henga ought to command the assault. The radioman stayed glued to Henga now. Henga gave orders over the radio, then spoke with his platoon leader.

The Owenga platoon leader issued instructions. Three dozen militia troops crowded against the stone wall. The section sergeants brought their whistles to their lips.

The troops psyched themselves up to go over the top. Jeffrey thought that, for farmers and shepherds and fishermen, they made tough and eager soldiers. These people lived close to and off of their land and the sea, and loved them both. They were fighting to protect their children and their homes. A few of the troops were women, and Jeffrey was jarred to see at least one married couple serving side by side.

A handful would stay by the wall, to hold a baseline the others could re- treat to in an emergency—another standard infantry tactic. Jeffrey ordered Harrison to remain with them. The young man had already done enough.

There was a *boom,* off on the right somewhere. A cannon shell rent the air. The ground shuddered as the shell burst in a heaving cloud of dirt and fumes.

The Saracen's aim was awful—its old gun barrel was really burned out, or the optical sights were badly aligned, or both. The shell hit much closer to the stone wall than the rock outcropping. Jeffrey and the oth- ers were pelted with earth, and shell splinters zinged against their stones and logs.

The way the dust and smoke dispersed showed the wind was getting stronger. It blustered insistently now, gusts screeching through the scat- tered trees and through every crack in the wall. The wind chilled Jeffrey and all those with him, drowning out the bagpipe player.

WHEN Bauer heard the shooting near the Naim River headwaters, and then his radioman couldn't raise the chief, he decided not to take chances. He blew the lock off the bunker door with his pistol. He had his experts disarm the atom bomb and move it inside, for protection from the crossfire that was sure to come very soon. Van Gelder knew it was touch and go whether they'd get the bomb set up again before they were forced to withdraw.

Now was his chance, if he ever had a chance, to stop the Germans before it was too late. He glanced at the ground, but there was nothing nearby he could use as a club. He hefted the thick ROE binder—it was heavy, and the closest thing he had to a weapon. With it, and with the grace of God, he might knock Bauer unconscious, or stun the man. Then if he moved fast enough he could grab Bauer's pistol, and use Bauer as a hostage or a shield, to make the enlisted Kampfschwimmer back off.

Every nearby member of Bauer's commando platoon turned toward Van Gelder as one. Their eyes bored through his soul. They gripped their rifles tighter, and put their index fingers through the trigger guards. Muzzles inched in his direction. Bauer didn't even bother looking at Van Gelder.

Van Gelder realized how transparent his scheming had been, and how hopeless was any idea of stopping this nuclear blast. He sighed from deep in his chest. Even treason as an escape was out of his reach. The enlisted Kampfschwimmer relaxed and went about their business, improving their defenses or emplacing the bomb—but several kept watching Van Gelder, and made sure he knew it.

Things might be out of his hands, but Van Gelder still had to make an inner personal moral choice. He did: he devoutly hoped the locals overran the Kampfschwimmer before the bomb was armed, and killed every one of the Germans. If Van Gelder himself died too, at least he'd meet his maker with his conscience clear. Near him the hard wind moaned around the satellite dish and the bunker. Its tortured cry reflected his dark mood.

The islanders' armored car opened fire. The shot was wildly off in range and direction. Bauer ordered two of his men to crawl forward with antitank launchers. His machine gunner finished building a shelter of stones atop the rock outcropping, for an excellent all-around field of fire.

Privately Van Gelder despaired.

*   *   *

JEFFREY heard the heavy machine gun taken from the armored car, now dug in among some bushes, suddenly begin to fire at its German counterpart from long range. The Kampfschwimmer with his light machine gun atop the rock outcropping was forced to answer back. Thus one German threat was kept fully occupied. Both weapons belched hot flame, threw solid streams of high-powered slugs, and spat out empty shell casings. They made a chattering racket as they dueled.

The platoon from Waitangi held their position to the Germans' rear. The next thing Jeffrey heard was them opening up with steady FNC fire, trying to pin down the rest of the Kampfschwimmer. The Saracen advanced, and fired its gun from closer in. This time the cannon round hit much nearer to the rock outcropping.

Henga set his jaw and nodded, and his sergeants blew their whistles up and down the line. SEALs and Owenga militia, and Jeffrey and Ilse, vaulted over the wall at a run. Some advanced upslope while others squeezed off covering rounds. Jeffrey flopped to the ground and aimed and fired his M-16. All around him friendly assault rifles crackled. He lunged to his feet and darted and zigzagged ahead. The others ran forward, or crouched and fired. Then they'd trade roles, crouching to fire or running instead. They were closing the distance to the Germans steadily this way, and taking scant incoming fire, but they had most of a thousand yards to cover, the length of ten football fields.

The Saracen fired another round. Jeffrey couldn't tell its effect. He was too busy reading the ground, using low spots and draws and boulders for cover. The wind sang in his ears, competing with the ceaseless reports of rifles and machine guns near and far. He tried to be as careful as he could, but it just wasn't in Jeffrey's nature to let those around him take all the risks.

There was a loud bang to Jeffrey's front, and he saw a flaming ball tear along, not at him but toward the Saracen. The way it would drift and then correct, Jeffrey knew it was a wire-guided antitank rocket. The Saracen was caught in the open. Jeffrey watched the crew bail out through the hatches just in time.

The rocket hit. In a flash its shaped-charge warhead burned right through the armored car's thin steel. Shell-propellant loads inside caught fire at once; flames shot from every orifice. There was a huge internal explosion as high-explosive warheads cooked off. The Saracen's turret blew into the sky, rolling end over end and trailing smoke. It thudded to the ground, upside down, a useless wreck.

"*Come on!*" Henga shouted to rally his troops. The heavy machine gun and light machine gun continued to argue vehemently. The supporting fire from the direction of Tuku poured in from the other side—flat trajectories beating the soil, at an angle not endangering Henga's line of advance but forcing the sniper and the rest of the Germans to keep their heads well down.

Jeffrey fired off three quick bursts on full auto, then lurched to his feet and pressed forward. As he ran he reloaded. He was painfully breathless, and sweating in spite of the chill. The bayonet fixed to his rifle reflected the sun. Soon the fighting would be hand to hand.

Van Gelder squeezed flat in a low spot as bullets poured in from three sides. The enemy heavy machine gun chewed away at the top of the outcropping. The steady stream of big incoming rounds made sharp rock chips spew everywhere. The German machine gunner screamed and his gun stopped firing, and Van Gelder saw his blood drip down.

Bauer's bomb specialists crawled out of the bunker in the outcropping. "Commander, we're done."

"Put up the sign, and give me the vial."

Van Gelder watched as one man fastened a preprinted poster to the inside of the bunker door. He left the door propped open. Bauer took the vial and placed it primly on the ground near the door.

In the shade, the vial glowed an eerie green. Van Gelder read the sign, in big block letters in English.

He was speechless with impotent rage. Bauer had lied to him *again,* by a factor of more than a hundred.

"It's a done deal!" Bauer shouted. "Nothing can stop it now."

"You—"

"*Watch out!*" a Kampfschwimmer yelled.

Van Gelder stood there, transfixed. A handful of enemy troops had crept very close, and now they aimed at Van Gelder like a firing squad. One of them looked too familiar.

Van Gelder stared. The woman stared back, then shouted something; she hesitated a moment too long. Bauer knocked Van Gelder to the ground, saving his life. Bullets snapped and whizzed and ricocheted, close by and right overhead.

"That's, that's . . ." Van Gelder stammered.

"What?"

"It's Ilse Reebeck."

Bauer didn't listen. "Save your nonsense for later." Bauer turned to his surviving men. They'd been falling back under pressure, tightening their perimeter, purely on the defensive now. *"Withdraw,"* Bauer ordered. He took Van Gelder by the arm and urged him away. Van Gelder glanced back, and saw troops from Waitangi joining the pursuit.

Van Gelder followed Bauer through the drainage ravine in utter resignation, retreating back the way they'd come, fleeing the scene of unspeakable Axis hypocrisy.

But Ilse Reebeck is here. She's alive. . . . How did she get here?

THE Kampfschwimmer retreated just as Henga's troops overran their positions around the rock outcropping. The Germans were falling back the only way they could, toward the naked cliffs and the sea. Most of Henga's force pursued them, angry and yet jubilant that they'd won. Clayton, his SEALs, and Ilse joined the chase. A few of the islanders held back, to treat their wounded and count their fatalities. The slope up to the rock outcropping held scattered injured, with medics in charge, plus several corpses joined by comrades in arms and their grieving relatives and friends.

Jeffrey held back too, glad to be alive. He approached the bunker carefully, his rifle aimed to his front. The only Germans he saw were clearly dead, and the bunker door stood open. The remnants of the SEAL tents and the hulk of the Land Rover smoldered; the ground was cratered by Saracen hits. The dead SEAL's burnt skeleton lay scattered, groups of bones still held together by remnants of sinew like tar.

Jeffrey noticed that dry grass by the Saracen turret was burning fiercely now; the brush fire was fanned by the wind, quickly spreading eastward, away from the battle zone but toward the main road and Owenga. There was another fire in the distance, where the spotter plane had gone down.

Montgomery came back. Silently, he began to gather the dead enlisted SEAL's remains. He used an entrenching tool with soil to stop the smoldering, then piled the bones on a poncho he lay on the ground. Montgomery looked very sad.

Ilse ran up to Jeffrey. She was panting, and had to lean forward with hands on her knees to catch her breath. "I . . . I saw . . ." She gagged at the stench of the place.

Jeffrey felt too grim to hear or care. *We didn't win this battle. We lost a larger one.* He was reading the sign taped to the door. He looked at the foreign object in the bunker, so out of place and threatening, obscene. A big timer in its side was counting down the seconds one by one.

"THE rest of them got away," Ilse said. "They rappelled using ropes down the cliff face." She paused and took deep breaths. "Right into the water wearing Draegers."

"Draegers? That doesn't make sense."

"Jeffrey, I—I saw . . . Gunther Van Gelder was with them."

"Who?" Jeffrey said distractedly.

"Jan's first officer. I know him, and he knows me. He saw me too."

"From *Voortrekker? Here?*" Jeffrey seemed shocked.

Ilse nodded, still panting.

Jeffrey grabbed her arms roughly. "Did you kill him?"

"He got away."

"That means *Voortrekker's* close, *really* close. . . . If this Van Gelder knows you're alive, they'll make the connection. They'll know *Challenger's* here."

"I—I know." Then Ilse read the sign. She gasped. It said the silvery casing held a tritium-boosted fission device with a yield of sixty kilotons. It said the weapon had foolproof antitamper traps, and shouldn't be touched. According to the timer, the weapon would go off several hours from now, at dusk.

Sixty kilotons was five times as strong as the bomb that wiped Hiroshima off the map. The whole of Chatham Island would be destroyed, turned into a charred and blasted radioactive wasteland.

"Do you think they're serious?"

A little vial sat on a fancy display bracket, like what someone would use on a shelf of cherished household knickknacks. Affixed to the bracket was a label: EXAMINE ME PLEASE.

Jeffrey picked up the vial. "Some kind of tritium compound, like they use to make luminous night sights . . . It looks real enough to me. I think this sample's meant to say they're *very* serious."

30

On Chatham Island

ILSE BOUNCED UNCOMFORTABLY as she rode with the SEALs in the back of a rickety farm truck. This was the best that Constable Henga could manage right after the battle, since the island's transport assets were rather limited. The truck kept backfiring, and the engine knocked, as the driver pressed forward as fast as he could—forty miles an hour, not nearly quickly enough. Never in her life had Ilse felt such need for speed. Lieutenant Clayton, an expert in disarming unexploded nuclear ordnance, said that even if he could get all his tools he shouldn't touch the bomb. The risk of setting it off by mistake while trying to defuse it was too great—the Germans used fiendishly clever antitamper booby-traps. If he tried to rig a shaped charge, to wreck the bomb's implosion lenses to make it fizzle, shock sensors would send the firing signal at the speed of light.

Ilse grimaced when the truck's transmission protested as the driver shifted gears to go uphill. The wind gusted so powerfully it caught the truck from the side and made the whole vehicle rock. The Tuku-Waitangi Road followed the towering headlands north along the west side of the island. On Ilse's left a strong surf pounded the base of the cliffs. The incoming waves were already visibly larger than when she and Jeffrey looked out to sea before the Kampfschwimmer attack. A massive tropical storm was hammering New Zealand and advancing relentlessly on Chatham Island from the west.

Jeffrey had taken a different route, rushing back to Owenga for the minisub to *Challenger*. His orders to Ilse and Clayton were very direct: Get to Waitangi immediately. Establish communications with Commander in Chief, U.S. Pacific Fleet, at the four-star admiral's Pearl Harbor base. Keep the Chatham Island civilians calm, and organize an evacuation before the bomb could blow. Jeffrey decided the SEALs should help, both with logistics and psychologically, their presence a reassuring sign that the islanders weren't abandoned. Jeffrey told Ilse her steady demeanor under stress was needed too: the lives of a thousand innocents were about to be torn to shreds. Ilse could smooth through countless family minicrises that might leave big, strong, scary U.S. Navy SEALs at a loss.

The driver reached the peak of the upgrade. The truck lurched as its transmission crunched and screeched. They started to go downhill, moving faster.

Ilse's mind raced on, sifting the facts, as she tried to grapple with the team's appointed tasks. She had never felt more grim. The entire population needed to be moved somehow to safety. The nearest usable land, the only dry land of consequence for many thousands of miles, was New Zealand itself.

New Zealand had major airports, with very large planes. But the Chatham Island airstrip was so short, any airliner that tried to land would simply run out of runway and hit the lagoon. The airstrip could take small propeller planes, of which New Zealand had a good number. But the winds of almost hurricane force would destroy such aircraft with ease, probably on their takeoff rolls, no matter how brave and skilled their pilots.

Constable Henga, sitting next to Ilse and talking constantly on his radio, ruled out escape by sea. As Ilse knew too well, the island's fishing boats could not survive the powerful winds and crashing swells that would batter them on the high seas in the hours to come. New Zealand had frigates patrolling the ANZA Gap, but even at flank speed the closest wouldn't reach the island soon enough—it was already after noon, and the bomb would go off at sunset. Relief ships from New Zealand couldn't possibly cover the distance in time. The handful of neutral merchant vessels in range, contacted and told of the problem, instead of helping turned to flee the impending fallout cloud.

On *Voortrekker*'s minisub

Images of bullets piercing bodies plagued Van Gelder's mind. His arms and legs and back were sore from running and climbing, from rappelling down a cliff face into the water, and from swimming into the minisub wearing Draeger gear. Even after he had toweled off and changed clothes, his hair was damp and his skin itched from dried sea salt.

He sat wearily in the mini's passenger compartment; he could tell from the way the little vessel handled that it was being driven at flank speed. He was surrounded by Kampfschwimmer all extremely pleased with themselves despite their losses on the island. They spoke to each other nonstop in low voices, reliving highlights of the action, enjoying a postcombat high.

Van Gelder coughed. His tongue and throat still tasted of burning rubber and flesh, and his mouth was coated with acrid dust.

"Try this," Commander Bauer said. He held out a thermos bottle.

"What is it?"

"Just what you need, my friend." Bauer drank, then smacked his lips with obvious relish and proffered the thermos again.

Van Gelder took a taste. He thought drinking right from the bottle was crude, but everyone else was doing it. The thermos held hot coffee strongly laced with schnapps. It cleared his throat quite nicely and went smoothly into his gut. He let the heat of the coffee, and the different heat of the alcohol, spread to his limbs. It reduced his fatigue and made him feel a little better.

Bauer made eye contact. "You did a good job back there."

Van Gelder glowered at him.

Bauer shrugged. "I couldn't tell you *everything* in advance, for security. Your reactions on the spot were perfectly normal."

Van Gelder just nodded, indifferent, feeling utterly defeated.

"Don't be so down on yourself. You think any of us enjoy endangering women and children? War is a brutal business. We're soldiers, so we fight."

Van Gelder stared into space.

Bauer touched his shoulder. "You've never been in a land battle before, have you?"

Van Gelder had to clear his throat. "No."

"It's different than you're used to, with all your fancy gadgets in the control room, isn't it?"

"Yes."

"You see whom you fight with, close up. You watch friends and enemies die. It *should* disturb a man of good character. . . . But afterward, the feelings of comradeship and achievement make us glow inside better than schnapps. Even our grief for the fallen is sweet as well as bitter, for they have done their duty and gone to a warrior's Valhalla."

"You left a man behind alive."

"My chief. Taken prisoner, yes. It couldn't be helped. He's a decent man. Don't worry, he won't talk."

Van Gelder knew that tears were coming. He held his head in his hands. To think of what he'd helped to do, and how he'd failed to stop it, and now the utter outrageousness of everything Bauer was saying . . .

Still Bauer tried to comfort him good-naturedly. The German knelt in the aisle and reached and held Van Gelder in his arms. "This sort of emotional crash is not uncommon. Each of us has been through it at one time or another, in our own personal way." Bauer asked his men for confirmation. Van Gelder heard them agree.

Bauer gently pulled Van Gelder's hands from his face. "I anticipated your stubbornness about the rules of engagement all along. It's the reason you were sent, remember. Now the Berlin-Boer Axis can move forward with Truth on our side. Come, let us spend a moment in worship together."

Bauer led his men, as in hushed tones they began to hum an old Germanic battle hymn.

It was the last thing Van Gelder needed.

They sent me just so they could say a special ROE man was there. They involved me in a major war crime, not really to justify the crime, but to give the outward appearance of justification. By implicating me they also made me a captive tool for further Axis exploitation . . . and they'll name me as a scapegoat to the Allies if we ever all get caught.

Bauer convinced Van Gelder to take another drink from the thermos. Van Gelder swallowed, then wiped his face. In the control compartment, the pilot altered course. The force of the turn showed Van Gelder they still hurried home to *Voortrekker* at top speed.

"I mean what I said," Bauer told him. "That you did a good job, for a beginner. If you hadn't shown some moral qualms, I wouldn't trust you now. But you're no beginner anymore. We want to make you feel one of us, an honorary Kampfschwimmer."

Each of Bauer's men shook Van Gelder's hand, and one of them tousled his hair. The enlisted Kampfschwimmer all sat down again.

"You and I need a good working relationship," Bauer murmured privately in Van Gelder's ear—insistently, almost threateningly. "Who knows when we might have more such keen adventures?"

Van Gelder said nothing.

"Besides," Bauer added in a normal voice, "as his number one you bring important news ter Horst will welcome, *Challenger*'s proximity, to stir your captain's battle lust."

On *Challenger*'s minisub

Jeffrey stood uncomfortably, squeezed in behind Harrison as the younger man piloted the minisub. The enlisted SEAL had the copilot's seat. The air in the control compartment was ripe, with Jeffrey and Harrison stinking of burnt cordite and stale sweat.

The mini came through the underwater safe corridor, past the small minefield protecting Owenga.

"Pilot," Jeffrey ordered, "ahead flank." They were still too far away to call *Challenger* using the mini's covert acoustic link.

Harrison acknowledged and worked his throttle. The battery-powered mini picked up speed—to all of sixteen knots.

Jeffrey was really annoyed with himself. He'd misread the entire situation during a seesaw firefight with Kampfschwimmer. Now, he was stuck in a race against *Voortrekker*'s minisub, somewhere out there in the depths. The enemy had a head start, and the German mini was faster, and the first to reach their mother ship could influence the outcome of the war.

"Copilot, show me a chart of this broad area."

The copilot worked his keyboard. A digital map popped on a screen. Jeffrey studied the bottom terrain with a seasoned, professional eye. He assembled what few facts he knew.

The whole Chatham Rise—a ridge of shallow water stretching west from Chatham Island all the way to the New Zealand coast—was heavily mined against enemy subs.

The Australian diesels, and *Challenger,* were arrayed in a line on the opposite side of the island, stretching more than a hundred miles to the east.

Mentally, Jeffrey drew a straight line on the chart: along the minefield on the Chatham Rise, through Chatham Island itself, and east through the positions of Commodore Wilson's battle group. *Voortrekker* had to be south of that line.

South of Chatham Rise was the Bounty Trough, shaped like a giant amphitheater in the sea floor, facing east, in water ten thousand feet deep.

South of the farthest, eastern flank of Wilson's battle group was a lengthy range of sea mounts, marching toward Antarctica. The sea mounts jutted from an abyssal plain that went down well past fifteen thousand feet.

Given the maximum cruising range of a German minisub, *Voortrekker* had to be somewhere between the grandstand of the Bounty Trough and the near side of the sea mounts.

To himself, as he began to plan the hunt and the combat, Jeffrey shook his head. There was an immense arena to cover, and the tactical uncertainties were huge.

31

Ninety minutes later, on *Challenger*

JEFFREY LEFT THE minisub nestled in *Challenger*'s in-hull hangar space. He climbed down the docking trunk and came out in *Challenger* proper, near the enlisted mess. Commodore Wilson stood there waiting for him.

Wilson looked stern and intense. "So *Voortrekker* beat the SOSUS, and they're somewhere right in the neighborhood, and their combat swimmers left a big bomb."

Jeffrey nodded. *That sure sums it up.*

"Your head's bleeding," Wilson said.

Jeffrey touched his forehead near the hairline. His fingers came away with blood. A nasty gash he'd received in the battle with the Kampf-schwimmer had opened up as he used the ladder down the docking trunk. The gauze he'd changed in the mini had soaked through again and was dripping. He dabbed at it with his handkerchief.

Wilson turned and started briskly for the control room. Jeffrey ordered Harrison to go lie down for some rest, then rushed to catch up with the commodore.

"How did you know, sir? And how did you know to come get us?" To

Jeffrey's pleasant surprise, *Challenger* had left her hiding place and rendezvoused with the mini much nearer the island than Jeffrey expected—right after that, *Challenger* turned back east and sped up to her top quiet speed, twenty-six knots.

"I'd ordered one of the *Collins* boats to keep trailing its floating wire antenna. Lieutenant Clayton reached Pearl Harbor like you told him, then the *Collins* heard from CINCPACFLT." By radio. "The *Collins* relayed on to me by covert acoustics."

CINCPACFLT was the acronym for Commander in Chief, Pacific Fleet, the operational boss of Pacific Ocean naval forces—in conversation pronounced "Sink Pack Fleet."

Jeffrey and Wilson took narrow, winding corridors, and went up steep ladders. They passed damage-control parties mustered at key points in the ship; some men wore fire-fighting gear. The men, including the newest guys, seemed confident and chipper and prepared. One senior chief, always irrepressible and outspoken, said they looked forward to the rematch with *Challenger*'s pesky foe. Jeffrey was proud of them all.

Jeffrey and Wilson reached the control room. Jeffrey felt good to be back. Now that he was on *Challenger,* he at least could *do* something. He tried not to think about Ilse and the SEALs, left stranded on the island because of military necessity—such were the burdens of command.

Lieutenant Commander Bell, Jeffrey's trusty executive officer, had the conn. COB and David Meltzer manned the ship-control station. Kathy Milgrom led the sonar chief and his men. As usual Jeffrey thought Kathy looked owlish, but she was alert and sharp—he reminded himself that owls were birds of prey who hunted by night. Lieutenant Sessions stood at the digital-navigation table with his own department's chief and their enlisted techs. Sessions was calm and earnest, as always. Jeffrey exchanged quick greetings with the crew.

"You're bleeding," Bell said as he shook Jeffrey's hand. Bell told the messenger to summon the medical corpsman. Bell was mentally charged up from taking command of the ship in such a crisis, if only till Jeffrey was back. Bell crackled with vital energy that was infectious—his whole head almost seemed to glow. Jeffrey drew comfort from Bell's steady presence at his side, and couldn't help smiling.

Smiling made Jeffrey's face hurt. The old wound in his left thigh ached and throbbed; it usually did when he was tired and under pressure.

"I need a shower and a change of clothes," Jeffrey said to the control room at large, apologetically. He knew he smelled awful, and must look frightful too. Everyone around him was so neat and clean.

"Later," Wilson said. "CINCPACFLT wants us immediately, live on voice."

"The seas are too rough, Commodore. We can't transmit like this on our two-way floating wire."

"Use your satellite dish."

"We'd need to come to periscope depth. An Axis spy bird might notice. With an enemy sub so near . . ."

"We don't have a choice. If we're lucky, *Voortrekker*'s so deep she's out of touch anyway."

To himself, Jeffrey shrugged. This was taking a serious risk. *It's up to Wilson and CINCPACFLT—a four-star admiral—not me.*

Jeffrey told Bell to bring the ship to periscope depth. Bell relayed orders to Meltzer and COB. The deck nosed up, and *Challenger* slowed. Jeffrey could sense the tension around him increase by the minute: the ship was exposing herself, surrendering stealth to achieve two-way communications connectivity.

Jeffrey felt and saw blood drip from his head to the front of his shirt. *Head wounds always bleed a lot, but I can feel my blood pressure rising a point as* Challenger *rises each foot.* Bell gave Jeffrey a doubtful look, concerned both for his captain and for the safety of their mission and the ship. The control-room crew shifted nervously in their seats and studied their glowing screens, apprehensively searching for threats.

Jeffrey began getting lightheaded, and sat down at the command console. The corpsman arrived with a medical kit.

"That needs stitches, sir."

"Do it, here."

"What was it, sir? Shrapnel cut? Rock fragment?"

"I can't remember."

The corpsman gave Jeffrey a local painkiller shot in his scalp, then an antibiotic in his arm, and opened a suture pack. He cleaned the wound and put in three stitches. Even though the skin grew numb, Jeffrey could feel it being tugged; it unnerved him to hear the sounds the needle and thread made as they pierced his scalp and then were pulled through.

As the ship reached periscope depth, she began to roll because of the strong seas topside. The corpsman hurried to tie off the final suture. It hurt despite the painkiller when another steep roll hit—the corpsman went one way and Jeffrey the other as they braced themselves.

At last the corpsman was done. Jeffrey thanked him and he left. At battle stations the corpsman's place was below, in his cubicle near the wardroom. The wardroom table would double as his operating theater if need be.

Jeffrey and Wilson put on headsets so they could conference-call with Pearl Harbor; Bell helped Jeffrey so he wouldn't hit his newly sewn-up cut. Jeffrey asked the messenger to bring him a mug of hot coffee with plenty of sugar. Jeffrey drank it down.

When the communications mast was raised at periscope depth, the radio room established contact with Pearl Harbor. Reception was scratchy, and came and went, because the antenna kept getting dunked.

CINCPACFLT personally came on the line. Jeffrey instinctively sat up straight. He was talking to one of the navy's most senior officers.

A half hour later, on Chatham Island

Ilse stepped out of the modest building that housed Waitangi's town hall. She needed a break from the tension and frenzy in Constable Henga's command post. She was losing her voice from endless talking and shouting. It seemed like she'd spent hours on the phone nonstop, helping call islanders and also answering questions in person, making sure everyone knew what to do. The hardest part was keeping up the front, to make it sound like the evacuation plan had a purpose.

For a respite Ilse looked out to sea, to the west. Waitangi Bay sparkled at her mockingly in the golden midafternoon sun. The bay was tossed by chop and whitecaps. The growing wind had backed, from out of the southwest now, and Point Weeding sheltered the bay from the worst of the surf. But out beyond Waitangi Bay were the waters of the much larger Petra Bay, which filled the whole left side of the island's I-shaped coastline. The waves in Petra Bay were very large. Ilse knew big sea swells were always the product of a distant major weather system, and in this case the source was the tropical storm now blasting New Zealand.

Repeated calls to mainland authorities, eight hundred kilometers away, only confirmed what Henga and Ilse and Clayton already knew. Those planes large enough to possibly fly in the storm had no way to land on the island—and even if by some miracle they could, the runway was much too short for them to ever take off again. Helicopters couldn't take off at all, as major cities like Wellington and Christchurch were pummeled by blinding rain and winds of sixty knots. They'd tried, but when the third helicopter in a row crashed and exploded, overburdened with barely enough fuel for the long round trip, the government called off further efforts. Ilse knew good men and women had been killed in the attempt.

Ilse turned in the other direction. Her heart sank as once more she saw conditions on the only road leading north toward the airstrip, an airstrip that had no planes. The narrow road was jammed by the occupants of the whole southern half of the island, and the sights and sounds of their useless exodus were heartrending. Rattletrap cars and trucks carried entire families and all the possessions they could move on such short notice. Axles squeaked as draft horses pulled overloaded farm carts, piled high with trunks and bursting suitcases and heirloom furniture, with their owners often on foot. Dogs of every size and breed barked, and a few had broken loose and were chased by their owners. Other people rode horses, and the horses sensed the human panic. They whinnied, and sometimes reared, and threatened to throw their riders to the ground.

The youngest children seemed more bewildered than scared, though many infants—like the horses—felt the panic and cried. Older children's reactions varied from fear to shock to resolve to traumatic denial. Their parents were often in no better shape. Ilse thought the scene could have come from any one of the major wars or disasters of the past century. These people were refugees. The problem was this time the refugees had nowhere to go.

Ilse looked southeast. Above the land in the distance hung a cloud of dense black smoke. The wildfires, started by the battle with the Kampfschwimmer, were spreading farther and farther. Owenga was in danger of being cut off.

Ilse looked due south. Somewhere there, on the higher ground, sat the infernal device left by the Axis.

Ilse was almost overwhelmed by everything. She went back inside.

Constable Henga corralled her at once. He looked harried and weary.

"The phone lines to Owenga just went out. The last I heard the road's been cut, by the fire and smoke and maddened sheep. We're taking people off by fishing boat instead, and bringing them through the lagoon on the downwind side of the island. The airstrip's on a spit of land. The boats can drop them there."

"Still no news of an airlift?" Ilse asked.

"No. Nothing's changed."

"What do you want me to do?"

"Get to the airstrip, and try to help keep people calm."

"But what's the point?" she said. "You heard Lieutenant Clayton. He doesn't even know if that timer readout on the bomb is telling the truth. It could go off any minute."

"For God's sake, don't tell anyone that!"

"How am I supposed to get to the airport? You saw the road."

"Can you ride?"

"Yes."

"Cross country?"

"Yes."

"Take one of the horses tied up in back. Just stay parallel to the road, then turn right at the fork by the lake. The middle of the island's so narrow it's impossible to get lost."

"Is there anything else I should do?"

"No. Just get up there. Try to prevent mass hysteria."

"How am I supposed to do that?"

"Ilse, look. We're all in this together. If everyone has to die, let them die with hope. Tell them to sing, to pray, anything. Tell them help will get here somehow."

Ilse went outside. An angry crowd had gathered, but people had their backs to town hall.

Ilse realized what was going on. *"Constable!"*

Henga came outside.

A mob was manhandling the captured Kampfschwimmer chief. Chief Montgomery was trying to restore order, but people in the mob were armed.

"Stop that at once!" Henga shouted. He fired three shots from his pistol into the air.

"It's *his* fault," people yelled. "He killed our friends. If we have to die, he goes first!"

"This lawlessness won't help anything," Henga shouted back.

But Ilse could read the mood of the crowd. Their rage was far beyond arguing.

The German's leg was bandaged where he'd been hit in the battle. Local men held him upright while others tied his hands behind his back. Others held Montgomery at bay, at gunpoint.

Someone threw a rope around a telephone pole. The mob pressed closer to watch. Ilse's heart pounded. She knew she should do something.

"Stop it," she yelled. "He's a prisoner of war! You can't do this!"

"He's a war criminal! We have witnesses!"

"No. This isn't right. Don't do it."

"Shut up, you. You aren't one of us. You brought this trouble when *you* came."

Someone tied a noose. They draped it around the German's neck and drew it snug.

Ilse wanted to look away, but an animal part of her felt the way the islanders did. Her life was as forfeit as theirs. Revenge was the only thing left.

Men grabbed the free end of the rope and pulled.

The German was yanked off his feet. He rose into the air. He kicked and struggled as his eyes bulged. The mob pressed even closer, standing underneath and all around to see. Ilse moved closer too.

The German's face turned purple and began to swell. His tongue popped out of his mouth and turned black. He still kicked wildly. He began to sway and twist back and forth in the wind. His hands fought desperately against the ropes that bound them. The noose bit even tighter, completely crushing his windpipe, pinching shut the veins in his neck like a tourniquet.

His brain screamed for more oxygen. His heart used its last reserves of power to try to comply, and pushed more blood up through his arteries. The German's face became a balloon, a dark purple balloon, streaked with patterns of ruptured blood vessels like tangled vines.

It seemed to go on forever. Ilse saw his clothing bulge with a giant reflexive erection. She couldn't stand it, and ran to the back of the town hall.

She chose a horse that looked relatively young and fit. It was a light gray mare, already saddled. Ilse mounted and rode from Waitangi. When she glanced back, the Kampfschwimmer dangled lifeless from the telephone pole. The lynch mob broke up and joined the procession north to the airstrip.

ILSE rode her horse up the narrow neck of Chatham Island at a fast canter. On her right were pristine sand dunes and beaches that led to the huge tidal lagoon. She saw a fishing boat chugging north there, its deck a microcosm of the scene of refugees and belongings along the road; another fishing boat, empty now, was heading back south for Owenga. On her left the surf crashed hard against the base of the bluffs, in the most open part of big Petra Bay. Mist sprayed skyward through blowholes, where the ageless seas had eroded channels through the cliffs. Ilse skirted peat bogs on low ground. Everywhere birds hopped or perched or swam or flew, well adapted to the trade winds that never ceased. Flowers and trees and bushes and vines overflowed the nature reserves she passed.

Chatham Island had such a multitude of beautiful pocket ecosystems, and soon they would all be destroyed.

Ilse pressed her horse onward, opening gates when she met fences too high to safely jump, and finally crossed the road through a gaggle of creeping autos. She paused to let her horse rest and drink from a stream.

She reached the airport. It looked like the world's most insane yard sale—crowds of people and jumbles of merchandise everywhere. Here, though, the people looked distraught and terrified.

Ilse saw why Henga had sent her. The handful of town council members and clergy were swamped by an ocean of distressed humanity. No one was really in charge. Islanders crowded willy-nilly into the few buildings by the airstrip, to get out of the wind. The others milled about aimlessly, or sat in isolation in their cars, or squatted abjectly on the ground. There were no arrangements for public sanitation. Stragglers continued to pour in from north and south. More boats arrived, with the handful of families from the other inhabited island in the Chatham group, Pitt Island. A few citizens with some presence of mind were making sure the others left the runway clear. People kept scanning the sky. Ilse knew there was really no point.

She did not feel like singing or praying—some of the islanders had already thought to do that anyway. She started back down the road to Waitangi.

Near the fork by the lake, she noticed a big cloud of dust approaching from the south. She urged her horse to go faster, to investigate. Then she reined up short. She heard a strange noise, like thundering and bleating. She saw them: tens of thousands of sheep, stampeding north to escape the wildfires raging out of control.

The old farm truck she'd ridden in before, its transmission failing now, was keeping barely ahead of the sheep. It stopped near her for a moment. Henga and Clayton and Montgomery rode in the cab. In the back were several body bags, the losses from the firefight, including Clayton's three enlisted men.

"Get back," Clayton told her. "You'll be trampled."

Montgomery fired several rifle shots at the sheep. He felled a few, but the others kept coming relentlessly. Ilse saw some sheep were partly burned, wild with pain, or bled where they'd crashed through fence railings or been torn by leaping barbed-wire enclosures.

"We have to divert them from the airport!" Henga said.

"*How?*" Ilse said. Once sheep and people met there would be many deaths.

"A barricade of cars!" Henga shouted. "Across the road by the fork! We'll divert them right up the island! Come on!"

The truck took off again. Ilse spurred her mount to a full gallop, dangerous for a casual rider and a partly trained horse. But time was now of the essence.

They reached the tail end of the refugee convoy, halted in a tangle of gridlock. The islanders, many of them sheep herders, understood the problem at once. They started their cars and trucks and rearranged them in a line, straddling the road and stretching well into the sands on either side. The front edge of the sheep stampede was getting closer. The ground actually shook. There were almost a quarter-million sheep on the island, and half of them were bearing down on the barricade.

The stampede reached the barricade. The air was thick with dust, and with the profoundly disturbing wailing of some hundred thousand crazed sheep. They began to press against each other and batter against the vehicles. They churned everywhere, and some sheep were trampled and crushed. The vehicles rocked and began to be shoved aside. Ilse's horse reared and she almost fell off; she tried to talk to it soothingly.

"Set them on fire!" Henga shouted.

"The sheep?" Ilse yelled.

"The cars. Quickly!"

Islanders wanted to save their things from the cars, but Henga said it was too late for that. He and Clayton and Montgomery went to work on the cars with their weapons. Everyone fled on foot, toward the airstrip. The line of cars burned fiercely as gas tanks exploded one by one. A wall of flame blocked the road; the sheep stampede was turned away. Choking smoke began to drift in the direction of the airstrip. Ilse turned her horse and started back that way.

When she got there the smoke kept up with her, and billowing sooty puffs sometimes blotted the clear blue sky. It added a surreal note to the situation at the airstrip, which resembled now a giant displaced-persons camp. As Ilse passed clumps of civilians, and even above the aromas of her horse, she smelled the islanders' fear—a sharply unpleasant, pungent, sour body odor. Many islanders were crying at the loss of their herds. The stampede of their beloved creatures, their livelihood of breeding stock and wool and mutton for export, brought home the ultimate scale of the disaster.

Then Ilse heard another strange noise. It came from the northeast. She turned to look.

She saw two black dots low above the water, and thought they were seabirds. Then she saw several more, much higher. The sun glinted off metal or cockpit glass.

Aircraft.

But there's no airbase in that direction for seven thousand miles.

The two dots resolved themselves into a pair of Harrier jump jets. The other aircraft lost altitude, and made a fly-by of the island in plain view of the crowd. One of them had a big propeller on each wing and a saucer over the fuselage; the others had a jet engine under each wing, plus two air-dropped torpedoes. Ilse knew the saucer held a special radar, for surveillance and air-traffic control. The others looked like S-3B Vikings, long-endurance antisubmarine patrol planes. Ilse and the islanders could read the markings on their sides. Big black letters said NAVY. They climbed again, and the Vikings proceeded east.

The two Harrier jump jets approached the airstrip, slowed, and hovered briefly. With a deafening whine they settled down in a cloud of flying dirt and smelly jet exhaust. On their sides were the letters USMC. United States Marine Corps.

Ilse knew they had to have come from a carrier, a big American aircraft carrier. It would have helicopters too, lots of them. The islanders weren't alone.

32

On *Challenger*

BELL STILL HAD the conn, and Jeffrey and Wilson studied a large-scale navigation plot. *Challenger* continued east, four thousand feet down, in the sweet spot of the deep sound channel. The ship was trailing a sonar-towed array, for the best possible detection of enemy subs. Everyone in the control room was at a very high state of alert. Jeffrey could see it in his people's necks and shoulders, and in their eyes and the set of their jaws. He needed them on their toes, but too much tension would drain them too quickly. He reminded his crew they could be at battle stations for many hours. "Keep on the ball, folks, but don't gives yourselves an ulcer or a migraine." Jeffrey watched some of the crewmen try to loosen up a little. They resumed their silent vigils at their stations.

"Overflights," Kathy Milgrom reported. "They sound like S-3B Vikings, Captain. . . . They're turning back west."

"Very well, Sonar," Jeffrey said. He knew from the conversation with the admiral at Pearl Harbor that the Vikings came from the USS *John C. Stennis*. The *Stennis* was one of the U.S. Navy's newest nuclear-powered supercarriers. She'd been rushed out of the naval base at San Diego days ago, because of *Voortrekker*'s approach, to help guard another portion of the Australia–New Zealand–Antarctic Gap. When word reached Pearl Harbor of the bomb on Chatham Island, the *Stennis* was ordered to make flank speed, and charge ahead of her slower, conventionally powered escorts, to try to organize an airlift. Soon, Jeffrey knew, she would even outdistance the nuclear subs that always scouted ahead of the rest of the carrier group, because the *Stennis* was many knots faster than those subs, faster than anything but the *Seawolf* class and *Challenger*—and *Voortrekker*.

By doing this the *Stennis* left herself very badly exposed.

"The Vikings will guard the shallower waters toward Chatham Island," Wilson stated. The Vikings had sonobuoys and magnetic anomaly detectors, plus their torpedoes. "I want the *Collins* boats to remain covering the main part of the line from Chatham Island to the north end of the sea-mount range."

Jeffrey nodded. The procession of sea mounts stretching south, to his mind, still defined the far edge of the theater of battle.

Wilson looked at the chart. "I want my *Collins* boats to move closer to each other, like *this*." He made a grouping gesture with his hands.

"Why closer, Commodore?"

"*Voortrekker* has eight torpedo tubes. Each of the diesels has six. I want their arcs of fire, the maximum range of their fish, to overlap. Ter Horst will be outgunned if he tries to push past them. . . . Once the diesels are repositioned, have them start to ping. With the Vikings and the minefields, they'll form a solid wall and force *Voortrekker* east."

Jeffrey understood. As operations officer, he filled in some practical details and relayed Wilson's orders to the secure communications room, next to the control room. Soon the lieutenant (j.g.) in charge there called back on the intercom to say the four Australian subs had acknowledged.

"Now look at these sea mounts," Wilson said.

Jeffrey studied the chart. The sea-mount peaks, extinct undersea volcanoes, were very deep. But each soared four or five thousand feet above the abyssal plain of the Southwest Pacific Basin. The sea mounts were significant terrain, the local high ground.

"*Voortrekker* almost certainly waited for her minisub in the Bounty

Trough somewhere," Wilson said. The gigantic undersea amphitheater, well west of the sea mounts.

"I concur, sir," Jeffrey said; he'd concluded that back in the minisub.

"The sea mounts give us good places to hide. We can ambush him, as he comes east to avoid our other forces."

"Can we really be sure he'll come east?"

"The bomb, Captain, the timing of the bomb. The weather, the geography, it's all part of the Axis plan. It has to be."

Jeffrey nodded. "Their ocean-surveillance satellites let them track the progress of the tropical storm, and told them when *Stennis* would get here."

"The *Stennis* is their next objective. Ter Horst intends to sink the *Stennis*."

"And the islanders were made into bait for the carrier," Jeffrey said angrily, "by planting the bomb." *That's typical ter Horst thinking.*

"But *Voortrekker* needs to move quickly, Captain, before the evacuation airlift is complete, or before the tritium warhead blows, whichever comes first."

Jeffrey nodded grimly. After that, the *Stennis* could withdraw and regroup with her escorts. *Yes,* Voortrekker *has to come east.*

Wilson looked again at the chart. "The northernmost sea mount is too obvious. If we hide ourselves there, ter Horst would expect it. He'll make a counterambush, and we're dead."

"You think we should hover behind the second sea mount south?"

"It's less obvious. Always do the unexpected."

Jeffrey hesitated. "But ter Horst will be thinking this too. He has similar charts. He'll outpsych us, sir, and know we're really behind the second sea mount, *because* the first one is so obvious."

Wilson frowned. "You mean we should use the first sea mount after all? Outpsych *him?*" Wilson thought, then shook his head. "I don't like this. It's too much of a gamble. Whichever sea mount we choose, the odds of getting it right are only fifty-fifty."

"Sir, with respect, maybe we should choose neither." Jeffrey pointed at the chart. "This spot of low terrain between the two sea mounts. It's almost like a sinkhole in the basin floor."

"Lurk there? It's deeper than our crush depth." *Challenger*'s official crush depth was fifteen thousand feet.

"Sir, when you were unconscious on the South Africa raid, we were forced down to sixteen thousand five hundred."

"I read your report, Captain. But that was before you took more battle damage, and before the New London refit." Wilson looked at Jeffrey over the top of his reading glasses. "Need I remind you that the repairs were hasty? And that we haven't taken the ship below ten thousand feet since leaving dry dock?"

"Sir, we *have* to do the unexpected. It's bad enough ter Horst found out we're here. We only have four tubes to *Voortrekker*'s eight." The closest *Collins* boat could never reach the scene in time to help. "Without regaining the element of surprise, we'll lose the one-on-one melee for sure."

"We could have a serious flooding casualty before we even meet him. We might have a hull implosion that deep, or be forced to do an emergency blow and make a racket and give ourselves away and be destroyed. CINCPACFLT said we're expendable in an equal exchange of losses with *Voortrekker*. He didn't tell us to go and commit sheer suicide."

"I know, sir. But I really think we need to use the sink hole, exactly *because* ter Horst won't expect it. . . . It's a calculated risk."

On *Voortrekker*

Van Gelder and ter Horst leaned over the digital navigation plot. The control-room air was cold and stale, and it was very quiet, with as much equipment as possible throughout the ship shut down for stealth. *Voortrekker* moved very slowly, at shallow depth—much speed would make a surface wake that might be seen from the air. For now *Voortrekker* mostly drifted with the surface currents, which in this area ran east. She used the sonar layer right beneath her to shield her minimal noise from the still-intact Chatham Island SOSUS line on the ocean floor so far below.

"Overlay the tactical plot," ter Horst said, almost whispering.

The navigator punched some keys. Van Gelder saw the icons now for the passive sonar contacts. Viking aircraft patrolled in the distance, their flight paths varying unpredictably. Four nuclear-armed *Collins*-class diesel submarines pinged in a line further east, as if to advertise their presence, as a dare. The line they formed was miles north of the SOSUS, and made a last but formidable enemy barrier to *Voortrekker*'s advance.

If one of the Vikings turned and came this way, Van Gelder knew, ter Horst would have to make an ugly choice: stay shallow, and risk being spotted by magnetic anomaly and bombed by atomic torpedoes, or else dive the ship through the layer, and be picked up by the SOSUS instead, with the same unpleasant end result. There was no way to know what the Vikings might do next. *Voortrekker*'s situation was very dangerous. Yet Van Gelder felt more at peace, back now on the vessel he loved—his home. He was doing a job he'd been well trained for, an undersea warship's first officer—a job he knew he was good at and he enjoyed.

"They're making a fence," ter Horst said. "They're pushing us *this* way." He touched his finger to the chart, tracing the line of sea mounts. "They're herding us straight toward *Challenger* on purpose. So, which sea mount is Fuller hiding behind?"

"Not the top one, Captain," Van Gelder said. "It's too obvious, and we could easily outflank him to the south and still have time to cut northeast and hit the *Stennis*. . . . I think he's behind the second one. And he'll have the sonar noise advantage, since he can just sit there while we have to move."

Ter Horst stared at the chart for what seemed a very long time. "I want to tell you a story about a spider, Gunther."

"A spider?"

"There's a type of spider that lives in the deserts of southwest America. It excavates a crater in the sand, then digs itself into the bottom of the crater. When an insect comes by, the beetle or whatever stumbles into the crater. It rolls to the bottom, and the spider springs forth and bites with its fangs."

Ter Horst moved his index finger, and caressed the sinkhole between the two sea mounts.

"No. We won't go past either sea mount. We'll do something different, and then sit still and make this Jeffrey Fuller come to *us*."

33

On Chatham Island

ACRID SMOKE FROM burning brush and burning cars blew across the runway. The air was thick with it, and the smoke went up Ilse's nose. Drowned sheep drifted in the lagoon. She heard the noise of countless others bleating wildly in the distance. Between her thighs, her winded, sweaty horse was nervous and skittish. Everything heightened the feeling of crisis and reminded Ilse that time was running short.

It seemed to her that every islander stood now to stare at the northeast horizon. The Harriers were good for moral support, and they got here first because they were fast, but they were single-seat fighters— useless for rescuing people. Then another dot appeared in the sky, growing larger. The crowd murmured with expectation.

When the plane got close there was a collective sigh of letdown. It was another large two-propeller job, not something that could land at the airstrip. Ilse turned her horse, to help the SEALs and the Harrier pilots organize the evacuees into small groups. The aircraft's engine noise changed, and Ilse looked back. As she watched, its engine nacelles rotated from horizontal to vertical. The aircraft slowed and then began to float, impossibly motionless in the air. It set down just like a helicopter, in a cloud of dust and engine fumes of its own. Ilse realized the plane was a Marine Corps tilt-rotor Osprey. She had heard of them but never seen one.

The islanders surged onto the runway and mobbed the Osprey. But the pilot shut down the engines. No one even opened a door. Ilse spotted Chief Montgomery and waved. She used her horse to push a way to the head of the crowd, to the cockpit. Montgomery followed right behind, walking in her horse's wake.

"Why are you just sitting here?" someone in the crowd yelled at the pilot. The pilot spoke on his radio, and said something to the copilot sitting next to him, but he ignored the civilians.

Someone else came up to the plane. Ilse recognized one of the ringleaders of the lynching of the Kampfschwimmer.

"Get us out of here! Look at the sun, it's late!"

Others in the crowd agreed. "This thing could hold two dozen people easy," someone shouted. Belligerent young men, whom Ilse suspected were drunk, began to bang on the aircraft's doors and on the fuselage.

"Hey. *Hey,*" Montgomery said. "We all agreed, the injured and women and children first."

"Fuck that," a lynching ringleader snapped. He pointed his shotgun at Montgomery.

In a blur Montgomery disarmed the man, then waved the shotgun's butt in his face. "I've had about enough of you."

Constable Henga forced his way closer. "You can still be arrested for murder. I should cuff you right now for disturbing the peace." The troublemaker backed down and slunk over to his cronies. Ilse could tell they were seething.

Montgomery turned to the pilot. He held out his ID. "Why aren't you taking people off?"

The pilot shrugged. "Orders, Chief. I was told to just wait."

At that the crowd became agitated again. People muttered, expressing disgust or veiled threats.

"It's the military mind," Montgomery said in his loudest stage voice. "Sometimes I don't understand it myself." His joke was just enough to stave off something ugly.

Then more aircraft appeared, three more Ospreys. They landed. The island's only ambulance drove up to one, and the volunteer paramedics transferred wounded from the battle. Next came two stretchers with old people who'd had heart attacks from stress.

The other Ospreys started loading passengers. But the crew chiefs wouldn't take any luggage or pets.

Ilse saw several children hugging their dogs or cats. The children were crying. They refused to leave the pets behind; one girl ran away with her kitten and hid behind a tree. The kids and their mothers were meant to be rescued first, and this latest mess was holding up the entire operation. One crew chief seemed prepared to grab the kids and club the dogs and cats and just get the people the hell off the island.

Ilse rode up to the crew chief. "The pets don't weigh much. Can't you make life simple, and just take them and go?"

He looked up at Ilse. "Ma'am, we have barely enough fuel to get back to the carrier as it is, if she keeps coming right at us as fast as she can. It's touch and go if we'll make it even then. If the wind shifts against us . . ." He shrugged. "We could all end up in the drink."

Ilse understood. The whole rescue mission was one desperate stretch. A sixty-pound dog weighed as much as or more than a youngish child. *But try to explain this to the child.*

"Look, okay," Ilse said. "What if we put all the pets in that hangar shed there? If there's room later, could you take them?"

"It's not up to me."

Ilse whispered, "Humor me for the kids."

The crew chief turned to the mothers. He told them what to do. A lady from the paramedics used small injections of sedative to keep the animals quiet.

The first group of refugees took to the air and headed northeast, with nothing but the clothes on their backs and what they could cram in their pockets.

Another Osprey arrived, with a heavy load in a cargo sling suspended under its belly. It put the load on the ground beside the edge of the runway and hovered. The Harrier pilots ran up and undid the sling. The Osprey set down and began loading passengers.

That's a hundred people off, so far. There are still nine hundred to go.

The sun was low in the sky now. Ilse was getting very worried. A Harrier pilot walked by her.

"What's in that big container?" she asked.

"A fuel bladder. Ten thousand pounds of helicopter fuel."

Ilse saw them now, a string of a dozen helos coming toward the airstrip. The air thudded steadily from the combined effects of their powerful rotors. Islanders cheered.

"Sea Stallions," the Harrier pilot said. "Each can carry fifty or sixty adults. . . . They're flying on the vapor in their tanks right now."

Another man in a flight suit came up to Ilse. "Are you Lieutenant Reebeck?"

"Yes." She recognized the pilot from the first Osprey.

"I got more orders. I need you and Chief Montgomery, and a Lieutenant Clayton, pronto."

"We're going to the carrier? But I want to be last. Take other people instead."

"No, ma'am. Not the carrier. My orders are to take you three to the south end of the island, and land near the bomb."

ILSE tied her horse to a tree and patted it farewell. She knew the horse would be killed when the bomb exploded, and would suffer horribly at this distance from ground zero. Fighting back tears, she asked Constable Henga to shoot it later instead. He promised.

Ilse made her good-byes with Henga. She hardly knew the man, yet he'd swiftly become a steady, reliable presence who gave her comfort amid the confusion and depression all around. Henga shook Ilse's hand firmly and turned back to helping supervise the airlift. He trotted to the runway, shouting something. Just like that, Henga had come into her life and left again. Ilse tried to get used to it, the intense interactions and sudden ripping apart that impacted human relationships during war. But it was very hard to get used to.

Ilse climbed into the Osprey through a passenger door in the side. The interior was austere; wires and cables and pipes showed everywhere. Much of the space was taken by extra internal fuel tanks, and by cable reels and equipment cases held down by straps and netting. Ilse and Clayton sat on one side at the front of the cargo compartment, with Montgomery on the other, facing them. The Osprey's crew chief sat next to Montgomery. Like the others, Ilse used an uncomfortable fold-down mesh seat. Everyone fastened their flight harnesses.

The pilot and copilot started up one engine and then the other. Ilse craned her neck to look out a porthole in the door, to watch. The propeller blades became a blur, and the aircraft vibrated heavily. The engine noise deepened in pitch and grew louder. The aircraft rose off the ground, going straight up, fast. Ilse had a panoramic view of the airstrip and the lagoon.

The engine nacelles rotated to horizontal. The ride to the SOSUS bunker on the south edge of the island was very quick. Ilse saw the road she'd taken, the town of Waitangi itself from high up, the smoke and flame of burning brush, and sheep limping or wandering aimlessly. Then she saw the burned-out hulks of the Saracen and the Land Rover.

The pilot set down in an open spot at a safe distance from the outcropping with the bunker; this area was upwind of the wildfires. The pilot shut down the engines. The crew chief took an equipment case and gave it to Shajo Clayton. He handed another to Ilse. Ilse saw hers was a replacement for her console that had been destroyed when the rocket hit her tent at the start of the battle.

ILSE glanced into the bunker. This late in the day the sun shone right through the open door. The bomb sat there in its gleaming stainless-steel casing, waiting patiently to explode. The timer said there were barely two hours left. It gave Ilse the creeps to be so close to the thing.

Clayton opened his case and set up a portable gamma-ray spectrometer sent by the carrier's radiological-control officer. Soon Clayton confirmed that the atom bomb was real and the vial held real tritium. Clayton began to take other measurements, for intelligence purposes.

Montgomery and Ilse gingerly worked around Clayton and the bomb, splicing the ends of cables severed in the battle. The Kampfschwimmer hadn't tampered with the undersea microphone line, but the feeder near the outcropping was cut in several places. Montgomery and Ilse repaired this damage next.

Ilse ran wires from the SOSUS equipment to the nearby Osprey, and set up her portable console inside. The satellite dish by the outcropping was much too damaged to use, but she was able to establish radio contact with the SOSUS center in Sydney using the Osprey's communications gear. She received an updated report. She ran the programs on her console to optimize the microphone line for conditions in the water, and passed the report to the first of the Australian submarines. Eventually an acknowledgment returned to her, acoustically, passed back along the line of diesel subs, saying *Challenger* had received the report. There was no sign of *Voortrekker* anywhere.

34

On *Voortrekker*

VAN GELDER LEANED over the sonar chief's shoulder. The feeling in the control room was tense. This maneuver was so chancy, Van Gelder could tell through subtle body language that even Jan ter Horst was unhappy needing to try it. But *Challenger's* unexpected presence—she was supposed to be in dry dock a hemisphere away—was a serious complication.

Ter Horst had had the sonar chief put the outside sounds on the speakers, amplified for clarity. Every time a *Collins* boat pinged from the north, all present in the control room heard it. To Van Gelder, the sound of each ping, intrusive, searching, and hostile, struck him physically, like the sting of a bee. It was only through supreme effort that he masked the outward signs of his stress. The sonar chief said the Australian boats were probably too far off to pick up *Voortrekker*—but that was based only on models and estimates, a fact which gave Van Gelder no comfort.

Voortrekker continued to run very shallow and slow, above the sonar layer, to hide from the enemy SOSUS. Her depth was barely thirty meters—one hundred feet. The SOSUS line now lay in the middle distance to the south. So close to the surface, even with her ceramic-composite hull, *Voortrekker* was still awfully vulnerable to magnetic-anomaly detectors on Allied aircraft because of all the steel and iron inside her. More Vikings had arrived from the *Stennis*. Based on their random but thorough search patterns, sooner or later one would come too close and spot *Voortrekker*. This put ter Horst under severe time pressure, at a point when he could least afford to rush.

From hard experience, Van Gelder knew there were different levels or stages of fear during undersea combat. At the moment, there was that steady, wearing emotional pressure of needing to stay undetected while on the move with the enemy near—when time seemed to truly stand still, and the noise of one's own breathing felt deafeningly loud. In contrast, there was the desperate, frenzied, action-filled panic when enemy nuclear torpedoes tore in at the ship—when the crew responded through rote training and gut instinct and sheer grit. The worst mental torture of all, for a submariner, was knowing that the situation could change from one to the other with savage, unforgiving suddenness.

Convinced that the sonar chief knew his job, Van Gelder patted his shoulder for encouragement, then returned to the command console. He scanned the tactical plot: combined with the SOSUS hydrophones, the Vikings and the *Collins* boats had *Voortrekker* sandwiched; Van Gelder was sure that this was exactly the Allied high command's intent. Keeping *Voortrekker* poised above the layer, far enough away from both the SOSUS and the enemy diesels, was like trying to balance a nine-thousand-ton nuclear sub on the head of a pin. Ter Horst was exactly the sort of captain who would try.

Van Gelder knew his crewmen and junior officers well. He knew each man's strengths and weaknesses. He knew the different way that each reacted to such stress, and they all showed it now. Some were sweating more copiously as every Australian ping seemed louder than the last in the oppressive silence of the control room. Others felt cold, especially in their limbs, and had to keep rubbing their hands to stay warm as *Voortrekker* made her slow progress. Others developed facial twitches, or cricks in their necks, as they sat there dreading the first word of enemy weapons in the water. Some suffered that impulse to turn into nonstop talkers, but they had to keep their mouths shut, and instead they'd shift uncomfortably in their seats and fidget.

Van Gelder was yet a different type. In moments of supreme danger, he felt tight from head to toe, so puckered up inside he would be constipated for days. He also felt a silvery tingling in his stomach and chest. The tingling, he always thought, was adrenaline. Sometimes Van Gelder believed this sensation was habit forming: it wasn't entirely unpleasant, because he felt eagerness as well as dread. Eagerness to carry on with his duties, in spite of the knowledge of closeness of death. Eagerness to prosecute the battle, to lead his men, to survive by doing smart, aggressive things . . . and above all eagerness to *win.*

This was one trait Van Gelder felt he shared with Jan ter Horst, however different the two might be in other ways. In a revenge match with USS *Challenger,* well away from populated land, Van Gelder had no moral qualms. To sink the enemy vessel would bring the war to a more rapid close.

When ter Horst judged he was far enough north of the final SOSUS hydrophone line, he ordered *Voortrekker* back to the bottom. But first, for even greater stealth, he told the helmsman to turn due south—to show both the SOSUS and the diesel subs the narrowest possible profiles—and then come to all stop. *Voortrekker* dived straight down while staying level—on an even keel—by taking in seawater ballast to make her heavy. This tricky task fell to the ship's chief of the watch, and Van Gelder maintained a careful eye.

Voortrekker dropped through the sonar layer, losing her cloak against the distant but still-potent SOSUS, and the tension in the control room became an almost solid entity. The *Collins* boats continued to ping, threatening in Van Gelder's ears like swarming, hungry mosquitoes.

The suspense rose even more, because as *Voortrekker* descended further, the weight of the water above her squeezed her hull. At depth, from this immense compression coming from all around, the hull would groan or pop—a dead giveaway of her presence, if someone were close enough to hear.

The sonarmen were kept very busy. The fire-control technicians hunched over their consoles, concentrating for their lives. Everyone waited on pins and needles for the first hull pop, and for whatever enemy response it might bring. The crew stayed absolutely still. The twitchers let their faces twitch. The neck-crampers suffered in motionless silence. The sweaters stopped dabbing their sweat.

Down the ship went, down. The control room seemed quieter than quiet. No one even dared to clear their throat. Van Gelder saw one new crewman, very young and scared, let himself drool rather than risk making noise by swallowing the saliva—his Adam's apple must be spasmed like a knot. Van Gelder understood, and wouldn't criticize the youth later. The air in and out of Van Gelder's own nostrils seemed louder than a hurricane.

The hull popped several times before *Voortrekker* reached the sea floor, in water three kilometers deep. Each pop, over the sonar speakers, made several crewmen jump in their seats. Van Gelder would have jumped too, had not his role as first officer demanded he repress his visible human side.

At last *Voortrekker* reached the bottom. Van Gelder watched, waited, listened, then reported to ter Horst: no reaction by the enemy. But Van Gelder felt compelled to warn that it was impossible to be sure *Voortrekker* truly remained unheard.

Satisfied enough, and annoyed by Van Gelder's caution, ter Horst ordered top quiet speed—thirty knots. His course was east, parallel to and halfway between the SOSUS and the diesel subs. For now, he'd hide as much as possible in gentle folds in the rolling bottom terrain.

All eight torpedo tubes held weapons with tactical atomic warheads. Ter Horst and Van Gelder entered their secret arming codes. They turned their special keys. On Van Gelder's weapons status display, eight warheads showed PRE-ENABLED.

Simultaneously, on *Challenger*

Jeffrey watched on his displays as *Challenger* snuck behind the first sea mount.

"Ordered way point reached, sir," Sessions said from the navigation plot.

"Very well, Navigator." The huge bulk of the sea mount ought to screen *Challenger* from *Voortrekker,* wherever ter Horst might be, and also block the sounds of *Challenger*'s hull popping on the way down.

Now comes the fun part.

"Chief of the Watch, retract the towed array."

"Retract the towed array, aye," COB said.

Full retraction of the long array took several minutes. As crucial as the time factor was, Jeffrey made himself be patient. From here, given his next intended maneuvers, dangling a towed array behind the ship would be a handicap.

"Chief of the Watch, rig for deep submergence." COB acknowledged again. "Helm, rig for nap-of-sea-floor cruise mode."

"Nap of sea floor, aye," Meltzer said. He flipped switches and typed on keys, and some of his displays showed the outside world in a different, more visual and intimate way.

"Helm, ahead one-third, make turns for six knots. Take us to the bottom, thirty degrees down bubble." Again Meltzer acknowledged. *Challenger*'s bow nosed steeply down. Everyone held on tight. No matter which way you sat, or what you gripped while standing, a thirty-degree down bubble was extreme. The crew became more reserved, as they thought of the test that Jeffrey would subject them to in the next few minutes. The test for them was staying focused and calm, as Jeffrey put *Challenger* through the ultimate test—a dive past official crush depth.

As they approached ten thousand feet, the hull began to protest. Kathy's people reported the hull pops each time. Eventually, the hull was so compressed from all sides that the deck in the control room started to warp. The crew grew even more quiet and cautious in their movements. This warping—this close, hard contact of structural members—was a danger sign that some of the ship's sound-isolation gear was no longer effective.

Jeffrey kept an eye glued to a depth gauge. He ordered Meltzer to come to a milder five-degree down bubble, to reduce the rate of descent now that they'd exceeded *Challenger*'s test depth. He also had Meltzer cut ship's speed to three knots.

Minute by minute, gradually, the ship went even deeper. Crewmen held their breaths. COB kept one hand poised by the emergency blow handles, just in case. Jeffrey pretended not to notice. Silently he urged his ship to hold together. He fought down his own concerns, but they fought back psychosomatically. He felt a stabbing ache in his thigh, and his forehead was sore despite the corpsman's shot.

Jeffrey studied the topography around him on the gravimeter display, to judge his progress through the terrain. The imagery was vivid and three-dimensional and sharp. The sea-mount slopes, above him now, were jagged and very steep. Their peaks loomed high over *Challenger* like mountains six thousand feet tall. The deep-sea-basin floor, just beneath *Challenger,* was mostly flat and smooth and fell off at a shallower angle.

Jeffrey had Meltzer turn south and hug the bottom—it was here that a towed array would tangle and drag. With Meltzer at the controls, his broad chest puffed out confidently, *Challenger* moved slowly toward the hollow in the ocean floor, the sinkhole.

On the way down to fifteen thousand feet, as the hull compressed even more, bits of heat insulation and paint chips crumbled and fell from the overhead. Crewmen squirmed. Jeffrey, with a blitheness he didn't feel inside, brushed the dust—like dandruff—off the shoulders of his khaki uniform shirt.

At sixteen thousand feet, water suddenly sprayed from a ruptured pipe in a forward corridor.

Crewmen gasped, but Jeffrey calmed them. He knew at once it was only internal cooling water, not the sea at outside pressure—a pipe joint failed from the flexing as components within the ship were squashed.

The sea itself wouldn't spray. It would roar in with a force past human comprehension, like being fired at point-blank by artillery howitzers.

COB quickly bypassed the broken section of pipe.

Through all this Wilson didn't say a thing. He didn't move a muscle, or even blink. He knew as well as Jeffrey did that—caught badly off-balance by *Voortrekker*'s sudden appearance this far north—*Challenger* very much needed both stealth and surprise. Jeffrey had convinced Wilson that this sinkhole sniper's nest was the ideal, the necessary point to lay an ambush.

Jeffrey dearly hoped now he was right in trying this. If he was wrong, death by hull implosion would be painful but swift, with little time for remonstrance.

Jeffrey made brief eye contact with Wilson, then had to look away. He was as concerned that he might disappoint his commodore as he was that he might sink his ship through such aggressive risk taking. Wilson had that effect on Jeffrey. His disapproval sometimes seemed more fearsome than death itself.

But *Challenger* held up. Jeffrey gave a silent cheer for the design engineers, the contractors, the skilled workmen and -women, everybody who built the ship and helped repair her. The control-room crew glanced at each other and nodded and grinned. They were proud of their ship, and she hadn't let them down once yet. They were also proud of their captain, however far out on the envelope he so often made them go. Jeffrey smiled to himself. This was exactly the attitude he wanted them to have right now.

It's time to put in place the sonar search plan.

Jeffrey ordered Meltzer to turn the ship due west and hover motionless. *Challenger*'s powerful bow sphere was aimed directly down *Voortrekker*'s route of advance. Using the side-mounted wide-aperture arrays, Kathy's people would do other passive sonar scans as well. The wide arrays looked out and up toward either flank of the ship, to the approach slopes and the near side of the first sea mount to the north, and the second to *Challenger*'s south.

The sonarmen would listen for *Voortrekker*'s flow noise, and for tonals from her machinery and electrical power supplies. They would also listen on ambient sonar, for echoes off *Voortrekker*'s hull from crashing surface waves and other ocean sounds. They would watch for a hole in the ocean too, a moving spot in the water that was too quiet— something large, blocking background noises from farther away, something that down here could only be the Boer ceramic-hulled sub.

Deep-capable nuclear torpedoes were loaded in all four working tubes. Jeffrey and Bell armed the warheads.

Now there was nothing to do but wait. Wait for *Voortrekker* to come and give herself away. Wait for Jan ter Horst to make a mistake.

Forty minutes later,
on *Challenger*

Jeffrey sat at the command console. He finished chomping a peanut butter and jelly sandwich to give himself energy. He washed it down with coffee to keep himself alert.

His eyes roamed over his console displays. On the gravimeter, the two sea-mount pinnacles towered, several miles away on either side of *Challenger*. On the tactical plot, the Australian diesel subs stretched in a line toward now-distant Chatham Island. Their pings were clearly detected by *Challenger*'s sonar signal processors—but at this long range, on the speakers, only the closest one was barely audible even to Jeffrey's trained ears. Antisubmarine aircraft continued patrolling, but none came in the neighborhood of Jeffrey's ship. *Voortrekker*'s location Jeffrey could only guess at.

Jeffrey settled in for a long wait. This was a part of undersea combat he always found difficult—the waiting—even in the New London attack simulator, or in training exercises at sea before the war. The adversary could show up in the next five seconds, or he might not be detected for hours. It called for all of Jeffrey's self-control, self-discipline, and patience.

Jeffrey did not especially like the present situation. The sudden appearance of *Voortrekker* on the wrong side of two SOSUS lines disrupted the whole strategic picture. The *Collins* boats were supposed to be vectored toward *Voortrekker* by the SOSUS, with plenty of notice in advance. They were supposed to form a scouting line, and act as bait, while *Challenger* secretly lurked in the deep to make the actual kill against ter Horst.

Now, caught out of position, the diesels could do little but form a conspicuous barrier—though granted a very potent one, with two dozen working torpedo tubes between them, all armed with nuclear fish. Instead, *Challenger* herself was the bait, the lure for *Voortrekker*, now that ter Horst had learned—through Van Gelder's spotting Ilse—that *Challenger* was somewhere in the area, not in dry dock.

The outcome of this surprise encounter battle hinged on ter Horst not guessing where Jeffrey was hiding, down in this sea-floor sinkhole. The existence of the sinkhole was an accident of local geology. Jeffrey wondered what he—and Wilson—would have done if the sinkhole weren't here. Jeffrey planned, once contact with *Voortrekker* was made, to let ter Horst go by. Then he'd fire a pair of nuclear fish straight up the bastard's ass.

Wilson returned from using the head.

"Anything, Captain?"

"Nothing, Commodore."

Wilson grunted.

A distant blast rocked the ship.

"Loud explosion bearing three two zero," Kathy reported. Northwest. "Range eighty thousand yards." Forty miles.

"What was it?" Jeffrey demanded. He had a terrible feeling in his gut.

"Noise spectrum matches Axis atomic torpedo warhead, Captain."

"Sir," Bell said, very worried, "that blast coincides with the eastern-most *Collins*-class boat." The intercom light from the communications room blinked. Bell answered, listened, hung up, then turned to Jeffrey. "Confirmed, Captain. Acoustic message fragment received, saying they were under attack, then nothing."

Damn. Ter Horst outsmarted me after all.

"Any counterfire, XO?" The *Collins* should've had time to shoot back.

There were three more sharp eruptions, same bearing and range. Kathy said they were Axis warheads set on highest yield, one kiloton. Their reverb thundered and roared.

So there was counterfire, but it was all ter Horst's, to smash the Australian torpedoes aimed his way.

"He found the seam in our forces," Wilson stated. "Between us and the closest diesel boat."

"You mean he realized we were here, in the sinkhole?"

Wilson nodded. He looked disgusted. "He'll charge northeast now, after the *Stennis*. He's opened himself the shortest possible route."

"We have to go after him, Commodore."

"Concur."

Jeffrey told Meltzer to make flank speed, on a course northeast. Jeffrey decided to stay near the bottom, because that's what Jan ter Horst would do.

"Get off a warning," Wilson ordered. "*Voortrekker* has supersonic antiship cruise missiles."

Bell handled the details for Jeffrey. A small autonomous radio buoy, with preprogrammed text in code, was released toward the surface.

Wilson looked at the tactical plot. *Challenger* kept accelerating, then began to vibrate as she neared flank speed. "Good," Wilson said. "With *Stennis* alerted, and us on his tail, we have *Voortrekker* in a pincers."

Jeffrey studied the plot. He wished Ilse was here, to help him read Jan ter Horst's mind. Jeffrey ran through what he knew of ter Horst, the way he'd fought last time they'd met. . . .

"Helm, *all stop!*"

Meltzer acknowledged. He sounded startled by the order.

"Just what are you doing?" Wilson said to Jeffrey. He shot him another of those piercing looks over the top of his glasses.

"I'm not sure yet," Jeffrey stated. "But I *am* sure what I'm *not* doing. I'm not going to do what ter Horst expects."

"Explain yourself."

"You said it already, Commodore. Sir, the pincers. *We're* his greatest threat, and his highest-value target. *Challenger,* not *Stennis*. He can't afford to leave us in his rear. . . . So he's *not* running after the carrier. He just wants us to think he is. He's *here*." Jeffrey pointed at the plot. "Hiding behind the first sea mount, on the opposite side from us. Waiting for us to come rushing past, preoccupied and practically sonar blind at flank speed."

"You mean it's a *trap?*"

"I believe so. He's a devious bugger." Jeffrey ordered Meltzer to head due north, right at the first sea mount, at twenty-six knots—half as fast as flank speed, but infinitely quieter.

"You realize if you're wrong," Wilson said, "you're giving *Voortrekker* such a head start that we'll never catch up. If he can sink the *Stennis,* and he leaves us in the dust . . ."

"I know, Commodore. I know. I don't think I'm wrong."

"Captain," Bell interrupted, "if we meet *Voortrekker* head-on, coming around the sea mount at short range, we'll be outgunned two to one. We can't possibly win the engagement."

"I know, XO. I know."

Simultaneously, on Chatham Island

Ilse sat in the Osprey, working her communications gear. She finished processing the latest round of oceanographic data from the sensors attached to the microphone line strung out into deep water. She started using that data to reoptimize the relay of reports from Sydney down into the sea, for use by *Challenger* and the *Collins* boats.

Meanwhile, in the bunker in the rock outcropping, the tritium-boosted bomb's timer was winding down. Shajo Clayton still carefully used his gamma ray spectrometer, taking readings from every angle and side, to try to gain some insight into the powerful weapon's design.

The weapon's very existence was deeply troubling to Ilse. The Axis had publicly sworn off building hydrogen bombs, to shrewdly pull the teeth from the Allies' thermonuclear arsenal: The Germans and Boers were sticking to tactical atomic weapons only, used almost exclusively at sea. The Allies thus dared not launch their H-bombs against the Axis, for fear of slaughtering millions of innocents in Europe and Africa—which would also outrage the world and risk catastrophic responses from Russia and China.

But now, the use of a tritium boost to a fission weapon on land was a worrisome step toward escalation. The bomb on Chatham Island fell in the gray area between a straightforward uranium or plutonium warhead, maxing out at two dozen kilotons, and a true sustained-fusion hydrogen bomb, which could yield many megatons.

The danger, the implications, were almost too large to contemplate. The blast would make the Axis look reckless and ruthless, but Ilse suspected this was the Axis regime's whole idea. How neutral countries reacted still had to be seen—they might well be impressed or intimidated. The mushroom cloud here would make the U.S. seem weak, lacking both in military initiative and adequate global resources to ever beat the

Axis back from their already-huge territorial gains. In some ways it was like World War II, except with no Allied successes to boast of at a Midway or an El Alamein or a Stalingrad. The explosion on Chatham Island would surely be destabilizing—and further instability favored the enemy side.

Ilse forced her mind back to little things she might control. To think too much, right now, was a sure route to panic or insanity.

In a window on her screen, she displayed the raw data coming from the SOSUS line. Suddenly the signal went wild. From working with Kathy Milgrom on *Challenger* in battle, Ilse knew the signature of a distant underwater atomic blast. It looked like a big one too, so it had to be Axis—Allied torpedoes used smaller maximum yields.

The Sydney SOSUS center immediately confirmed her take. She typed fast, to send a report to the Australian subs, who'd surely detected the blast on their sonars already. It took some time to hear back. Their response had to be repeated, then pieced together from fragments, because of distorting reverb from the blast and then three others which followed.

The answering message said contact had been lost with the farthest *Collins* boat in the line, after it barely had a chance to say it was being attacked.

A vital section of the chain—the acoustic link between Chatham Island and *Challenger*—was severed.

Sydney was extracting useful data from the SOSUS. They heard enemy torpedo-engine noises and fleeting whiffs of *Voortrekker* at flank speed. They gave an estimate of ter Horst's course before he disappeared into the bubble clouds of the undersea nuclear blasts. *Voortrekker* was last heard heading northeast, past the first sea mount and toward the distant *Stennis*.

But Ilse had no way to warn *Challenger* now. The gap between the third Australian sub, the last in the line that survived, and *Challenger* was too large for the acoustic link to function, even if the roiling bubble clouds didn't intervene. And the *Collins* boats were much too slow and too far away to help.

Jeffrey and his crew were on their own.

Ilse looked at her wristwatch. She badly wanted to leave the island now. The Osprey pilot queried via satellite.

Commander in Chief, Pacific Fleet told them to stay exactly where they were and keep working. Another Osprey came over from the airstrip. It landed next to Ilse's, then just sat there.

On *Challenger*

Jeffrey stared at the gravimeter. The first sea mount was very close. Its vast bulk reared almost a mile above him as *Challenger* followed the ocean floor at twenty-six knots. The mood in the control room was concerned and apprehensive.

"Either stop, or change course," Wilson said. "You can't drive *through* the mountain."

Jeffrey almost wished he could, or could at least *see* through solid rock. The gravimeter could do precisely that, since matter was transparent to gravity. But as long as an enemy sub kept moving at all, the mass of its hull and reactor shielding would go undetected by the gravimeter's computer methodology.

There was no positive proof, and Jeffrey could be horribly wrong, but he simply had to play his hunch: he was firmly convinced ter Horst was somewhere right on the other side of this undersea extinct volcano, waiting for him.

"He has twice as many tubes," Bell said, "twice our rate of fire."

Jeffrey didn't need to be reminded. This was the problem he'd been agonizing over all along. Jeffrey could fire four torpedoes at a time before needing to let the repaired autoloader machinery push new units into the breaches of the tubes. *Voortrekker* could fire eight at a time. No matter how Jeffrey divided his fire between *offense*—fish aimed at *Voortrekker*—and *defense*—fish used to smash torpedoes ter Horst aimed at *Challenger*—the enemy would triumph. Ter Horst could smash all Jeffrey's fish and still have four from that very first salvo to blow *Challenger* to smithereens.

"We have to change the rules of the game," Jeffrey said. "Somehow."

"Like use a decoy?" Bell suggested.

Jeffrey shook his head. "He'll be expecting decoys."

"Then *what?*" Even Wilson seemed to be feeling the pressure now.

Jeffrey examined the tactical plot. He stared and stared, as if he were waiting for it to speak to him. Turn to port, or to starboard? Follow the mountain clockwise, or counterclockwise? He tried to forget what was really at stake and make it just a sport, like football or soccer.

Jeffrey gestured with his hands, and thought out loud. "If we go *this* way, he could catch us as we come round *there*. If we go *that* way, he could catch us *here*. With the sea mount blocking the line of sight till the very last minute, first contact will be at extremely short range. There'll only be time for one salvo. . . ."

"All of which we knew already," Wilson said.

Jeffrey gazed and gazed at the gravimeter. He had to find *some* way to redefine this tactical problem, to completely alter the parameters of the whole scenario . . . and do it fast.

Jeffrey knew he was good at thinking on his feet, with the clock ticking. He trusted his own capacity for leaps of intuition, that mysterious way in which his mind didn't have an idea he needed, and then suddenly the idea was simply there, and glaringly obvious. Jeffrey hoped his own brain didn't let him down this time.

"Hah!" A broad grin came to Jeffrey's face. His stomach tingled brightly. "We don't go *either* way."

"You mean force *Voortrekker* to come to us?" Bell said.

"We'll still be outgunned two to one," Wilson warned.

"No, we won't. . . . We'll outgun *him* two to one."

"*What?*"

"Commodore, patience, please. XO, listen, here's the deal. I want to send our fish out and around ahead of us. Launch them from just where we are, so *Voortrekker* won't hear them coming till too late. Program them to follow the side of the sea mount in a semicircle, and start their homing searches when they're well away from us." Jeffrey also told Bell to have the weapons disarm before they could complete the circle and come back in *Challenger*'s face.

"Understood, sir, but how does that improve the odds?"

Jeffrey snapped out firing orders in rapid succession. He sent four Mark 88s, deep-capable atomic torpedoes, around to the left. He told Bell to reload smartly. They armed the warheads and Jeffrey sent the next four around to the right—and reloaded again. Jeffrey sent four more left, had Bell reload, then sent four more to the right again.

Now Challenger *has* sixteen *weapons in the water, and ter Horst doesn't even know it yet.*

"All units running normally," Kathy reported. The Mark 88 torpedoes attacked at seventy knots.

"Now *that* should keep him busy," Jeffrey said. Bell nodded and smiled. The whole mood in the control room lifted.

Commodore Wilson patted Jeffrey on the back. "Thinking outside the box. You never cease to amaze me, Captain."

"Thank you, Commodore. . . . Now comes the tricky part. Helm, right ten degrees rudder."

Meltzer acknowledged. *Challenger* turned.

Almost half my ammo supply is irrevocably committed, and we're about to stir up a hornets' nest on the other side of this hill.

Jeffrey ordered Bell to reload, yet another salvo of weapons, but this time Jeffrey didn't fire. He did tell Bell to flood and equalize the tubes and open the outer doors.

"Helm," Jeffrey ordered, "use left rudder as needed. Follow the sea mount, counterclockwise. *Now* it's time to put ourselves between *Voortrekker* and the *Stennis.*"

35

On *Voortrekker*

"It's only a matter of time now," ter Horst said. "I expect we'll hear him to starboard, not to port. He'll head northeast from the sinkhole to cut me off, bypassing the sea mount from counterclockwise."

Van Gelder knew now the spider, in ter Horst's story before, was supposed to be Jeffrey Fuller.

"Understood, sir," Van Gelder said. *Voortrekker* waited quietly on the north side of the first sea mount, to ambush *Challenger* from the rear as Fuller raced to save the American carrier.

"He thought he'd use the *Stennis* as flypaper to draw and hold me, to lure me straight on toward *Challenger*. Instead I've done an end-around and turned the game on its head. That *Collins* boat, Gunther, the datum we made by sinking her, they're *our* flypaper for *Challenger*."

Van Gelder nodded. He might dislike ter Horst's politics, and might despise the man's twisted sense of honor and ethics, but Van Gelder couldn't deny his captain's impressive natural tactical skill.

Van Gelder eyed a chronometer—the bomb on Chatham Island should explode soon. Something flashed on his screen, and the sonarmen reacted like they'd been hit by cattle prods. Van Gelder thought the bomb had gone off prematurely.

"Hydrophone effects," the sonar chief shouted. "Near field! *Four torpedoes in the water!* Mean bearing two seven zero!" To *port,* not to starboard, coming around the mountain clockwise, from the *west.*

"Return fire, Number One," ter Horst ordered. "Destroy them all, then send four more of ours in that direction. They'll find *Challenger* by active search."

Van Gelder rushed to issue commands. The weapons dashed from the tubes. Now all eight tubes were empty.

"Four more torpedoes in the water! Inbound, bearing zero six zero!" Coming around the sea mount from the other way—from starboard, east. Torpedoes began pinging everywhere now.

"He can't be two places at once!" ter Horst shouted. "We're caught in the middle!"

"We need time to reload and arm," Van Gelder warned.

"Helm," ter Horst snapped, "left full rudder. Flank speed ahead."

"Torpedoes at zero six zero are gaining fast."

"Launch noisemakers and jammers!"

Voortrekker's first wire-guided torpedoes intercepted the first incoming group, to the west. Van Gelder pressed the firing buttons; the four warheads exploded, barely outside lethal range of his own ship. Even set on their lowest yield, one-tenth kiloton for self-defense, *Voortrekker* rocked and shimmied. Everything in the control room shook. Loose objects went flying. Van Gelder was tossed like a rag doll against his seat belt. His eardrums rang as if his skull would crack.

Blast waves bounced off the sea-mount face, and caught *Voortrekker* viciously in the stern. The ship veered more and more leftward, aimed straight at the sea mount, a solid mass of basalt. The danger showed all too vividly on the gravimeter—*Voortrekker* was still accelerating to flank speed, and she'd built up huge momentum.

"Hard right rudder!"

The helmsman complied. *Challenger*'s second four torpedoes detonated against the noisemakers and jammers back behind *Voortrekker*'s stern. Again *Voortrekker* was hammered. Between the latest tight turn at high speed, and the new shock waves from starboard, *Voortrekker* went into a snap roll. She banked wildly and dived out of control, aimed at the sea floor. The gravimeter faithfully showed the hard volcanic bottom coming at Van Gelder fast. The helmsman and chief of the watch struggled to save the ship from a fatal collision with terrain.

"Four *more* torpedoes in the water!" the sonar chief shouted. "Four more torpedoes closing in to port!"

"Snap shots, tubes one through four!" ter Horst ordered.

"They're too close!" Van Gelder yelled.

"Do it!"

The weapons leaped from the tubes. Van Gelder saw on his tactical plot that they might never intercept in time.

Amid the maelstrom of throbbing nuclear fireballs and roiling bubble clouds all around, *Challenger*'s weapons tried to home on *Voortrekker* rather than spots of tortured water. Van Gelder's fire-controlmen tried to home on the inbound weapons.

It was chaos. Detonations shattered the sea, and almost shattered *Voortrekker*. Gaps appeared in the sea-mount wall as the blast forces started big avalanches. Rubble pounded *Voortrekker*'s hull.

"We need to get out of here," Van Gelder shouted above the noise. "The whole mountainside could bury us alive!"

"Helm, steer two one zero!" Southwest. "Maintain flank speed!" But one hard turn after another had slowed the ship, because the rudder acted like a speed brake.

"Hydrophone effects!" the sonar chief shouted once more. "Four *more* torpedoes, bearing zero five zero." From counterclockwise again. "Torpedoes closing fast!"

"*Where are they all coming from?* Number One, noisemakers! Jammers! God *damn* that Fuller! Push the reactor to a hundred twenty percent!"

On Chatham Island

Ilse knew enough from past experience how to interpret the raw signals showing on her console screen from the SOSUS. Those were torpedo-engine noises. She recognized the distinctive tonals of *Voortrekker*'s Sea Lion weapons and *Challenger*'s Mark 88 fish.

Torpedoes began to detonate. All went off very deep. It was so fast paced and confusing she had no idea who was winning or who'd been sunk. Then she caught a glimpse of data that looked like *Voortrekker* moving southwest, her reactor systems and pump-jet propulsor straining at fifty knots.

Four more torpedoes were in the water suddenly, on the near side of massive bubble clouds impenetrable to the SOSUS hydrophones. These new torpedoes belonged to *Voortrekker*. As Ilse watched they spread out, doing seventy-five knots each. On her console their signal strengths just grew and grew. When they were right on top of the SOSUS line they exploded. The signal went completely dead. Ter Horst had nuked the SOSUS.

Most of the fallout that breaks the surface will disperse and settle and age before it reaches South America. But the local ecological catastrophe has begun.

CHALLENGER warily circled the first sea mount twice, through the lingering reverb and bubble clouds, then steered slowly southwest.

"Where is he?" Wilson said. "I have trouble believing he simply ran back the way he came."

Jeffrey looked at all the sensor readings. There was no sign of *Voortrekker* anywhere. Viking planes from the *Stennis*, and P-3C Orion land-based maritime patrol planes that were finally able to take off from New Zealand, had peppered the entire area with active sonobuoys. These special sonobuoys could operate down to *Voortrekker*'s crush depth—the terrain around the sea mounts was covered like a carpet. The three nuclear subs that were escorts for the *Stennis*, though many knots slower than *Challenger*, were converging on the area in a wide sweep from the northeast and east. The three surviving *Collins* boats, after snorkeling to recharge their batteries, were pinging aggressively and moving down from the north.

"Captain," Kathy Milgrom called. "An Orion dropped a signal sonobuoy. . . . I think it's for us."

"Put it on speakers."

Above the churning water and roaring echoes of the recent nuclear battle, Jeffrey heard a series of siren tones, varying in length and pitch. After a pause, the signal repeated. Bell looked up the signal code in his digital database.

"It says to come to periscope depth and copy satellite message traffic."

Jeffrey sighed. He *really* hated exposing himself in a war zone. But he remembered what Wilson had said, about being a true team player and grasping the bigger picture. *Periscope depth it is.* Jeffrey was about to give the orders to Meltzer and COB when he glanced at a chronometer.

"Commodore, I suggest we wait for the Chatham Island bomb to go off first. It won't be long."

Simultaneously, on Chatham Island

Ilse sat staring at her useless console. She was in radio contact with Sydney, but that was all. No new data came in from the SOSUS, and *Challenger* was much too far away for her to reach on the separate acoustic link.

Ilse wasn't even sure if *Challenger* had survived that raging undersea melee. Sydney's supercomputers were trying to make detailed sense out of the raw data received before the line was cut. But the navy captain in charge of the processing center said this could take hours. The Axis bomb, only a hundred yards away from Ilse and the pair of Ospreys, would go off in minutes. Shajo Clayton had already packed his gear and was sitting in the Osprey's cabin next to Ilse and Chief Montgomery.

Everyone had their gas masks ready, in case the radiation count should start to rise. But the atomic sub-on-sub battle had been a hundred miles away, and Chatham Island was safely upwind. Tactical fission

weapons, especially ones set off deep underwater, produced far less surface carcinogens and radiation than hydrogen bombs in the air. The
tritium-boosted Axis weapon about to explode at ground level was infinitely more worrisome.

Ilse saw crewmen leave the other Osprey. They used hoses and a
portable pump to transfer fuel from its tanks into Ilse's Osprey. Through
the open cabin door she asked them what was going on. "Orders."

Ilse glanced at Clayton and Montgomery. They shrugged.

After a while the pilot of Ilse's Osprey slid open the cockpit's side
window. "That's it! We're full!" The other men rolled up the hoses and
dumped them on the ground.

A large helicopter appeared from the north. It set down quickly, and
the crew from the other Osprey trotted over. The passenger compartment door popped open, and the crewmen from the Osprey climbed
inside. Through the helicopter's portholes, Ilse could see many dogs
pressing their noses to the glass. The helicopter took off. It headed
northeast, toward the very distant *Stennis*.

Ilse looked at the abandoned Osprey. "They're just leaving it here?"

"Guess so," Montgomery said. "I think we took all its fuel."

"Why didn't they come with us instead? The crew?"

"Dunno."

The crew chief told Ilse to disconnect her console. She unplugged the
coaxial cables and fiber-optic lines and handed them out the door. The
crew chief coiled them and tossed them a safe distance from the aircraft,
so they wouldn't be sucked into the engine intakes. Then he pulled out
flotation vests—life jackets—and passed them around. He showed Ilse
how to put hers on. He pointed to the tabs that would activate the
compressed-gas bottles to inflate her vest if needed.

The pilot and copilot ran through their takeoff checklists. The engines started. They warmed up, grew much noisier, and the Osprey
jumped into the air.

Using the setting sun and the island as reference points, Ilse could see
the aircraft was heading south.

"We're going the wrong way," she shouted above the engine noise.

"Orders," the crew chief said.

Ilse glanced at her watch. *This is really cutting things close.*

As the plane fought for altitude, the aircrew cycled the engine nacelles to horizontal. The engines strained powerfully and the aircraft quickly gained speed, heading away from the island as fast as it could. The crew chief handed out dark goggles.

"When I say so, keep your heads down. After the flash, count to ten before you look so you won't be blinded. The metal of our fuselage should stop most of the gamma rays. Our inside's lined with boron shielding, to absorb the neutrons."

"Is that just to make us feel better?" Montgomery asked.

The crew chief shrugged. "If you get leukemia in ten years, you'll know why."

"Terrific."

Clayton gave Ilse the leaded apron he'd worn while he studied the bomb.

"Drape it over your torso. It'll, you know, help protect your reproductive organs."

Ilse nodded. "Thanks." She did want children someday.

Ilse glanced out a porthole. The red-orange sun was touching the horizon, half masked by a solid barrier of thick, dark clouds that were bearing down on the island from the west. She realized this was the leading edge of the tropical storm from New Zealand.

She glanced outside in the other direction. By craning her neck, she could barely see Chatham Island shrinking behind them. The island was shrouded in dusk, but the yellow glare of fires was easy to see, enveloping the whole area of Owenga. There was another fire in the middle of the island, near the airstrip. Ilse could also just barely make out the flashing navigation lights of that final helicopter, far away, well past the far end of the island.

"Goggles," the crew chief shouted.

Ilse put hers on, put her head in her lap, and covered her head with her arms; the lead apron was folded between her thighs and her abdomen. She heard Chief Montgomery, his voice muffled, say, "My mother always told me it would've been safer to join the army." Clayton chuckled, and Ilse felt herself on the verge of giggling hysteria.

The aircraft went into a steep dive, and leveled out right above the water. Ilse guessed this was to put the horizon, the bulge of the earth, between them and the initial weapon burst.

"Any second now," the crew chief shouted.

The whole world turned blindingly white, despite Ilse's goggles and the shield of her arms and thighs. The suddenness of it was so shocking Ilse forgot to count to ten. The aircraft began a steep, aggressive fight to regain altitude. Ilse turned to look out the window.

Even at this distance she could feel the radiant heat. She had to squint against the glare. Light came through the aircraft portholes and cast harsh black-and-white shadows inside. She realized the internal lighting had failed from the electromagnetic pulse. At least the Osprey, with its avionics shielded, still flew.

A giant dome of mist and molecular plasma blossomed over Chatham Island. It dissipated and the broiling fireball revealed itself. Ilse could see the airborne shock wave spreading, a leading edge of moisture condensation moving at the speed of sound. The surface of the ocean roiled an angry white, foaming from the blast force that passed through the ground into the sea. The shock front moved through the water much faster than through the air. Ilse watched its expanding disk pass underneath the Osprey. Closer to the island, illuminated by the swelling fireball, a local tsunami expanded outward fast.

The unbearable heat of the initial flash and the rising fireball had done their work. The entire island was outlined in flame. The spreading landward shock wave swept up burning debris, dying sheep, telephone poles and houses, and flung everything into the air. In some places the force of the pressure wave would snuff the fires, in others they'd burn redoubled.

The fireball continued to rise and expand and cool. A pillar of black smoke and vaporized earth and rock was sucked up at its base. The suction grew stronger and stronger. Now burning cinders and flaming wreckage were drawn from all around, inward toward the pillar and up inside.

The airborne shock front reached the Osprey, and with it the first noise of the nuclear blast, like a volcano going off. The aircraft was thrown forward by the shock wave. Ilse held on as the plane shook madly. The starboard engine stalled. The shaking went on and on. The aircraft began to go down, not by choice this time. In panic Ilse yanked her life-jacket tabs. The flotation vest inflated in an instant and squeezed her chest uncomfortably.

Above the rumbling, roaring sound still coming from Chatham Island, the remaining Osprey engine grew even louder, and the engine's transmission noise became ragged and strained. But both propellers kept turning. Ilse could hear the pilot and copilot reciting a checklist to each other, shouting to be heard above everything else. The ocean was coming up fast, as the heavily loaded Osprey struggled to stay in the air. Finally the aircrew got the second engine restarted. Ilse was bathed in sweat.

One more time, she looked back to the island. The mushroom cloud was easily five miles high and rising. It tilted east because of the wind. The fireball no longer glowed, but lightning flashed at its top and inside the pillar. The pillar of smoke and debris continued getting thicker. It turned a reddish brown, like smog, from ionization effects. A purplish fluorescence lingered on the mushroom cap, from intense radiation.

The crown of the mushroom cloud kept rising, so high now it was nicely lit by the last rays of the sun from beyond the horizon; its east side hid in shadow, but its west side showed a fluffy, rosy pink. The water around the south end of the island wildly churned, as boulders and wreckage plunged out of the sky. The tiny spot of land that used to be Chatham Island was a solid sea of fire, a radioactive wasteland for centuries to come.

36

Simultaneously, on *Challenger*

IN THE CONTROL room, Jeffrey's eyes roved everywhere critically, in anticipation, making sure his ship and all aboard her were ready. By instinct and feel and long experience he assessed each crewman's state of mind, their level of energy, their spirit. Overall, he was satisfied, considering what was about to happen, and what hadn't happened yet. *The bomb, and* Voortrekker.

He quadruple-checked the speed log and the depth gauge on his console. Jeffrey had *Challenger* hovering stationary, in the deep sound channel at four thousand feet. Hovering reduced her self-noise. Using the deep-sound channel optimized the range of her passive, listening-only sonars.

Jeffrey reread the gyrocompass again: the ship was aimed to give the best coverage, tactically, to her side-mounted wide-aperture arrays. The starboard side pointed northeast toward the distant *Stennis*, just in case, and the port side faced the opposite direction, southwest—which now seemed *Voortrekker*'s most likely route of escape. Jeffrey's sonar-status repeater showed that a towed array was deployed, strung out in the gentle current—to leave no blind spots, and to search for very-low-frequency noise.

"Still no datum on *Voortrekker* anywhere, Captain," Kathy reported.

"Very well, Sonar," Jeffrey acknowledged crisply. "Maintain search. Put passive sonars on speakers."

Jeffrey listened to the noise that began to fill the control room. From all around his ship, the *Collins* boats and active sonobuoys pinged.

The sound of freedom, he told himself, those friendly active sonars sounding in the deep. *Challenger* didn't ping, to disguise her location. She did use out-of-phase noise-canceling emissions, so *Voortrekker* wouldn't by chance steal an echo off *Challenger's* hull.

Jeffrey eyed the ship's chronometer. He realized Bell and Wilson were looking at it too.

"Soon now, sir," Bell said. He didn't sound happy. Wilson was stoic, expressionless.

As the three of them watched, the chronometer's minute hand crept toward the detonation time of the Axis bomb. From a hundred miles away on Chatham Island, it would take almost two minutes for the waterborne shock wave's diminishing force to hit the ship. Sound traveled through seawater at almost a mile a second—five times as fast as through air.

Earlier than Jeffrey expected, Kathy reported a powerful seismic rumble. He'd forgotten the speed of sound was even higher through the earth than through the sea.

So the bomb didn't fizzle. Now the Axis has sent their message to the world, and escalated the stakes another notch. Jan ter Horst can claim another triumph.

The sonar chief and his men were ready for what would happen next. Jeffrey was surprised by the intensity of the noise when the waterborne shock wave hit. It began as a roar that rose to a thunderclap crescendo. The roar continued while Chatham Island was shaken by the blast, and energy from the rising fireball pounded the land and the sea. The infernal commotion died off slowly, as more shock waves rebounded off near and far bottom terrain. The ocean itself seemed to protest, when reverb echoed through clouds of tiny particles throughout the water, and as noises reflected off temperature layers and blobs and sheets and schools of fish and plankton teeming everywhere.

Kathy had already put her staff to work. After several minutes of on-board supercomputer time, she reported to Jeffrey.

"No hostile contacts on ambient sonar or hole-in-ocean mode, Captain."

"Very well." Jeffrey had used the acoustic illumination from the blast to try to locate *Voortrekker,* like one humongous sonar ping. But the enemy sub had truly vanished.

The diminishing airborne shock wave at last passed overhead, the final thing to arrive from Chatham Island. A faint rumble and strident hissing came from above on the speakers, as if from a distant storm. Jeffrey knew the geopolitical storm had only begun.

It was time to answer that call from CINCPACFLT. Jeffrey ordered Meltzer and COB to bring *Challenger* to periscope depth.

On the Osprey

The Osprey's copilot told Ilse she was wanted on the radio.

The crew chief helped her take off her life vest and gave her a fresh, uninflated one. He handed her his flight helmet, complete with headphones and throat mike. He showed her how to use the mike, and plugged the wires into a jack near her seat.

Ilse found herself in a high-level conference call. Reception was riddled with lingering static from the nuclear blast, and the voices were distorted from the hyper-encryption processes, but the other people on the call were intelligible. Commodore Wilson and Jeffrey were speaking from *Challenger.* The commander in chief of the Pacific Fleet was speaking personally from his base in Hawaii.

The purpose of the call was to try to grasp Jan ter Horst's intent. CINCPACFLT, the four-star admiral, was a gentleman about it, but he made clear to Ilse he was aware she'd once been very close to ter Horst.

Everyone reviewed what they knew: the disposition of Allied strength, forming a cordon across that entire part of the ANZA Gap; the fact that ter Horst had used four valuable nuclear torpedoes to destroy the final SOSUS line by brute force; the fact that there was no contact whatsoever with *Voortrekker* anywhere.

"Could he just be sitting somewhere nearby, on the bottom?" the admiral asked.

Jeffrey admitted it was possible, but Ilse disagreed. "Jan isn't stupid, Admiral. He knows when he's outnumbered. He knows that by just sitting there, he'd let the nuclear subs from the *Stennis* escorts close in on him more and more and work cooperatively with *Challenger*."

"So talk to me, Lieutenant Reebeck. Tell me what you think he'll do."

"He'll want to even the odds. He'll also want to sink *Challenger*."

"How will he do that?"

"I'm not sure I'm the best one to answer that, sir."

Jeffrey jumped in. "Let's look at what we know. *Challenger* and *Voortrekker* are the two fastest vessels in this theater, when running submerged at flank speed. They're also weatherproof, Admiral."

"Yes, yes. I know. A nuclear submarine can steam right under a category-five typhoon as if it isn't even there."

"Right, sir," Jeffrey said. "And no surface ship or aircraft can make that claim."

"You think he headed west, then, toward the tropical storm? But that would take him right at New Zealand, and the storm will pass through fairly soon."

"I understand, Admiral. I don't think he's heading west."

The conversation paused. Ilse sensed frustration from the others on the call.

"What about the bottom terrain?" CINCPACFLT said. The admiral mumbled something in the background. Ilse suspected he was asking his aide for a chart. Ilse asked the crew chief if they had any on the Osprey. He said the cockpit had digital navigation aids.

Ilse went into the cockpit. The aircrew were intent on their controls, and kept checking the status of all the Osprey's vital systems. It was dark except for the glow of instruments. The view outside, forward and sideways and up, was dazzling. Ilse could see countless richly colored stars, coming down to a smooth and unobstructed vast horizon. She recognized the Southern Cross, and even made out the Magellanic Clouds, a pair of small galaxies that orbit the Milky Way. The Osprey still headed south, to give Chatham Island and its fallout cloud the widest possible berth.

Ilse looked more closely inside the cockpit. She saw that all the instruments were really digital images on display screens. The artificial horizons and the gyrocompasses looked just like regular ones, but they were video pictures, not actual instrument dials.

Ilse plugged her helmet wires back in, then apologized to CINC-PACFLT for dropping off the call. She asked the copilot to bring up a nautical chart of the area. The one he had didn't show bottom terrain, so she needed to go by memory.

The admiral must have had a chart on a laptop or monitor in his office now. "I see these volcanic bottom ridges run north–south," Jeffrey concurred.

"So if he isn't just hugging the bottom till things blow over," CINC-PACFLT said, "and he isn't heading toward the tropical storm and New Zealand, and he isn't heading northeast toward *Challenger* and our other main-line forces, what *is* he doing? . . . Lieutenant Reebeck, would he just retreat toward home, South Africa? Maybe he feels he's accomplished enough, with this explosion on Chatham Island."

"No, Admiral. With respect, sir, Jan ter Horst is not someone to ever feel he's done enough."

"We were talking about *Voortrekker* trying to even the odds," Jeffrey prompted. Ilse noticed that Commodore Wilson was letting Jeffrey do all the talking on *Challenger;* Wilson seemed good at knowing when to give Jeffrey his head.

"So where can he take on your vessel one to one, Captain," the admiral asked rhetorically, "with no interference from other forces? What can he do by using his speed, and where can he go to lose my ships and aircraft?"

"There's *nowhere* he can go, Admiral," Jeffrey said. "We can hunt for him everywhere. Even without the SOSUS working, Vikings and Orions from the *Stennis* and New Zealand can blanket the area. *Voortrekker*'s crew can't live forever in hiding, sir, on just the charge she's got in her batteries and the air she's got in her tanks. Eventually they'd have to power up the reactor, run other equipment, move, make some noise. We'll hear it."

"I wish I had your confidence, Captain," the admiral said, "but I don't want to take the time pressure off ter Horst for any reason. Miss Reebeck, help us out here."

Ilse thought carefully. "Well, Jan is always one to pull something outrageous. His only weakness, if you could call it that, is he feels the constant need to outdo himself."

"Which means? . . ."

Ilse looked at the chart. *His vessel's superior speed . . . the need to avoid the surface ships and aircraft, even aircraft ten times as fast as him . . . his personal drive to meet* Challenger *head to head for a rematch. A rematch with no outside interference.*

"Oh, God," Ilse said out loud.

"Repeat, please?" the admiral said.

"I think I know where he's going."

"*Where?*" Jeffrey said.

Ilse looked at the map on the cockpit screen. What she saw was on the screen. It wasn't sea-floor terrain. It was something huge, almost five hundred miles across, up to two thousand feet thick, and on the surface.

"He'll head due south."

"Why south?" CINCPACFLT said.

"*All* the way south. Antarctica. The Ross Ice Shelf. He's going to run under the Ross Ice Shelf and wait for *Challenger* to come in after him."

On *Challenger*

CINCPACFLT told Ilse to get off the line. The admiral continued the conversation via satellite with Wilson and Jeffrey. The admiral ordered *Challenger* to head south at top speed, using the bottom ridge terrain for acoustic concealment. Aircraft would concentrate their search along the route to the south, ranging between Chatham Island and the local sea mounts at one end, and the Ross Sea leading to the ice shelf at the other. They'd try to make contact with *Voortrekker* while *Challenger* tried to catch up.

Jeffrey insisted that special rules of engagement be put in effect. Wilson concurred. Those aircraft, and any friendly ships or submarines, had to hold their fire no matter what. Dropping sonobuoys was one thing, but Jeffrey didn't want anyone dropping depth charges or shooting torpedoes and hitting *Challenger* by mistake.

The admiral agreed. All supporting forces would confine their roles to searching for the enemy only. He ended the call.

"Chief of the Watch," Jeffrey ordered, "lower all masts and antennas."

COB acknowledged and flipped some switches. "All masts and antennas retracted."

"Rig for deep submergence."

"Deep submergence, aye," COB said. He altered the lineup of pumps. The word was passed on the sound-powered phones. More men were stationed to monitor backup depth and pressure gauges. Others went aft, to engineering, to be available in an emergency.

"Helm, rig for nap-of-sea-floor cruising mode. Make your mean course one eight zero." South. "Make your depth ten thousand feet."

"Nap of sea floor, aye," Meltzer said. "Make my mean course one eight zero, aye. Make my depth ten thousand feet, aye."

Meltzer reconfigured his console displays. He pushed his control wheel forward. *Challenger* dived for the bottom.

Crewmen took deep breaths, or flexed their fingers, to try to unwind. The ship was making another excursion to test depth, after a recent nuclear battle.

"Helm," Jeffrey said, "ahead flank."

Meltzer acknowledged. *Challenger*'s speed began to mount.

The ship herself seemed to act with a feeling of purpose. At times like this, Jeffrey could most vividly tell that *Challenger* was alive, with a heart and soul as real and distinctive as any person's.

Wilson came up to Jeffrey and cleared his throat.

"Commodore?"

"I'm not questioning the logic here. CINCPACFLT agreed."

"Sir?" Wilson was visibly fretting, which was exceedingly rare for the man. He got Jeffrey worried too.

"What if we're wrong, Captain? You said it yourself. We're *Voortrekker*'s single biggest threat. . . . What if this is all a trick? Ter Horst knows now that Ilse Reebeck is alive and on the scene. What if he intentionally *used* that?"

Jeffrey was shaken. "You mean, sir, used her attempt to read his mind, and turned it against us?"

"What if he got *Challenger* to rush south on a hopeless wild-goose chase while he slips past us and heads north?"

On the Osprey

As uncomfortable as the sideways canvas bucket seat was, fatigue and the steady droning of the Osprey's engines made Ilse start to nod off. She was surprised by a tap on the shoulder. It was the crew chief.

"We got more orders. We keep going south. Next stop is the Mc-Murdo base. No midair refueling available, given the timing and the geography."

"You mean Antarctica?"

"Yeah. The west end of the ice shelf. See all this equipment from the *Stennis*?" He gestured at the reels and boxes under the cargo straps and netting. "Same gear you were using on the island. You're gonna set up on the edge of the shelf instead. Lieutenant Clayton and Chief Montgomery are supposed to help you."

"But that must be two thousand miles from here!"

The crew chief nodded. "Should take eight or nine hours."

"We have enough fuel?"

"Barely. This particular aircraft has the Osprey's extended fuel package, for long-range ferrying flights. That's why you were put on it to begin with, as a contingency plan. That's why we topped off from the other Osprey on the island."

"But *two thousand miles?*" There was no dry land along the route for them to make a forced landing if need be.

"Depends on the headwinds, Lieutenant. Keep your fingers crossed." He pointed out a porthole, at the ocean. "We run short and have to ditch, it's *really* cold and wet down there."

37

Six hours later, on *Challenger*

JEFFREY LAY ON his rack in his stateroom, trying to get some sleep. His natural inclination was to stay awake, and stay in the control room, until the final issue with *Voortrekker* was resolved. But the Ross Ice Shelf was two full days' flank speed steaming time ahead. Commodore Wilson ordered Jeffrey to rest.

Lieutenant Commander Bell had the conn. Jeffrey reminded himself his captain's stateroom was just aft of the control room, and he was only seconds away if Bell needed him. Knowing it didn't help Jeffrey relax. His born personality was to always be in the thick of things. But being captain meant you had to delegate, come what may. Jeffrey tossed and turned.

His mind ran back to his skirmish with *Voortrekker*. The engagement so far was a seesaw battle of deadly guessing and counterguessing: Jeffrey used the sinkhole, but ter Horst figured it out. Ter Horst then hid behind the first sea mount, but Jeffrey knew it. Jeffrey launched torpedoes around both sides of the sea mount, but *Voortrekker,* with her better rate of fire and her sophisticated noisemakers, escaped. Ter Horst nuked the last part of the SOSUS, then disappeared.

To himself, Jeffrey had to admit that so far ter Horst was winning. The next time they met, there might not be a sea mount for Jeffrey to hide behind and play tricks. If *Voortrekker* reached the Ross Ice Shelf and Jeffrey had to go underneath it after him, with no possible means of support . . .

Jeffrey's mind wandered to his conversation with his father at the Pentagon. *Dad, you were right. Being a war hero is something no one in their right mind should ever want to be by choice. The chances of failure are much too great. The responsibilities are almost crushing. The constant brushes with death, even if you do survive, leave permanent scars on the soul.*

A messenger knocked on the door. Jeffrey, fully dressed, got up gratefully.

"Sir, Sonar heard another message buoy. They want us on the radio, smartly."

Jeffrey went to the control room. Even though Bell had the conn, only the captain had authority to expose the ship by raising a mast at periscope depth. Jeffrey took the conn and gave the orders.

CINCPACFLT was on the line again. He told Jeffrey and Commodore Wilson that the Axis bomb blast was already having serious negative diplomatic repercussions around the world. Rather than be angered by the destruction of Chatham Island, Asian neutrals were being self-protective realists. Pragmatically, they saw the big mushroom cloud, so soon after the New York raid and Diego Garcia, as exactly what it was meant to be: a sign aimed in their direction of the Berlin-Boer Axis's unstoppable momentum. Jeffrey was stunned to hear from the admiral that National Security Agency intercepts indicated Thailand—a supposed good friend of America—had decided to join the Axis if *Voortrekker* reached the Pacific and began to run amok.

Then came a much greater shock. Japan might have made the same eavesdropping intercept about Thai intentions, because the Japanese government formally announced to the world that they were a nuclear power. Tokyo owned homegrown tactical atomic weapons, and would use them in self-defense against any threat from any quarter. To prove it, they set off an underwater blast well east of Hokkaido. Long-standing international nonproliferation treaties had been shattered, but Tokyo offered no apologies.

Jeffrey saw that the Pacific Rim was fast becoming destabilized. CINCPACFLT said that the president of the United States was meeting with the cabinet and the Joint Chiefs in an emergency session right now. CINCPACFLT hinted that desperate measures were being discussed. When Jeffrey asked what he meant, the admiral darkly hinted it might be time to think the unthinkable, like back in the worst days of the Cold War—but he couldn't or wouldn't give specifics.

He was interrupted by his aide, then he came back on the line. The admiral said both Russia and China had harshly denounced the Japanese, and were putting their nuclear forces on a heightened state of alert.

Jeffrey knew now the situation was getting out of control. CINCPACFLT must be under enormous pressure from Washington to show a positive result, to sink *Voortrekker* once and for all as a way to get things calmed down. The admiral passed that pressure on to Jeffrey and Wilson. The admiral reminded them, coldly, that *Challenger* was expendable in a one-for-one exchange, if that's what it took to destroy ter Horst.

The admiral needed to put the conversation on hold to take another urgent call. It lasted for some time. During the pause, Jeffrey mulled over everything he and Wilson had just been told—it was a lot to absorb.

Jeffrey, a keen student of military history all his life, began to have a vision of the world on the brink, not just like in the Cold War, but more like in World War I: Both sides throwing more and more force into what was supposed to have been a short and simple fight. Both sides increasingly appalled by their own horrific losses, yet driven by noble emotions—or by blindness and stupidity—to fight even harder and pay an ever-mounting price in blood. Nations not involved at first being asked or pressured to choose sides. The fog of war, the onrush of snowballing events, the lack of adequate time to think through crucial decisions of awful weightiness—the need for far more wisdom than any man or woman might ever hope to have in real life—could lead to Armageddon.

Still the admiral was on his other call. While Jeffrey waited, he reminded himself that ongoing tactical atomic war at sea, without escalation to a thermonuclear exchange, had been a standard doctrine for the Soviet Union in the bad old days, and was also espoused in the early Cold War by the French. Many American experts, in the twentieth century, had argued for its practicability too. This was exactly the approach the Berlin-Boer Axis had been taking. But was everything coming unglued?

The admiral was back on the line; he said that other conversation was classified.

Almost at once, the aide interrupted the admiral again. The admiral said an Orion from New Zealand heard something on a sonobuoy. The admiral wanted Jeffrey to speak directly to the aircrew. They were quickly patched into the call.

The Orion's pilot said they were near the edge of the Bounty Platform. Jeffrey knew this was a shallow plateau, south of the Bounty Trough, which plunged abruptly to thirteen thousand feet. The edge of the Bounty Platform was ideal terrain in which *Voortrekker* could try to stay concealed if she was heading toward Antarctica.

The admiral ordered Jeffrey to proceed there immediately—two hours' flank-speed steaming time to the west-southwest. Commodore Wilson objected that it might be a false alarm, drawing *Challenger* out of position.

"What's that?" came over the radio from someone on the Orion.

"*Missile launch!*" another voice yelled. "Two, three, I see four!"

"Where? *Where?*" the pilot shouted; Jeffrey heard a rising whining roar, picked up by the aircraft's cockpit microphones, as its four engines strained to maximum power.

"From underwater! Closing fast in our five o'clock! Break left!"

"I can't see them! *Where are they!*"

"Break left! Left! Left! Harder! Left!"

"Chaff! Flares! Launch infrared flares!"

"Left! Left! Left! *Left!*"

"*Jesus!*"

There was the sound of an explosion. All contact with the Orion was lost.

Jeffrey felt like a corkscrew was twisting up his spine. "That has to be him. Polyphem antiaircraft missiles, launched in sets of four through a torpedo tube."

"Concur," CINCPACFLT said. "There's your datum, Captain. Get off the line and get over there and sink the SOB."

"Sir, I will, but I want to make a request."

"Be quick."

"We need more firepower, Admiral. I want support from other Orion aircraft. And I want the rules of engagement changed. If their sonobuoys detect two submarines in chase, they should assume the one in front is *Voortrekker,* and drop their weapons. Also, if I launch a radio buoy asking for torpedoes with such-and-such a firing solution, I want the Orions to drop."

The admiral hesitated only a moment. He said something to his aide. The aide responded. There was a pause. The admiral came back. "Approved, Captain, though there'll be some delay to get more Orions on station." He gave Jeffrey a time reference, and a rendezvous point for the planes. "We'll take care of the aircraft ROEs from here. . . . Now good luck to you. Dive and get the hell over there."

Jeffrey gave helm orders. *Challenger* drove to the bottom crevasses and resumed flank speed.

The only saving grace in this is that we're expendable, and Voortrekker *isn't to the Axis, so I can take the greater risks.*

Commodore Wilson was clearly unhappy about the tactical picture. Jeffrey knew he knew CINCPACFLT was a naval aviator by background, not a submariner. He had advisors who wore gold dolphins, but even so he'd see things differently than Jeffrey and Wilson would.

"Why did ter Horst shoot down that airplane?" Wilson said.

"It held sonar contact on him," Jeffrey said.

"Why was it even *able* to make sonar contact? At such depth, in such broken volcanic terrain, with *Voortrekker* so stealthy?"

"Luck?"

Wilson shook his head.

"You mean he *wanted* to be found?"

"He showed us where he is, for sure. He's saying, Come and get me.

He knew that using those missiles, the Orion would have time to make a radio report. He could have simply blown it out of the sky in an instant, with a nuclear torpedo underneath, like he did to the *Reagan*'s jets at Diego Garcia. But he didn't. He used slow missiles. *Why?*"

"But the blast from a torpedo would have given his location just as well, maybe better. Louder."

"No. We might have all thought the Orion set off its own weapon by mistake. Misread the ROEs, maybe, and dropped on a false contact, say a large biologic, then got knocked down in the blast. This way, ter Horst left no doubt whatsoever. He taunted us."

Jeffrey saw Wilson's point. "He's laying a trap again. He sits still, on ground of his own choosing. We go charging once more into the breach, and get it on the chin."

38

On the Osprey

ILSE WOKE UP in dim red lighting, very stiff and sore. The solid whining drone of the aircraft's engines, the steady vibrations they made in the fuselage bulkhead and mesh seat and deck, were reassuring. In the back of Ilse's mind was still the fear of crashing into the sea.

She looked at her watch: a few more hours to go to reach Antarctica. Outside the nearest porthole was only darkness. It was the middle of the night, Chatham Island time. Clayton and Montgomery were sleeping, but Ilse felt wide awake. The crew chief also was awake. He and Ilse shared coffee from a thermos and ate cold rations right from the khaki plastic packages.

Which meal is this? Breakfast? Dinner? From her wide-ranging travels through latitude and longitude, from north to south and east to west, on airplanes and in submarines, she was horribly jet-lagged.

When they finished eating, the crew chief collected the trash.

Ilse was troubled by something. She whispered so as not to awaken Clayton and Montgomery. "Chief, I know it's not for me to say, but there's an international treaty that officially demilitarized all of Antarctica. The U.S. and a bunch of other countries signed it. Aren't we violating that?"

"Lieutenant, ma'am, the Axis has broken treaties left and right."

"But that doesn't mean we should do it too."

"Of course not." The chief touched the side of his nose. "You're an oceanographer, right? We're on an oceanographic research expedition. Nothing illegal in that."

"But you—I mean we—we're carrying weapons." Pistols and M-16s.

The chief touched his nose again. "That's just for self-defense. You know, like if we're attacked by polar bears."

"You know as well as I do there aren't polar bears at the south pole. And I hardly think we'd be mauled by a pack of mutant killer penguins."

The chief shrugged. "The minute that Axis sub you're after crosses the sixtieth parallel south, they violate the treaty outright. After that, all bets are off. Till then, you're just a scientist, and we're just driving the bus."

Ilse was very unhappy. She did *not* like the idea of personally defiling one of the last truly pristine places on the planet. To bring war down here, to the bottom of the world, was an appalling thought, even if she could tell herself that *Voortrekker* was the reason, the cause, the excuse.

The crew chief read her mind. "Cheer up, Lieutenant. Want to see something you don't see every day?"

"Sure. I guess. Okay."

She followed the crew chief into the cockpit. She looked out through the front windscreen. The sun was coming up, or so it seemed. The horizon was a beautiful violet-pink. The only problem was, sunrise was directly ahead of the plane, and the plane was heading *south,* and sunrise always came from the east. The eastern horizon was *dark.*

"Antarctic summer," the pilot said. "Pardon the contradiction in terms." He smiled. "The land of the midnight sun. The more south we get now, the higher the sun will be in the sky. At McMurdo, this time of year, the sun never sets, you know, all twenty-four hours."

Ilse nodded. It was one thing to understand the theory, but quite another to be observing it firsthand, especially in the middle of a war.

"Want to see something else really cool?" the pilot said. "Again, pardon my pun. Look down at the water."

"I can't see anything. It's still pitch-dark."

The pilot flicked a switch. One of the cockpit displays showed a video image looking down at the ocean. "Low-light-level television. The camera's in the nose."

Ilse studied the picture. "Those are all icebergs?"

"It's the consolidated pack-ice barrier. Warmer weather, icebergs calve off the edge of the shelves. Sometimes the sea itself will freeze, then break up from wave action in a storm. That's where the flat stuff comes from."

Ilse saw an almost solid mass of pieces of ice, stretching ahead of the plane. Some were large and very flat, others were iceberg pinnacles the size of houses or small mountains, and some were innumerable jagged fragments pushed and piled together. As she watched, Ilse could see everything was in constant motion up and down from the sea swells. Some icebergs tumbled end over end, because their irregular shapes made them unstable. The view on the display shifted constantly; the plane was moving fast. Ilse peeked at the pilot's air-speed indicator. They were doing 275 knots. After a few minutes the ice fragments petered out, and the water was mostly open.

"What happened?"

"The inner edge of the barrier. The wind and currents tend to push the smaller icebergs north, away from the Antarctic coast. You get this giant ring around the whole continent. That's the summer pack-ice barrier."

The pilot turned a knob. "Now it's passive infrared." He made the camera look down and backward.

Ilse could see the ice and the water were very cold, but the infrared imagery was sensitive enough that she could see slight differences between the temperature of the water and the ice. Parts of the larger icebergs were also slightly warmer, where they'd caught the sun during the previous daylight hours at this latitude.

"Pretty amazing," Ilse said.

"That's nothing. Wait till you get to McMurdo, and on from there."

On *Challenger*

After the conversation with CINCPACFLT, and then the discussion with Wilson, Jeffrey was faced once again with the quandary common in undersea warfare: how to get from A to B quietly but quickly. It was always made much harder when the enemy could be waiting for you somewhere along the route.

Wilson went to his stateroom—whether to work or rest he didn't say.

Bell and Jeffrey looked at each other. Sometimes it almost seemed to Jeffrey the two of them communicated telepathically.

"Sprint and drift, Captain?" Bell said.

Jeffrey nodded. "Sprint and drift. You have the conn. Send a messenger for me in ninety minutes . . . sooner, of course, if anything untoward happens."

"This is the XO," Bell announced. "I have the conn."

"Aye aye," the watch-standers responded.

Jeffrey went to his stateroom. He didn't bother turning off the lights, and lay down on his rack, above the covers, fully dressed. He put an arm across his eyes to keep out the light. He needed to rest, and to think. At times like this he gave thanks for his position as captain. On a nuclear submarine, only the captain slept in privacy.

Jeffrey felt *Challenger* pick up to flank speed. After a few minutes of this, the ship slowed to bare steerageway. Jeffrey knew Kathy's people would be searching all around for any sign of *Voortrekker* or other threats. Then the ship sped up again. Jeffrey pictured Bell giving commands and Meltzer reacting. He pictured everyone back in Engineering, responding to each new engine order. Jeffrey pictured the sonarmen, working their equipment hard every time the ship stopped.

This was sprint and drift in action: a burst of speed to cover some distance, then a halt just long enough to listen for new sonar contacts without distracting self-noise—and if nothing dangerous was detected, then another burst of speed.

Jeffrey felt the ship slow down again for the next thorough sonar search. It would take some time to reach their destination, the edge of the Bounty Platform where the Orion had been shot down. Jeffrey wondered if anyone had survived; he hoped a combat search-and-rescue operation was under way.

Challenger sped up. Jeffrey realized he wouldn't get any sleep like this. He let his mind wander, to the bigger situation. Regrettably, as captain, there were things he couldn't discuss with others, even with his XO.

From what CINCPACFLT said or implied, Allied diplomacy was failing in many foreign capitals, and people might be losing their cool in Washington as well. Thanks to the Axis upping the ante of aggression to a new level, premeditated opportunism and selfish greed—or simple hysteria—were gripping Asia and much of the rest of the world. Orders had come from the top: Sink *Voortrekker* at all costs. Ter Horst and his ship now were symbols, and a symbol—by working in the realm of human ideas—could have more crucial influence than any person or weapon system.

It seemed sadly ironic to Jeffrey that, though it was the Berlin-Boer Axis that had obliterated innocent Chatham Island, many neutrals saw this not as something abhorrent but as a sign of Axis strength.

Jeffrey sighed. Ironic, yes, he told himself, but it was all too consistent with long-term history, armed and economic conflict between nations. The myth that big wars were over forever had been exactly that: a dangerous myth. Promises between embassies sometimes melted away under stress. International coalitions came and went like the tides, or shifted treacherously like sandbars in a hurricane. A country might act like your friend in one confrontation or crisis, and then become an obstruction, or your mortal enemy, in the next.

At last the messenger knocked. Jeffrey walked to the control room. He studied the navigation plot and the sonar data, then took the conn.

As *Challenger* drew closer to the position where the Orion had gone down, Jeffrey altered his tactics.

"Helm, ahead two-thirds, make turns for twenty knots. Right ten degrees rudder, make your course two seven zero." Due west.

Meltzer acknowledged. A steady twenty knots would keep the ship on the move but allow good sonar sensitivity—and stealth.

"New passive sonar contacts," Kathy said a few minutes later. "Aircraft-engine noises, approaching from northeast and northwest."

"Very well, Sonar. . . . Messenger of the Watch, request the commodore in Control." Wilson was there in seconds.

The aircraft flew overhead. Three passive sonobuoys dropped nearby, evenly spaced so their water impacts signaled "dot dot dot," the Morse code letter *S*, for submarine. The planes were clandestinely saying hello.

"Friendly aircraft are two Orions and two Vikings," Kathy announced.

"Release the radio buoy," Jeffrey ordered. The buoy was programmed with a recognition password, plus instructions for the planes. *Challenger* had completed her quiet, prearranged link-up with the supporting aircraft.

The planes began to scour the area with their sensors. They used a wide variety of search patterns, from racetrack-shaped oval orbits to S-curve back-and-forth sweeps to ladderlike snaking zigzags.

They were acting outwardly as if *Challenger* weren't there. But in each aircraft's flight plan was an overall course to match *Challenger*'s, and an underlying trend beneath their other maneuvers to move westward at twenty knots—matching *Challenger*'s tactical speed.

This way, with *Challenger*'s four working tubes augmented by airdropped torpedoes on several long-endurance antisubmarine planes, *Voortrekker* could be killed by overwhelming pulses of atomic firepower.

Jeffrey felt slightly disappointed. He had hoped for better than four planes. This meant he needed to plan ahead more cautiously than he'd wanted to.

Between them, the Orions and Vikings would have twelve fish, though they couldn't drop them all at once or the weapons, lacking guidance wires, would interfere with each other. If each plane dropped *half* its torpedoes in a salvo, and *Challenger* fired all her tubes, then Jeffrey's ship and the planes could between them shoot ten torpedoes—six plus four—compared to *Voortrekker*'s eight. This was the advantage Jeffrey wanted, but with just a dozen fish on the planes, he could only count on *two* such ten-versus-eight salvo exchanges. Those two salvoes had better really smash home, because after them the planes would be out of ammo and *Challenger* would once more be outgunned.

Time passed as *Challenger* moved west. Kathy's people, and the aircraft, searched the entire location where that Orion had been shot down. There were no signs of survivors, or of *Voortrekker*.

The search went on. Jeffrey's whole world contracted to the control room—to this dimly lit space enclosed on all sides by hard metal walls and hard deck, hemmed in by the low metal overhead heavy with stark-naked pipes and purposeful rivers of wires. This box within *Challenger*'s hull, this constricted compartment stuffed with people and electronic gear, became Jeffrey's entire universe.

A frustrating two hours later Bell said, "We've been all over the area, Captain. Nothing."

"Why hasn't ter Horst attacked?" Wilson said.

"I don't know," Jeffrey said.

"He has to be aware we're here by now. He can hear the aircraft circling just as well as we can."

Jeffrey nodded. "Maybe he hears them, Commodore, but doesn't know *we've* arrived, or he thinks we aren't coming."

"Sir," Bell said, "we could do two things at once if we ping. Be absolutely sure the whole world knows where we are, and maybe have a better chance of picking him up on active search."

"Commodore?" Jeffrey asked.

"I concur."

Pinging here was very dangerous for *Challenger*. But Jeffrey simply needed to take the chance. The Orions and Vikings were useless if they had nothing to shoot at, and *Voortrekker*, one way or another, had to be found.

"Sonar," Jeffrey ordered, "go active."

Kathy acknowledged crisply. The rest of the crew seemed eager more than nervous, as if they wanted to just get on with the fight and get it *done*.

Jeffrey was pleased. He'd noticed that—since explaining to the crew about CINCPACFLT's orders that, in extremis, they were expendable in an even exchange with the Boer sub—they'd all become a bit cocky, and morale had risen a notch. It was as if CINCPACFLT had made everyone on *Challenger* feel very special and needed.

Good. Courage—like fear—is contagious. Let my people sense my own eagerness to conclude this grudge match with ter Horst. Let that feistiness, this desire for a hard scrap with the enemy, make the rounds of my ship and infect everybody aboard.

The bow sphere emitted a deafening high-pitched screech. The sonarmen worked their consoles.

"No new contacts," Kathy reported.

Jeffrey held his breath. That ping would have given *Voortrekker* a foolproof firing solution on *Challenger,* wherever ter Horst was hiding. Everyone waited and waited. There were no enemy torpedoes in the water.

"Sonar, go active again. Use low frequency."

Again the bow sphere pinged, a deep and powerful rumble that made everything in the control room shake. Time passed. Nothing.

"He's not here," Wilson eventually stated, carefully expressionless.

Crap. Jeffrey realized now that *Voortrekker* shooting down the Orion had been another of ter Horst's tricks. CINCPACFLT, Wilson, Jeffrey, Bell, all of them had fallen for it.

Jeffrey and Bell made eye contact, and again they seemed to read each other's minds:

We were *supposed* to think the shoot-down was a lure for *Challenger.* We were *supposed* to think *Voortrekker* was running south and baiting us. We were *supposed* to rush this way.

All the while, *Voortrekker* was sneaking back northeast, with her nuclear torpedoes and her Kampfschwimmer team and her supersonic antiship cruise missiles. Toward the USS *John C. Stennis.* Toward the vulnerable U.S. Navy bases in Hawaii and San Diego and Guam. Toward America's vital shipping lanes to the whole Pacific Rim. And toward more pseudo-neutral clandestine tender ships, with lots more torpedoes and missiles, not to mention naval mines.

"God damn it," Jeffrey said out loud.

39

WILSON HAD JEFFREY launch another message buoy. It sent a warning to the *Stennis*. It told the Vikings and Orions to depart and try to close the gap left in the anti-*Voortrekker* cordon near the line of sea mounts where the *Collins* boat had gone down—and where *Challenger* had left unguarded her former hiding place in the sinkhole. Kathy reported as the aircraft-engine noises receded into the distance.

"Helm," Jeffrey ordered, "make your course zero six zero." East-northeast. "Ahead flank." Meltzer acknowledged.

Challenger accelerated. The shaking that always occurred at flank speed began again. Mike cords and light fixtures on the overhead jiggled. Consoles squeaked gently in their shock-absorbing mounts. Crewmen gulped down mugs of coffee so they wouldn't splash.

Jeffrey knew the crew around him felt glum. Jan ter Horst had outwitted them again. To himself, Jeffrey had visions of *Voortrekker* running rampant, sinking carriers and tankers and troopships right and left. Nuking Pearl Harbor. Sending Kampfschwimmer to commit more atrocities in San Francisco and Los Angeles. Allied forces would be drawn to protect the U.S. homeland's western front, away from the Battle of the Atlantic, forces badly needed there to keep Great Britain in the war.

"Captain," Kathy said, "request alter course thirty degrees to starboard and reduce speed. We have an anomalous reading on the starboard wide aperture array."

Jeffrey perked up. *Could it be we've found ter Horst after all?* "Helm, make your course zero nine zero. Slow to ahead one-third."

Challenger turned; Meltzer's rudder application helped the ship slow down.

Kathy jolted. "*Torpedoes in the water!* Bearing two five zero, range ten thousand yards, *four torpedoes closing!*" Five miles distant, west-southwest.

"Did an aircraft drop by mistake?" Wilson said.

"Negative! Definite Sea Lion torpedo-engine noises!"

As one, the crew were alarmed and electrified by the news.

"Helm," Jeffrey ordered, "ahead flank. Make a knuckle. Make your course zero three zero." Jeffrey would run from the inbound weapons at an angle, to force their seeker heads to lead the target.

"Captain," Bell said, "inbound weapons were well dispersed when first detected. Assess weapons were swum out by *Voortrekker* at torpedo stealth speed several minutes ago."

Meltzer jerked his rudder wheel back and forth, to make the distracting knuckle in *Challenger's* wake. Jeffrey felt the ship bank hard to port and then to starboard. She leveled off. "Steady on zero three zero, sir."

Jeffrey's heart was racing now. "Fire control, launch noisemakers and jammers." Bell acknowledged.

"He was here the whole time," Wilson said dryly. "He was waiting for us to second-guess ourselves and send the aircraft away."

"We need to call them back."

"Do it."

Jeffrey ordered Bell to send off a message buoy, but this would take precious time. *Well, I got my wish.* Voortrekker *launched an attack.*

I should have known that sending the aircraft away would make us vulnerable. . . . Did my unconscious mind want *this to happen?*

I can't wait for the planes to return. I've got to retake the initiative.

Jeffrey stood up, and rocked on the balls of his feet from excitement. With his left hand he gripped a stanchion on the overhead. With his right he pointed to Bell.

"Fire Control, range to incoming torpedoes?"

"Range now eight thousand yards. Closing by one thousand yards per minute."

And when they reach four thousand yards—in only four minutes—those one-kiloton warheads will be in lethal range.

Jeffrey had to do something in self-defense.

"Fire Control, tubes one, three, five, and seven. Snap shots, target the incoming torpedoes."

"Four tubes fired electrically!"

"Reload, more Eighty-eights!"

"Captain," Kathy said, "friendly aircraft are returning."

But the message buoy wasn't ready yet.

They must have heard the ruckus over their radio link to the sonobuoys. . . . Of course, I knew they would. I think I planned this all along, without even knowing it—luring Voortrekker *into the open by sending the planes away, and having the planes come back on their own when ter Horst did break cover.*

But Jeffrey's satisfaction with himself evaporated fast. *Voortrekker* could surely hear *Challenger*'s noises as Jeffrey's ship made flank speed to evade the incoming Sea Lions. Ter Horst would pursue to close the range, to make Jeffrey's counterfire less effective.

We're in a chase with Voortrekker, *and we're the leading ship. I told the Orions and Vikings to attack the leading ship. . . .*

Ter Horst is a fucking genius. He figured out my rules of engagement. He's turned our own planes against me.

"Helm, hard left rudder! Make your course two five zero."

Challenger banked violently to port. Meltzer fought to hold her nose up and avoid a snap roll. The ship lost speed from the turn, then accelerated again toward fifty-plus knots.

"All tubes reloaded!" Bell called. They armed the warheads.

Something else tickled the back of Jeffrey's mind. *Why did ter Horst fire only four torpedoes? When's the next group coming?*

The initiative. You must *take back the initiative, any way you can.* Half blind at flank speed, Jeffrey still had no detection on *Voortrekker* herself.

"Sonar, go active, high frequency."

There was a deafening screech from the bow sphere.

"New active sonar contact!" Kathy yelled. "Designate the contact Master One. Contact depth and speed confirm it's *Voortrekker!*"

Voortrekker must have been hiding in a fold in the bottom terrain. Now she was coming at *Challenger,* just as Jeffrey had guessed. Kathy relayed the data to Bell. Bell worked out a firing solution.

Suddenly there were four atomic blasts in the distance. Kathy said they were Sea Lion warheads, going off on the surface. Jeffrey realized ter Horst had made a big electromagnetic pulse in order to jam the Orions' and Vikings' reception from sonobuoys or radio buoys. Now Jeffrey was out of touch and couldn't change the ROEs.

"Fire Control," Jeffrey ordered. "Make tubes one, three, five, and seven ready in all respects including opening outer doors. Firing point procedures, all tubes at five-second intervals. On Master One, match sonar bearings and *shoot!*"

"Four tubes fired electrically!"

"All units running normally."

"Spread the weapons out under wire-guided control. Keep them well away from our units intercepting the inbound Sea Lions. Reload!"

Bell acknowledged. Jeffrey had never before expended atomic torpedoes at such a prodigious rate. Given his orders and the tactical picture he had no choice. Jeffrey could easily lose this fight.

The double-edged swords of those aircraft were drawing nearer.

"Fire Control, Navigator, work up an intercept course on Master One, smartly."

Bell and Sessions did. Jeffrey gave the helm orders. *Challenger* banked into another turn and charged at *Voortrekker,* following in the wake of Jeffrey's torpedoes.

"What are you doing?" Wilson said.

"Forcing *Voortrekker* to run. I'll ram him if I have to."

On *Voortrekker*

Gunther Van Gelder listened on the sonar speakers, and studied his tactical plot. His ears still rang from *Challenger*'s latest ping.

"Aspect change on enemy contact," the sonar chief reported. "Enemy turning rapidly to port."

"He's coming back at us," ter Horst said. "Good. Helm, steer one eight zero." South, away from *Challenger*. "Flank speed ahead."

Voortrekker was struck by four vicious thunderclaps, none of them far off. The sonar speakers cut their volume automatically, but even so the ocean roared, and everything in the control room shook. Van Gelder's skeleton rattled inside his body, and his head rang like a bell. He forced himself to concentrate, to eye his weapons-status screen. "Our four torpedoes aimed at *Challenger* all intercepted and destroyed!"

"Four more torpedoes in the water," the sonar chief yelled above the noise. "American Mark 88s, constant bearing, closing fast!"

"Number One, launch counterfire."

Van Gelder fired a Sea Lion at each of the inbound Mark 88s. The weapons dashed from the tubes, and turned, and ran back at the pursuing enemy weapons. The tubes were empty now.

"Reload," ter Horst ordered. "Snap shots, all eight tubes, target is *Challenger*, maximum yield." Ter Horst and Van Gelder rushed to arm the warheads.

"Shoot!"

"All tubes fired."

"Units are operating properly," the sonar chief reported. Then, "Aircraft signatures. Multiple inbound aircraft."

"Aircraft type?" Van Gelder demanded.

"Multiple types. Twin turbofans . . . and quadruple props."

"Vikings and Orions, Captain. They're back, as you predicted."

On *Challenger,* minutes later

Jeffrey was impressed by the pilot commanding the foursome of friendly aircraft. In smooth coordination, they used their superior speed to fly wide of the surface mushroom clouds, then dropped more sonobuoys on the far side of ter Horst's low-altitude electromagnetic pulse.

Jeffrey watched impatiently, on tenterhooks, as Kathy's people tracked the planes' maneuvers and Bell's men updated the tactical plot—as best as they could through the harsh acoustic sea state of kiloton-class detonations. *Challenger* had very advanced signal processors, which to some degree could cut through the disturbances of a nuclear blast—the algorithms focused the hydrophones tightly in one direction, and tuned out all but selected sound frequencies, to ignore distracting noise from somewhere else.

Soon, the Orions and Vikings flew past *Challenger* along her port and starboard sides. Ahead of the ship, they launched their first salvo of Mark 54 lightweight atomic fish. As the weapons descended on parachutes, the pilots turned away hard.

Jeffrey knew the aircraft crews would be wearing uncomfortable protective suits. The planes would try to avoid the fallout plumes from the Sea Lions and Mark 88s that had already gone off on the surface or deep in the sea. Now, the Vikings and Orions fought for distance from the impending effects of their Mark 54s.

Jeffrey heard a *smack* on the sonar speakers as each of the six Mark 54 torpedoes hit the water. Then he heard their engine sounds above the noise of other torpedoes and countermeasures and roaring nuclear bubble clouds. He heard the *plops* as more sonobuoys rained down. Some began to ping, and others were passive, but their capabilities compared to *Challenger*'s were limited—and ter Horst could always try to create more electromagnetic jamming. At best, this engagement would be total, violent chaos, and there was now a real risk that *Challenger* could be sunk by a Mark 54.

The 54s began to ping. Kathy and Bell reported *Voortrekker* turning from south to west, to jink out of the air-dropped torpedoes' active sonar search cones. Jeffrey had no choice but to follow. He ordered Bell to fire four more Mark 88s at Master One on her new course. Ter Horst was hugging the bottom, at fifteen thousand feet, to exploit every possible layer of temperature and salinity and biologics to separate *Voortrekker* from the Allied planes. Jeffrey told Bell to run his Mark 88s a thousand feet above the sea floor.

"We have to force ter Horst to stay deep. If he can get shallow enough, he'll launch antiaircraft missiles."

"Understood," Bell said.

Jeffrey and Bell ran through their litany of arming procedures and firing commands. Four Mark 88s dashed through the sea. Now ten atomic torpedoes all together were chasing *Voortrekker,* or trying to. Some of the air-dropped Mark 54s lost their target when *Voortrekker* turned. Ter Horst launched another salvo of counterfire, escalating the contest another notch.

Some of the Allied torpedoes homed in on each other in the confusion, and blew. Then *Voortrekker's* counterfire torpedoes began to detonate. The ocean was ripped apart by a solid wall of underwater shock waves and unbearable noise. Million-degree pulsating fireballs plunged for the surface. A local part of the ocean entered a state of searing disruption, never seen in nature short of impact by an asteroid.

Challenger was battered by the shock forces. Several control-room consoles failed, and intercom circuits stopped working. The phone talker relayed damage reports from elsewhere in the ship: A handful of crewmen had suffered concussions or broken bones. One balky auxiliary turbogenerator had to be shut down. Cooling-water pipes had broken. Other equipment had ceased to function.

But *Challenger* kept fighting. Now she was chasing *Voortrekker* due west. Outside *Challenger's* hull—which suddenly seemed very fragile amid this mounting hellish maelstrom—sonar conditions were so poor that Jeffrey was beginning to lose situational awareness. He fought to keep straight in his head the ever-shifting geometries of the battle, and to predict what his opponent, ter Horst, would do next.

On *Voortrekker*

Voortrekker rocked and fishtailed from the force of her own exploding warheads back behind the stern. The disturbances of the blasts

formed a hydrographic nightmare separating her—and her sensors—
from *Challenger*.

"Captain," Van Gelder warned when the noise was no longer too loud
for him to be heard, "navigator and gravimeter both indicate escarpment wall of the Bounty Platform lies dead ahead on this course."

Ter Horst smiled. "Don't you think I see it too?"

On *Challenger*

Jeffrey held on tight to his armrests as *Challenger* charged half blind
through the churning, roiling water of the most recent nuclear blasts.
Many atomic torpedoes had gone off by now, yet so far not one weapon
had succeeded in reaching killing range of either sub.

With the ocean around them so distressed, Jeffrey ordered Meltzer to
take the ship a few thousand feet shallower, to avoid a bottom collision.
Even so, COB constantly needed to juggle variable ballast, as local buoyancy varied from the heat and the trillions of tiny collapsing pockets of
high-pressure vapor. Radioactive seawater rushed through *Challenger*'s
main condensor cooling loops, but those loops were self-contained and
shielded, and the polluted water went right back out of the ship.

Jeffrey had no idea what he would find on the other side of the blast
zones. But now that he'd made contact with *Voortrekker*, he couldn't afford to be cautious and let her get away.

Once through the cauldron of tortured water, the first thing Kathy's
people heard was a Sea Lion coming right at them. Jeffrey ordered a defensive snap shot. Bell intercepted the weapon just in time. The detonation punched *Challenger* in the nose. She twisted and squirmed as she
thrust through the latest blast zone. Meltzer worked the bowplanes and
sternplanes aggressively to keep the ship under control.

Once on the other side, Kathy reported *three* sonar contacts, all
sounding like *Voortrekker* running away at flank speed.

"He launched two decoys," Wilson said.

"Sonar, ping, high frequency."

The bow sphere screeched. The echoes came back. The sonarmen went to work—decoys were launched from torpedo tubes; they were much smaller than *Voortrekker* herself. *Challenger*'s signal processors would know the difference, even in these conditions.

"Leftmost contact is the true one," Kathy reported.

Jeffrey ordered Meltzer to alter course, fifteen degrees to port, to keep up with *Voortrekker*.

"Captain," Kathy said, "aircraft returning for a reattack."

Jeffrey hoped they didn't attack the wrong ship.

"All tubes reloaded," Bell said.

"Sir!" Kathy said. "Contact with *Voortrekker* lost! Last detected in close proximity to the Bounty Platform escarpment wall!"

"Did he collide with it?" Jeffrey demanded.

"Negative, sir. We heard both decoys hit the wall, but no datum on *Voortrekker*."

"What's he doing *now*?" Wilson said.

On *Voortrekker*

"All stop," ter Horst ordered.

The helmsman acknowledged.

"Back full until we lose headway."

It took a little while for *Voortrekker* to shed her forward momentum. She came to a halt.

"Chief of the Watch, rise on auto-hover using variable ballast only, maximum rate of ascent. Helm, hug the escarpment wall using auxiliary propulsors only."

The ship began to ascend on an even keel, quickly but very quietly. Van Gelder watched the gravimeter. The whole wall rose straight up, from five thousand meters deep to only two thousand—a solid wall of rock three kilometers high. Van Gelder saw that this particular portion of the wall was topped by a sea mount whose peak was even shallower, only six hundred meters deep beneath the surface. Now Van Gelder understood why ter Horst had ordered *Voortrekker* to turn this way when the two flank-speed decoys were launched.

The sonar chief reported the enemy aircraft were closing in to drop more weapons. Everyone in the control room heard *Challenger* ping once more.

Ter Horst looked at Van Gelder and laughed. "You see, Gunther? Each time, I think several moves ahead of Fuller. He's trying to find us against the escarpment wall. But we're so silent since we stopped the propulsor shaft, he can't hear us. Since we're moving up like an elevator, perpendicular to his bow sphere's line of sight, his pings won't even get a Doppler shift off our hull."

On *Challenger*

"Where *is* he?" Jeffrey said. "Where did he *go?*"

"Careful," Wilson said. "Think it through."

Jeffrey realized he'd begun to lose his self-control. This was exactly what ter Horst planned and wanted to happen. Jeffrey made himself stay focused. Every second counted now. He was glad he had Wilson to backstop him in this endurance marathon against ter Horst's brilliant mind.

"He's blending into the escarpment wall," Jeffrey said. "It's the only explanation why we can't find him anywhere on active or passive search."

"Why hasn't he fired more torpedoes at us?" Bell asked.

"He'd give himself away, and be pinned against the wall. He surely hears the aircraft coming around again, just like we can."

"But this is his best chance to overwhelm us, Captain, *immediately*, before the planes reattack. He has to have figured out by now we have only four tubes working."

"The aircraft!" Jeffrey said. "That's it! He's gone shallow on auto-hover. He's going after the aircraft!"

On *Voortrekker*

"Depth six hundred meters," Van Gelder reported. *Voortrekker* was at the peak of the sea mount atop the Bounty Platform wall, still being masked by terrain. "Sets of four Polyphem missiles loaded in torpedo tubes two, four, six, and eight."

"Aircraft approaching fast on attack runs!" the sonar chief called out.

"Aircraft courses indicate a wide spread bracketing us," Van Gelder warned.

Ter Horst glanced up at the overhead, as if to look through to the sky. "They seem to know, or they guessed, that we're using the escarpment wall."

"Sir," Van Gelder urged, "they'll drop weapons any moment."

"Tubes two, four, six, and eight, shoot."

Van Gelder watched the tactical plot. Sixteen antiaircraft missiles broached the surface. Four enemy aircraft dropped a total of six Mark 54 torpedoes—ter Horst's missiles were too late.

"Reload all tubes," ter Horst snapped. "Helm, flank speed ahead. Steer one eight zero. Thirty degrees down bubble. Back to the bottom smartly."

Voortrekker's bow nosed steeply down. Only Van Gelder's lap belt kept him from sliding right out of his seat. *Voortrekker* picked up speed, running south, along the edge of the Bounty Platform wall, moving as fast as the ship could go.

Simultaneously, on *Challenger*

"Launch transients!" Kathy shouted. "Missile motors igniting! Flow noise! Flank-speed datum on *Voortrekker!*" Kathy fed the range and bearing and depth to Bell. He issued orders to his weapon-systems specialists. Jeffrey fired four more torpedoes, at five-second intervals.

"Six air-dropped Mark 54s in the water," Kathy said.

"I think we've got him now," Jeffrey said. Here was the second combined salvo, from *Challenger* and the aircraft. *This one better do the job.*

"Aircraft are turning away," the sonar chief said. "Multiple missiles in the air, closing on friendly aircraft."

Jeffrey cursed to himself.

"Torpedoes in the water!" Kathy shouted. "Four Sea Lion torpedoes."

"Sea Lions are on intercept course with friendly weapons," Bell said.

"Reload!" Jeffrey ordered. He wanted revenge for the Orions and Vikings that were about to die.

"Eight *more* Sea Lions in the water!" Kathy said.

Does Voortrekker *know where we are?*

"Master One's torpedoes fanning out in a wide spread," Bell reported. "Assess as random shots, but some are threats to *Challenger*."

Jeffrey fired four more defensive shots. "Reload!" Soon enough, *Voortrekker* would trace the Mark 88s back to their source, and draw a bead on *Challenger* that way. There was a real danger that at this rate *Challenger* would run out of torpedoes—but the same thing applied to ter Horst. Jeffrey dreaded another inconclusive draw. It made him determined to fight all the harder. He was very glad he'd left New London with a full complement, some sixty fish on the torpedo-room racks and carried in the tubes.

Jeffrey fidgeted while the torpedo-room autoloader gear ran once more through its mechanical cycle—he prayed the hydraulic machinery would hold up under the nuclear battering, and under such constant heavy use. Again he and Bell armed the warheads. He had Bell fire *another* salvo.

Jeffrey listened to the cacophony on the sonar speakers. His mind tuned out the sounds of the separate airborne battle, which was now beyond his control. Even so, there were sixteen enemy torpedoes in the water, plus eighteen from *Challenger* and her supporting aircraft, audible against a constant backdrop of *Challenger*'s hissing flank-speed flow noise and the continuing rumbling reverb from all those earlier nuclear blasts. In this madness of crisscrossing fish it was a toss-up whether Allied weapons really outnumbered ter Horst's—and there was the definite possibility of a double kill, with both ships sunk, maybe even by their own torpedoes.

It began, the latest melee of detonations, and *Challenger* was buffeted. Kathy's people lost all contact with *Voortrekker*.

This is no place to linger. Jeffrey's ship was very low on ammo—and the swarm of atomic torpedoes would continue to hunt for targets and explode.

Jeffrey hoped Ilse was right, that ter Horst's ultimate refuge was the ice shelf, so that Jeffrey knew which way to go to maintain the pursuit. He hoped the doomed aircraft overhead had at least convinced *Voortrekker* to keep running in that direction, south.

"Helm, make your course one eight zero." The ship still was doing flank speed. If Jeffrey slowed, he'd be quieter, but this was not the time or place for quiet. Yet he needed to take steps to protect his command. It was too late to protect the local environment, and for this Jeffrey knew he'd feel a lasting inner shame.

"Fire Control, launch noisemakers and jammers. . . . Launch two decoys, flank speed, in a spread to right and left."

Simultaneously, on *Voortrekker*

Van Gelder listened to the racket on the sonar speakers as almost three dozen nuclear torpedoes screamed every which way. Some ran at each other on intercept courses. Others ran at *Challenger* or *Voortrekker*, or toward the face of the Bounty Platform wall, or homed on bubble clouds as if they were hulls. A few tore off uselessly into the distance, their firing solutions or guidance systems awry. The combined noise almost drowned out the sixteen antiaircraft missiles flying overhead, and the straining engine sounds of the evading enemy aircraft.

The first things to connect were the antiaircraft missiles. As the sonar chief called out each event, Van Gelder heard a series of muffled thuds when each missile warhead detonated. The warheads were high-explosive only, but the blasts nearby and right above transferred sound down into the water. Then Van Gelder heard a series of smacks and drawn-out watery tearing noises, as the enemy aircraft one by one broke up and plunged into the sea. Van Gelder knew some of the planes had fifteen people in their crews, to fly them and man all the antisubmarine gear.

Those who survived the missiles, using parachutes to jump to safety or life rafts when their aircraft ditched, would suffer the immediate effects of all those nuclear torpedoes about to blow. Van Gelder knew not one of the downed aircrew still breathing would do so for much longer. Blast force, searing heat, and intense radiation would kill them for sure. The worst part would be the waiting, wondering where and when the first nuclear fireball would break the surface as the survivors bobbed in the sea.

But the aircraft had already done their worst. They'd managed to drop their last Mark 54s.

Ter Horst ordered more noisemakers and decoys. Van Gelder rushed to comply. Soon, he knew, the fearful noise of all those torpedo engines coming and going would be drowned out by sounds infinitely more frightening and deadly. He wondered what the whales and dolphins hearing all this felt, the ones that weren't already dead or deaf or in too much agony from internal injuries to care.

On *Challenger*

Nuclear torpedo warheads began to detonate near and far. Jeffrey's body and his ship were punished by forces worse than any he'd ever experienced. It was impossible to follow what was happening, either on the data screens or in his head. Kathy and Bell and their people struggled to keep track of inbound torpedoes and keep their own on proper course.

More warheads blew. Jeffrey's brain seemed to bounce back and forth inside his skull. His teeth hurt. He thought his rib cage or his lungs would burst apart. Damage-control reports came in from all over *Challenger*. Jeffrey's vision was too blurred to read his console now, and his eardrums ached too much for him to hear.

Blood dripped onto his vibrating console screen—the stitches on his forehead had opened up. The noise and shock effects redoubled as additional warheads blew. Blast waves bounced off the escarpment wall and came back at the ship. *Challenger* surged and heaved and shivered.

Commodore Wilson lost his grip on a stanchion and was knocked right off his feet.

Yet more warheads blew, much too close.

Bell leaned close and bellowed something urgently in Jeffrey's ear.

"*What?*"

Bell repeated himself, and tried to talk with his hands, using improvised sign language. Finally Jeffrey understood.

"Flooding in the trash-disposal lockout chute!"

The disposal chute was like a small torpedo tube, aimed straight down through the bottom of the ship, near the galley and mess spaces. At fifteen thousand feet, water was powering in under pressure at almost four tons per square inch—this could be a fatal wound.

Jeffrey's response was automatic, instinctive. "Chief of the Watch, emergency blow! Helm, plane up!" Jeffrey's own voice sounded distant, disembodied, from the painful ringing in his head. COB pulled the special emergency-blow handles. Meltzer yanked back hard on his control wheel.

Bell, as executive officer, ran aft to take charge at the flooding. Through the phone talker, Bell said they couldn't even get close until the ship reached much shallower depth. The sea was jetting in with such tremendous force that three crewmen had been dismembered. The spray was taking the paint right off the bulkheads; the injured being treated on nearby dining tables were injured further by flying objects thrown by the incoming sea.

The rate of influx in tons per minute was heavy. COB did everything else he could to lighten the ship, pumping all variable ballast. At this depth the pumps sounded overstressed, asthmatic. High-pressure air continued to roar into the forward and aft main ballast tanks.

Challenger seemed to stagger and hesitate. She wasn't coming up, even with the propulsion plant still running at flank speed and Meltzer using the sternplanes to try to drive the ship up hard.

Jeffrey's head began to clear more. Now he heard the separate roar of the inrushing sea, even from this far forward in the control room. The air became pungent and cold. Jeffrey's eyes stung and his mouth tasted salt. Freezing seawater mist, as if from a giant atomizer, was drifting from the flooding site.

That mist came straight from a nuclear battlefield. "COB, stop the fans! Everyone, emergency air-breather masks!"

Jeffrey donned his mask and watched a depth gauge. He eyed the readings on COB's control panels. The constant fulminating noises from outside, coming right through the hull even with the sonar speakers off, made it difficult to concentrate. Jeffrey realized things were very bad. *Challenger* was getting heavier, and wasn't coming up. The breather mask badly hurt his injured scalp. Blood dripped down Jeffrey's face and puddled by his jaw inside the mask. *Another* aftershock hit, punishing the ship, and it tore at Jeffrey's stitches enough to make him grit his jaw. But he had much bigger problems.

"COB, forget the air. Use hydrazine!" The compressed air blowing into the main ballast tanks, at this great depth and outside pressure, simply wasn't working fast enough. Meltzer's attempt to drive for the surface wasn't helping—everything he tried on the bowplanes and sternplanes just made the bow tilt steeply up, turning the deck into a hillside, making it that much harder for the damage-control parties to work.

It was time for measures Jeffrey had hoped he'd never need. The hydrazine charges were built into the forward and aft main ballast tanks. Hydrazine was rocket fuel.

The charges ignited with the noise of a moon shot taking off. The buildup of searing high-pressure fumes forced water out through the bottom of the tanks. *Challenger* lost weight at last, and started to rise. Bell said it was touch and go, whether they'd reach shallow depth before too much water came in and pulled the ship back down.

Jeffrey stared at the depth gauge, and he prayed. From all around outside the ship, shock waves and fireballs continued to rumble and throb. They mercilessly pummeled *Challenger* like the raging legions of Satan. *Challenger,* almost helpless now as a warship, struggled for the surface, for her life. Up there, Jeffrey knew, waited many bomb-tossed tsunamis and glowering mushroom clouds, a different sort of hell.

Simultaneously, on *Voortrekker*

Atomic warheads exploded everywhere. The endless pounding and nerve-shattering noise made it impossible for Van Gelder to think. Console screens went blank as system after system crashed.

"Update the tactical plot," ter Horst ordered. "I need to know what's happening out there!"

The first thing to come back was the gravimeter, immune as it was to sonar conditions. Van Gelder could see the vertical wall of the Bounty Platform, very close and looming high above. Atomic torpedoes were going off against the wall. Parts of the wall disappeared as they gave way, since the gravimeter couldn't track moving objects.

"Avalanches!" Van Gelder shouted.

"I can't hear you!" ter Horst yelled above the constant noise of warhead detonations and their echoes off the surface and the bottom and the wall.

Van Gelder tugged at his captain's sleeve and pointed at the gravimeter screen.

"Helm, left thirty rudder, *smartly!*"

The helmsman must have lost his hearing too. Van Gelder ran and grabbed the control wheel and pointed at the new course on the gyro compass. The helmsman nodded, and took back the wheel. Tumbling boulders smashed against the ship. Van Gelder knew that if the stern-planes or rudder or pump-jet were hit, *Voortrekker* would become a helpless sitting duck.

More boulders impacted, but the helm continued to respond. An underwater tsunami surge caught *Voortrekker* from starboard. It shoved her away from the escarpment wall, not a moment too soon. Van Gelder heard the crashing roar as tons of rubble rained down.

A Mark 54 torpedo dashed through the top of a nearby bubble cloud. It began to ping, and homed from way above on *Voortrekker*'s hull.

"Suppress the echoes!" ter Horst shouted.

"Unable to comply," the sonar chief yelled back. "It's in our baffles!" The inbound weapon was back behind the stern, in the ship's blind spot for sonar out-of-phase cloaking emissions.

Ter Horst ordered a defensive countershot.

Another Mark 54 charged through another bubble cloud, ahead of *Voortrekker*. Would those Allied aviators get their revenge?

"We're caught in the middle," Van Gelder yelled.

"Intercept them," ter Horst snapped.

Van Gelder fired two Sea Lions. From the force of the continuing avalanche, and the energy of tortured water outside, and *Voortrekker*'s lurching maneuvers as more shock waves hit, the fiber-optic wires to the Sea Lions broke.

Both Sea Lions detonated awfully close, on their preprogrammed backup timers. *Voortrekker* was smashed from bow and stern.

Damage reports piled in.

"Port- and starboard-side torpedo autoloaders out of action!" Van Gelder said. "Starboard-side loading chute vital welds have cracked. All starboard-side torpedo tubes not usable!"

Ter Horst cursed. Van Gelder realized the aviators had achieved something after all: the odds were evened up with *Challenger*, four torpedo tubes to four.

Another torpedo came at *Voortrekker* from the stern. It was a Mark 88, from *Challenger*, running very deep.

Voortrekker's four functioning torpedo tubes were empty. With the autoloader equipment broken, it would take minutes to load one tube by hand. Noisemakers were no good this deep—they'd be strangled by the outside pressure. A decoy would be just as slow to load as a torpedo, and a decoy might not work. Ter Horst ordered Van Gelder to get a tube reloaded, any way he could. Van Gelder passed urgent orders to the torpedo room, and the men began to work with block and tackle.

"Where's *Challenger*?" ter Horst demanded.

"All contact lost," the sonar chief said.

"Even pinging would be useless," Van Gelder yelled. "Acoustic sea state is off the scale!" Outside, the ocean all around them rumbled like a hundred live volcanoes.

"Helm, steer one eight zero!" South again. "Phone Talker, tell Reactor Control to push it to one hundred twenty percent!"

Voortrekker had no choice but to try to outrun the incoming weapon.

The Mark 88 was almost twenty knots faster than *Voortrekker*. Van Gelder watched his screens as *Voortrekker* ran toward the Antarctic at fifty-three knots herself. He wasn't sure if the enemy weapon would run out of fuel before it reached its warhead's lethal range. He wasn't sure if his men could get one tube reloaded for a countershot before it was too late. He wasn't sure where *Challenger* was, or what condition Jeffrey Fuller's ship was in. Van Gelder wasn't sure if ter Horst could avoid more enemy fire before he reached his next objective, the relative sanctuary of the immensely thick Ross Ice Shelf.

Van Gelder prayed. The one thing of which he felt deeply sure was that there was an afterlife, and in the afterlife he would be judged.

40

Two hours later, on the Osprey

Ilse watched through a porthole as the tilt-rotor Osprey came in for a landing at the McMurdo base in Antarctica. The base consisted of a runway made of ice and dozens of low, functional, military-looking buildings, all clustered into a natural bowl leading to rugged hills. McMurdo was on a peninsula at the south end of Ross Island, which was frozen into the western edge of the Ross Ice Shelf. Unlike the smaller ice shelf in the Antarctic's Weddell Sea, which was on the other side of the continent and also much farther north, and which broke up periodically—some said due to global warming—the Ross Ice Shelf was solid as a rock. On rare occasions the shelf did calve huge icebergs off its outer edge, but—ironically—in this part of Antarctica recent temperatures were actually trending *colder*.

The Osprey quickly refueled, then took off again, heading east along the outer edge of the ice shelf. Now, in the strange perpetual late-summer twilight here at latitude seventy-seven south, by looking backward Ilse could see Mount Erebus, more than twelve thousand feet high. Mount Erebus loomed in the very center of Ross Island. Erebus was an active volcano, with a lake of molten lava in the crater at its peak;

smoke drifted from the crater. The north face of the mountain glowed a lovely scarlet, lit by the low sun. The south face hid in shadow.

To northward, as the Osprey followed the ice shelf, stretched the Ross Sea, leading to the endless open water of the Great Southern Ocean that circled Antarctica. Ilse watched as the Ross Sea was tossed by wind that came from the south, from the frigid high ground at the geographic south pole itself, a thousand miles inland. She noticed occasional icebergs in the water, and large flat floes. She saw brash ice—broken fragments—at the base of the edge of the shelf, where the freezing water rose and fell with the tides.

The edge of the shelf was a rugged cliff two hundred feet high in most places. The cliff plunged straight into the sea, and Ilse knew the ice of the shelf stretched hundreds of feet farther down—unlike the north pole ice cap, which averaged only twenty feet thick in wintertime, the Ross Ice Shelf varied in thickness from six hundred to two thousand feet or more, year round. The body of the shelf—larger than Texas, California, and New York combined—was formed by the merging of giant ageless glaciers, flowing down constantly from the massive mountains hundreds of miles farther south. The shelf was a hybrid, because it also grew by the freezing of seawater on its underside, and by the steady compacting of snow by wind and gravity on its upper surface. It was so-called fast ice, because it was anchored fast to the shore on all but its outer, north-facing, edge. Yet it floated, just like an iceberg, supported by buoyancy. It took up the entire inner part of the huge Ross Sea.

The ice and snow of the top of the shelf were stark and beautiful. There were strange optical effects, from the coldness of the air and from its dryness away from the sea. By a peculiar mirage, which Ilse knew was common here, she could see the tops of the first mountain range which rose far inland. The mountaintops looked hard and black, and much too close.

The ice shelf glistened in breathtaking shades of aquamarine, turquoise, and teal. Some parts were blindingly white, others translucent green. Ilse sometimes saw fissures and crevices, or small slush lakes atop the ice where the sun warmed snow on its surface. In some places the ceaseless wind had polished the surface smooth; in others the ice was grooved and channeled. But mostly the top of the shelf was featureless. It simply went on, mile after mile, massive, solid, dehumanizing in its size and its loneliness, and ending always in that sharp cliff face that just kept stretching farther and farther east.

The sea beyond the ice shelf wasn't so lonely. Often Ilse saw seals and penguins. They swam between the bergs and floes to feed on teeming schools of fish, or climbed up on the ice to rest. Overhead, Antarctic birds—petrels of different types, and albatrosses—flew and swooped. In the open water between the multishaped fragments of ice, Ilse saw the huge, fast forms of orcas—killer whales, glossy black with white markings. The killer whales hunted in organized groups, using strategy, and baby seals and penguins were their prey. This was the natural order, since long before the human species even knew Antarctica existed.

Now mankind had come to make war, Ilse reflected, defiling this wild and virginal landscape. Ilse and Clayton and Montgomery were hunters too, like the orcas. A machine of war, *Voortrekker,* and the men inside, were Ilse's prey.

"We're here," the crew chief yelled above the engine noise. They were somewhere near the middle of the shelf edge, almost an hour's flight from McMurdo. Ilse heard the now-familiar change in pitch as the nacelles rotated to point straight up, and the Osprey shifted to vertical landing mode. The aircraft put down gently in a cloud of prop-blown snow. The cliff face, and the sea below it, were just a few hundred yards away.

Ilse was wearing extreme-cold-weather clothing that they'd given her at McMurdo. She was glad, because the heating in the passenger compartment was weak, and sitting still she got chilled. She and Clayton and Montgomery unbuckled their flight harnesses. The crew chief opened the door. A blast of very dry, very cold air blew in.

Ilse stepped outside, into a different world. The sky was surprisingly clear. At first she couldn't distinguish anything. Then her eyes adjusted to the lighting, and to the environment. She saw Sno-Cats, half concealed behind small manmade ice hillocks. The Sno-Cats—these were older models with the engine compartment in front—had four articulated half-track treads instead of wheels, and big, heated passenger compartments. Sno-Cats were the transport vehicle of choice here on the White Continent. Ilse noticed that these ones had their high-visibility orange paint jobs hidden under a hasty coat of whitewash, for camouflage. Peering around, she noticed troops, garbed all in white. Even their rifles were completely white. Then she saw that some of the soldiers had huskies with them, on leads. Even the K-9 dogs were white.

A soldier came out of a hole in the ground. No, a hole in the ice— there was no ground in the normal sense for hundreds of miles in any direction. He smiled and introduced himself. He was a tough, wiry gunnery sergeant in the U.S. Marines. Marine Recon to be specific, an elite within an elite. He obviously expected Ilse. She realized the marine encampment had been set up here to support her.

Ilse's conscience still bothered her. "Isn't all this illegal?"

"Weapons are allowed by treaty for law-enforcement purposes, ma'am. Technically, I'm here as a United States marshal. You three," he said to Ilse and Clayton and Montgomery, "raise your right hands, and say, 'I swear.'" They did. "Congratulations. You're deputy U.S. marshals."

Ilse wasn't even an American citizen, but she didn't say anything.

A corporal came over and handed each of them white M-16s and ammo magazines. "You know how to operate this?" the corporal asked Ilse. She nodded impatiently.

"It's lubricated by powdered graphite," the corporal said, "so the mechanism won't freeze."

"Thanks." *For so-called summer, it is horribly cold.*

"Okay," the gunnery sergeant yelled above the wind and the noise of the Osprey. "It's time you people get to work."

Clayton and Montgomery helped Ilse carry her underwater listening gear into the sergeant's hole in the ice. She saw that it was the entrance to an ice shelter, an underground bunker cut using axes and chain saws. There was a heater, electric lighting, some tables and chairs, piles of rations and sleeping bags, and a chemical toilet behind a canvas screen.

All the comforts of home.

Electrical cables were quickly strung from the Osprey, anchored snugly to stakes driven into the ice, and then their free ends with the plugs and jacks were fed into the bunker. The Osprey took off, heading out to sea in helicopter mode, stringing a hydrophone line into the water, off of the reels in its cargo bay and through the open rear ramp. As Ilse watched, the Osprey flew some miles due north, then turned northwest and eventually disappeared beyond the horizon. Another Osprey arrived from McMurdo. It also deposited cable ends for Ilse's gear. It took off and flew out to sea, also trailing a hydrophone line. This one turned northeast.

Ilse realized the two Ospreys had laid a listening grid in the water—which was about two thousand feet deep—in the shape of a giant Y. Ilse went back into the ice bunker and connected all the cable ends to her portable console, the one supplied by the *Stennis* to its Osprey that had brought her here. She hooked up the console to the fuel cells the marines had brought from McMurdo as a low-observable power supply.

It was warm enough in the shelter that Ilse could lower her hood and open the front of her parka. In short order her improvised listening post—like a nonmoving double sonar towed array—was in business. With the cables strung out into deeper water in their Y arrangement, she should get good targeting data on *Voortrekker* if ter Horst came anywhere near the middle part of the shelf.

Clayton and Montgomery operated portable satellite communications gear. They quickly established a link to the radio grid which included the SOSUS center in Sydney and the air-wing commander on *Stennis,* plus McMurdo, McMurdo's supporting air base at Christchurch, New Zealand, and CINCPACFLT himself in distant Pearl Harbor.

The gunnery sergeant came down the steps cut in the ice, and he pushed past the white canvas windscreen. "All set, ma'am?"

"Yes," Ilse replied. "What are all your troops here for?"

"The Germans. Their base isn't far from McMurdo. They have Sno-Cats too, and we know they're on the move."

"You mean you think they'd attack us? *Here?*"

41

ONCE MORE, IN his stateroom on Wilson's orders, Jeffrey tried to get some rest. This time he'd undressed for proper sleep, but sleep mostly eluded him. His bunk shook steadily as *Challenger* drove southward, running deep at flank speed. The race against *Voortrekker,* the final race to the Ross Ice Shelf, was on.

Jeffrey's mind ran back to the events of the last twenty-four hours. *Challenger* reached the surface after COB's hydrazine emergency blow. On the photonics mast display screens, everyone in the control room saw the massive waves and forest of mushroom clouds from the latest battle with *Voortrekker*. The effects were bad, both inside and outside the ship.

Bell supervised damage control, as the crack in the garbage-disposal lockout chute was permanently sealed off so *Challenger* could dive again. Bilge pumps quickly removed the seawater that had flooded in.

The pieces of the men killed by the blasting influx of the sea at depth were put in body bags, and the body bags were stored in the ship's freezer; they were thoroughly segregated for sanitary reasons from the dwindling supply of frozen food. The smashing force of the influx had left much of the galley and mess spaces a scene of destruction as well as of death. Aluminum, stainless steel, and plastic lay on the deck or hung from the overhead, twisted into unrecognizable heaps. Broken wires and pipes were hastily repaired or bypassed. Shattered glass, twisted utensils, torn and soaked seating upholstery, all were gathered up.

The radiology-control officer, a lieutenant (j.g.) from engineering, supervised a radioactive-contamination survey of the insides of the ship, and of ship's personnel—the dosages weren't high enough for acute radiation sickness, but longer-term health problems weren't ruled out. The fans were restarted and particle filters worked at cleaning the air. A painstaking freshwater washdown cleansed areas that showed any traces of fallout; the tainted water was pumped into shielded tanks, and from there was pumped overboard. The crew, wearing their respirator masks and protective gloves, scrubbed all exposed surfaces with absorbent, treated cleaning cloths. The cloths were stored in special bags, tagged as radiological hazards, and placed in the designated holding area back in Engineering. A lot of the crew's clothing, soaked by the polluted sea, went into those disposal bags. One enlisted men's shower stall was used as the dedicated decontamination shower. Precautions were taken so no fallout was tracked around on shoes.

The corpsman and his assistants paused from treating the wounded to hand out iodide tablets, to help fight absorption of radioactive iodine by the thyroid gland. Other medications aided excretion of the heavy-metal fission waste, uranium and plutonium and thorium. The corpsman redid the stitches in Jeffrey's scalp and told him he'd definitely have a lasting scar.

It was hours before the crew could come out of their air-breather masks. Jeffrey, as captain, conducted a brief memorial service for the dead. He exhorted the crew to ever greater efforts of teamwork and stamina, for revenge. To himself, he felt very drained. In private, Bell and COB consoled the men most affected by the loss of close friends—but no one was unaffected by the three deaths.

Now, as Jeffrey lay in his rack and stared into space in the dark, he told himself the insides of the ship—and the mind-set of his people—were more or less okay. A few men, including maybe him, had undoubtedly absorbed some of the undersea fallout carcinogens. Radiation's impact on the body was a statistical thing. In twenty or thirty years, some cancer cases would show among the crew, in lungs or bones or worse. Maybe, Jeffrey hoped, in twenty or thirty years, these cancers would be treatable.

It's like exposure to Agent Orange in Vietnam, or the Gulf War syndrome in the nineties. The immediate wounds of battle are only one price of the war. Veterans continue to suffer for the rest of their lives from posttraumatic stress disorder and from diseases caused by environmental toxins.

The seas around the battle site would stay radioactive for far too long. The airborne fallout, right around now, ought to be reaching Latin America. The effects would be what the effects had been since the very start of the war: fear, and increased starvation. Local fishing industries would be devastated, because no one would eat the fish. Children would go malnourished, because their parents wouldn't feed them milk, because of the strontium-90 in the grass and in the cows. People would seal up their homes, or hide in improvised bomb shelters, or wear gas masks as they tried to resume their daily lives.

It's Chernobyl all over again, or the 1940s and '50s and early '60s, with their hundreds of open-air nuclear-weapons tests, including some the U.S. set off in New Mexico and Nevada. Eventually, the fallout would blow over, or people would just stop caring and give up and take their chances. The unlucky ones would get sick. Diplomatic protests would be filed, and public protests might turn into riots, but so far nothing had helped to stop this war or tone down the violence.

Jeffrey realized he'd dozed off when he woke suddenly in a cold sweat. He'd been having a nightmare. He couldn't remember the dream, but he felt the emotional hangover. Dread, anxiety, anger, and above all guilt: Bell, as fire-control coordinator, was sure that they'd hurt *Voortrekker* in the latest action yesterday. But Kathy Milgrom said rerunning the sonar tapes detected hints of *Voortrekker* fleeing south at flank speed.

All this destruction and death and pollution is happening here, spilling into the South Pacific and now toward Antarctica too, because of

Voortrekker. Ter Horst is here, making all this happen, and forcing me *to make it happen, because I failed to destroy him last time, two months ago.*

A messenger knocked on Jeffrey's door.

"Coming." Jeffrey dressed quickly, in a clean blue cotton jumpsuit that zipped up the front.

"Sir," the messenger said. "Commodore Wilson wants you in his office." The messenger handed Jeffrey a mug of black coffee. "Don't worry, sir, the water's clean, and the coffee grinds weren't affected."

"Thanks." Jeffrey drank it down. He was good at getting by on little sleep, and at waking up and becoming alert in an instant, but this time the lingering mood of that guilt-ridden nightmare wouldn't disappear.

He knocked, and Wilson told him to enter. Wilson was alone in the office that used to be Bell's stateroom.

"Good morning, Captain." Wilson looked drawn and haggard. There were deep bags under his eyes. He wore his reading glasses, but he was squinting, as if he was suffering one of his headaches or was having trouble seeing properly.

"Good morning, Commodore."

"We need to make another status check with CINCPACFLT," Wilson said. "It's time. Have Bell bring us to periscope depth."

"Sir, that's very risky under these circumstances, don't you think?"

"We can't hope to defeat ter Horst if you act like a lone wolf. I already told you, antisubmarine warfare is a team sport."

Wilson handed Jeffrey the stateroom's intercom mike. "Give your XO the orders. When we make radio contact, have it piped in here. We need privacy in case classified information has to be discussed."

"Or in case alarming developments need to be kept from the crew?"

Wilson nodded. "Morale is always a prime consideration, Captain."

Jeffrey did as he was told. He felt the ship slow and then nose upward. In a few minutes *Challenger* leveled off, rolling near the surface in the stormy seas. The communications officer, in the radio room, put CINC-PACFLT through on the stateroom's speakerphone.

The admiral sounded exhausted and worried. Jeffrey wondered if he'd gotten any sleep since the last time they talked. The conversation was short and to the point.

"Gentlemen," CINCPACFLT opened without preliminaries, "the Pentagon more than a day ago prevailed on Commander in Chief, Central Command, to free up two of the *Los Angeles*–class fast-attack subs that were escorting the *Ronald Reagan* in the Indian Ocean. These two submarines are now moving quickly toward the west edge of the Ross Ice Shelf."

"That's good news, Admiral," Wilson said.

"Unfortunately, as you both can guess, these vessels are badly in need of a refit after eight months deployed at sea in a theater of battle."

This presented two problems, as Jeffrey well knew. He wasn't sure if the admiral, a naval aviator, fully appreciated them. Jeffrey glanced at Wilson, and Wilson glanced back as if to say, Go ahead.

"Their quieting gear, Admiral," Jeffrey said, "sound-isolation pads and the like, will be worn, so the L.A. boats will be noisy. And their hulls will be fouled with sea growth from months of service in the tropics, sir, so they'll be slow."

"So my staff informs me, Captain. The *Reagan* is more vulnerable, too, to attack by Axis submarines with her undersea escorts depleted, but the risk simply has to be taken."

"Understood," Wilson said. The lumbering *Collins*-class diesel subs that had formed his original battle group were left in the dust now, far to the north.

"In addition," the admiral went on, "Commander in Chief, Atlantic Fleet, was ordered to send two *Virginia*-class fast-attack subs from the South Atlantic into the Pacific. They'll converge on the eastern edge of the Ross Ice Shelf, if they make it through the Drake Passage." The Drake Passage lay between the southern tip of Argentina, at Tierra del Fuego, and the northern tip of the jutting Antarctic Peninsula.

"The problem here is that Argentina, reacting to snowballing global tensions in the aftermath of the Chatham Island blast, has reasserted her age-old claims to exclusive territorial rights to the Peninsula. The regime in power just declared a two-hundred-mile-wide zone of exclusion, like the British did around the Falkland Islands thirty years ago."

"I'm sure that point hasn't been lost on anybody," Wilson said.

"Concur," the admiral said.

"Admiral," Jeffrey said, "the exclusion zones from the Peninsula and Tierra del Fuego will overlap."

"Yes. Argentina has issued a notice to mariners that all submarines transiting the Drake Passage are to surface and be boarded for inspection, or they'll be depth charged without warning."

"Jesus," Wilson said under his breath. He sounded disgusted and disturbed.

"Our analysts and our people in-country there see the hand of Axis agents behind this," CINCPACFLT responded. "Hardball backroom lobbying, covert psychological-warfare ops, use of moles or threats or outright bribes, the Axis is trying it all. . . . I can tell you both categorically our state-of-the-art *Virginia* subs will *not* be boarded by any upstart Argentineans. They've been ordered to defend themselves if attacked."

Jeffrey ran his hands through his hair, thinking. It was touch and go whether the two *Los Angeles*–class subs would reach the ice shelf before ter Horst did. It was touch and go whether the *Virginia* subs would reach the shelf at all—on the way, a war might start between the U.S. and Argentina.

"Commodore, Captain," CINCPACFLT said, "under the circumstances, with so many friendly subs converging on your area of operations, I feel the need to modify your rules of engagement."

"Sir?" Jeffrey said.

"All aircraft will be restricted to searching for *Voortrekker,* but will *not* drop any weapons."

Jeffrey nodded, although the admiral couldn't see. So close to the south magnetic pole—which was actually in the Ross Sea near Mc-Murdo—the planes' magnetic anomaly detectors would be useless. Now, sonobuoys were the only meaningful tools they had.

The admiral was interrupted by his aide. When he came back on the line, Jeffrey heard heightened concern in his voice.

"I'm informed our recon satellites have detected troop movements by both Brazil and Argentina, along the stretch of border they share in the middle of South America. . . . As you both know, those two nations have fought all-out wars with their neighbors in the distant past, and smoldering skirmishes more recently."

"Latin America has a very long memory," Jeffrey said.

"Yes. It seems hostilities are rising anew, amid all the other escalating worldwide suspicions and tensions and encroaching fallout. Argentina's own continuing economic crisis isn't helping any."

Jeffrey pondered this. "Brazil once ran a nuclear-weapons program, Admiral, but they said they gave it up as a gesture of peace some twenty years ago."

"Brazil still operates nuclear reactors, and our agents have been saying since this Berlin-Boer War broke out that she might have renewed her efforts to build fission weapons for self-defense."

"That's just what we need," Wilson said.

"Argentina may or may not have been given atom bombs by the Axis, on the excuse of maintaining parity with Brazil. The CIA isn't sure. But if that happens, the Axis's real purpose of course will be to destabilize South America for entirely selfish reasons."

"The U.S. would be directly threatened from the south," Jeffrey said. *A third* front riding hard on Voortrekker's *opening of a second.*

"Oil and natural gas and other vital raw materials in South America could be lost to the Allies if that happened," CINCPACFLT said. "One of our few surviving major export markets might be lost, and our balance of trade goes the rest of the way down the toilet. The Panama Canal might even be destroyed."

Jeffrey and Wilson stared at each other, shocked that the world could be coming apart so badly and so soon.

"Everything," the admiral stated, "*everything*, hinges on *Challenger* continuing in hot pursuit and sinking *Voortrekker* once and for all. Your basic orders are therefore reaffirmed. If *Voortrekker* reaches the edge of the Ross Ice Shelf intact, you go in after her."

Again Wilson and Jeffrey stared at each other, as the hard reality behind this seemingly simple command sank in.

Jeffrey knew the clearance in the water—between the bottom of that thick ice and the mud and rock of the Antarctic continental shelf below—would be very tight. The ice shelf was almost five hundred miles wide along its outer edge. It extended as much as four hundred miles toward shore before touching dry land.

"Admiral," Jeffrey said, "the underside of the ice shelf has to be the least explored place on earth."

"That's right, Captain. I'm told scientists know more about the far side of the moon than they do about what lies under the Ross Ice Shelf. . . . My aide says I have another call, from my superiors. I need to get off. Good luck."

Four hours later, on the Ross Ice Shelf

After eating and using the toilet, Ilse went back to her console. Chief Montgomery kept an eye on its readouts in the meantime, just in case it picked up something besides biologics and wind and waves and icebergs. Ilse had given Montgomery and Clayton basic training in how to work the console, so it would have full-time coverage without exhausting her prematurely. It was still too early for *Voortrekker* to get near the shelf, given the distance ter Horst needed to travel and the top speed he could go.

Just as the marine corporal handed Ilse a steaming cup of coffee, something registered on her console screen. She sat down and played it back and tried to make sense of the data. The noise, or rather noises, came from far off to the northwest. They looked like a pair of nuclear detonations—underwater, not surface or air bursts. The yields, she estimated using software on her console, were both about one kiloton. She thought they might be Allied air-dropped depth charges.

Then Shajo Clayton said he had Sydney and the *Stennis* on the line, both wanting to speak to Ilse. Aircraft from the *Stennis* had heard the blasts on their sonobuoys. Sydney, lacking any working SOSUS lines of their own due to *Voortrekker*'s tampering, asked Ilse to relay her raw data via the satellite link. She entered the commands on her keyboard to do so.

As she finished her coffee, Sydney and then the *Stennis* came on the line again. In addition to the carrier's air-wing commander, who was a navy captain, the rear admiral who commanded the whole *Stennis* battle group was on the call.

The Sydney supercomputers hadn't needed long to do their work. The blasts Ilse detected were two Sea Lion warheads, definitely torpedoes launched by *Voortrekker*. Embedded in all the reverb and aftershocks were the unmistakable sounds of two *Los Angeles*–class hulls imploding as they fell through crush depth.

42

Two hours later, on *Challenger*

KATHY MILGROM REPORTED hearing another signal sonobuoy in the distance. Once more, Jeffrey realized, his ship was being summoned to periscope depth. He suspected it might have something to do with the torpedo explosions Kathy's men detected a couple of hours ago, a hundred miles ahead of *Challenger*'s location. Those explosions probably gave a datum on *Voortrekker*, so it ought to be relatively safe to expose the antenna mast again—unless ter Horst had counted on Jeffrey thinking exactly that, and he'd doubled back in ambush.

Kathy had reported a heavy Allied air-dropped depth charging of the area of *Voortrekker*'s datum, some minutes after the original blasts. This surprised Jeffrey, since *Los Angeles* boats were supposed to be working in that area. It also violated the latest rules of engagement.

It was possible one of the depth charges had killed *Voortrekker*, but based on experience so far, Jeffrey wasn't taking chances.

When CINCPACFLT came on the line, he insisted on speaking to Wilson in absolute private. Wilson went into the secure communications room and threw everyone there out.

Jeffrey waited nervously while *Challenger* steamed slowly south with her antenna mast exposed. Bell and his fire-control technicians used the photonics masts to scan for surface and airborne threats, but they didn't report any contacts. The electronic-support-measures room didn't detect any threats from enemy radars. Even so, Jeffrey was frustrated. Every minute *Challenger* lingered like this with a mast raised, ter Horst gained a further lead in the race to the shelf. These repeated excursions to periscope depth wasted time, since *Challenger* had to proceed at less than ten knots, to avoid damage to her masts by water drag. Jeffrey hoped Washington, and CINCPACFLT, weren't starting to micromanage his efforts.

Jeffrey was disturbed that Wilson was sequestered with the admiral for so long. It had to be something important. He occupied himself by pacing around the control room, looking over the shoulders of the weapon-systems specialists and sonarmen.

Wilson suddenly dashed out of the radio room.

"Take her deep! Evasive maneuvers! CINCPACFLT reports inbound Shipwrecks!"

So *Voortrekker* was still alive, and from some satellite or acoustic link had gotten targeting data on *Challenger* near the surface. Jeffrey snapped out helm orders. The deck dropped out from under him as the ship dived hard and turned away at flank speed. Soon the long-distance airborne depth charging began. Shipwrecks were supersonic antiship cruise missiles, built in Russia and tipped with Axis atom bombs. These Shipwrecks might have plunging warheads, designed to go off deep beneath the sea.

Crewmen held on tight and sweated it out. They stared at their consoles or at the overhead, or scrunched their eyes tight closed. *Challenger* reared and bucked with each warhead's detonation—underwater detonations, as Jeffrey feared, where they did far more damage to a submarine. Echoes of the blasts hit from the surface and the bottom. Aftershocks hit as each throbbing fireball rose to the surface and burst into the air. Jeffrey kept giving helm orders, to try to dodge and outguess ter Horst's missile-targeting pattern.

Jeffrey's jaw was grimly set and his hands were balled into fists. There was no way he could fight back, there was nothing he could do but struggle to barely escape—and he hated it.

Some missiles hit very close. Fluorescent light fixtures shattered. More crewmen suffered injuries, and above the noise of the warheads Jeffrey was anguished to hear his people grunt or curse or cry out in pain.

The merciless high-tech depth charging continued.

More pieces of equipment failed. Manifolds cracked and leaking compressed air roared, making the moisture in the control-room air condense as fog. Jeffrey had trouble seeing even as far as the back of Meltzer's head. Jeffrey waved his hands but the fog wouldn't dissipate. It made the air grow cold. He yelled more evasive helm orders, and *Challenger* twisted and turned.

Another warhead blew. *Again* freshwater pipes somewhere nearby began to spray. Above the rumbling roars from outside Jeffrey heard the water rush along the deck. He looked down as it sloshed around his shoes. Chiefs snapped out firm orders, and once more the tired damage-control teams rushed to make repairs.

Challenger shook from a very near miss. The lights went out for a moment, then came back on, the ones that weren't broken. There was a terrible pressure in Jeffrey's inner ears from all the noise, and his entire body ached from the constant pounding. He was dimly aware of more casualty and damage reports, but he left that to Bell as he fixated on maneuvering his ship so they might survive. Where would the next warhead plunge? Advance warning from sonar was useless—the missiles were forty times as fast as *Challenger* at flank speed. Jeffrey made another guess, knowing everyone's life was at stake, and ordered Meltzer to double back hard.

There were twelve detonations in all before it subsided.

Jeffrey and Bell looked at each other, surprised to still be alive. It was the most terrifying thing Jeffrey had ever experienced.

"That was *Voortrekker*'s entire vertical launch array," Bell said.

Jeffrey nodded—he didn't trust himself to speak.

"He's the shrewdest bastard I know," Wilson said as he shook himself off from the pounding. "He's created another datum, but he knows Allied aircraft in his area have already exhausted their weapons. The nearest surface warships that could launch Tactical Tomahawks at him are way north of Chatham Island, near the *Stennis*, and totally out of range."

Tomahawks are subsonic anyway, Jeffrey told himself, *and* Voortrekker *would be long gone before they reached ter Horst's missile launch point.*

Jeffrey had to clear his throat. "He's playing tag, making us come after him again and playing with our minds."

Jeffrey glanced at Wilson. The commodore's face was ashen, even more than it ought to have been from the depth charging.

"My office. Now."

Jeffrey followed. They went inside and Wilson locked the door.

"I think the whole world's going insane," Wilson said.

"Sir?"

"CINCPACFLT heard from the Pentagon, and from Miss Reebeck's listening post on the ice shelf."

"And?"

"Ter Horst sank both the fast-attacks from the *Reagan*. The whole western hook of our pincers is gone."

"Christ," Jeffrey said. "That's almost three hundred men killed, in those two crews."

"There's nothing left between *Voortrekker* and the ice shelf. This Shipwreck missile blitz at us was meant to prove the point."

Jeffrey nodded.

"There's a major blizzard brewing near the south pole," Wilson stated. "It's forecast to start coming north across the Ross Sea tomorrow."

"Perfect weather for *Voortrekker* to try to break back out through what's left of our cordon." Jeffrey suddenly blanched. "*That's* what he wants. This is what he wanted all along! He lures all our fast-attacks down toward the ice shelf, then busts back north and uses his superior speed to leave them way behind. The entire South Pacific gets denuded of Allied nuclear submarines, and he takes out the *Stennis* and goes on from there."

"Yes. Precisely. Key people in the Pentagon, reviewing events of the whole past week, have concluded that aerial depth bombings will not sink *Voortrekker,* because ter Horst is too smart and his ship is much too stealthy. Those same key people, reviewing events of the most recent forty-eight hours, now question *Challenger*'s ability to destroy *Voortrekker* one on one."

"But—"

Wilson held up a hand. "If we do pursue him under the Ross Ice Shelf, there's still a big question of how we'll even find him there."

Jeffrey hesitated. "I know. I've been thinking about that."

Wilson took a deep breath, and looked Jeffrey right in the eyes. "Here's the deal, Captain. There are two *Ohio*-class strategic missile submarines on patrol in the Great Southern Ocean."

"Boomers?"

"The idea was they'd be safe from any interference there, being so far from the war zone. Now it seems the war has come to them."

Jeffrey waited. He could tell from Wilson's facial expression that he was leading up to something. Something very bad.

"The rules of engagement are revised again. They now are irrevocable. I am to borrow your minisub to depart from *Challenger,* and shift my overall command to the closest boomer. The boomers are equipped with new low-frequency active towed arrays. Combined with the *Virginia*-class ships now hopefully working through the Drake Passage, and the submarine escorts from the *Stennis* hurrying down, they will form another undersea battle group. With additional reinforcements on the way, we will guard the edge of the shelf, in case *Voortrekker* tries to break out."

Jeffrey nodded. "That all makes sense, except for what I said before." That the bunching of Allied subs near the shelf was exactly what ter Horst wanted.

Wilson disregarded Jeffrey's remark, and Jeffrey suspected he had a reason. "*You,* Captain, are to pursue *Voortrekker* under the ice shelf, *alone.* This way, any contact you make, you know for sure is hostile. From the time you go under the shelf, you have twenty-four hours. If by the end of that period you do not reemerge and indicate that you have positively destroyed *Voortrekker,* and *Voortrekker* has not been detected exiting from under the shelf by our other assets, both boomers will be ordered by the President to launch all their missiles against the top of the shelf."

Jeffrey was speechless. The air in Wilson's office suddenly felt suffocating. "Use *thermonuclear weapons?*"

"Yes. Our own hydrogen bombs, dropped on an uninhabited wasteland."

"Sir, this is madness!"

"I know. CINCPACFLT didn't make the decision. He just passed it on to me. All the old Cold War thinking, about using hydrogen bombs to destroy enemy submarines at sea, seems to have been pulled out of the files and dusted off and is rearing its ugly head again. . . . It's been thought through, and it does make twisted sense. The ice shelf is pure freshwater, so radioactive fallout will be minimal. The steam will condense in the cold, so it won't spread far. There's nothing on the Ross Ice Shelf to burn, so there'll be no nuclear winter. The ice shelf floats, so there'll be no change in sea level when it breaks up. . . . The inertia of the seawater under the ice, and the normal dying-off of explosion seawave energy with distance, will prevent a catastrophic tsunami beyond the north edge of the shelf. We know that much from multimegaton tests at Enewetak Atoll in the 1950s."

"But that's—that's four dozen ballistic missiles, between two Trident subs! With several independently targeted warheads in each missile!"

"Yes. The W-88 warhead. I don't know exactly how many warheads per missile. There were treaties, but the real facts are highly classified. The variable yields of each W-88 will be set to three hundred kilotons. Their launch trajectories and detonation times will be determined by computer, then coordinated by atomic clock. The simultaneous detonation of some sixty or a hundred megatons, spread out over the thick, strong structure of the central ice shelf, will generate a dynamic pressure underneath strong enough to smash *Voortrekker*'s hull."

"And *Challenger*'s, too, if we're still under there."

"Yes."

"But even if it works, it risks global escalation."

"I know. Nobody asked me. The mood in Washington is that we have to be better listeners to the rest of the world for once, and the rest of the world right now wants and respects gestures of power and strength, of determination and will, and that alone. The Axis made their gesture, at Chatham Island. Now it's our country's turn to make a stronger gesture."

"And *this* is it?"

"I'm sorry. We don't have to agree it's right. We *do* have to obey our orders."

Jeffrey stared at the deck as it all sank in. Wilson was correct, of course. In a sick way, it did make sense. The U.S. had set off a hydrogen bomb in the atmosphere in the 1950s that by itself had a yield of fifteen megatons. There was fallout near Bikini Atoll, and radiation sickness and cancer deaths, but life went on. The largest single bomb the Soviets tested in the atmosphere had a yield of over *fifty* megatons. Again, life went on. Now the U.S. proposed to unleash something even bigger, also in the open air, if need be.

"Sir, I protest. This is a defamation, an—an act of utter lunacy. They can't possibly be serious." Jeffrey thought hard, then brightened. "They're bluffing. Or, or it's disinformation, meant to be leaked to the Axis, to get them to back down, to get ter Horst to turn away from the shelf. . . . Yes, that's right. It must be a disinformation bluff!"

Wilson shook his head sadly. "CINCPACFLT made it perfectly clear. Washington, the president, they're serious. This is absolutely secret, a last-ditch trap for ter Horst, and the Axis is not to know a thing. We're turning his use of the ice shelf on its head. Instead of a sanctuary for *Voortrekker,* it's to become the ultimate nutcracker. . . . The handful of friendly or neutral scientists, at ice stations or at the pole, will be flown out as soon as possible. Fortunately the weather hasn't turned yet and full winter hasn't hit."

"What are they being told?"

"Just that there's danger of tactical nuclear fallout. We're blaming it on the Boers, which *is* more or less true. . . . The Germans down there are being left to fend for themselves."

"But what about Lieutenant Reebeck and the SEALs?"

"Rendezvous coordinates will be prearranged in code, so as not to tip off ter Horst or the Germans. Lieutenant Reebeck and Clayton and

Montgomery are to transfer back to *Challenger,* using your minisub after it returns from the boomer without me, when you go under the shelf."

Jeffrey at least was glad for that. "I can use Lieutenant Reebeck's help on our search strategy."

Wilson nodded. "So now you have your orders, Captain, and your ultimate motivation: Get in under there, find and track ter Horst any way you can. Destroy him, and come back out, all in twenty-four hours. It's that, or the Antarctic becomes an ecological catastrophe for centuries to come, and the world teeters on the brink of a final holocaust."

43

Later that day, on the Ross Ice Shelf

ILSE DIMLY SENSED shaking. She moaned in protest, then rolled over to go back to sleep. The shaking continued. She flopped onto her back inside her sleeping bag. The air was so dry her eyes were scratchy and hard to pry open. Her mouth was parched, and her tongue felt swollen and cottony. She was so zonked by the strange Antarctic perpetual twilight, she had trouble remembering where she was.

She woke up enough to see Shajo Clayton's friendly, reassuring face, looking down at her as he poked her shoulder to rouse her.

"Your watch again," Clayton said. "It's almost *that* time," he added with keen anticipation. He handed Ilse a mug of steaming cocoa.

"Thanks." Ilse could see Clayton's breath, and her own, in the air of the ice-shelter bunker. She saw Montgomery manning the hydrophone console.

"Nothing yet," Montgomery said. "It ought to be soon, if ever."

Ilse nodded. Still in the sleeping bag, she drank the cocoa quickly, to clear her muckmouth and help her rehydrate. Then she realized how cold it had gotten the last few hours, and how damp and uncomfortable she was. The slightest sweat from her skin pores, and the moisture from her breath, condensed in the bag while she slept. Now, despite the wicking effect of the artificial fibers, she felt freezing water and even bits of ice against her body.

Clayton looked away while Ilse changed to her daytime clothing: fresh long underwear, her Special Warfare diving dry suit, socks and outer clothing, special boots, and her parka and mittens. Again she saw her breath, and the air was so dry it seared as it went down her throat. Dressing, she gave herself static electric shocks.

"I need a minute of exercise." Ilse put on her insulated face mask, woolen hat, and tinted goggles, and pulled thick gauntlets over her mittens. She raised her parka hood and, thoroughly bundled up, went outside.

It was *exceedingly* cold. In the Antarctic, in mid-February, it changed from summer to winter awfully fast. Out here, on this stark, open landscape, Ilse reminded herself that half the world was at war, and she was waiting now for more shooting to start. She felt terribly exposed and vulnerable.

She bent and stretched and ran in place and perked up. She looked around. The sun was to the east now, and the surface of the vast ice shelf was a mix of frosted silver and yellow and gold. Above her head she saw the moon, pale and almost full, higher in the sky than the sun ever got down here. The sky was clear except to the south, where heavy clouds were forming—the mirage of the distant mountains was gone, hidden now by a solid wall of gray that Ilse suspected was falling snow. The wind, as usual, came from the south—it was a lot stronger than when she'd first arrived. *That snow must be the leading edge of the blizzard.*

Ilse glanced toward the sun. It gave no warmth. But she saw a beautiful visual effect, a parhelion, like a rainbow or sun dog but more complex. The parhelion was caused by ice crystals in the upper atmosphere. There were arcs and shafts of light, and false suns too, optical illusions, surrounding the real sun in the center. Parhelions were extremely rare outside Antarctica, and Ilse had never seen one before. The ice crystals were another sign the blizzard was on the way.

Ilse knew the wind put great stresses on the ice shelf, and made for odd acoustic effects; sound carried amazingly here. She heard occasional cracks like rifle shots, strange noises like a freight train rumbling through a railroad tunnel, and weird inhuman moans and cries. Out to sea, as before, seals and penguins and orcas hunted and played, and she could faintly hear their barking and braying, carried against the wind. She heard roaring, thunderous splashes too, against the base of the ice shelf cliff. The powerful tide was coming in, raising the surf.

The marine gunnery sergeant, making the rounds of his concealed positions, saw Ilse. He came over and said hello, and they went into the ice shelter.

Refreshed and more awake now, Ilse sat at her console and resumed her vigil for signs of *Voortrekker*. Clayton and Montgomery asked the sergeant what the local Germans were up to.

"Last report I got, they were fiddling with some of the ice-core-sampling boreholes, you know, left by the scientists that got flown out. A few of the bores go all the way through the shelf and into the water. Intelligence thinks the Germans are laying listening gear or something."

On *Voortrekker*, approaching the Ross Ice Shelf

Van Gelder and ter Horst each read the same intelligence report on their screens. The information came from the German troops working on the Ross Ice Shelf. The data was kindly passed along by an aircraft from the Russian science station on the Hobbs Coast, east of the ice shelf. The aircraft had dropped a few transducers into the water to relay the data to *Voortrekker* by covert acoustics. One of the transducers fell in range of *Voortrekker*, as intended.

Ter Horst finished reading long before Van Gelder did. Van Gelder wasn't surprised—Jan ter Horst was a fast and voracious reader, with a superb memory and almost total recall.

"Well," ter Horst said, "now we know exactly where Fuller's forward listening post is set up."

"I expect they put it near the middle of the ice-shelf edge, Captain, for the best all-around coverage against us."

"We need to oblige them for all the trouble they've taken on our behalf. The easiest way to maintain contact with *Challenger* is to give them another datum on us, and let Fuller keep coming our way. . . . If he loses us completely now, things could get rather messy. We do need to destroy him under the shelf, before we turn back north."

Van Gelder nodded. "Otherwise we'd have him in our rear again." Like when ter Horst had first wanted to stalk the carrier *Stennis*.

"An unattractive proposition, and an unacceptable risk, especially with all the other Allied forces gathering against us, and with half our torpedo tubes unusable. This report says the American air force is scrambling B-52s with atomic depth bombs, sustained by midair refueling, besides everything else."

The autoloader for the port-side tubes had been fixed, after a lot of exhausting effort supervised by Van Gelder, but the starboard tubes were hopeless without dry-dock work.

"As paranoid as I am, Gunther, I think those faulty welds were simple overhurried workmanship, not sabotage. You were right all along, my friend. We pushed our luck, rushing into battle straight from a shakedown cruise."

"We've done well anyway, Captain."

But ter Horst was talking mostly to himself. "No, our first priority is definitely to sink *Challenger* under the shelf." She was the Allies' only ceramic-hulled sub in this hemisphere, the only vessel that could threaten *Voortrekker* on anything like equal terms.

Ter Horst and Van Gelder studied the navigation chart and gravimeter. *Voortrekker* was following a long trough of deep water, twenty-five hundred meters down. The trough slanted southeast, from the volcanic terrain of the Mid-Ocean Ridge behind them, toward the east end of the Ross Sea, dead ahead. Van Gelder thought of this local area as neutral-to-friendly territory: the helpful Russian base was nearby, while the American base at McMurdo was far away at the west end of the Ross Sea and the shelf. The German base was even further west than McMurdo, but the German forces—passed off as scientists—had aircraft and Sno-Cats to get around.

Van Gelder skimmed the last part of the intelligence report. It said the Americans had issued a warning that an atomic battle would occur—they offered air transport for any research teams who needed to evacuate. The Russians ignored the warning, since they wanted to monitor the crucial battle firsthand. The German troops, of course, were also staying, to fight.

Van Gelder pointed at the chart. "We can turn due south *here*, sir, and aim to pass under the shelf edge *here*. That would put us thirty miles east of their hydrophone setup. We ought to be heard for sure by the enemy listening post, if we make a burst of flank speed in the shallower water there." Because the Americans' hydrophone line was so lengthy, it could pick up very long wavelength—low-frequency—flow noise and tonals from a goodly distance, sounds which would be missed by any small air-dropped sonobuoy.

"Yes," ter Horst said, "we'd be heard for sure, but *too much* for sure. Let's go here instead." He pointed at a different place on the chart, further east of the listening post. "We need to make this subtle, Gunther, like we don't know the post is there, and they detected us through their own cunning."

Ter Horst talked to the navigator. The lieutenant ran calculations, then reported back. Ter Horst gave the helm orders. *Voortrekker* turned south and climbed out of the trough, toward the Antarctic continental shelf below and the Ross Ice Shelf above.

Ter Horst glanced at Van Gelder and smiled. "This sequencing should work perfectly. The listening post ought to have just enough time to make their sighting report before the German troops on the shelf get there to take them out."

On the ice shelf

Ilse watched her console intently. The time-and-motion estimates said *Voortrekker* ought to come by very soon. The wind was even stronger—Ilse could hear it right outside from down in the ice shelter. The wind also made noise on the sea, which her console detected and filtered out. But the sky still was light, and a nice blue-green translucence shone through the ice shelf's surface, which formed the roof of the dugout bunker.

Just now Montgomery slept, looking to Ilse like a big polar bear in a white Gore-Tex cocoon. Clayton came inside from getting fresh air. He brushed a sprinkling of snow off his parka. He said flurries were beginning to blow from the south.

The changing weather agitated the huskies chained outside—some of them barked and howled. Ilse heard whistling, then a loud crack. *The ice shelf, reacting to the wind stress again.*

The marine corporal threw himself into the shelter. *"Incoming!"*

Montgomery bolted awake.

"The Germans are attacking!" the corporal yelled.

This hit Ilse like a slap in the face. *They must've swung in from the south, using the blizzard to hide from Allied recon.*

Ilse heard more cracks, and stuttering roars, and bangs, and sharp concussions. The whole ice shelter shook. *Rifles, machine guns, grenades, and . . . and* mortars?

The corporal's radio crackled. It was the gunnery sergeant calling from another dug-in position. He wanted to know Ilse's status.

"Tell him we haven't made contact yet."

The corporal repeated this into the radio. The sergeant said they'd try to hold the Germans back. The corporal dashed outside.

"What if *Voortrekker* comes a different way?" Clayton asked. "If he doesn't get close enough to your listening grid, we'd never hear him."

"Negative information is still good information. It tells *Challenger* and the rest of our forces where *not* to look. We can't just pack up and run."

Enemy mortar rounds began to land more briskly. Their fire was marching back and forth, as if searching for Ilse or her satellite uplink or her cables into the water. The shelter shook again from a near miss. Bits of ice broke off the ceiling and pelted Ilse and her console. Mortar shrapnel pinged against the steps into the bunker. Acrid fumes blew in and made her cough.

Shit. Maybe they're attacking now because they know ter Horst is coming this way.

The noise of firing, both incoming and outgoing, grew heavier.

The gunnery sergeant crawled down the steps and flopped into the shelter. "We're outnumbered. They have Sno-Cats working around both flanks. We're in danger of being pushed into the sea."

"I can't leave yet," Ilse said.

"Don't be crazy."

"You don't understand what's at stake."

"I've got orders from McMurdo to get you to the rendezvous drop-off *now*."

"From McMurdo? Not Pearl Harbor? It isn't McMurdo's decision."

"*From* Pearl, *through* McMurdo, I think. I don't know."

"Christ," Ilse said. Another mortar shell landed close. Ilse and the sergeant ducked instinctively. A big part of the roof crashed down.

"That's it! Grab what you need and clear out. Head for the nearest vehicle." The sergeant looked at Clayton and Montgomery. "A static defense is hopeless now. Our best chance is an aggressive-maneuver battle." Both SEALs nodded.

Ilse and Clayton and Montgomery grabbed the equipment cases with their diving gear. Ilse took one last, longing look at her console read-outs. Still no sign of *Voortrekker*.

They left the bunker, crouching against the flying slugs of lead and fragments of steel. The corporal pointed them toward a Sno-Cat. He pulled the pin from a grenade and popped the spoon, poised to throw it down the steps to destroy the console and the bunker as they withdrew.

Above all the other noises, Ilse heard her console beep.

"*Wait!*" she screamed.

The corporal cursed, and shouted, "Grenade!" He tossed it in the safest direction he could, and everyone near him lay flat. Ilse slid down the steps into the bunker. She felt the concussion through the ice floor as the grenade went off nearby. On her console screen she saw the data: *Voortrekker*, at flank speed. She memorized the time, the range, the bearing. She climbed out of the bunker.

"Okay!"

This time the corporal threw in a satchel charge. Everyone ran for their lives. As they clambered into the Sno-Cat, the satchel charge blew. The whole roof of the ice bunker blasted into the sky. A tall column of smoke and shattered ice lingered in the air.

Enemy machine-gun rounds began to find their Sno-Cat.

"It's armored," the corporal said. "The window glass is armored too." The corporal turned to the driver. "Move out!" The Sno-Cat lurched into motion, heading east. Its winterized diesel engine roared. Its four separate half-track treads, two on each side instead of wheels, gave the Sno-Cat impressive traction.

Ilse jumped when a heavy machine gun mounted atop the back of the Sno-Cat suddenly opened up. It bellowed and the whole vehicle shook. Bright tracer rounds streaked through the flurries, strobing and piercing into the distance.

Ilse could see other white Sno-Cats following hers in a loose combat formation now. They too had improvised gun positions built into their roofs. She could identify the friendly Sno-Cats by small black stars stenciled on their sides.

She saw flashes behind her, further off, and caught her first glimpse of the enemy Sno-Cats—the machines, made in the U.S. by the Tucker Corporation, had been marketed worldwide before the war, and the Axis knew a good thing when they saw it.

Ilse turned to Clayton. "That was a solid detection on *Voortrekker*. I know what I need to know."

"Jeez, that cut it close."

Ilse nodded.

"The only problem now," Montgomery said, "is how in hell do we make the rendezvous in secret with all these Germans on our ass?"

The corporal glanced in the rearview mirrors. "There's more of them than of us." Ilse thought this observation might be true, but wasn't helpful. Her Sno-Cat bounced and pitched as it hit a series of sastrugi: ice carved by the steady endless wind into low rock-hard ridges like speed bumps.

The battle turned into a running, slashing dogfight. Ilse's heart was in her throat as incoming tracer rounds flashed by on both sides of her vehicle. The heavy, glowing tracer rounds plunged on ahead of her Sno-Cat, moving infinitely faster.

Mortar rounds began to land on the ice near friendly Sno-Cats—the Germans had big mortars mounted in some of their vehicles, firing through openings in the roofs. The mortar bursts on the ice were like near misses from enemy battleship shells. Snow began to blow more heavily, as the front edge of the blizzard closed in.

"More ammo!" the gunner in back of Ilse's Sno-Cat yelled.

"I'll do it," Ilse said. She got up and went in back. She began to hand up the heavy boxes of .50-caliber machine-gun belts each time the gunner ran low. Incoming rounds hit the window at the back. They pitted the bulletproof glass and obscured the outward view. The gunner kept firing from his semiprotected position in the roof. Ilse could hear Clayton talking on the corporal's radio, to the gunnery sergeant in another Sno-Cat, but she couldn't make out what they said. Her ears were ringing as the .50-caliber weapon kept up its pounding right above her.

A German mortar hit an American Sno-Cat dead-on. The vehicle blew apart in a livid ball of red fire. Flaming fuel spread quickly, and there was a pyre of thick black smoke. Ilse saw two burning figures crawl out and then collapse.

"This isn't working," Clayton said. "We can't afford to just keep dodging and hope the Germans run out of mortar shells before we all get killed. McMurdo's completely snowed in. We can't get air support!"

A mortar round landed near Ilse's Sno-Cat. A big piece of shrapnel punched through the driver's-side window and took off the driver's head in a spray of gore. The vehicle swerved, skidded sideways, and slowed. Montgomery grabbed the controls—he knew how to operate the vehicle from his SEAL cold-weather training. Then the machine gunner was hit, and he flopped into the passenger compartment. Blood squirted from a fatal wound in his neck. The corporal took over the machine gun. Ilse kept handing him ammo from the pile of boxes. The boxes were running low.

Clayton's radio crackled. He responded, then put the radio down. "Hold on!"

The Sno-Cat and the other friendlies all made tight U-turns, and charged straight at the Germans at top speed. Clayton held a satchel charge in his lap. The corporal had shifted his gun position with the turn, to fire forward. He chose one German Sno-Cat and tried to chew into its engine compartment with his bullets as the distance closed. It worked: something under the enemy Sno-Cat's armored front caught fire. A tread broke off the suspension system. The target spun wildly and slipped onto its side, remaining treads still churning in the air. The corporal fired at the now-exposed fuel tank. Ilse watched the German Sno-Cat blow sky high.

We're still outnumbered.

German bullets slammed the front of Ilse's Sno-Cat. She could see the tracer rounds as they ricocheted off the armor and into the sky. The external air filter and both exhaust pipes were riddled. Some slugs smacked the front windshield. Again the glass was pitted and crazed; now the view was obscured by bullet hits as well as blood. The smell of the blood inside the Sno-Cat was coppery and thick.

"Get ready," Montgomery shouted. The friendly and enemy vehicles were very close now, all driving at each other as fast as they could.

Clayton cracked the passenger door. He yanked the cord that fired the fuse of his satchel charge. As Montgomery steered the Sno-Cat right down the side of an enemy vehicle, Clayton tossed the live charge onto the hood of the German Sno-Cat. The satchel charge blew a moment later. The concussion was so strong it shoved Ilse's Sno-Cat sideways, but her vehicle kept running. Behind her, the enemy Sno-Cat was destroyed. She saw other American Sno-Cats try similar tactics. Friendly and enemy vehicles burned, and raised more smoking pyres.

A Sno-Cat running out of control crossed Ilse's path, with flames shooting out of its back. As ammo cooked off inside in sparkling flashes, it plunged off the cliff at the edge of the shelf, leaving a trail of smoke.

Through a spattered and sooty side window, Ilse saw an American and a German Sno-Cat collide head-on. The crews bailed out and continued the fight at close quarters, with rifles and bayonets—an American husky went for a German soldier's throat. They were left behind as the surviving American Sno-Cats wheeled in unison to charge the depleted German formation again. The Germans swung inland, to try to catch the Americans from the flank.

More bullets pounded Ilse's Sno-Cat. The corporal at the machine gun was killed outright. He fell into the rear of the passenger compartment, on top of the corpse of the private. Counting the headless driver whom Montgomery had shoved aside, there were three dead in the vehicle now.

But there was no time to think about that. Ilse climbed into the semi-enclosed gun position, bringing up boxes of ammo with her. The wind whistled strongly here, and the stink of vehicle exhaust and burnt cordite was choking.

She gripped both handles and tried to test the weapon but nothing happened. *"What do I do?"*

"Lift the safety toggles with your index fingers," Montgomery shouted as he drove. "Push the firing button with your thumbs!"

It worked. The long .50-caliber weapon kicked on its mounting; it was very hard to control. Above the din of the weapon and the engine noise and the wind, Ilse heard Clayton talking on the radio, coordinating tactics with the Marine Corps sergeant in command.

Clayton told Ilse which German Sno-Cat to target, one that had finished a wide sweep to the south and then turned toward her. Montgomery steered the Sno-Cat to face the incoming threat, and charged. Ilse held on as they came through the turn. She began to fire at the driver of the enemy Sno-Cat. She aimed, then corrected, by watching where her tracers hit. The enemy gunner fired back at her. Bullets hit the armor plates welded at McMurdo to form the firing position. Ilse cringed at each impact, and wanted to scream, but she kept her thumbs on the firing button. Beneath her the Sno-Cat vibrated and bounced, and in front of her the machine gun recoiled and bucked. It spewed out hot spent shell casings the size of cigars, along with links from the ammo belt the weapon devoured voraciously.

As the two vehicles closed the range, throwing up clouds of snow and fragments of ice, Ilse fired at the enemy driver. Eventually, her bullets would chew through his bulletproof windshield glass; her machine gun's barrel began to glow red hot. Eventually, the enemy gunner's bullets would find the chinks in her firing position, and kill her as the private and corporal had been killed.

A bullet struck Ilse hard. There was blinding pain in the whole left side of her head. Blood spurted down her chin and all over her neck and soaked her parka. She could only see out of one eye, and thought her left eyeball must be gone or else her goggle lens was covered with her brains. She felt lightheaded and suddenly very cold. She struggled to stay conscious and keep firing. *If I can only live long enough to kill that enemy driver . . .*

It worked. The German Sno-Cat's whole windshield caved in. The vehicle slewed sideways and stalled as Ilse's Sno-Cat thundered by. Clayton threw another satchel charge. It landed next to the enemy vehicle and detonated. When Ilse tried to see, the German Sno-Cat lay on its side, on fire. Montgomery steered due east again, parallel to the cliff edge, toward the rendezvous. Blood still poured from Ilse's head. Her remaining vision began to grow dim.

She slumped down from the machine gun, into the passenger compartment, and collapsed onto the shaking, rocking, blood-drenched deck.

Clayton heard the noise she made and turned. With her one good eye she read the horror in his expression, and knew for sure she was finished. She was afraid to touch her head, for fear of the mess that would be there where her face and skull once used to be. She was too weak to move at all now. She started to black out. Strangely, she welcomed death. Then she remembered she had one more job to do.

Clayton came back toward her. She used every last ounce of will and fought to blurt out the coordinates of her contact on *Voortrekker,* so Clayton could tell Jeffrey after the rendezvous.

Clayton told her not to talk. He knelt and cradled her head and opened a first-aid kit. She expected a final morphine shot, to die in drug-induced bliss.

Ilse repeated the coordinates weakly. She begged Clayton to write them down or memorize them before it was too late. She felt herself slipping fast.

Clayton pressed a wad of gauze to the side of her head, and held it snug with tape. He gave her a local painkiller shot.

"It's just your ear. I think your left earlobe is shot away."

Clayton gingerly pulled off her bloodstained goggles, and Ilse could see with both eyes.

Ilse felt alive again. The power of suggestion—her mistaken belief that Clayton knew she was dying—wore off fast.

Which is fine, and maybe now I get a Purple Heart, but we still have a lot of big problems.

"Who's following?" Clayton yelled to Montgomery.

"I can only see one Sno-Cat. I *think* it's friendly. The snow's so thick it's hard to tell."

"How do we make the rendezvous without being spotted and giving everything away?"

"Try to contact the other vehicle."

Clayton used the radio. The other vehicle was friendly—it belonged to the gunnery sergeant. "We need someone to drive while we suit up," Clayton told him.

Ilse heard the encrypted radio crackle a response.

Both Sno-Cats slowed. The sergeant ran from the other vehicle, and took over the driving from Montgomery.

Montgomery and Clayton helped Ilse strip down to her dry suit, then don her diving equipment. They had trouble getting the dive-mask strap around her wounded ear. Ilse tested her Draeger mouthpiece. The respirator's system was working fine, but she had trouble holding the mouthpiece between her teeth—the left side of her face was numb from the painkiller shot. Clayton and Montgomery suited up and grabbed other gear.

"GPS and inertial nav match closely," the marine sergeant shouted. This far south, it was hard for the Axis to jam the Global Positioning Satellite signals the way they did in other battle zones. "We're almost there. . . . Get ready." The sergeant steered closer to the edge of the ice shelf. The other American vehicle followed.

They slowed down only slightly.

Clayton popped the passenger door. "Ilse, you first."

Oh God. Ilse aimed for a snowbank, and threw herself from the vehicle. She hit and slid and rolled. She saw her blood staining the snow. She tried to move, and thought no bones were broken. Clayton and Montgomery crawled to her fast. The two friendly Sno-Cats roared on into the distance.

"Down," Clayton shouted.

Ilse dug into the buildup of snow and prayed her white camouflage getup would work.

Two German Sno-Cats roared by, barely yards away, pursuing the American ones. *It's a good thing we weren't run over.*

Clayton and Montgomery waited for the German engine sounds to fade. They hurried to rig rappelling lines at the very edge of the ice shelf, down the two-hundred-foot-high cliff into the sea; they used their ice hammers to drive rope anchors firmly into the top of the shelf.

Ilse peeked over the edge. *Now comes the really scary part.*

Although the cliff face, facing north, was sheltered from the blizzard's screaming wind, the tide was still coming in and the surf was strong. Big waves crashed against the base of the cliff, throwing up spray and tossing sharp, broken pieces of ice. Other chunks of ice, some of them very big, banged against each other or against the base of the cliff. This noise from left and right, stretching beyond the horizon, was like constant grinding thunder.

The air temperature was dropping fast now—it was way below zero degrees Fahrenheit, even before the wind chill—and the driving snow made it harder to see. But to Ilse, the spots of open water looked slushy, almost like oatmeal, as if the whole Ross Sea was starting to freeze. Farther out, Ilse saw the dorsal fins and upper bodies of killer whales, cutting between the ice blocks. The hungry orcas raised their ugly snouts out of the water, looking for prey on the floes.

"You okay for this?" Clayton shouted.

"I *have* to be," Ilse said. "It's the only way back to *Challenger.*"

Montgomery checked her diving rig one more time. He used six-foot lanyards to clip him and her and Clayton together. He connected the scaling ropes to the fittings on their belt harnesses. He threw all their excess equipment over the cliff, into the water, to get rid of it. Ilse reminded herself the cliff face continued straight down far below the waves, all the way to a depth of eight hundred feet, maybe more.

The three of them started rappelling down the cliff.

The breaking waves roared loudly now, and drove high up the cliff as if groping for Ilse personally. The banging of the broken floes below was frightening. The threesome halted against the vertical cliff of the ice shelf, holding just above where the foaming waves were reaching. Ilse was glad for her dive mask, as painful as it was, because it protected her eyes from the freezing spray and from ice bits that flew like shrapnel here.

"We have to time this just right," Montgomery yelled above the noise. "Into the trough between two big ones, and between the big pieces of ice!"

Clayton and Ilse nodded. Ilse glanced below doubtfully; she knew those larger chunks of ice weighed many tons, but she'd be damned if she let Clayton and Montgomery see her scared.

"When I count to three," Montgomery shouted, "we let go and drop, *together*. Understand?"

Clayton and Ilse said they did.

"If one of us hesitates, all three of us could be killed."

A very big wave crashed, and water drove up the face of the cliff, drenching Ilse and the two SEALs. Ice fragments hit Ilse's body. Sea spray froze on her dive mask. She gripped her Draeger mouthpiece desperately in her teeth. She held her legs together, with her knees slightly bent. She looked up, away from the water, and pressed her mask firmly in place with one hand.

"One . . . two . . . *three*."

Ilse released her climbing-rope fitting. She and Clayton and Montgomery, all tethered together, dropped like stones. Ilse watched as the top of the cliff seemed to recede into space. Then she hit the water and plunged deep.

The grip of the cold was a shock to her body. She fought to steady her breathing. Her face mask flooded at once. She tasted salt, where water had forced its way past her mouthpiece. Now her face was frozen numb and she could barely see.

She felt the crystal-clear and indigo-colored water surge as the next big wave came in. She and Clayton and Montgomery swam deeper, fighting for sheer survival, trying to not be smashed against the rock-hard face of the cliff.

Ilse was tumbled and buffeted by the power of the breaking wave. She heard its noise through the water. She felt both lanyards jerk at her waist, as the force of the water tried to tear her and Clayton and Montgomery apart. She made herself keep breathing evenly. If she held her breath, or inhaled at the wrong moment, an upward heave by the water could burst her lungs.

At last they got deep enough for comparative safety from the waves, but now they were so deep their pure-oxygen Draegers could give them convulsions. It was darker at fifty feet, though streaks of Antarctic sunlight did come down between the floes. In a race against time and against their own bodies' physical limits, they swam and used the undertow to carry them farther out to sea.

Montgomery activated a low-power sonar transponder. In a few minutes, as Ilse froze and tried hard not to drown, a big dark shape loomed below. It was the ASDS minisub from *Challenger,* holding as steady as it could.

Then Ilse saw other big, dark shapes in the water. *Killer whales. Drawn by us flailing around.*

The orcas moved to attack. Ilse made urgent hand signals to Clayton and Montgomery. They swam down under the minisub as the killer whales closed in. They made it through the bottom hatch just in time. Clayton slammed the hatch shut and dogged it tight. Water sloshed in the lockout chamber, and Ilse's eardrums hurt: the waves were so high, it had been hard for the minisub crew to keep the air pressure in the chamber properly equalized to the outside sea.

The ASDS crew followed the next step of diver recovery: the air pressure dropped gradually, for adequate decompression from their brief dive to sixty feet. The pressure reached one atmosphere, normal. Ilse, chilled to the bone, shivered uncontrollably, afraid now she was going into shock from her wound. Clayton and Montgomery hugged her to share their body warmth.

The hatch to the control compartment was opened from the other side. Ensign Harrison peered in, looking clean and dry and bright and cheery—then Ilse noticed Harrison wore lieutenant (j.g.) collar bars.

Harrison looked at the soaked, bruised, exhausted, bandaged threesome huddled in the lockout trunk.

"And how is everybody?" Harrison said.

44

On *Challenger,* approaching the Ross Ice Shelf

USS CHALLENGER WAS at battle stations, rigged for ultraquiet. Jeffrey sat at the command console, shoulder to shoulder with his executive officer, Bell. Commodore Wilson was gone, working now from the boomer sub according to CINCPACFLT's plan, and Ilse and the SEALs were back aboard.

Ilse sat at a sonar console next to Kathy Milgrom, Ilse's regular place at battle stations, only feet from Jeffrey. After getting as much sleep as they could on the demanding journey south, COB and Meltzer manned the ship-control station again. Harrison—finished driving the mini-sub—was *Challenger*'s relief pilot. Lieutenant Sessions, no longer the commodore's part-time executive assistant, was once more Jeffrey's full-time navigator.

The medical corpsman sewed Ilse's ear and changed the dressing. He gave her antibiotics and a painkiller shot—now she wore her sonar headphones with the left earcup over her cheek, so it wouldn't bother the wound. On Jeffrey's orders, the corpsman gave Jeffrey and Ilse, as well as Kathy, Sessions, and Bell, special medical stimulants. The stimulants would keep them wide awake for the next oh-so-crucial twenty-four hours. After that, they'd crash, but by then, Jeffrey knew, it wouldn't matter; Lieutenant Willey the engineer, or the weapons officer, could take the conn—if anyone on *Challenger* was even still alive.

Jeffrey had Clayton and Montgomery working damage control in the forward parts of the ship. The SEALs' great upper-body strength, and their steady nerves under fire, would help reinforce and stiffen all those younger men in *Challenger*'s crew—some of them still so inexperienced—who'd have to fight the fires and flooding. Jeffrey was sure that in the battle to come, Bell's damage-control parties would be busy. Jeffrey was grateful that the dozen civilian contractors on board since New London all had volunteered to stay, instead of leaving with Wilson, to also help as needed on emergency repairs.

Jeffrey pondered the awful responsibility he now bore. He thought back on all the military history he'd devoured since he was a kid. Jeffrey knew history would be the ultimate judge of the fateful decisions and actions happening now around the world. He dearly hoped the future world would be one that was free, not one controlled by the Axis. Jeffrey also hoped he wouldn't be recorded on the pages of history as a failure today.

Jeffrey remembered the last thing Commodore Wilson had said before he climbed into the minisub. "I've told you everything I know, and taught you everything I can. It's all on your shoulders now, Captain, and I do believe you like things that way. If you succeed, I'll give heartfelt thanks for your safe return. If you do not succeed, I *assure* you the boomers will launch. Then God help every one of us, and maybe I'll see you in hell." Wilson shook Jeffrey's hand. Jeffrey knew that Wilson was a loving husband and caring dad, but to his naval subordinates he always showed reserve. Wilson wasn't into touching or glib handshakes, so the gesture on parting, that firm, warm grasp of Wilson's hand in Jeffrey's own, reemphasized the somberness and importance of the moment.

Jeffrey still felt the afterglow of Wilson's strong, determined grip, and knew it was his best way, as both a man and an undersea-battle-group commander, of wishing Jeffrey good hunting. Wilson had to be very worried what would happen to his wife and children if things turned bad. Jeffrey knew how worried he felt for his own parents, and for his two older sisters and their spouses and their kids—all back in America's homeland, maybe targeted right now by Russian or Chinese ICBMs.

Wilson left it to Jeffrey whether or not to tell his crew about Washington's decision, and the reasons for it. Jeffrey mulled this over. As the outer edge of the ice shelf came up fast, he decided to do what he'd always done: share everything, and keep his crew fully informed. Jeffrey addressed the control room; phone talkers relayed his words throughout the ship.

"You all need to know exactly what's happening, and why. Listen carefully. Above all, don't react until I'm done, because I'm going to *tell* you how to react. I expect each and every one of you to follow my lead in this, with as much self-discipline as you've ever shown obeying any order in your life." Jeffrey summarized the deteriorating global military and political situation since Chatham Island had been destroyed by an Axis tritium-boosted weapon. In spite of themselves people gasped or grimaced when Jeffrey told of Japan setting off an atom-bomb test, and of Argentina and Brazil on the verge of going to war.

Jeffrey explained the president's decision, that *Voortrekker* simply could not be permitted to reach the Pacific. He tried to justify as best he could Washington's choice, that in extremis a demonstration of massive force would have to speak for the U.S. and her allies now that diplomacy had fizzled and the world was already half mad.

Jeffrey described the boomers' fateful rules of engagement, and *Challenger*'s time limit to destroy *Voortrekker* and get the word out. He paused to let it all sink in, then reminded the crew what was truly at stake—for *Challenger,* for the war effort, for world peace, and for the environment.

"The way to react, people, is to do what I shall do. Focus on your sense of duty, and on your love of your families and of your country and your ship. Pray if you think it helps, when you have time. Put in a prayer for me too, 'cause I think I'll be too busy." That brought a few chuckles, or sober nods. "Then put aside any thoughts of future or past. Forget about the outside world as we together go under the shelf. Forget all except the immediate battle when we engage the enemy. Rely on your shipmates as you always do, and perform your work to the best of your abilities, and concentrate on nothing but the task at hand."

Challenger, twenty minutes later

In the control room, Jeffrey and Bell intently watched their displays. Kathy and Ilse busily overviewed the incoming data. Around them sixteen other crowded people concentrated on their jobs. *Challenger* used every sensor she had—short of pinging on the bow sphere or trailing a towed array—to feel her way forward and locate the enemy. The outer edge of the Ross Ice Shelf lay dead ahead.

The gravimeter mapped the sea floor on the shallow Antarctic continental shelf. At short range, the image from the gravimeter was very sharp. But the gravimeter wasn't useful for looking *up*—it couldn't distinguish seawater from ice, because the density difference was small.

Challenger instead looked upward using her hull-mounted photonics sensors, in passive low-light TV mode, with maximum image intensification. Other imaging sensors looked down or to the sides. *Challenger* also used her tight-beam, low-power, active under-ice sonar, mounted in the sail tower. Emitting on sonar at all was risky but necessary.

The ship hugged the sea floor at sixteen hundred feet. The bottom of the massive ice shelf often came down almost that deep—*Challenger* measured sixty-five feet from the bottom of her keel to the top of her sail, and the clearance in some places would be tight.

Jeffrey saw the outer edge of the shelf, hard and dark and unforgiving, looming just ahead of him. He ordered a status message sent by the covert acoustic link, telling Wilson the hunt for *Voortrekker* was on. Soon Wilson's acknowledgment came back. Jeffrey ordered a timer readout windowed on a control-room main display screen, in large red numerals. It said 24:00:00, and then the seconds started counting down. Jeffrey knew he actually had maybe five minutes less than that to get Wilson the all-clear code. The forty-eight missiles would launch—taking short, flat trajectories—timed so every H-bomb blew when the timer read 00:00:00.

Jeffrey watched the various images windowed on his console, as Ilse and Kathy gave a running commentary. When *Challenger* went under the shelf, the cold-water anemones and starfish on the bottom petered out. Soon the strange Antarctic fish, with black fins and white antifreeze for blood, grew fewer and fewer. Going in further, even the phytoplankton petered out—no sunlight could penetrate the many hundreds of feet of opaque ice, laced as it was with tiny air pockets, plus algae and lichens and bits of soil and rock all scoured from the land by ancient glaciers.

The water became clean and clear. There were no seals or penguins or orcas here. With no open water close enough to let them reach the surface to breathe, marine mammals that ventured too far under the shelf would drown.

There wasn't even bioluminescence now. The underside of the Ross Ice Shelf was a desert. The noise of crashing waves and smashing floes died off into the distance, back behind *Challenger*'s stern.

Jeffrey ordered the photonics sensors switched to active line scan. The laser scanning beams might be picked up by the enemy, but with the lack of any outside lighting to amplify, the risk in using the blue-green lasers had to be taken. The pictures turned from color to black and white, but were very crisp and detailed.

"Boulder field dead ahead on the bottom," Meltzer called out at the helm.

Jeffrey saw it on the gravimeter.

"Volcanic bombs," Ilse said, doing her job as combat oceanographer. "Thrown here ages ago, when the shelf was smaller."

"Very well, Oceanographer. Helm, evade."

Meltzer turned the ship to avoid the boulders. As *Challenger* passed, Jeffrey could see the lava bombs on the line-scan pictures. Some were shaped like giant teardrops, blobs of magma that had solidified as they flew through the air and hit the sea. Others were jagged, the size of cars or cottages, granite and basalt heaved in a violent eruption out of some Antarctic volcano crater long before the start of recorded history.

The undersurface of the ice shelf was more jagged than Jeffrey expected. Big stalactites hung down, like ones of rock would from the ceil-

ing in a limestone cavern. There were cracks and crevasses in the bottom
of the ice shelf too, and also bummocks—pressure ridges—projecting
downward toward the Ross Sea floor.

"What causes that?" Jeffrey said.

"The main body of an iceberg is freshwater, you know," Ilse said.
"Here as well, when new ice forms by freezing onto the bottom of the
shelf, the salt gradually leaches out. The process forms these stalactites.
They're hollow: ice outside, extra-salty brine in the middle."

"Would hitting them damage us?"

"I doubt it, they're fragile, but there'd be noise, like breaking glass."

Jeffrey grunted—one more way to make a datum for ter Horst.

"The pressure ridges," Ilse went on. "I wasn't expecting them to be so
extensive either. I think that's from the conflict of such extreme forces.
The glaciers and prevailing surface winds push from the south, against
the tides and waves and occasional strong gales shoving from the
north. . . . And come to think of it, a lot of this ice started on the shoreline ages ago. Where the glaciers cross the coast they're a broken jumble
of angular shapes and ragged edges."

On the photonics displays, *Challenger* passed a group of what looked
like huge ice steps or platforms or slabs, attached to and projecting
down from the roof—that was what Jeffrey called the bottom of the ice
shelf now, *the roof.*

Jeffrey eyed the steps and slabs. "What made those things?"

"I'm guessing, but I suspect they're fragments left when big chunks
of the shelf calved off. There'd be secondary projectiles, and some
would be shoved back under the shelf by a backwash when the main
bergs tumbled away. . . . Older pieces would be frozen solid into the
roof. Newer ones might still be loose."

"Loose ones we could try to shove aside, if we had to?"

"I think so."

"What's *that?*" There was a giant boulder, scratched and with its
edges rounded, sticking partway down from the roof.

"Glacial origin, I think, carried out this far as the shelf advanced. It
must have been stuck there for millennia."

"Think there'll be more like that?"

"Probably. The whole underside of the shelf may be studded with them."

"Could they be shaken loose by torpedo blasts?"

"Probably."

"Terrific." *One more thing to worry about.*

"They may fall on their own, from time to time, as their weight makes them slowly ease down through the ice. Some of the boulders on the sea floor here look glacial, not volcanic."

Jeffrey studied the imagery. He saw what Ilse meant. "Sonar? *Your* assessment?"

"These conditions are extremely unfavorable, sir," Kathy said. "We're getting multiple reflections off all the ice and boulder surfaces. Even our own minimal self-noise seems to be coming back at us from everywhere at once. . . . And the water temperature is so steady and constant with depth, Captain, we won't be making direct-path sonar contact at any distance. The sound-speed profile makes all sound rays bend *up,* so the paths will curve and bounce off the bottom of the shelf repeatedly."

Jeffrey nodded.

"They'll reflect back toward the sea floor," Kathy continued, "and bounce even more. Each bounce distorts and weakens any coherent sound waves badly, both as to direction and signal intensity, sir. The pressure ridges and ice slabs and crevasses we're seeing, the boulders of different shapes and composition, this bottom mud from erosion silt combined with volcanic ash, they're almost impossible for us to model and adjust for. . . . With respect, Captain, *Voortrekker* chose a good place to hide."

"Very well, Sonar."

"Enemy visual contact!" Bell hissed urgently.

"Helm, all stop!" Jeffrey studied the imagery. His heart pounded, and he hoped it didn't show. He realized he'd been taken in by the alien beauty of this strange seascape, and almost forgot ter Horst could be lurking for him anywhere.

"What is it? An Axis minisub?" Something long and big was hugging the underside of the ice, half concealed by the ridges and steps.

"No incoming fire," Kathy reported. "No tonals or mechanical transients."

"Oh, God," Ilse said.

"Give me a proper report," Jeffrey snapped.

"It's a dead whale, Captain."

"Helm, get closer."

The whale floated upside down, with its belly against the ice.

"I can't believe it," Ilse said. "It's a *right whale.*"

Jeffrey couldn't tell if Ilse was delighted or horrified.

"They're endangered," Ilse said. "They were almost hunted to extinction, but they'd started to come back. Most of them are in the North Atlantic. I had no idea they came anywhere near here!"

"Why is it so far in under the shelf?"

"Deafened, or brain damage, I think. Too close to a nuclear battle in the Atlantic somewhere. It must've wandered through the Drake Passage, disoriented. It ended up under the shelf, too far in to get back out again in time. It suffocated."

"You mean like when a sick whale beaches and dies?"

"I think so. It's awful."

Challenger moved on. Close above them, everywhere for miles around, loomed the impenetrable thickness of the dark and massive ice shelf. Jeffrey almost felt its great bulk pressing on him personally. Close beneath, everywhere under the shelf, the sea floor seemed to press from the other direction. In most places the distance between was less than the length of a football field—a headroom shorter than *Challenger* was long. Ice bummock and protruding boulders made things even tighter.

"Sir," Bell said to break the uncomfortable silence, "I feel the need to advise that our weapon effectiveness will in different ways be both degraded and enhanced by these conditions." Bell's reports, like Kathy's, became formal recitations using standard phraseology—which might seem regimented, but was needed for the good of the ship.

"Talk to me, Fire Control."

"The sonar seekers in our fish will be just as confused as our hull arrays, or more so. But with the roof and the floor in close proximity, the usual spherical attenuation model for warhead power in deep water won't apply. Any weapon blasts, either high explosive or nuclear, will have much more effective force, much greater lethal range, than we're used to."

"Understood, Fire Control. We need to plan for that. Very well."

"Sir, I also want to reemphasize that we are no longer expendable. A double-kill in this situation would be a serious disadvantage for the Allies. Unless we survive and get out and confirm *Voortrekker*'s destruction, the boomers launch."

"Captain, I concur," Kathy said. "A tactical atomic duel far in under the shelf will be impossible for friendly forces to follow and interpret, either from out at sea or from atop the shelf. Even if we sink *Voortrekker* and do survive the action, there'll be no way for the outside world to know it unless we escape to tell them so in time."

"Sir," Ilse said, "I also have to concur. The blizzard will make the ice shelf shift and flex. Compacted ice is strong, but it *flows,* just like a glacier. Any boreholes cut through the shelf, old ones or new, will pinch off rapidly. And up on the surface, in winds of maybe seventy knots and a wind chill of eighty below, our troops will have a battle just to survive. Forget about them doing useful work establishing listening posts or relay stations to monitor us and give us any aid."

"Understood, everybody," Jeffrey said. "So let me throw in my two cents. We're just like that dead whale. If we get in trouble, or lose propulsion power, we're stuck down here. We do an emergency blow, we simply bob against the bottom of the shelf and wait to die."

Jeffrey knew there was no way they could go shallow to ease the outside pressure if there was flooding. There was no way to snorkel and get fresh air to vent the boat, if they had a fire or toxic-substance spill.

"That ice is much too thick for our weapons even on highest yield to make much of a dent in it. And there's no way to launch a radio buoy, or trail a floating wire antenna, either. . . . So we have to stop being pessimists, people, and all make sure we get things right the first time."

Jeffrey's officers acknowledged. None of them seemed sheepish—they'd been doing their jobs.

"Sir," Sessions said, "as navigator, given what the strict conditions are for mission success, I recommend we establish the concept of a bingo point."

"You mean like with an aircraft," Jeffrey asked, "the time when half your fuel's gone so you better head home?"

"Yes, sir. Given the physical obstacles we're encountering, and the unknown track we'll have to follow pursuing our target, there will come a point when we need to turn back or we'll be caught under the shelf ourselves, and die when *Voortrekker* dies, when the hydrogen bombs come raining down."

"You put that all too aptly, Navigator. . . . I didn't mean that as a put-down. It's a very good idea. Establish an estimate of time till bingo point."

"Captain, I'd need a lot more data to come up with a meaningful figure, and the figure will change depending on what course we steer and what terrain conditions we encounter."

Jeffrey reluctantly saw Sessions's point. "Well, what's your initial best guess, for starters?"

"Right now? Let's use half the hours remaining until the boomers launch."

"Concur. Pass the time-to-bingo-point to the vertical display. We'll put it under the time-to-boomer-launch number, in green below the red. When the green runs out, we know we better turn back."

Sessions acknowledged.

"If Antarctica has to perish," Jeffrey said, "at least we can make good our own escape. And that's not a selfish statement, people. If those boomers launch, the world is gonna be in a really big mess, and our navy will need us bad."

Everyone nodded somberly.

Jeffrey began to plan ahead, and felt somber indeed.

This place may be a wonderland of strange, chaotic ice and rock formations, but to a submariner it's a navigational and tactical nightmare. It's like ter Horst and I are two half-blind, half-deaf enemies, fighting with blunt knives and twelve-gauge shotguns in a maze in a house of mirrors. Besides that, the house is on fire and we're not even sure where the exits are.

"Pressure ridge dead ahead," Meltzer reported. "Volcanic ridge below it on the bottom. Clearance is inadequate, Captain."

"Very well, Helm. Turn left as needed and find a way through."

On *Challenger*, one hour later

Jeffrey's first major decision had been for *Challenger* to go under the Ross Ice Shelf a bit to the east of Ilse's former listening post. This was partly for better stealth and concealment, since to go precisely under her abandoned ice bunker would be too obvious. Also, given Ilse's datum as *Voortrekker* neared the shelf, this maneuver put *Voortrekker* almost certainly east of *Challenger*—and that told Jeffrey which way to search for ter Horst.

Again Jeffrey felt the incredible weight of the ice shelf pressing down, and the different drastic pressure of the running of the clock. He straightened his posture, as if to fight back—and also because he knew every person in the control room would take their mental and physical cues from his body language.

Jeffrey drew a deep breath. At times of such supreme tension, like most people, his senses were always heightened. The normal odors around him seemed strangely enhanced. The traces of ozone from electronic equipment made Jeffrey's nose tingle. The nontoxic cleansers, and lubricants and paint, always left a smell in the air in a submarine, but now that smell was particularly pungent and metallic. It seemed to leave an aftertaste as it went down Jeffrey's throat when he breathed. The ripeness of unwashed clothes and unbathed people all around him seemed even more ripe than only minutes before.

Jeffrey's vision was heightened, too. Objects he looked directly at appeared harder and sharper than normal. Colors—like a red fire ax, or a yellow battle lantern—were so vivid they almost throbbed. Sometimes there was a barely perceptible halo effect around things in Jeffrey's peripheral vision.

"Fire Control," Jeffrey said to Bell. "From here our lives are very simple. We have to solve two tactical problems."

"How do we find ter Horst, and then how do we kill him and get away."

"Well and succinctly put. Oceanographer, Sonar, Navigator, we need a pregame huddle. Fire Control, take the conn."

Bell acknowledged. Ilse and Kathy joined Jeffrey and Sessions around the navigation plot. The main display on the digital table showed the Ross Sea and the shelf.

"Throw things in the stew pot, people," Jeffrey said. "Let's stir them around and see what we get."

Kathy Milgrom spoke first. "We know passive sonar doesn't work well here, and pinging could give our position away disastrously."

"That leaves nonacoustic means," Jeffrey said. He'd been thinking about exactly this already, but he wanted his officers to participate and make contributions. He knew they'd do a better job of implementing a plan if they had a share in forming it.

Sessions brightened. "Temperature gradients, Captain, from the heat in *Voortrekker*'s steam-condenser cooling-loop seawater discharges."

"Good," Jeffrey said. "That ought to work well here, since the natural water temperature is so constant and cold."

"I concur," Ilse said. "And chemical sniffers. We already know the water under the shelf is very clean and pure. No manmade pollution, or nearby passing ships, or wrecks, to confuse the issue."

Kathy nodded. "There's always some leakage of lubricants and hydraulic fluids in any submarine's wake, no matter how thorough the seals. Propulsion shafts and torpedo-tube doors, rudder and sternplane and bowplane fittings, and antennas and periscope masts. From the seams around moving parts, fluids seep and mix with the seawater."

"So *Voortrekker* ought to be leaving a trail." Jeffrey made this a firm statement, not a question.

Ilse thought for a moment. "The trail should be fairly stable. No wave mixing down here, and gentle currents if any."

Bell, who couldn't help listening since the others were standing only a few feet aft of the command console, added something. "We pounded *Voortrekker* good in our last encounter, Captain, near the Bounty Platform. They'll probably have even more chemical leakage than usual."

Jeffrey nodded curtly. Then he noticed he was holding himself more aloof from the crew. With Wilson gone, Jeffrey was for the first time the ultimate command authority present on the ship. He found himself already becoming more demanding and less collegial. He understood

Wilson's behavior better, and began to see him as a role model, not an antagonist. Jeffrey was pleased with this, and felt good.

Now, speaking of antagonists, just where do we pick up ter Horst's non-acoustic trail?

"Nav," Jeffrey ordered, "show me the bottom terrain under this part of the shelf."

Session turned to his assistant. The senior chief typed on his keyboard. A different digital chart came up, and as Jeffrey watched the display zoomed in.

Jeffrey studied the chart. He eyed the contour lines. "So the Antarctic continental shelf is more like a doughnut than a plateau."

"That's right," Ilse said. "The shelf doesn't just rise gradually to the shoreline, like on other continents. There's so much ice all over Antarctica, eons of snow building up and compacting, it forms a layer in many places ten thousand feet thick. All that added mass pushes the whole tectonic plate down. It presses furthest in the middle, over dry land and the pole." Ilse ran her fingers along the nautical chart. "You get this shallow ring along the edge of the continental shelf, but then the water gets deeper again toward shore, before the bottom rises at the actual coast."

Jeffrey pointed at a place on the chart. "Here." A shallow spot, the high part of that outer tectonic ring, where the clearance between the sea floor and the ice-shelf roof was tightest. "We go *here,* we narrow our search for *Voortrekker*'s trail from three dimensions to two. Navigator, plot a course to this way point."

"Aye aye, sir," Sessions said. He and his senior chief went to work.

Jeffrey strode decisively back to the command console. "I have the conn."

"Aye aye, sir," Bell acknowledged. "You have the conn."

"This is the captain. I have the conn."

The watch-standers all crisply said, "Aye aye."

"Fire Control, when we reach my chosen way point, we turn east. When our temperature and chemical sensor readings spike, we know we're hot on *Voortrekker*'s tail."

"Understood," Bell said. "But our opponent can mimic our thinking, Captain, and *Voortrekker* has temperature and chemo sensors too."

45

VAN GELDER WATCHED his displays, fascinated by the weird conditions under the Ross Ice Shelf.

"Gunther," ter Horst said, "now that we see what it's like down here, I want your recommendation on what to put in our working torpedo tubes. I intend the melee to be fast and savage once contact is made, and we can't count on having time to reload."

Van Gelder was sure that Fuller and his executive officer were holding just such a discussion. Van Gelder thought very carefully: The choice of first-use weapons could make all the difference. "One tube for an off board probe, sir, for better scouting into areas with narrow clearance."

"Agreed. Reconnaissance must be the prelude to attack."

"One nuclear torpedo, and one high-explosive torpedo, to keep our options open, Captain. The engagement range could be very short once we find *Challenger*, possibly too short for a nuclear warhead."

"I concur," ter Horst said. "That leaves us one more tube in our crucial first salvo. What do we put in it? Not a decoy, we can't kill *Challenger* with decoys. So, a second nuclear Sea Lion, or a second Series Sixty-five?" *Voortrekker*'s high-explosive torpedoes were Russian exports, Series 65s, wide-body weapons with three times the warhead charge of the American Mark 48 Improved ADCAPs.

"I think it's a question of balancing offense and defense, sir. We can use our antitorpedo rockets against an inbound conventional weapon." The antitorpedo rockets were mounted in nonreloadable recesses on the outside of the ship. They homed on an inbound weapon and fired a blast of depleted-uranium buckshot, to destroy a high-explosive warhead, but their rocket motors burned out at only one kilometer—far short of the lethal range of an Allied atomic torpedo. "Sir, I recommend the last tube have another Sea Lion. That increases our offensive power. Or instead, it lets us use one Sea Lion against *Challenger* and one for self-defense, in case Fuller shoots at us with nuclear Mark 88s instead of high-explosive ADCAPs."

"Hmmm . . . I disagree. I want two Series Sixty-fives, not two Sea Lions. It gives us more flexibility."

Van Gelder wondered what decisions they'd make on *Challenger*.

"Load the tubes," ter Horst ordered.

Van Gelder passed commands. He and ter Horst armed the one Sea Lion's nuclear warhead.

"Sir," the sonar chief called out, "contact on acoustic intercept!"

Van Gelder turned. "What is it?"

Ter Horst glanced up eagerly from his console. "*Challenger?* Her under-ice sonar?"

"Er, no, Captain," the chief said. "It's an acoustic message burst. The format shows it's friendly."

"What's the message source?" Van Gelder asked, surprised.

"Range and bearing indicate it's a microphone, sir, lowered through a bore in the ice shelf a number of miles away."

"Pass the data to the communications room," Van Gelder ordered.

"Sir, the message is very garbled by the bad sonar conditions. . . . Sir, it's repeating."

Van Gelder waited impatiently.

"If they're trying to reach us at all," ter Horst said, "it must be something important."

"Well?" Van Gelder snapped at the sonar chief. Van Gelder was surprised at his own irritation. *Easy, Gunther. Everyone's under pressure. That might be okay for junior people, but first officers don't ever let it show.*

"The signal was cut off, sir," the sonar chief said. "It's like it just stopped, in the middle of a burst."

"No more repeats?" ter Horst asked.

"Wait, please. . . . No, nothing, Captain."

"The wire must have been cut," Van Gelder said, "by the shelf ice flowing and flexing in this storm." He could hear the shelf on the sonar speakers, reacting to the hurricane-force blizzard high above. Creaking and groaning and boinging sounds came from the speakers.

"Concur, sir," the chief said. "I think the transducer wire snapped in the middle of the retransmission."

"Did we get enough to decode?" ter Horst said. Now *he* sounded impatient, but that was a captain's prerogative.

Van Gelder eyed the data and ran programs on his console. "The supercomputer needs to clean up the signal a lot more than I can." He relayed the available data to the communications room.

In a few minutes Van Gelder's intercom light blinked. He answered, listened, then spoke to ter Horst.

"Sir, we got most of the message intact. The header says it's in captain's personal code."

"Send it to my console. . . . Look away, please." Ter Horst entered his special passwords. Then he read.

Van Gelder averted his eyes from ter Horst's screen, since the message must be top secret. He heard ter Horst laugh so hard he slapped himself in the side. Then ter Horst leaned over and reached, and actually squeezed Van Gelder's chin.

"Gunther, Gunther, Gunther. You'll never believe this. They've paid us the ultimate compliment. This is fantastic!"

"Sir?"

"Either our code breaking is even better than I thought, or we must have an extremely well placed source in the Allied command. Anyway, it seems the enemy questions Fuller's ability to defeat us one-on-one. They've given him twenty-four hours, and then they're going to shoot hydrogen bombs all over the top of the shelf."

"Just to destroy *us?*" Van Gelder was shocked.

"Japan detonated an atom bomb. Oops for America there! And Brazil and Argentina seem on the brink of war, thanks to meddling from our *agents provocateurs.* The Allies are really at their last extreme. And all because of *us!*"

"It's wonderful, Captain." Van Gelder wished he meant it. He began to understand the true implications of everything he'd done. It went far beyond the small tactical view. World sanity was collapsing like a stream of dominoes.

"This *is* wonderful!" ter Horst exclaimed. "It gives me a new idea, a whole new approach to our battle plan."

"Sir?"

"This couldn't possibly be better, even if I'd arranged it all myself in my wildest dreams."

"I don't think I completely follow you, Captain."

"Think of it! We destroy *Challenger,* then sneak out carefully before the deadline and avoid detection by other enemy forces all inferior to us. . . . Then the Allies shoot a bunch of hydrogen bombs at the ice shelf. *Then* we reappear in the Pacific, not dead but quite alive."

Van Gelder saw where ter Horst was going with this. "And sink the *Stennis?*"

"The United States will be humiliated, utterly discredited everywhere, nuking the Antarctic for nothing, after crowing that we were destroyed. Their president will have to resign, Gunther, they'll be so broken by their rash stupidity. . . . The Allied coalition will fall apart at the seams, and neutrals will flock to sign on with our side. We'll control half the world, maybe more. American voters will have their congressmen *begging* us for an armistice by then, pleading for mercy as we dictate terms. We'll *crush* their economy, force them to disarm altogether. They'll be plunged into mediocre impotence for a hundred or a thousand years. . . . *I love it!*"

Van Gelder didn't know whether to be elated or horrified. Ter Horst's scenario, so rosy for the Axis, might easily instead become a global thermonuclear firestorm.

The navigator interrupted just then.

"First Officer, sir, we have reached the designated course way point."

"Very well. . . . Captain, it's time."

"Thank you, Gunther. Better and better."

Ter Horst gave helm orders. *Voortrekker* stopped going south, farther in under the ice. She sidestepped east, then turned around to feel her way back north. She began to describe the second half of a big meandering circle under the shelf.

"Excellent, excellent, Gunther. I think we've left enough of a trail that Fuller can't possibly miss it. When we finish doubling back, we hide behind that nice pressure ridge you found, and our ambush setup will be absolutely perfect."

Simultaneously, on *Challenger*

On the sonar speakers, Jeffrey heard the ice shelf make strange rushing and banging sounds as it was battered by the storm raging topside.

On the gravimeter, he saw the bottom terrain become more rugged. The gravimeter also picked up larger boulders frozen into the ice shelf. On the display, they seemed to float in space above the sea floor like blimps. This eerie environment began to give Jeffrey the creeps. He realized that with all these dangling boulders, an enemy nuclear sub could afford to hold perfectly still if it wanted—its reactor shielding mass concentration wouldn't stand out on Jeffrey's gravimeter.

"Captain!" Kathy called out. "Contacts on acoustic intercept!"

"*Voortrekker* pinging? Her under-ice sonar?"

"No, sir. Message bursts. Transducers dangling down through the ice."

"For us?"

"Negative. Format indicates Axis origin. . . . They're repeating. . . . Transmission ceased abruptly."

Jeffrey remembered what Ilse had said about the ice shelf pinching off boreholes. "Did we get enough to try to decode?"

"I'm not sure," Kathy said. "I'll pass the data to the communications room."

"XO," Jeffrey said, "go there. Help the comms officer, keep an eye and give him encouragement. See if he can extract anything, anything useful at all." *Challenger* received high-baud-rate data dumps each time Jeffrey and Wilson talked to Pearl Harbor—this was one advantage of raising the satellite dish in a war zone. That data included the latest guidance on breaking Axis naval codes.

Bell left the control room, and the other officers played musical chairs. Sessions took over as Fire Control. His senior chief, the assistant navigator, became the acting navigator. Jeffrey asked Meltzer, who'd been at the helm awhile now, if he wanted a break. He agreed and traded with Harrison. Now Harrison had the wheel, and Meltzer took the relief pilot's seat.

"Captain," Ilse called. "Chemo-sensor contact. Temperature sensor contact. Definite contact on wake of an unidentified submarine."

"Unidentified means *Voortrekker*," Jeffrey stated. "Oceanographer, relay your data to the ship-control station. Give the helmsman steering cues so we follow the trail and track *Voortrekker* down."

"Yes, sir," Ilse said.

Jeffrey grabbed the intercom mike. He recalled Bell to the control room.

"Nonacoustic contact on *Voortrekker*," Jeffrey told him. Bell resumed as Fire Control. Bell's eyes looked slightly wild, probably from excitement and concern, exaggerated by the corpsman's stimulant. Bell had a wife and newborn son back in the States. But Bell's voice was firm and clear—he was steady and focused.

Sessions returned to the navigation plotting table. He carefully kept track of their course as *Challenger* twisted and turned. The ship went farther and farther in under the ice shelf, following *Voortrekker*'s lingering signs of intrusion. Jeffrey knew Sessions's data might prove vital as that red countdown timer ran down: any weapons fire under the shelf would knock loose big chunks of the roof, creating added obstructions. *Challenger* might have no choice but to go back out the same way she'd come, and even *that* might not work. The green number under the red—Sessions's estimate of time to the turnaround bingo point—guaranteed nothing in terms of survival.

Some while later, Bell's intercom light blinked. Bell answered. He listened, then said, "Are you *sure?*" Bell turned to Jeffrey. "Captain, they've broken a piece of that enemy message. All the supercomputer could get is the fragment, 'twenty-four hours.' "

"Twenty-four hours?" It fell into place for Jeffrey at once. "There's only one possible reason the Axis would try so hard to get such a message to *Voortrekker*. The deadline for the H-bombs. They found out somehow. *They know,* and that means Jan ter Horst knows."

"Torpedoes in the water!" Kathy screamed.

46

On *Voortrekker*

TER HORST MADE sure Van Gelder saw he was gloating. At the very last moment, ter Horst had changed his weapons-loading scheme. Every tube held a powerful high-explosive Series 65.

"All tubes fired!" Van Gelder said.

"Reload," ter Horst ordered, "all working tubes, more Series Sixty-fives."

Van Gelder relayed commands. He watched his weapons status screen. The port-side autoloader shuffled units on the holding racks in the torpedo room, then rammed one through each open tube breech door. The doors were closed and locked.

"Reloaded."

"Flood and equalize and open outer doors. Tubes two, four, six, and eight, match generated bearings and *shoot.*"

"All tubes fired." Four more big 65s screamed from the tubes, a second salvo. Now eight were in the water all together.

Van Gelder watched his tactical plot. The weapons technicians steered the units through their fiber-optic wires. They came at *Challenger* from almost every direction, from behind the slabs and bummocks in the ice-shelf roof, and past big boulders and terrain ridges on the roofed-in Ross Sea floor.

With half his tubes unusable, ter Horst was forced to leave *Challenger* one escape path. He'd purposefully chosen south, further in under the shelf.

On *Challenger*

"Eight torpedoes in the water," Kathy shouted. She called out bearing after bearing of the incoming threats.

They're closing in from all around us.

Jeffrey heard their engine noises scream. With the 3-D quadraphonic of the sonar speakers, and sound rays bouncing and bending crazily outside, each torpedo seemed to come from everywhere at once. Kathy's people needed the signal processors to sort things out.

"Sonar, weapon *types?*"

"Series Sixty-fives, Captain."

Ter Horst is somewhere close. Too close to go atomic.

"Fire Control, stand by on antitorpedo rockets."

"Ready on AT rockets, aye."

"Target each incoming weapon, smartly."

Bell began to launch the antitorpedo rockets. "Targeting is difficult, Captain."

The rockets were very maneuverable on their own, but they weren't wire guided. Their sensors were meant for a clean, straight shot at an inbound weapon in open water.

Rumbling roars began as each small rocket left its launch bay. The roars mixed with the screams of the inbound torpedoes.

Jeffrey's chest tightened as he heard the 65s begin to ping in terminal homing mode. Clearance between the roof and floor was tight, so tight that *Challenger* dared not go to flank speed and run. *If I use noisemakers now, while we're cramped by all these obstructions, they'll blind us as much as or more than they confuse ter Horst's torpedoes. I could run us straight into one of his inbound weapons by mistake.* Jeffrey ordered all stop, then told Harrison to hover motionless near the roof, to try to hide amid the crags and projections.

A 65 homed on a pressure ridge near *Challenger*'s hull and detonated. The blast force hit, then echoed harshly. *Challenger* shuddered and jumped. Above the echoes came the sound of breaking glass and shattering ice, as stalactites and bummocks were smashed. Ice shrapnel and loosened boulders slammed against the ship, and *Challenger* rolled and pitched uncontrollably, as if trapped in some disgruntled giant's cement mixer. Harrison and COB fought to hold *Challenger* steady.

The sudden change from being the ultraquiet hunter to being the prey amid such immense sonic mayhem badly stretched everyone's nerves. Just like that, Jeffrey told himself, the ocean had gone from the silence of a literal tomb to the inhuman cacophony of an all-out naval engagement. He forced himself to make the mental transition as fast as he could, and to exude by sheer charisma a steadying presence for his crew.

An antitorpedo rocket connected with a Series 65: There was a sharper, high-pitched *crack,* then the rocket warhead's burst set off the explosives in the torpedo. Again *Challenger* was pounded. Blast waves reflected unforgivingly from the roof and from the bottom, from ice-shelf pressure ridges hanging down and sea-floor ridges sticking up. The surviving 65s bobbed and weaved, as somewhere out there *Voortrekker* steered them with deadly intent.

More torpedoes and AT rockets blew. The noise drowned out the engine sounds of the remaining 65s, which still bore in on *Challenger* from all sides. On Jeffrey's order, Bell blindly launched more rockets—a desperate move. One hit on *Challenger*'s hull by a 65 and they were finished.

We're totally on the defensive now.

"Sir," Kathy shouted, "acoustic sea state is too high! We're losing situational awareness!"

"Captain," Bell yelled, "unable to update tactical plot. True range and bearing to remaining Sixty-fives unknown."

On the imagery from the photonics sensors, Jeffrey saw a huge fragment of roof ice streaming by. It tumbled madly, propelled by conflicting shock waves. It barely missed *Challenger*'s bow. *That chunk must weigh hundreds of tons.*

Another Axis torpedo detonated against the bottom, mistaking a large volcanic bomb for *Challenger*. An antitorpedo rocket hit something, but there was no secondary blast of a torpedo warhead this time, just more echoes and reverb and buffeting. The laser-scan photonics pictures grew dim, as bottom mud was stirred up higher and higher and ice shrapnel flew or floated on all sides.

There were more punishing explosions, much too close.

Jeffrey couldn't shoot back. He had no target. No one and nothing on *Challenger* could tell him where *Voortrekker* was.

That bastard ter Horst's ambush setup was perfect.

"Strongly recommend clear datum!" Bell urged. Submariner talk for "Run for your life."

Jeffrey stared at the gravimeter. The bottom still showed crisply—the image was immune to ice shrapnel and billowing silt and noise. Jeffrey saw hovering boulders—frozen into the ice shelf—suddenly disappear, as they were blasted from the roof by other Series 65 near misses on *Challenger*. He saw the same boulders appear again when they hit the floor and stopped moving. Some landed dangerously close to *Challenger*'s delicate stern parts and made loud thumps.

More 65s and AT rockets hit things and went off, or embraced each other and blew in double eruptions as Bell had intended. Some of Bell's intercepts were on weapons that by skill or sheer luck in the chaos had located *Challenger*—those enemy 65s were halted dangerously near.

Each blast slammed the ship sideways. She rolled to port and starboard hard, surging and heaving from the aftershocks. Everyone was tossed against their seat belts or knocked to the deck. Each blow, each blast, each hair's-breadth escape left the control-room crew more disoriented.

Challenger's hull was still intact, but this punishment couldn't go on. The under-ice sonar picture was totally garbled. Forced to improvise in impossible conditions, Jeffrey brought up older data, from before the ambush began. He prayed he wouldn't hit new slabs or fragments dangling down.

Bell was right, to clear datum. Ter Horst had bested Jeffrey *again*. He'd seized the initiative *again*. When Kathy reported yet more 65s in the water, another incoming salvo, there was no choice left to Jeffrey but to flee. There was only one sure gap in the ring of inbound enemy weapons.

"Helm, make your course one eight zero!" South. "Maximum practical speed! . . . Fire Control, launch noisemakers and jammers, *now!*"

On *Voortrekker*

"Sir," Van Gelder said, "enemy appears to be running south."

"Good," ter Horst said. "Send the remaining torpedoes after him."

"Captain, all wires have been broken by warhead blasts or secondary projectiles. Torpedoes must rely on preprogrammed instructions."

Ter Horst sighed. "Well, so be it. I didn't think sinking him would be *that* easy. We accomplished our main objective. We forced *Challenger* farther in under the ice. . . . Helm, sidestep the area of disrupted water and ice chunks. Then proceed due south."

"Understood," the helmsman said.

"Sonar," ter Horst ordered, "reestablish contact on *Challenger*'s tonals as soon as possible."

The sonar chief acknowledged.

"See what I'm doing, Gunther?"

"Trying to scare Jeffrey Fuller?"

"I'm using our secret weapon. We know he has that twenty-four-hour deadline. If we push him in far enough, toward the point of no return, he'll start to crack. . . . For now, we soften him up. In the next melee at a time of *my* choosing, we'll go nuclear and blast his ship to pieces."

47

CHALLENGER RAN SOUTH, weaving through a maze of obstructions, and then slowed for better sonar sensitivity. The crew was settling down from their latest battering, and *Challenger*'s most important equipment continued to function. Jeffrey listened to the rumbling on the sonar speakers, the echoes of the battle still dying off in a broad arc sternward of his ship. The ice shelf right overhead continued to protest from those torpedo blasts, and from the blizzard. Everyone in the control room could hear groaning, rushing, creaking sounds coming from above— the thick shelf reacting to massive horizontal and vertical forces. Unlike the lingering torpedo noise, the blizzard sounds were getting stronger.

Jeffrey glanced to his left. Bell stood between Ilse and Kathy, leaning over their shoulders as they worked at their consoles. At Jeffrey's orders, they were hurrying to analyze sound recordings of the skirmish with *Voortrekker,* to learn whatever they could.

"Sir," Bell said, "we're pretty sure *Voortrekker* is down to four tubes now. Ter Horst's rate of fire, and his tactics, both point to four weapons per salvo, not eight. I conjecture he took damage from the aircraft he shot down. That's good news."

Jeffrey considered this carefully. "It is good news. It evens the odds. But considering what's at stake here, XO, fifty-fifty odds aren't good enough."

"Understood, sir." Bell returned to his console. Ilse gave Kathy more help in figuring out and adjusting for the unique acoustic conditions under the shelf. Kathy and her sonar chief and their technicians struggled toward Jeffrey's next goal: regaining contact on *Voortrekker*. Jeffrey very much wanted that first contact to be on ter Horst's vessel, not on more of his incoming weapons.

Except for the noises from outside, and the clicking of keyboards, and the murmuring of the sonarmen, the control room was very quiet.

Challenger continued more or less south, farther in under the ice. Jeffrey windowed Sessions's navigation plot. *Challenger*'s actual course was a snaking path, for two reasons: Harrison, at the helm, needed to avoid the obstructions in the shelf roof and on the ocean floor. Also, since the terrain was too constricted to stream a towed array, the ship had to turn right or left to expose the wide-aperture arrays toward north—ter Horst was undoubtedly out there somewhere, pursuing. Hearing him, before he heard and pinned down Jeffrey, required sifting through confusing raw data with every ounce of supercomputer power, signal-processing acumen, experience, and talent that *Challenger* and her sonar people possessed.

Jeffrey watched the red and green digital timers tick away each second, to the bingo point and the ultimate deadline. He reminded himself that when that red timer ran out, Jeffrey would have helped make naval history, whatever that history might say. The thought made him feel alert and alive—it was *not* just a cliché that he'd trained for this moment his entire adult life.

The part of Jeffrey that went through dread or doubt was very deeply repressed. He could sometimes sense it, that weaker human element, grating against his consciousness, and he forced it down even deeper. His job was to make sure the history books of the future said something favorable about him today. Recognizing this gave him an adrenaline rush, the latest of many, and he savored the sensations for all they were worth.

Jeffrey planned ahead, trying to project his next move, and ter

Horst's next move, and Jeffrey's countermove, and ter Horst's countermove to that.

Part of this is like playing chess. Whoever can see clearly the most moves ahead can win. . . . I need a better plan than what little I've got right now.

Jeffrey considered his options carefully. He talked with Bell, and they drew sketches on Jeffrey's console with their light pens.

At last, Jeffrey sensed excitement among the people to his left.

"Contact reestablished on *Voortrekker*," Kathy reported. "Contact is a multipath reflection contact."

"Where is he?" Jeffrey said.

"Somewhere north of us, sir, as expected. Beyond that, range and bearing are impossible to determine."

"Show me your waterfall display."

Kathy passed the data to Jeffrey's screen. He saw a dozen different lines, on different bearings near due north, each gradually tracing down the waterfalls of broadband noise. Normally, each of these lines would indicate a separate submarine contact on exactly that bearing. Now, Jeffrey knew, all of them were distortions of *Voortrekker*. All of the lines were faint, meaning a weak or distant contact. Some lines faded out altogether, then others would appear from somewhere else.

Kathy clicked on each waterfall contact, then showed Jeffrey the tonals on that bearing. The wide-aperture arrays picked up medium-frequency sounds from some of *Voortrekker*'s machinery, such as harmonics from the fifty-Hertz line hum of her main high-voltage electric supply. As Jeffrey watched, there were twelve, then ten, then fifteen ghost images of *Voortrekker* on his screen.

Jeffrey ordered Harrison to try making different turns, to hold ter Horst at the outer edge of detection range. Jeffrey couldn't afford another direct confrontation yet. Until he thought of some conclusive way to more than even the odds, the chance of *Challenger* being sunk was too great—and if she were sunk those hundreds of hydrogen bombs would fall.

"He holds contact on us too, sir," Bell reported. "Every time we go left, the cluster of data on him turns left with us. Whenever we jink right, he follows us right."

"Signal strength increasing!" Kathy said.

Bell looked at Jeffrey meaningfully. "He's making a lunge at us, sir."

"Does he know where we are, Fire Control?"

"I doubt he's tracking us well enough for a firing solution, *yet*."

"Helm, head south more."

"South, aye aye," Harrison said.

"Signal strength of contact on *Voortrekker* decreasing," Kathy said. Ter Horst was falling behind.

Jeffrey pondered. "Fire Control, what if he puts another weapon in the water, and lets it rely on its onboard homing sonar?"

"He'd probably just waste ammo, Captain, and he has to be running low. Its software would be swamped with contacts seeming to come from a dozen different places at once. If the weapon pinged, it'd be blinded by returns from projections and boulders everywhere, each one of them looking like a submarine hull."

Jeffrey nodded. He'd thought exactly that himself—based on what he was seeing on *Challenger*'s own sonar screens—but he wanted Bell to check his reasoning. Bell used to be *Challenger*'s weapons officer, and Jeffrey trusted his knowledge and instincts on torpedo performance in extreme environmental conditions like this.

"Signal strength increasing!" Kathy reported.

"Another lunge," Bell said. "He likes to play cat and mouse."

"He's getting on my nerves. Helm, increase speed two knots."

"Aye aye." Harrison sounded uptight. He concentrated intensely on his displays and steering cues. COB and Meltzer watched, giving him advice and moral support.

"Signal strength of contact on *Voortrekker* dropping," Kathy said. In a little while she added, "Signal strength now holding steady. Assess the range is constant again."

"He's matching our speed," Bell said. "He's feeling his way, just like we are."

"He wants to push us farther in under the ice," Jeffrey said. "And I think I see why."

"Sir?"

"He knows about our time limit. He knows we have a bingo point.

He's trying to frighten us by making us think we'll never get out alive."

"Understood."

"But we do have one advantage. We *know* he's aware of our deadline."

"How does that help us, Captain? It means he knows a double kill down here would be a disastrous defeat for the Allies. It puts us completely on the defensive, which isn't the way to win against ter Horst."

"Let him push us farther in, XO, if that's what he wants. It gives us at least one tactical edge. *We* get to scout our way ahead of *him*. That gives us superior knowledge of local acoustic and terrain conditions."

"Understood," Bell said. "But how does *that* help us, sir?"

"I'm not sure yet. . . . Oceanographer."

"Captain?" Ilse said.

"I want to talk to you about Jan ter Horst."

On *Voortrekker*

On the sonar speakers, Van Gelder heard the lingering effects of the high-explosive skirmish, left well behind to the north. *Challenger's* noisemakers gurgled weakly, making their last dying gasps. There were scraping and crunching sounds as loosened pieces of ice, all of them buoyant, jostled each other. They floated up and settled against the bottom of the shelf, making distant bangs and thuds. There was a sharp concussion, then throbbing echoes that went on for minutes, as the last wayward Series 65 torpedo homed on something it thought was a target.

Looking forward of *Voortrekker,* using the bow sphere and both side-mounted wide-aperture arrays, the sonar chief held vague contact on *Challenger.* The signals surged and faded as *Voortrekker* and *Challenger* moved. Sound rays took different paths at different times in different places—splitting and rejoining, bouncing off the sides of pressure ridges, reflecting off hard but irregular boulders in the roof or on the floor. Data from *Challenger* would carom first off the ice of the shelf and then off the mud on the bottom, bending and zigzagging up and down, over and over, confusingly. It was impossible to have more than the vaguest idea where *Challenger* was.

The chemical and temperature sensors were of little tactical use now, since *Challenger*'s real path twisted and turned so much. To try to follow it exactly would only waste time, and also risk losing the primary contact. Worse, such delay, or such predictable maneuvering by ter Horst, might set *Voortrekker* up for a trap exactly like the one *Challenger* herself had just barely escaped.

Ter Horst interrupted Van Gelder's thoughts. *It's as if he reads my mind.*

"Patience, Gunther. For now we simply keep herding him toward his doom. When he thinks it's becoming too late to ever get out in time, and he and his crew start to buckle, *then* we strike. With a broad spread of Sea Lions set on maximum yield, we'll smash his hull wide open with what targeting data we've built up by then."

"What if he turns and fights?"

"We'll hear it right away. We fire at him then, that much sooner."

"Sir, as your first officer I feel compelled to state a devil's-advocate argument."

"I'm listening."

"Wouldn't it be safer if we just tried to sneak away now? We're closer to the shelf edge than Fuller. We may already have him scared enough he'd willingly break contact."

"Don't be silly. If we do that, we give up the protection of the shelf, the whole positional advantage we worked so hard for, and we expose ourselves to Allied forces with Fuller still in our rear. I dearly want to sink *Challenger* by my own hand, Gunther, *here*. I suppose you could call it an ego thing."

"Yes, sir." *Ter Horst is more self-aware than I sometimes give him credit for.*

"Besides, if we let *Challenger* survive, and Fuller gets out a warning, the boomer launch is called off. I really, *really* want those boomers to launch."

On *Challenger*, one hour later

"Tell me again about Jan," Jeffrey said.

"I already did ten times."

Jeffrey ignored Ilse's impatient tone. "Do it again. We need to sweat every detail. . . . Tell me what he's like, from a submariner's point of view."

"I'm not sure I'm the right person to answer that."

"Come on, Lieutenant. This is your third mission with my ship. You were with us every step of the way last time we faced ter Horst. Talk to me."

Jeffrey sat at the command console. Ilse stood, leaning against the corner of his console so she could face him easily. This way, she didn't have to crane her neck from her seat at a sonar workstation, and her wounded ear would hurt her less.

Ilse sighed, then took a deep breath. "He's clever, aggressive, inventive. He's outgoing, charming, a very good liar. He's ruthless, shrewd, and brave. He's religiously devout, and really thinks God's on his side."

"The old-line Boer theology?" Bell broke in.

Ilse nodded, gingerly, to protect her ear. "They think a passage in the Bible gives them the right to enslave all blacks."

Bell made a face—he was African American. "So where does this get us with ter Horst, Captain?"

"We need to understand his tactical personality better, to have a chance of beating him. We need to see how he might become predictable, if we take a close enough look at his psyche."

"That's another thing about Jan," Ilse said. "He's completely unpredictable. He does it on purpose. He *flaunts* it."

"Then let's see what we know about him lately," Jeffrey said. "Maybe we can spot a pattern. . . . First, there was Diego Garcia, an unquestionable success for him, and one he accomplished at high personal risk. Then he nukes a helpless civilian island. He sinks a virtually defenseless *Collins* boat. He takes more risks to shoot down half a dozen Allied aircraft he could've simply tried to avoid. He sinks two old, slow, noisy *Los Angeles*–class boats, taking both on at once. Then, he exposes himself to even *more* risk by revealing his position, to fire that salvo of cruise missiles at us the last time we went to periscope depth."

"You make him sound like a bully, Captain," Bell said.

"Does that mean then that on some level he's a coward?" Jeffrey asked. "I'm not saying his tactics were wrong or distorted or reckless. They *worked*. I'm saying that in each instance, another commander might've done something different, an equally good alternative approach in each scenario. What ter Horst did tells us something specific about ter Horst."

Ilse shook her head. "He may act like a bully, but there's no way Jan's a coward."

"No, you're right, coward's not the right word. But is he on some level insecure, overcompensating, pushing people around for fun or sadism?"

"Jan may be a sadist at times, but he sees it as justified by serving a higher cause. And I can tell you unequivocally, he is in no way whatsoever insecure." Ilse gave Jeffrey a meaningful look. He got the impression she was reminding him, pointedly, exactly how intimately she knew the man.

"But is he a show-off?"

"Lord, is Jan a show-off."

"So he's human, he *does* have needs. He needs constant achievement, right? And he needs an appreciative audience."

"Um, definitely."

"If we wanted to get him to snap, how would we do it?"

"I don't think Jan is someone you could get to snap. He's a born predator. Snapping other people is what he does for a living."

"Everyone has their breaking point," Jeffrey said. "What are ter Horst's hot buttons?"

"I'm not sure what you mean."

"What things bother him? What does he *really* dislike?"

Ilse thought a while. "Well, in the context of the war, I can see three things. He would hate to be outsmarted. He would hate a nasty surprise. And he would *hate* to ever be thwarted."

"We've already hit him with a little of all three, Captain," Bell said. "At the first sea mount, you outsmarted him by sending our fish around both sides of the mountain. He did get a nasty surprise, too, us being in this theater at all so soon, not stuck in dry dock. And he's been partly thwarted, at least, by you driving him back from the *Stennis* and forcing him to flee here."

"Is ter Horst afraid to die?"

"No," Ilse said. "He doesn't feel fear of anything in any normal sense."

"Let me put that differently. Wouldn't he *mind* dying, if he had any choice? Doesn't he really, *really* want to live?"

"Um, yes. I think I follow you now. If he's dead, he can't enjoy his own big ego anymore, and he loses his earthly audience of admirers for his greatness. . . . Even with *his* ego, and his fanatic religious beliefs, he has to know that in heaven, assuming there is such a place, he'd be way down the totem pole compared to God and the attending angels."

Bell couldn't help grinning at how Ilse put that.

"If we had to hit him with more of the things he dislikes," Jeffrey went on, "would a constant stream of them be better over time, or should we go for one big avalanche at once?"

"The avalanche. Definitely. He's much too tough to be bothered by continual smaller upsets." Ilse turned to Bell. "He's had enough small upsets already, just like you said, XO. He's still *very much* in the fight, and seems to have the advantage of us right now."

Jeffrey frowned. He didn't like defeatist talk from subordinates. "That's not for you to say, Lieutenant."

Ilse apologized.

Jeffrey accepted. "What I'm hearing in all this is that maybe we could use ter Horst's own ego against him."

"You mean, sir," Bell said, "that he's so self-impressed he may be brittle?"

"You beat me to the punch line, XO." Jeffrey was pleased: Bell was sharp, and was thinking what Jeffrey was thinking. "Ter Horst must be flying high at the moment, from a string of big successes. Even his being here under the shelf, he can give himself the credit for. It *was* his idea, and it *is* the perfect place for him to kill *Challenger* one-on-one."

Ilse and Bell waited for Jeffrey to say more.

"We have to make the final battle be more than a question of technical insights and gadgets. We fought him to a draw that way last time, off
South Africa. If we try something like that again, he'll be expecting it,
and we'll be too predictable ourselves. Down here there won't be a
draw." Jeffrey pointed at the big red timer.

"So just what are you suggesting?" Ilse asked.

"We become unpredictable, by adding another level to the conflict, a
sort of guerrilla-warfare mentality on top of the tactical contest. If we
surprise and outsmart and thwart ter Horst badly enough, and get the
timing of it right, we can flood him as a person with negative emotional
inputs. That works on his brittleness, maybe just enough to give us an
edge."

Ilse looked skeptical.

"Say it," Jeffrey told her.

"What you're suggesting is an awfully speculative proposition."

"It's constructive risk taking," Jeffrey said coldly.

"So what's the plan?" Bell asked. He seemed to be stepping in to break
up the tension between Ilse and Jeffrey.

Good. That's what XOs are for.

Jeffrey debated with himself how much more to tell them. He did
need his people as sounding boards, and he didn't want to stifle anyone's initiative.

"Frankly, I'm not sure yet. I feel things starting to jell up here." Jeffrey
pointed to his head. "But one or two big pieces of the puzzle are still
missing." Jeffrey surreptitiously glanced at Harrison and Meltzer and
knew he'd have to make a fateful choice. Inside, he felt regret.

Jeffrey made eye contact with Ilse and Bell. "I *can* tell you now, you
aren't going to like what I come up with. . . . We have to start to act the
opposite of what ter Horst expects, and I'll have to be even more ruthless than he is, as hard as that may be."

"How?" Ilse said.

"To begin with, from now on, as far as we're concerned, there's no
deadline and we're happy if we die."

48

Several hours later, on *Voortrekker*

VAN GELDER GAVE ter Horst a status report—*Challenger* was continuing south, at about seven knots, apparently the best speed she could safely make in these difficult conditions, where the risk of a terrain collision was very real. *Voortrekker* persistently kept pace, responding each time Fuller tried to turn—cutting him off, forcing him ever farther in beneath the ice. The tension was getting high enough on *Voortrekker;* it had to be reaching the breaking point on *Challenger.*

Ter Horst acknowledged Van Gelder's report. Then Van Gelder saw him stare into space.

"Sir, is something the matter?"

"I was imagining what it would be like down here."

"Captain?"

"When the H-bombs drop. Forty-eight Trident missiles on those two American submarines. Each with several warheads, somewhere between four and ten hydrogen bombs per missile. That's at least two hundred separate warheads. . . . Above, there'd be the coordinated flashes of the weapon bursts, low-altitude air bursts probably for maximum effect. So many of them, such an amazing thing to witness if you could. Then

there'd be the mushroom clouds, hundreds rising thick and strong together. The heat, the shock waves, the blast winds, the radiation. But
down *here*, Gunther. What would it sound like down *here*? What would
you see? What would you feel? How long would it take to die?"

Van Gelder shivered. "I expect it would be over quickly, sir. The shelf
is so thick it's strong as steel. I think it would act as a squash plate, and
not break up at once. The dynamic overpressure, beneath it, would be
instantaneous, wouldn't it?"

"Yes, I think you're right. Even a ceramic-hulled vessel would be
crushed like *that*." Ter Horst snapped his fingers for dramatic effect.
"Fuller won't feel much. It's a shame. A fast and almost painless death
for him." Ter Horst sounded tired.

"Should I have the messenger bring you a coffee, Captain?"

"No, I've had plenty already. . . . I ought to have rested more, on the
way down."

"Do you want to go to your stateroom, sir? I can wake you if anything
happens."

Ter Horst pointed at all the displays: the photonics imagery, the
gravimeter, the under-ice sonar, the broadband waterfall ghost images
of *Challenger* ahead. The navigation plot, and the estimated time to
turnaround, to the point of no return.

"Things are too critical, Gunther. . . . This is one more advantage we
have over *Challenger*. As my first officer, you're command qualified.
Fuller's exec is not. He hasn't had his commanding-officer training yet."

Van Gelder nodded. Because of foreign aid received from Britain
in the early Cold War, South Africa's submarine fleet followed Royal
Navy procedures. The second in command went through the training and testing course for making captain before he took up his duties as first officer. He might or might not get that ultimate
promotion, his own ship, but he had the preparation and the knowledge. In the American navy, prospective captains didn't take the
training course until *after* their executive-officer tour. Man for man,
Fuller's XO should be weaker in tactics and leadership than Van
Gelder was.

"I'll just put my head down here," ter Horst said. "You take the conn."

"Aye aye, sir. I have the conn."

"Poke me in the shoulder if there's any change. If not, wake me one hour before Fuller needs to head back north or be trapped by the bombs. Meanwhile, keep up the pressure on *Challenger.*"

"Yes, Captain." Van Gelder saw what ter Horst was doing by taking a nap: when the time came, *Voortrekker*'s captain would be refreshed, while Jeffrey Fuller would be run ragged. "Sir, should I have someone get you a blanket?"

"You're very considerate, Gunther. But no, thank you, I'm fine." Ter Horst folded his arms on his console top, cradled his face, and quickly went to sleep.

Van Gelder took command as the slow but steady chase continued. Minute by minute, mile by mile, *Voortrekker*'s margin of safety dwindled just as much as *Challenger*'s did. *Face it, Gunther, this is the scariest tactical gambit ter Horst has ever come up with.*

A few hours later, on *Challenger*

Jeffrey studied his screens. *Voortrekker* was still there, following somewhere close behind him, matching course and speed with every move *Challenger* made.

"It's like playing Simon Says," Jeffrey told Bell.

"Sir?"

"When we go right, he goes right. Left, left. If we speed up, he speeds up. Slower, slower. See what I mean?"

Bell smiled. "That's funny, Captain. Simon Says."

Jeffrey glanced at the time remaining to bingo point. "We've led them around by the nose long enough." *Me fleeing more and more southward is credible to ter Horst, given how he shocked us in that ambush with his Series 65s, plus the threat of* Voortrekker's *Sea Lion firepower now. . . . But to win I need to beat him to the punch this time.* "I think we've got our enemy as lulled by this routine as they're ever gonna be. . . . XO, it's time we shake things up."

"Sir?"

"He'll be planning something, his decisive attack, for around the time he estimates we need to head back north."

"Er, concur. He has to destroy us by then or he's stuck here himself. And that would be the point of maximum psychological pressure on us."

"He *thinks*. I'm going to reshape the parameters of the game now. Reshape them drastically."

"Captain?"

"Fire Control, change the loads in torpedo tubes one, three, and five. Load nuclear Mark 88s." Tube seven held an off-board probe, not deployed yet.

"*Nuclear* weapons, Captain? With this terrain and these short engagement ranges?"

"Do it, Fire Control." The latest rules of engagement allowed Jeffrey to go nuclear at his choice—better a few kiloton torpedo blasts under the ice than dozens of megatons above.

Jeffrey watched his weapons-status screen. He and Bell armed the warheads.

"Preset all warhead yields to maximum."

"That's dangerous under the shelf, Captain. Remember, their force will be amplified."

Jeffrey knew Bell was simply doing his job as devil's advocate. "Maximum yield."

"Aye aye."

Jeffrey thought out loud, and explained his intentions to Bell. "We can't use a decoy down here, any better than *Voortrekker* can. The fiber-optic wire would snag against one of these projections. It'd tangle and break. We'd lose control of the unit, and we can't see well enough ahead to preprogram it effectively."

"Concur."

"Besides, something the size of a torpedo trying to act like us down here is too small. Ironically, with all these reflective surfaces under the shelf, diffraction patterns of the decoy's noise would tell *Voortrekker*'s wide-aperture arrays that the decoy was tiny, hence wasn't really *Challenger*. Isn't that right, Sonar?"

"Yes, sir," Kathy said.

"Very well. Fire Control, launch the off-board probe."

"The probe is also torpedo sized, Captain."

"Launch the probe."

"Aye aye."

COB took control of the probe at his console.

"Chief of the Watch, use the probe to scout to our front. Find me a nice, big pressure ridge a few miles ahead, if you can."

COB acknowledged.

Jeffrey pulled a writing pad and pencil out of a drawer in his console. "XO, I want to modify a pair of our ADCAP torpedoes, like this." Jeffrey drew a sketch.

"Jeez, I don't know, Skipper. It'd take cutting, and welding too."

"We could use diamond cutting wheels instead of torches to make the cuts, right?"

"But sir, the heat and vibration, so close to all that fuel and high explosive inside the weapons . . . all while we still need to fight the battle with *Voortrekker*? We could have an accidental detonation right in the torpedo room, and do a *Kursk*. . . ."

"We don't have any choice, XO. Have your weapons officer get on it right away. The contractors can help."

"Yes, sir. I just want you to know how risky this is."

Jeffrey pointed at the red number on the countdown clock. It kept going down every second. "You don't need to remind me about risk."

Jeffrey cleared his throat. "Lieutenant Meltzer, take the helm." Meltzer left the relief pilot's seat. He and Harrison changed places.

"XO, you have the conn."

Bell acknowledged. He looked surprised and uneasy. Sessions took over as Fire Control.

Now comes the really hard part. But I have to do this.

"Harrison, my stateroom, now."

A few minutes later, on *Voortrekker*

"Captain," Van Gelder said, "wake up!"

"Eh? What? What is it?"

"*Challenger* has increased speed to almost twelve knots!"

"Course?"

"Course is due south."

"He's running *farther* in under the shelf? It doesn't make sense."

"*Challenger* accelerating. Speed now *fifteen* knots."

"He's gone insane. He must know he can't possibly lose us like this. The added noise just makes him easier to follow. . . . Helm, increase speed. Do not break contact!"

The helmsman acknowledged. *Voortrekker* sped up. Van Gelder felt the ship bank more steeply, as she dodged to port and then to starboard to avoid the obstructions between the shelf and the floor.

"First Officer," the navigator said, "time to enemy's turnaround point at new speed has dropped very sharply."

Van Gelder acknowledged. He knew the navigator's estimate of *Challenger*'s point of no return assumed all along that she'd egress from under the shelf at maximum practical speed. Now, the faster *Challenger* ran in deeper under the shelf—everything else being equal—the longer it would take her to get back out, because the distance to be covered on the way back would be greater. *Complicated to think about, but that's why being navigator is a full-time job.*

Van Gelder saw ter Horst look at the navigator's revised time estimate on his screen.

"He's forced my hand, unintentionally, Gunther. We need to destroy him, *now.*"

"Concur, Captain." If they followed *Challenger* for very long at this speed, both ships would be trapped beneath the ice. Van Gelder remembered ter Horst's musings before his nap, about the hundreds of thermonuclear blasts, the overpressure, the crushing of hulls.

"Fuller must have cracked, or he's panicking, or he just hates me so much he's committing suicide to make sure I'm destroyed."

"We could still turn back, Captain, and leave him to his fate."

"*No.* I intend to murder him once and for all myself." Ter Horst glanced again at the turnaround-margin display. The green number was running down to zero fast. "There's still time. Make tubes two, four, and six ready in all respects, including opening outer doors. Preset all Sea Lions to maximum yield. Fire a fan spread, to cover the cluster of bearings on our multipath contacts to *Challenger.*"

"Ready."

"Preset all weapons to home on passive sonar if their guidance wires break."

"Preset!"

"Tube two, shoot!"

"Unit is operating properly."

"Tube four, shoot!"

"Unit is operating properly."

"Tube six, shoot!"

"Unit is operating properly."

The weapons technicians steered the Sea Lions at *Challenger.* Because the torpedoes were so small and so maneuverable, they could attack at their full speed, seventy-five knots. *Challenger* was helpless. The weapon wires caught on ice slabs or boulders, and snapped. Van Gelder reported when this happened.

"It doesn't matter, Gunther. We have him dead to rights."

"Yes, sir."

Ter Horst sighed. "After all that, it seems so *easy* now. . . . I never thought I'd feel such letdown, when I ought to feel delight. My most worthy opponent, about to perish. We escape, and the H-bombs fall. What can I possibly do for an encore after *this?*"

"All Sea Lions closing on terminal runs. . . . Sir, all three weapons converging. They appear to have picked up the real, main contact. All weapons approaching lethal range on *Challenger.* . . . No return fire so far."

"Of course not. We've taken him completely by surprise. He doesn't even have Mark eighty-eights in his tubes for useful countershots."

Van Gelder studied his tactical plot. "Any second now!"

Ter Horst ordered the sonar speakers turned off.

The water under the shelf erupted in three massive explosions. The echoes and reflections of the blast waves blended into one continuous uproar. Ice fragments were blown back from the blasts with such force they pelted *Voortrekker*'s conning tower and bow dome. Boulders fell from the roof or were hurled to bounce along the bottom. The ice shelf cried out in protest, vibrating and crackling and singing and crunching wildly overhead.

More ice banged against the hull. The noise outside was so loud it was something Van Gelder felt more than heard. His brain was overwhelmed by sensory inputs. Everything in the control room bucked and shook. *Voortrekker* rolled and pitched. The helmsman fought his controls to little effect.

The ship began to experience a whole new problem. The heat of the fission detonations, trapped under the ice, spread out sideways. It began to alter *Voortrekker*'s buoyancy. Ter Horst shouted orders. The chief of the watch struggled to keep the ship on an even keel. Despite his and the helmsman's best efforts, *Voortrekker* became too heavy in the atomically heated water.

"Chief of the Watch," ter Horst bellowed, "collision alarm."

Van Gelder could barely hear the alarm against the overwhelming decibels around him. He held on tight as *Voortrekker* thudded against the bottom, stirring up the muck, scraping against the boulders before she recovered.

The hellish punishment outside went on, declining only slightly. Crewmen shook their heads to clear the ringing in their ears. Damage reports came in to Van Gelder's screens, or over the intercom, or were relayed by the phone talker. There were repairs to be done, but nothing vital. Crewmen had been injured, but none of their wounds seemed critical.

When it became possible to shout intelligibly, ter Horst ordered, "Tube eight, launch the off-board probe."

"Tube eight, launch the probe, aye aye!" Van Gelder said.

"Probe is operating properly!"

The probe slowly advanced ahead of *Voortrekker*. The noise getting through the hull began to die down, somewhat, but the control-room sonar screens showed nothing but meaningless snow.

"I'll take control of the probe myself," ter Horst said. "We need to make absolutely sure that *Challenger* is destroyed."

Van Gelder realized this was just an excuse. Ter Horst, characteristic of the man, wanted to count coup over *Challenger*'s remains. There was no way Fuller's ship could have survived.

The imagery from the probe came in through the fiber-optic cable. Its active sonar side-scan data was distorted by ongoing reverb from the triple blasts, and by chaotic sound-ray paths with all the new ice fragments and atomic bubble clouds. As the probe neared ground zero, ter Horst switched its cameras from laser line scan to passive low-light-level TV. Van Gelder was surprised by this, but then saw why.

"Look at that," ter Horst said. "That red-yellow glow in the background, hugging the roof. That must be from cooling plasma from the fireballs." Ter Horst was enraptured. The otherworldly glow faded slowly, and he switched back to active line-scan mode. He also tried to gather data with the probe's sonars.

Van Gelder was amazed by the readings on his screens, and by what he saw on the pictures from the probe.

The fireballs' thermal energy had disrupted sound propagation terribly—the side-scan pictures from near the blast site warped and rippled disturbingly. The weapons' kinetic energy had knocked giant slabs from the roof. Some slabs stood on end, jammed between the shelf and the bottom, blocking access to the site of *Challenger*'s wreck.

"I will not be deterred," ter Horst said. "I *will* see *Challenger*'s carcass."

So much bottom muck was stirred up that the TV pictures from the probe were almost useless now. Then the fiber-optic cable caught on something and snapped. The backup acoustic download link was useless.

"Launch another probe, smartly!" Ter Horst used a lighter touch on his joystick. He felt for gaps between the giant vertical slabs. He sent the probe through a gap. He turned its side-scan sonars and laser cameras to maximum power. He began to feel his way around, using what the probe's sensors could make out from short range.

Van Gelder saw a big upside-down crater blasted and melted into the shelf roof by a Sea Lion. There was a matching, mirror-image crater right below it, in the ocean floor. Minutes passed.

"Aha!" Ter Horst had spotted some wreckage. He overlaid the line-scan TV picture on the active sonar picture and had the computer merge them, to try to get a better look. "What do you think that is, Gunther?"

Van Gelder stared at the murky, distorted imagery. "If I didn't know better, sir, I'd say that's a fragment of minisub hull."

"Of course. Smashed inside *Challenger*'s hangar, then thrown clear when the mother ship herself was hammered apart."

Ter Horst searched for more wreckage. He drove the probe back and forth across the blast site repeatedly. His frustration began to mount. "Where is it? There should be more. *Much more!*"

"*Torpedoes in the water!*" the sonar chief screamed. "Two, three, *four* torpedoes in the water off our stern. Wide fan spread, range is short and closing fast. *American nuclear Mark eighty-eights!*"

Ter Horst's face turned white. "*What?*"

"Sir," Van Gelder urged, "we need to evade."

"God *damn* Jeffrey Fuller. He sacrificed his own minisub as a super-decoy to fool me. He worked around behind us while I chased his cursed mini as its sonars gave off recordings of noise like *Challenger* would make. He sacrificed one of his own crew to get at *me.*"

"*Captain.*"

"Yes, yes. Launch noisemakers and jammers. Gunther, give me data for nuclear countershots."

"Noisemakers, jammers, aye aye. . . . Sound conditions are too chaotic, acoustic sea state is too high. Unable to give reliable data for countershots on inbound weapons."

Ter Horst cursed. "Helm," he snapped, "make maximum practical speed."

"Course, sir?" the helmsman prompted, alarmed.

"Course? *Away,* away from the inbound torpedoes." There was only one direction. "South!"

"Sir," the navigator shouted, "advise that with this course and speed we will be trapped under the ice!"

"*Don't you think I know that?* Gunther, fire a fan spread north!"

"Sir, we're low on ammo."

"For Christ's sake, so is he! *Obey my orders!*"

"Fan spread north, aye aye."

"Sir," the sonar chief called, "inbound weapons signal strength increasing rapidly. Range is closing very fast."

"Helm, increase speed! More! *Faster!* God *damn* him!"

49

On *Challenger*

JEFFREY MENTALLY HELD his breath as the green timer at the front of the control room ran down toward zero and *Challenger* continued south. He sensed his crew become uneasy in a new way, and he couldn't blame them. To settle them with a firm grip, he coldly told Sessions to take the green number off the screen.

This is it, the start of my final big push, to try to shove ter Horst through a looking glass of his own making. Shove him through to the far side, the losing side, to see if I can make him crack like glass. Jeffrey wondered how ter Horst would react, personally, if Jeffrey's efforts succeeded. *Would ter Horst become abusive to his crew, or a raging screamer, or just shut down inside, or what?*

Jeffrey waited for reports from Sonar and Fire Control. Outside *Challenger*, all around, thunder still rumbled continually from the echoing reverb of *Voortrekker*'s three earlier atomic detonations, the first such weapons ever set off in Antarctica.

One way or another, today, those three won't be the last. Jeffrey's own fish were running southward, and *Voortrekker* would surely launch counterfire. Jeffrey felt self-revulsion at having to contribute to this defiling of the environment—but he shook it off so he could carry on with his duty. *Minimize the damage,* he told himself. *Win and you can minimize the environmental damage.*

Data from Sonar and Fire Control flashed onto Jeffrey's screens.

"*Voortrekker* running south now, Captain," Bell said. "She's launched noisemakers and jammers. . . . *Voortrekker* has fired torpedoes. Torpedo courses near due north, torpedoes no threat to *Challenger* . . . *Voortrekker*'s speed impossible to estimate, but appears to have increased substantially."

"Good, good," Jeffrey said. He'd had *Challenger* quietly sidestep east, after deploying the minisub, and he let *Voortrekker* keep on moving south. Then Jeffrey snuck his Mark 88s out and around behind ter Horst, hiding them at first in the noise of ter Horst's own weapon blasts against Jeffrey's ASDS minisub. The end result was that *Challenger* and *Voortrekker* traded places—now *Challenger* was closer to the ice-shelf edge, and Jeffrey was the pursuer, not the pursued. His Mark 88s churned through the water ahead of him.

Jeffrey smiled like a wild animal. "We have ter Horst on the run, XO. . . . Helm, maintain chase, but keep a safe distance until our units blow."

"Understood, sir," Meltzer said. The relief pilot's seat was empty. Jeffrey's conscience tortured him, and he ordered a qualified senior chief to take the position.

"Captain," Bell said, "our weapons are being confused by bubble clouds and ice debris from *Voortrekker*'s Sea Lion shots at our minisub."

"As expected."

"Units will detonate in one or two minutes, sir."

"Very well."

Sending Harrison off in the mini was the hardest order Jeffrey had ever had to give. Harrison volunteered, when Jeffrey had explained what needed to be done and why. Jeffrey thanked Harrison, but inside he knew the truth. Harrison was too young to grasp the meaning of his own mortality. Too young to really comprehend that he wouldn't be around to bask in the rewards of his valor, that he'd just be dead.

When I said I needed to become more ruthless than ter Horst, I wasn't kidding.

When this is over, if we survive, I'm putting Harrison in for the Medal of Honor. I'm just sorry it has to be posthumous. . . . It seems such an empty gesture, to take his parents' son away and give them back a little case with a piece of metal and cloth, and tell them he was a hero.

As if to emphasize Jeffrey's culpability, the water heaved and smashed at the ship when *Challenger's* outbound weapons detonated. The effects were the same as when *Voortrekker's* Sea Lions went off against *Challenger's* mini: noise, heat, bubble clouds, smashing boulders, tumbling slabs of ice. Ship damage and crew injuries.

But this time the shelf above reacted differently—and when *Voortrekker's* errant Sea Lion countershots blew, the reaction became even worse. The new phenomenon eclipsed anything Jeffrey had met before.

Jeffrey watched as the outside pressure readings fluctuated madly. Sea pressure drove the control room's depth gauges, and their readings became meaningless too.

"The shelf is flexing up and down!" Ilse yelled.

Then *Challenger* began to be shoved forward and backward. It went on and on, and wasn't a propulsor malfunction, and nothing Meltzer did could stop this crazy, sick-making back and forth. Jeffrey wondered what the hell was happening.

Ilse explained it. "Entire shelf reverberating from atomic blast effects! Water under the shelf is sloshing due to bottom protrusions shifting toward and away from the shore!"

Jeffrey heard a terrible, menacing, crackling noise, immensely strong but far away, carried through the body of the shelf, then down through *Challenger's* hull. The crackling became a deep, protesting rumble. There was a drawn-out, ripping, tearing *boom.*

The pressure fluctuations and the sloshing grew even stronger. New roaring and crashing, and watery rushing, sounded from all sides.

"Conjecture massive piece of outer edge of shelf has calved!" Ilse shouted. "Conjecture new iceberg is many miles across and wide!"

Jeffrey ordered Meltzer to keep pressing ahead, south, to stay on *Voortrekker's* tail. *That newborn giant berg makes everything harder.*

Sessions pointed out that, according to the latest estimate maintained on his navigation console, *Challenger* had gone in past the point of no return.

But Jeffrey now was fixated on his goal. "Very well," he acknowledged formally, by rote.

It took minutes for the atomic shock waves and fireball energies and reverb to die down somewhat, and for the motions of the ice shelf to subside. To avoid ter Horst pulling an opportunistic vanishing act in the chaos, Jeffrey ordered Kathy to ping on the bow sphere.

Kathy reported that *Challenger* gained a definite contact on *Voortrekker*, still south but also west of where Jeffrey expected. Kathy assessed that *Voortrekker* could hear *Challenger*'s ping, too. Jeffrey ordered a course change westward, to channel *Voortrekker* south. He used the threat of point-blank nuclear fire to force ter Horst to keep his distance. Jeffrey dearly hoped ter Horst didn't decide to come close and take Jeffrey with him. Bell warned that acoustic and terrain conditions would gradually improve—to the point when *Voortrekker* could get a usable firing solution on *Challenger* from farther away.

"Very well, Sonar, Fire Control." Jeffrey put steel in his voice.

Then Bell pointed out something else. "Captain, even if your tactics do break ter Horst's focus, we still have his first officer to contend with. He'll be command qualified, sir."

Jeffrey frowned. "Oceanographer?"

"Captain?" Ilse said.

"This Gunther Van Gelder, the guy you ran into on Chatham Island. Is he ter Horst's yes-man, or is he good?"

"I don't know Van Gelder well. We met at parties and banquets a handful of times when I was Jan's date. Jan held court and did most of the talking."

Jeffrey nodded impatiently. He forced himself to be a good listener while Ilse got to the point.

"I can say Van Gelder is not a yes-man. He's modest and even-tempered, but very capable, or Jan would never have picked him. Jan's crew is the best they've got. They're proud, and devoted to their captain."

"Does Van Gelder have a weakness or a blind spot?"

"If he does, it might be that he feels morally troubled about the war. But I don't see how that helps us. He's not the sort to turn traitor, or start a mutiny, or anything like that."

On *Voortrekker*

Van Gelder watched his screens nervously, reacting to what had been done to him and ter Horst and their ship. Now everything was reversed: Fuller showed his willingness to go nuclear here, and *Challenger* hounded *Voortrekker* mercilessly—farther and farther in under the ice.

Van Gelder eyed the navigator's countdown clock and nodded grimly to himself. The green number that showed *Voortrekker*'s time remaining to turnaround and escape from the shelf had suddenly fallen past zero, with *Challenger*'s clever trap and Fuller's jarring change of tactics. Now the green number actually showed a negative figure, the ever-expanding margin by which *Voortrekker* missed her deadline to survive. The red number, *Voortrekker*'s paltry lifespan until the enemy missile subs launched, kept ticking down second by second—*Voortrekker* was doomed.

"Hundreds of them," ter Horst said. "Hundreds of them. All flying and falling through the sky. Then their fission triggers ignite, and the hydrogen starts to burn, like in a star. Hundreds of stars, shining over the Ross Ice Shelf. Shining through the ice, saying hello."

Van Gelder was alarmed by ter Horst's mood and tone of voice. The captain sounded dreamy and withdrawn. Van Gelder searched for something diplomatic to say, to get ter Horst to respond with a purpose, to bring back the ter Horst he knew.

"Sir," Van Gelder urged, "recommend deleting time-to-turnaround from countdown clock." The useless negative number was just eroding crew morale.

"Leave it up. It fascinates me." *Voortrekker* continued south, since ter Horst had the conn and he didn't issue new helm orders.

Van Gelder thought fast. The situation was truly desperate, but ter Horst was reacting passively, maybe pushed beyond rational thought. He would surely recover soon, but by then it might be too late for constructive action. *This Jeffrey Fuller is good. Much too good.*

But he isn't suicidal. Something doesn't make sense.

Van Gelder double-checked with the sonar chief and the navigator. *Challenger* was still in pursuit, still playing cat and mouse with the tables turned.

If we ran out of time to be a safe distance from the shelf when the H-bombs explode, then Challenger *also ran out of time.*

Why would Fuller subject his ship to intentional self-destruction? It can't be so he's sure he's got us pinned under the shelf, to prevent us sneaking out like ter Horst wanted—leaving the U.S. to nuke the shelf needlessly. Ter Horst's plan for that went by the boards already: we're decisively pinned and Fuller has to know it.

So what is Jeffrey Fuller doing?

Van Gelder had a flash of insight. It wasn't the first time this had happened during combat, that strange and inexplicable discontinuity in his brain, when Van Gelder's mind was struggling in confusion and then suddenly the insight was simply *there*.

He knew how Fuller intended to survive. It was brilliant, but it was much too late, starting now, for *Voortrekker* to try the same thing.

Van Gelder began to form another plan. He saw how *Voortrekker* might yet get away: *Challenger* would be *Voortrekker*'s ticket home, if Van Gelder could play things just right.

If it works, I'll turn the tables on this Fuller just like Fuller turned the tables on ter Horst. I'll yank Fuller's whole ingenious gambit out from under him, and use an even nastier one in return.

As much as time was of the essence, now more than ever, Van Gelder's worst mistake would be to let ter Horst sink *Challenger* too soon. That possibility was very real, if ter Horst reacted out of vengefulness or spite—which were the only things ter Horst had left, unless Van Gelder did something drastic *now*.

Van Gelder explained his plan. He had to go through it twice for ter Horst to fully understand. Ter Horst was aghast at the audaciousness, the deviousness of it. Crewmen in the control room murmured or squirmed.

Van Gelder realized he'd suffered tunnel vision. So intent was he on his captain, he'd forgotten for that split second that the rest of the crew was there.

Van Gelder saw he'd blundered at this crucial juncture, and squandered his value as first officer, as a backstop to ter Horst: he'd kept his grip when ter Horst lost it, in public. He'd out-thought his captain in front of the crew, in the face of the enemy. While they were all under terrible stress, he came up with an answer ter Horst hadn't seen.

The dwindling still-aggressive part of ter Horst knew it too. Anger rose in ter Horst's eyes, driven by embarrassment and jealousy.

Van Gelder felt deep regret, but he knew what he had to do and he couldn't stop now. If survival meant indirectly humiliating his own commanding officer on the record, so be it. If they lived, and later in retribution ter Horst ruined Van Gelder's career, the sacrifice was needed to save the ship.

"Captain, you're tired," Van Gelder said gently, to preempt any irrevocable outburst from the man. "Sir," he added more firmly, "let me take the conn for just a while."

Minutes later, on *Challenger*

"How are they coming in the torpedo room?" Jeffrey asked.

Bell palmed the intercom mike and called. He spoke to the weapons officer. Bell held the mike and turned to Jeffrey.

"It's touch and go, Captain. At least we haven't had an explosion or fire down there yet."

"Tell them to hurry up. Our lives depend on it."

"Captain," Kathy called out, "we've lost passive sonar contact with *Voortrekker*."

On *Voortrekker*

Van Gelder had the conn. He'd ordered the helmsman to slow down suddenly, but continue on course. This ought to make *Voortrekker* drop off *Challenger*'s passive sonar screens, and lure Jeffrey Fuller into closing the range.

Next to Van Gelder, ter Horst sat, outwardly quiet but watching and listening.

Van Gelder dreaded what ter Horst might do next: The man alternated between seething rage and anguishing self-pity. Nothing prevented him from taking back the conn and acting impulsively. Van Gelder had no objective grounds on which to officially relieve his captain of command—intuitions on someone's moods, and intangible looks in eyes and reading of faces, wouldn't stand up under any court-martial's scrutiny. But Van Gelder didn't trust ter Horst to have the iron will and unerring sense of timing needed to destroy *Challenger* and yet escape the H-bomb blasts. Van Gelder trusted only himself.

It was a weird and sad business for Van Gelder to see his captain so reduced. Ter Horst's ego lay stripped to its underlying childishness. His former tactical IQ was mostly dysfunctional now, ironically crushed between the hammer of Fuller's greater skill and creativity—and the anvil of Van Gelder's own.

"Messenger of the Watch!" Van Gelder snapped.

"Sir?"

"Have the Kampfschwimmer leader come to the control room."

Commander Bauer appeared a minute later. He seemed surprised to find Van Gelder in evident charge. Bauer glanced at ter Horst and was startled by what he saw, but the German immediately covered up any reaction. Bauer turned his attention to Van Gelder and conducted himself professionally.

"You requested my presence, First Officer?"

"Your two surviving dialysis divers, they're able to make another sortie?"

"Of course."

"And you carry high explosives? Demolition charges, for underwater use?"

"Yes, we have materials for blasting and cutting."

"Load what you need into the minisub, smartly." Van Gelder told Bauer what had to happen.

"I'll go myself," Bauer said, "to make sure things are done properly, especially the last part." Bauer shook Van Gelder's hand good-bye.

50

On *Challenger*

"STILL NO PASSIVE sonar contact, Captain," Kathy reported. "Assess loss of contact is not due to change in sound propagation conditions. Conjecture contact has reduced speed and is evading."

"Go active, sir?" Bell prompted.

Jeffrey thought this over. "No. I did that once before."

"Trail him on nonacoustic sensors?" Ilse suggested.

Jeffrey worked his jaw back and forth. He knew there was consternation all around him in the control room, that now of all times they'd lost their target. But Jeffrey wouldn't let his people's worries annoy or distract him. The chess match with the enemy had reached the endgame phase, and Jeffrey was fully engaged.

Bell opened his mouth to say something, but Jeffrey waved a hand to cut him off. Whoever was making the calls on *Voortrekker,* something didn't add up. *Voortrekker* must be sneaking to the side, to lay another ambush. Ter Horst might well gain twisted satisfaction in sinking *Challenger*—in winning this duel dramatically—even if *Voortrekker* herself were then destroyed by an outside force, the H-bombs. That seemed more in character than ter Horst going for a self-immolating mutual kill from sheer orneriness.

Jeffrey began to debate with himself whether *Voortrekker* would use nuclear or high-explosive weapons now, whatever ter Horst's or Van Gelder's motivations.

Then he had a better idea. "I think I know where they are. They're where we'd least expect them to be, dead ahead, to the south. They probably stopped completely the moment they slowed to break our sonar contact. . . . Fire Control, we'll do what they least expect *us* to do. Reload all tubes with conventional ADCAP units. Helm, maintain course and speed."

Jeffrey intended to get in very close. Quickly, *Challenger* closed the range to *Voortrekker*'s last known datum.

Jeffrey measured the minutes that passed by what remained on the big red timer. He didn't think beyond that deadline, and to him nothing else mattered. *Challenger* was a machine, and the crew were cogs in that machine. Jeffrey would use them all as tools with equal, heartless dispassion. Jeffrey needed to keep up the pressure on *Voortrekker*, and stay in ter Horst's face, to win the final melee. Hanging back was a losing proposition.

Jeffrey realized *Voortrekker* held one terrible advantage—the Boer ship could merely go dormant and run down the clock, since they had nothing more to lose. Maybe *Voortrekker* wasn't lurking dead ahead. Maybe she hadn't turned to the side and doubled back to lay an ambush, either. Maybe she'd snuck off somewhere to hibernate, leaving Jeffrey to chase his own tail in ultimate frustration—while ter Horst's pyrrhic victory was to have the last laugh on his foe.

"Passive contact on the bow sphere!" Kathy called out. "Weak but good contact on *Voortrekker*, bearing one eight zero!"

Jeffrey sat up straighter. Exactly where he'd expected all along, to the south. *Challenger*'s relentless dead-on approach found *Voortrekker* in her place of concealment. Jeffrey nodded to himself. *This* was where ter Horst and Van Gelder had hoped to lay their ambush, while Jeffrey passed to either flank, looking for them somewhere else.

"Captain," Bell said, "we have an adequate firing solution. Advise target is too close to own ship for safe use of atomic warheads."

Also exactly as Jeffrey expected, and intended. If it was too close for Jeffrey, it was also too close for *Voortrekker*, without them taking fatal self-damage. Jeffrey knew he was gambling on the enemy's drive to outlive him, if just for a while, gambling on their instinct to put off their own deaths to the last. Jeffrey told himself this was the right time and place for a gamble, and to him the odds looked good. Besides, the gamble was necessary.

"Maintain course and speed."

It's now or never. If Voortrekker *can hit back at me badly enough, the whole show's over.*

Jeffrey gave firing orders. "Match sonar bearings, and *shoot.*"

One after another, four ADCAPs leapt into the water and dashed at *Voortrekker*. Jeffrey instantly told Bell to reload tubes one and three with more ADCAPs.

Voortrekker tried to return the fire, but her sonar or other systems must have been damaged in the earlier nuclear skirmish under the ice. The weapons she launched, also high-explosive warheads—Series 65s— rushed through the sea in the wrong directions. The wires to Jeffrey's ADCAPs broke.

Torpedoes began to detonate. The effects were gentler than last time, with yields measured in hundreds of pounds of TNT instead of hundreds of tons. Even so, the noise and buffeting were vicious. Crewmen and consoles jostled and shook. Each blast was like a *whang* or a *vroom* that hit sharply, then echoed from everywhere. The control room felt like a house caught in a cluster of earthquake tremors: sudden, scary vibrations came through the deck, and any objects hung or suspended swayed to and fro, out of synch. As much as Jeffrey had expected all this, the powerful sensory overload was something he never could get used to.

Kathy and Ilse struggled to clean up the signals and make sense of what was happening. They relayed their data to Bell.

"Hits on *Voortrekker!*" Bell shouted. "Definite hits on *Voortrekker!*"

"Sounds of emergency main ballast blow!" Kathy yelled. "Heavy flooding sounds on *Voortrekker!*"

Jeffrey listened to the sounds on the sonar speakers. They were atrociously unsettling, and grated on his nerves. He knew a submarine never died gracefully.

So it wasn't a fast-paced final running shoot-out after all. It was more a wearing-down in stages, of material damage to vessels and of emotional damage to crews, and we won it by a nose. In the end, both ships stood their ground and fired one salvo, and Voortrekker's *missed.*

Still, something deep in Jeffrey wasn't satisfied.

"Launch an off-board probe," he ordered. "I want to make perfectly sure."

Ten minutes later

Jeffrey stared at the imagery from his probe. "I think it's a trick. That's only their wrecked minisub." Jeffrey handed control of the probe to COB. Jeffrey shivered when the probe showed a limbless torso float by. But COB found no other wreckage.

Bell grimaced. "That's the same decoy strategy we just pulled!" *Voortrekker* was still alive somewhere.

Jeffrey's adrenaline poured on the coals, and his heart began to race. Any moment Kathy would call more torpedoes in the water, and Jeffrey was sure the new 65s wouldn't miss. But the faster Jeffrey fled the scene, the more he'd be sonar blind and the more fire-control data he'd give to *Voortrekker.*

Face it, buddy, you walked right into the pit trap, congratulating yourself along the way. It hurts now, doesn't it?

It was unbearable to sit there feeling so exposed. The enemy could be anywhere, and it could be fatal if Jeffrey sat still but fatal sooner if he ran.

I'm fully committed. Press on.

Jeffrey told Kathy to ping. The bow sphere emitted an eardrum-taxing screech. The sonarmen made out nothing like a moving submarine.

"What's *that?*" COB asked as he piloted the probe, still searching for clues.

"What?" Jeffrey said. "Where?"

"Sir," Ilse interrupted. "I'm getting something on chemo-sensors."

"Peroxide fuel from their minisub?"

"No. This reads like diesel oil."

"From her emergency diesel engine," Bell said. "That proves nothing, Captain. They could have pumped some overboard to fool us."

"I *do* see something," COB said.

"Put it on main screen," Jeffrey ordered.

There was a big dark shape in the gloom, barely picked up by the active cameras on the probe.

Bell's intercom light blinked. He answered; it was the torpedo room. "Captain, those modified ADCAPs are as ready as they'll ever be."

"Load them in tubes five and seven."

Bell acknowledged.

Jeffrey studied COB's imagery. "Chief of the Watch, send the probe in closer. Raise laser line-scan power to maximum."

The big dark shape was *Voortrekker*, the real *Voortrekker*, with over a hundred men confined inside. Jeffrey's initial reaction was not to rejoice, but to feel a sharp pain in his gut. It was impossible for him to see an undersea warship mortally wounded without on some level sharing her distress. Jeffrey felt a flash of anxiety and awkwardness at the sight, even though the vessel and her crew were enemy.

Voortrekker had come to rest at a very steep angle, with her stern down in the bottom muck and her bow against the underside of the shelf. A black cloud billowed near her middle, like squid ink. It floated up and pooled under the ice. *Diesel oil.*

On the sonar speakers, Jeffrey heard a steady roar: seawater flooding a submarine's punctured hull. As he watched and listened, there were more roaring and gurgling sounds. *Voortrekker*'s bow lost the last of its positive buoyancy, and the hulk settled on the bottom with a grinding thud.

Simultaneously, on *Voortrekker*

The control room was intensely quiet. Van Gelder thought it remarkable—and not in a nice way—to be sitting still with the deck so steeply tilted. The front of the compartment was higher than his eye level, and he was glad for the support of his seat back and headrest. Crewmen who had to stand, or sat facing sideways, braced themselves as best they could. Now and then, Van Gelder felt slight motion, and heard gentle grinding from forward—from *above*, really—as bottom currents or lingering blast effects tugged at the ship, while her broken nose pressed up against the bottom of the shelf.

It was dark in the control room, and dank, and cold, and getting colder. Van Gelder was soon able to see his breath in the harsh light cast by battery-powered battle lanterns. Inside his shoes, his toes froze. His hands, exposed, were half-numb lumps of ice. Van Gelder had to fight the urge to stamp his feet to stay warm. He waited, chilled in every way, for reports.

"We're getting laser scattering from a line-scan camera now," the chief of the watch said in an undertone.

"They've sent a probe to check us out," Van Gelder whispered, "the same way we did to them before. They found the wreck of our minisub, and thought it was a trick."

Ter Horst smiled weakly. "It was, Gunther, but thanks to you not the sort of trick they think. That was very clever, to launch your Sixty-fives in the wrong direction on purpose, as if we tried to aim at *Challenger* but missed."

Van Gelder also fired one of his own Series 65s, with its warhead charge cut to a third, at his own minisub, while the mini's sonars emitted a noise signature like the mother ship. This was to emulate the sounds of an ADCAP hitting *Voortrekker*—a critical part of Van Gelder's deception plan.

Now, *Voortrekker* herself played dead in plain sight. Within the hull, with no heat because the reactor was scrammed, it was literally as cold as a crypt. Van Gelder thought the analogy was apt.

Van Gelder was letting Fuller think *Voortrekker*'s minisub decoy failed, and one or more of *Challenger*'s weapons impacted with the real target—which was precisely what Fuller would *want* to believe. The first trick, the obvious one with the mini, was a mental sleight of hand, meant to make this Fuller believe the second trick was *real*.

I killed Bauer and his divers so that Voortrekker *could live. God forgive me, but Fuller did the same to one of his crew.*

Van Gelder saw men near him put their hands under their armpits. Some of them shivered. But their discomfort was unavoidable.

Minutes before, while high-explosive torpedo warheads exploded near and far, Van Gelder had put his plan in full effect. He'd blown the stern main ballast tanks with noisy hydrazine, to make sure *Challenger* heard, and blew the bow tanks using compressed air. This was to make it seem as if *Voortrekker* had tried to save herself, by a reflexive crew response that was useless here—deep under the ice shelf, an emergency blow did no good. Van Gelder quickly vented the stern tanks, to imitate the sound of air escaping a broken hull; he permitted enough seawater to refill the tanks from below to make *Voortrekker*'s stern sink to the bottom. With her forward ballast tanks remaining blown, the ship stayed light at the bow.

Van Gelder sent steady flooding noises, invented by *Voortrekker*'s signal processors, through the active wide arrays. He scrammed the reactor for quieting, after rigging the ship for reduced electrical, getting by on the battery banks alone. As the last warheads detonated, by remote control he'd fired the charges planted by Bauer's divers—for the visual effect.

"Increasing laser line-scan strength," the chief of the watch reported. "Enemy probe moving closer."

Again, Van Gelder waited. As unobtrusively as he could, he rubbed his hands slowly back and forth along his thighs. The warmth of the friction, the movement, helped restore some circulation. He was afraid that when he needed to work his keyboard or his touch screens, his achingly icy fingers wouldn't respond.

"Probe still moving closer, sir."

"*Now*, Gunther," ter Horst whispered. "Let them think we're going down by progressive flooding. We'll fool them better if it happens while they witness it, so they see what they desire to see."

Van Gelder shivered, in a different manner. The eerie way ter Horst's breath condensed in the cold as he spoke, the odd way stray shafts of light from the battle lanterns played across ter Horst's conflicted face, and the splashes of red from the console displays, made Van Gelder think his captain looked like a vampire.

But ter Horst was right. It was time. Van Gelder cleared his throat. "Chief of the Watch, vent all forward ballast tanks."

"No, Gunther, don't vent them. They'll spot the bubbles with the probe, and know we're still under control. Bring the air back into the ship." Ter Horst sounded subdued and spoke more slowly than usual, as if he were slightly dazed or depressed and couldn't shake it off. The effect on Van Gelder was very disturbing.

Van Gelder gave the order. His eardrums hurt as the internal air pressure rose. *Voortrekker*, with negative buoyancy now, began to subside toward an even keel, as her bow fell to the sea floor. It hit with a satisfying crash.

On *Challenger*

"Look at that, Captain," Bell said as he examined the probe picture of *Voortrekker* on the bottom. "Her whole bow's been blown off. The sonar dome is gone. The bow sphere is completely gone."

"You're right," Jeffrey said. "We really hit her good."

"Should I launch the modified torpedoes now?" Bell glanced nervously at the red countdown timer. There was little more than an hour until the hydrogen bombs would drop.

"Not yet. I want to make absolutely sure."

"Sir," Bell said, "I think she's really sunk. *Look* at her."

Jeffrey shook his head. He was suspicious. *Voortrekker* should have put up a much harder fight.

Unless . . . Unless there was a *reason* they didn't put up a harder fight.

On *Voortrekker*

Now *Voortrekker* sat on the bottom, down slightly at the bow and listing a few degrees to starboard. The control room continued growing colder, as the whole ship was chilled by the polar seas in which she was immersed. Though the bow sphere was gone, *Voortrekker* still had some forward coverage from sonars on the conning tower.

"The enemy probe is coming closer again," the chief of the watch reported quietly.

"Four port-side torpedo tubes still functional," the weapons officer said. In nuclear submarines, the tubes were aft of the sonar bow sphere, and tilted outward from the torpedo room—so weapons would clear the sphere, which was outside the main pressure hull.

"Use tubes two and four," ter Horst mumbled. "There'll be less mud, higher, higher up the hull."

Van Gelder nodded. "I intend to fire as soon as we get a good launch transient from *Challenger*." *Voortrekker*'s hull arrays were all in working order.

"Two torpedoes in the water," the sonar chief said. "ADCAP engine sounds." The report electrified everyone in the compartment.

Van Gelder's chest tightened. Very soon he'd know if his whole intricate plan would succeed or fail. If he did fool Fuller, and then sank *Challenger*, and the hydrogen bombs didn't fall, *Voortrekker* would limp back to South Africa, steaming the whole distance in reverse.

Everything depended on what these two ADCAPs did. Would they rush for the edge of the ice shelf, almost a hundred miles away, with a message saying Fuller had triumphed? Or would they rush at *Voortrekker*, to finish her once and for all, if Fuller had pierced every veil of Van Gelder's ploy?

Van Gelder waited, impatient yet dreading to know what the ADCAPs did. He prayed they headed due north.

"Enemy torpedoes are inbound!" the sonar chief screamed.

Van Gelder's heart sank. He thought of how best to defend his ship, of how to fight back. His mind flashed to all the awful things he'd helped do in this war, out of a misguided sense of patriotism and honor. He thought again of ter Horst's vision, of hundreds of manmade suns shining harshly on Antarctica. Those suns might set the world on fire.

"*Challenger* has gone to flank speed!"

Van Gelder battled with himself. Antitorpedo rockets? Series 65s? Atomic Sea Lions? Which should he use? What did it matter?

The tragedy of my life was to be a good man on the wrong side. I'll never know if Fuller's trick to get out an all clear works. But soon I'll know if I'm bound for heaven or hell.

"*Challenger* withdrawing! *Challenger* is moving behind our stern!"

If I shoot at Challenger, *I might or might not sink her. Even if I do sink* Challenger, *then Fuller won't get off his other ADCAPs, the special ones, and the shelf will be nuked for sure.*

"Signal fading," the sonar chief shouted. "*Challenger*'s signal now lost in our baffles!"

But the inbound torpedo engine sounds were very loud and close.

In the final clash of wills, Jeffrey Fuller came up with the winning ploy. He shattered my equilibrium with these two ADCAPs. Then he used my own hesitation, and my ship's inability to maneuver, against me. Now I don't know where he is, and I'm sure he'll launch more ADCAPs back there in my blind spot, where my antitorpedo rockets are useless.

"What are you planning next, Gunther?" ter Horst asked. There was such dependency and trust behind the question, it almost broke Van Gelder's heart.

There was only one choice left. A series of nuclear snap shots, around behind the stern—wild shots under the best of circumstances. In such obstructed terrain, with no towed array deployed, even that tactic would probably fail—and Jeffrey Fuller had to know it.

What does duty mean here? Which orders are legal or illegal now? Van Gelder decided not to shoot, to try to save Antarctica and maybe save the world. This meant far more than any chance of taking Fuller with him. . . . Van Gelder closed his eyes. He pictured the natural, warm, embracing sun of his homeland far away, remembering wistfully the final time he basked at the Durban beach resort before this terrible war.

On *Challenger*

Jeffrey fired two more ADCAPs at *Voortrekker*'s stationary bottomed hull from behind the target's stern. He watched the live data feed through the weapon-guidance wires, and listened on the sonar speakers. His first two ADCAPs, their wires now snapped, continued to home on *Voortrekker* from off her bow—*Challenger's* bow sphere could hear them pinging.

At Jeffrey's orders, Bell also had two atomic Mark 88s poised in torpedo tubes one and three, armed and ready to fire just in case.

Both of Jeffrey's first two ADCAPs hit *Voortrekker* as she sat there, one forward and one aft of her reactor compartment. Jeffrey's second pair ran straight up *Voortrekker's* baffles, then struck against her sides.

The blasts were small but powerful. Above their aftershocks, Kathy reported heavy flooding noise. Here in the blind spot of *Voortrekker's* active wide-aperture arrays, the flooding sounds had to be real. The enemy's genuine death throes went on and on, crunching and cracking and thudding and groaning as bulkheads and internal equipment gave way.

So Voortrekker was playing possum after all. If I'd believed what ter Horst and Van Gelder wanted me to believe, and not fired at their ship, my all clear message would be on its way—and well-aimed Sea Lions fired in ambush could be punching through my hull. That's how close a thing it really was.

I'll never know why they didn't use antitorpedo rockets against my first two ADCAPs at least, or Sea Lions at the last moment. Were they out of the right type of ammo? Were their tubes all hampered by wreckage or mud?

"Captain," Bell said. "We *must* launch the modified ADCAPs."

Bell's right. The game isn't over yet, by a long shot.

"Tube five, shoot. Tube seven, shoot."

"Both units operating properly," Kathy reported.

"Now we wait."

Challenger was in much too deep to ever get out from under the shelf in time. And with the terrible sonar conditions, from where *Challenger* was she had no way to send a signal that *Voortrekker* was destroyed.

Taking account of this from the beginning, Jeffrey had ordered Bell to alter two ADCAPs, removing their large explosive charges to put in extra fuel tanks instead, cannibalized from other weapons. With their onboard sonars programmed to ping the all clear code that Wilson and Jeffrey arranged in advance, the ice shelf might be saved.

The weapons ran at seventy knots, and with double their normal fuel load they ought to run for an hour. Preset to avoid instead of home on any targets, they were so small and maneuverable that they could rush out toward the shelf edge past obstructions that would hold *Challenger* to a crawl: their onboard sonar would help them avoid the worst ice ridges and boulders, once they outran their fiber-optic guidance wires.

The big remaining question was, would these jury-rigged messengers work, and in time? Would their hastily modified fuel systems keep running? Would their coded pings, as they neared the ice-shelf edge, be picked up by friendly forces or sonobuoys soon enough? Or would both ADCAPs break down, or crash into an ice slab or a rock? Would that new giant iceberg Ilse heard calving off the outer shelf get in the way and ruin everything?

Once submarine-launched ballistic missiles took off, they could not be recalled. There was no way to deactivate the fusion warheads, no missile shield positioned down here in Antarctica.

Around Jeffrey in the control room, people fidgeted or sweated or prayed. As Jeffrey waited, he began to understand how the enemy submarine crews he'd killed in this war must have felt in their final moments. Wondering if some tactic to save themselves would work or if they'd die. Knowing they'd exhausted every alternative and there was nothing more they could do. Thinking of their loved ones, or of God, or raging at their fate. It was more horrible to go through this than Jeffrey had ever imagined.

Jeffrey thought again of his crew, his courageous and loyal crew. He grabbed the mike for the 1MC, the shipwide public-address system. The 1MC was noisy, and hadn't been used in more than two weeks, but this way everyone would hear Jeffrey's voice directly.

"This is the captain. Remain at your posts but secure from battle stations. Secure from ultraquiet."

It seemed such a small gesture, but at least like this they could stand down from full alert, and make their final preparations in whatever private manner each of them might choose.

Eventually the ADCAP guidance wires snapped. The messenger torpedoes were on their own. There was no way to tell their status. There was no way for the crew to hear, if and when they transmitted.

The red timer counted down to the final minute. The remaining sixty seconds ticked away. No one spoke. People hardly dared to move or breathe. Jeffrey wondered if he'd feel much pain.

Finally the timer read 00:00:00. Jeffrey waited for the end. Nothing happened.

Epilogue

Fifteen days later

**Bachelor Officers Quarters,
Naval Submarine Base, New London, Connecticut**

CHALLENGER HAD JUST returned to her home port. Now she was back in dry dock, in the hardened underground pens across the river from the base, and most of her crew were on leave. It was after midnight, and very cold outside, and Jeffrey sat at his desk in his steam-heated room. On the desk, beside his glowing laptop and a battery-operated reading light, loomed many files and diskettes, the relentless burden of paperwork from his job as captain of a U.S. Navy warship. Also on his desk was a land-line phone.

Jeffrey was torn. He looked again at the phone, then once more opened a document on his computer. The document was a request form that a member of his crew be transferred off the ship. He'd already filled in the name—Ilse Reebeck—but that was all. He had trouble knowing how to say things in the proper light, to not hurt her professionally, or hurt himself. Jan ter Horst was dead, and Jeffrey had no idea what *Challenger*'s next mission orders would say. As good as Ilse's work might be, was this lull the proper time for final closure with her too?

Jeffrey hesitated, hands poised over the keyboard. The words just wouldn't come. Jeffrey asked himself again why he was doing this. He did feel guilty, that Ilse's continuing presence on the ship might become a distraction to him—she was, after all, besides everything else his ex-girlfriend. But none of that was Ilse's fault. *Am I being vindictive, rejecting her because she rejected me? Is overtiredness making me impulsive, or downright silly?* Jeffrey closed the document, but saved it.

His mind turned to his other problem: the phone. For about the tenth time that evening, he considered calling his dad. Jeffrey told himself it was very late, too late to call until tomorrow. And tomorrow, his father would be at work, and he might be in meetings all day.

Then Jeffrey told himself his father was a night owl, which was probably where Jeffrey got that trait. Then he told himself that, if his mom was home from the hospital, she'd need her rest, and it would be bad to disturb them after midnight. Then he told himself his dad was a practical man, and if his mother was asleep he'd turn off the phone, and Jeffrey would just get their voice mail. Jeffrey wasn't sure he wanted to leave a voice mail.

Jeffrey reached for the phone, hesitated again, picked it up, and put it down. His heart pounded. He wanted so desperately to speak to his dad. Jeffrey was feeling the blues, that loneliness mixed with edgy boredom that always crept up on him after the immediate pressures and passions of combat died down. He wanted to start where he'd left off with his father, that morning at the Pentagon. He wanted to tell his dad how much he'd thought about that conversation, how much he'd learned about himself and war since then. And he simply wanted to touch base with his family.

Jeffrey had already written the letters to the parents of his crewmen who'd been killed. It was the hardest thing he'd ever had to do, especially the ones for Harrison—since his parents were divorced, Jeffrey had to write *two* letters. But Jeffrey did it, all of it, in longhand using a pen until his hand cramped. He'd tried to sincerely share and ease the pain of the living, those who had to carry on after their loved ones were gone, their sons or husbands or fathers lost forever.

Jeffrey chided himself that after such a grim task, calling his own dad to say hello ought to be easy. But Jeffrey feared rejection, badly. Some of the things his father had said last time, about war and Jeffrey's career choice, were bitter, and hurtful because they were true. It might be too late now to make amends.

Jeffrey grabbed the phone and dialed his father's home number. As the phone began to ring, his chest grew tight once more with nervousness.

"Hello?"

Jeffrey had to clear his throat. "Dad, it's Jeffrey." He waited in abject fear for his father's response.

"Jeffrey! Where are you? . . . Can you say?"

"Do you have a secure line there, Dad?"

"Privilege of office, son. I was promoted again last week. Wait." Jeffrey heard a tone. "Okay, I'm secure at this end."

Jeffrey pressed a button on his phone, and there was a beep. "I'm secure. . . . I'm in New London, at the base."

"I heard things went very well."

"I can't talk specifics, Dad. I don't think you have the clearance." But Jeffrey was tremendously relieved—his father was glad to hear from him.

"Yeah, well, half our problem is Washington's as leaky as a sieve. I've been hearing stories about you. Besides, haven't you seen the papers?" Physical newspapers were harder to fake or hack or alter than on-line websites, so papers were preferred for news of how the war and the economy were doing.

"No. I literally just got back. I've barely had time to catch my breath."

"You're a hero, son. They decided to let out the news about you sinking *Voortrekker*. It's on all the front pages, nationwide. I'm hearing rumors from my contacts down here that they're going to give you the Medal of Honor."

"That's probably just twisted, Dad. The medal's for one of my crew.

He deserves it, not me. . . . I set off atom bombs in Antarctica. I'm not any kind of hero."

"No, son. What I heard is the Medal's for *you*. And I also heard, though I won't say more over this line, that you prevented something worse down there than anything *you* did. Something much, *much* worse, if you know what I mean."

"I can't comment on that, Dad." Jeffrey was shocked. His father was right—even in wartime, the Washington leaks and competitive social grapevine seemed to overweigh vital secrecy.

"So don't comment, son. Just listen. The way this war's been going, the country really needs heroes, and you're *it*. Congress has to approve the Medal. They will. They're doing it for themselves, for the photo ops and to make their voters feel good, a lot more than they're doing it for you. That's how Washington works. I've been here long enough to see."

"I guess you have."

"That doesn't mean you don't deserve it. You do. That little ribbon on your uniform, the blue thing with the tiny white stars, is gonna be very career enhancing, son."

"But—"

"Just take it, Jeffrey. Accept it. Don't make waves, and *don't* be an ass. For God's sake, admirals will have to salute *you* now, once the thing comes through."

Jeffrey nodded, then realized his father couldn't see him over the phone. It all began to sink in. Jeffrey had been so busy simply trying to survive, hour by hour and minute by minute with *Voortrekker* under the ice shelf. After that, he'd been much too drained to think about the bigger picture—just as Commodore Wilson, still his boss, had lectured him before. Now Jeffrey, through his father's prodding, at last understood the wider implications of his own success, of the fact that he *had* survived, and prevailed, and met that fearsome twenty-four-hour deadline.

Still, Jeffrey was embarrassed just to *think* of getting so much attention. Photo ops with politicians were not his idea of fun. He changed the subject. "How's Mom?"

"Good, Jeffrey. Great. The spots they saw on her liver on the scan last time? They decided they were benign. She's already had the radiation therapy, and they're doing chemo now. She's back at Sloan-Kettering for a few days. The way they do it, the dose is some kind of cocktail that's targeted at the cancer cells, and it's just one big treatment, by IV. You feel like hell for a week or two, but it's over so fast you hardly lose much of your hair."

"That's good, Dad. Real good." Jeffrey had to hold the phone away, as he felt a different sort of relief. An immense burden lifted. Tears came to his eyes, tears of gladness.

"Hello?" his father said. "You still there?"

Jeffrey needed to clear his throat again. He had an idea. "Dad, I was hoping we could try to get together soon. Maybe we can both of us take the train, and meet halfway in New York, and visit Mom."

"When could you get away?"

"Day after tomorrow."

"I'll clear my schedule. If we meet at the hospital midafternoon, we'll spend visiting hours with your mother, then you and I can do some celebrating. Dinner in a restaurant."

"That would be terrific, Dad."

Jeffrey's father chuckled. "Don't expect filet mignon. Mind you, there's a war on. But we'll find someplace good."

"It's set, then?"

"Yup. I'm looking forward to it, Jeffrey. Your mother will be really happy to see you. We're both very proud of you, son."

They hung up.

Jeffrey sighed. He still had all that paperwork. He reopened the form about Ilse's transfer. He struggled. Was he being selfish, or weak, wanting to get rid of her? The navy had plenty of other oceanographers who could hold their own in submarine combat, who were U.S. citizens and male. But was Jeffrey being prejudiced, or sexist? He'd been *ordered* to take Ilse into his crew. Was he being insubordinate to disagree and try to undo the arrangement? What did the past between them have to do with the future, anyway? They were both mature adults.

Is my job as captain to be insistent, or to cope?

Jeffrey was so embroiled in battle with himself, he was startled when the radiator stopped hissing. He glanced at his watch. Zero one hundred, 1:00 A.M., on the dot. Jeffrey was startled again by a knock on the door. He closed the document, shut his laptop, and got up.

Standing there in a white silk blouse and nice blue jeans was Ilse. "Um, hi," she said. "I . . . I missed you. Can I come in?"

Glossary

Acoustic intercept: A passive (listening-only) sonar specifically designed to give warning when the submarine is "pinged" by an enemy active sonar. The latest version is the WLY-1.

Active out-of-phase emissions: A way to weaken the echo which an enemy sonar receives from a submarine hull, by actively emitting sound waves of the same frequency as the ping but exactly out of phase. The out-of-phase sound waves mix with and cancel those of the echoing ping.

ADCAP: Mark 48 advanced-capability torpedo. A heavyweight, wire-guided, long-range torpedo used by American nuclear submarines. The Improved ADCAP has even longer range, increased speed, and an enhanced (and extremely capable) target-homing sonar and software logic package.

AIP: air-independent propulsion. Refers to modern diesel submarines that have an additional power source besides the standard diesel engines and electric storage batteries. The AIP system allows quiet and long-endurance submerged cruising, without the need to snorkel for air, because oxygen and fuel are carried aboard the vessel in special tanks. For example, the German class 212 design uses fuel cells (see below) for air-independent propulsion.

Alumina casing: An extremely strong hull material which is less dense than steel, declassified by the U.S. Navy after the Cold War. A multilayered composite foam matrix made from ceramic and metallic ingredients.

Ambient sonar: A form of active sonar that uses, instead of a submarine's pinging, the ambient noise of the surrounding ocean to catch reflections off a target. Noise sources can include surface wave-action sounds, the propulsion plants of other vessels (such as passing neutral merchant shipping), or biologics (sea life). Ambient sonar gives the advantages of actively pinging but without betraying a submarine's own presence. Advanced signal-processing algorithms and powerful onboard computers are needed to exploit ambient sonar effectively.

Antarctic convergence: The area in the Great Southern Ocean (the name given to the sea surrounding Antarctica) where warmer water from more temperate climates first meets the cold water nearer the Antarctic. The result is a zone of dramatically unpredictable weather, and of confusing sonar conditions.

ARCI: Acoustic Rapid COTS Insertion. The latest software system designed for *Virginia*-class fast-attack submarines (see below)—COTS stands for commercial-off-the-shelf. The ARCI system manages sonar, target tracking, weapons, and other data through an onboard fiber-optic local area network (LAN). (The ARCI replaces the older AN/BSY-1 systems of *Los Angeles*–class submarines, and the AN/BSY-2 of the newer *Seawolf*-class fast-attack subs.)

ASDS: Advanced SEAL Delivery System. A new battery-powered minisubmarine for the transport of SEALs (see below) from a parent nuclear submarine to the forward operational area and back, within a warm and dry shirtsleeves environment. This permits the SEALs to go into action well rested and free from hypothermia—real problems when the SEALs must swim great distances, or ride while using scuba gear on older free-flooding SEAL Delivery Vehicle underwater "scooters."

ASW: antisubmarine warfare. The complex task of detecting, localizing, identifying, and tracking enemy submarines, to observe and protect against them in peacetime, and to avoid or destroy them in wartime.

Auxiliary maneuvering units: Small propulsors at the bow and stern of a nuclear submarine, used to greatly enhance the vessel's maneuverability. First ordered for the USS *Jimmy Carter,* the third and last of the *Seawolf*-class SSNs (nuclear fast-attack submarines) to be constructed.

Bipolar sonar: A form of active sonar in which one vessel emits the ping while one or more other vessels listen for target echoes. This helps disguise the total number and location of friendly vessels present.

CACC: command and control center. The modern name for a submarine's control room.

CAPTOR: A type of naval mine, placed on or moored to the seabed. Contains an encapsulated torpedo, which is released to home on the target.

CCD: charge-coupled device. The electronic "eyes" used by low-light-level television, night-vision goggles, etc.

COB: Chief of the Boat. (Pronounced like "cob.") The most senior enlisted man on a submarine, usually a master chief. Responsible for crew discipline, and for proper control of ship buoyancy and trim at battle stations, among many other duties.

Deep scattering layer: A diffuse layer of biologics (marine life) present in many parts of the world's oceans, which causes scattering and absorption of sound. This can have tactical significance to undersea warfare forces, by obscuring passive sonar contacts and causing false active sonar target returns. The layer's local depth, thickness, and scattering strength are known to vary by many factors, including one's location on the globe, the sound frequency being observed, the season of the year, and the hour of the day. The deep scattering layer is typically several hundred feet thick, and lies somewhere between one thousand and two thousand feet of depth during daylight, migrating shallower at night.

Deep sound channel: A thick layer within the deep ocean in which sound travels great distances with little signal loss. The core (axis) of this layer is formed where seawater stops getting colder with increasing depth (the bottom of the thermocline, see below) and water temperature then remains at a constant just above freezing (the bottom isothermal zone, see below). Because of how sound waves diffract (bend) due to the effects of temperature and pressure, noises in the deep sound channel are concentrated there and propagate for many miles without loss to surface scattering or sea-floor absorption. Typically the deep sound channel is strongest between depths of about three thousand and seven thousand feet.

ELF: Extremely Low Frequency. A form of radio which is capable of penetrating several hundred feet of seawater, used to communicate (one-way only) from a huge shore transmitter installation to submerged submarines. A disadvantage of ELF is that its data rate is extremely slow, only a few bits per minute.

EMBT blow: emergency main ballast tank blow. A procedure to quickly introduce large amounts of compressed air (or fumes from burning hydrazine) into the ballast tanks, in order to bring a submerged submarine to the surface as rapidly as possible. If the submarine still has propulsion power, it will also try to drive up to the surface using its control planes (called *planing up*).

EMCON: emissions control. Radio silence, except also applies to radar, sonar, laser, or other emissions that could give away a vessel's presence.

EMP: electromagnetic pulse. A sudden, strong electrical current induced by a nuclear explosion. This will destroy unshielded electrical and electronic equipment and ruin radio reception. There are two forms of EMP, one caused by very-high-altitude nuclear explosions, the other by ones close to the ground. (Midaltitude bursts do not create an EMP.) Nonnuclear EMP devices, a form of modern nonlethal weapon, produce a similar effect locally by vaporizing clusters of tungsten filaments using a high-voltage firing charge. This generates a burst of hard X rays, which are focused by a depleted-uranium reflector to strip electrons from atoms in the targeted area, creating the destructive EMP electrical current.

ESGN: The latest submarine inertial navigation system (see *INS,* below). Replaces the older SINS (ship's inertial navigation system).

Fathom: A measure of water depth equal to six feet. For instance, one hundred fathoms equals six hundred feet.

Firing solution: Exact information (or best estimate) on an enemy target's location, course, and speed, and depth or altitude if applicable. A good firing solution is needed to preprogram the guidance system of a missile or torpedo so that the weapon won't miss a moving target.

Floating wire antenna: A long, buoyant antenna wire which is trailed just below the surface by a submerged submarine, for stealth. Such an antenna can receive data at a higher baud rate than ELF radio (see above). Recently, floating-wire-antenna technology has been developed to the point where the wire is able to transmit as well as receive, allowing two-way radio communication while the submarine is completely submerged. (To transmit or receive radio data at a very high baud rate, such as live video imagery of a target, the submarine must come to periscope depth and raise an antenna mast out of the water, which might compromise stealth.)

Frequency-agile: A means of avoiding enemy interception and jamming by very rapidly varying the frequency used by a transmitter and receiver. May apply to radio or to underwater acoustic communications (see *gertrude,* below).

Frigate: A type of oceangoing warship smaller than a destroyer.

Fuel cell: A system for quietly producing electricity, for example to drive a submarine's main propulsion motors while submerged. Hydrogen and oxygen are combined in a chemical-reaction chamber as the "fuels." The by-products, besides electricity, are water and heat.

Gertrude: underwater telephone. Original systems simply transmitted voice directly with the aid of transducers (active sonar emitters, i.e., underwater loudspeakers), and were notorious for short range and poor intelligibility. Modern undersea acoustic-communication systems translate the message into digital high-frequency active sonar pulses, which can be frequency-agile for security (see above). Data rates well over one thousand bits per second, over ranges up to thirty nautical miles, can be achieved routinely.

Gravimeter: A device which measures the gravity field gradients around a submarine. Using special mathematics, a detailed, three-dimensional map of local sea floor terrain is then displayed in real time on a computer display screen. Gravimeters make no emissions, and their operation cannot be detected by an enemy. Gravimeters cannot detect moving objects, but they are immune to bad sonar conditions.

Halocline: An area of the ocean where salt concentration changes, either horizontally or vertically. Has important effects on sonar propagation and on a submarine's buoyancy.

Hertz (or Hz): cycles per second. Applies to sound frequency, radio frequency, or alternating electrical current (AC).

Hole-in-ocean sonar: A form of passive (listening-only) sonar which detects a target by how it blocks ambient ocean sounds from farther off. In effect, hole-in-ocean sonar uses an enemy submarine's own quieting against it.

Hydrophone: An underwater listening device. In essence a hydrophone is a special microphone placed in the water. The signals received by hydrophones are the raw input to passive (listening-only) sonar systems. Signal-processing computer algorithms then continually analyze this raw data to produce meaningful tactical information—such as a firing solution (see above).

INS: Inertial Navigation System. A system for accurately estimating one's position, based on accelerometers which determine from moment to moment in what direction one has traveled, and at what speed.

Instant ranging: A capability of the new wide-aperture array sonar systems (see below). Because each wide-aperture array is mounted rigidly along one side of the submarine's hull, sophisticated signal processing can be performed to "focus" the hydrophones at different ranges from the ship. The target needs to lie somewhere on the beam of the ship (i.e., to either side) for this to work well.

IR: Infrared. Refers to systems to see in the dark or detect enemy targets by the heat which objects give off or reflect.

ISLMM: improved submarine-launched mobile mine. A new type of mine weapon for American submarines, based on modified Mark 48 torpedoes, and launched through a torpedo tube. Each ISLMM carries two mine warheads which can be dropped separately. The ISLMM's course can be programmed with way points (course changes) so that complex coastal terrain can be navigated by the weapon, and a minefield can be created by several ISLMMs with optimum layout of the warheads.

Isothermal: A layer of ocean in which the temperature is very constant with depth. One example is the bottom isothermal zone, where water temperature is just above freezing, usually beginning a few thousand feet down. Other examples are 1) a surface layer in the tropics after a storm, when wave action has mixed the water to a constant warm temperature, or 2) a surface layer near the Arctic or Antarctic in the winter, when cold air and floating ice have chilled the sea to near-freezing point.

Kampfschwimmer: German navy "frogman" combat swimmers. The equivalent of U.S. Navy SEALs and the Royal Navy's Special Boat Squadron commandos. (In the German language, the word Kampfschwimmer is both singular and plural.)

KT: Kiloton. A measure of power for tactical nuclear weapons. One kiloton equals the explosive force of one thousand tons of TNT.

LIDAR: Light direction and ranging. Like radar, but uses laser beams instead of radio waves. Undersea LIDAR uses blue-green lasers, because that color penetrates seawater to the greatest distance.

Littoral: A shallow or near-shore area of the ocean. Littoral areas present complex sonar conditions because of the bottom and side terrain reflections, and the high level of noise from coastal shipping, oil drilling platforms, land-based heavy industry, and so on.

LMRS: Long-term mine reconnaissance system: A remote-controlled self-propelled probe vehicle, launched from a torpedo tube and operated by the parent submarine. The LMRS is designed to detect and map enemy minefields or other undersea obstructions. The LMRS is equipped with forward and side-scanning sonars and other sensors. Each LMRS is retrievable and reusable.

MAD: Magnetic anomaly detection. A means for detecting an enemy submarine by observing its effect on the always-present magnetic field of the earth. Iron anywhere within the submarine (even if its hull is nonferrous or de-Gaussed) will distort local magnetic-field lines, and this can be picked up by sensitive magnetometers in the MAD equipment. Effective only at fairly short ranges, often used by low-flying maritime patrol aircraft. Some naval mine detonators also use a form of MAD, by waiting to sense the magnetic field of a passing ship or submarine.

Megaton: A measure of power for strategic nuclear weapons. One megaton equals the explosive force of one million tons of TNT. (A megaton also equals one thousand kilotons.)

METOC: Meteorology and Oceanography Command. The part of the U.S. Navy which is responsible for providing weather and oceanographic data, and accompanying tactical assessments and recommendations, to the navy's operating fleets. METOC maintains a network of centers around the world to gather, analyze, interpret, and distribute this information.

Naval Submarine League (NSL): A professional association for submariners and submarine supporters. See their website, www.navalsubleague.com.

NOAA: National Oceanic and Atmospheric Administration. Part of the Department of Commerce, responsible for studying oceanography and weather phenomena.

Ocean Interface Hull Module: Part of a submarine's hull that includes large internal "hangar space" for weapons and off-board vehicles, to avoid size limits forced by torpedo-tube diameter. (To carry large objects such as an ASDS minisub externally creates serious hydrodynamic drag, reducing a submarine's speed and increasing its flow noise.) The first ocean interface has been ordered as part of the design of the USS *Jimmy Carter,* the last of the three *Seawolf*-class SSNs to be constructed.

PAL: Permissive action link. Procedures and devices used to prevent the unauthorized use of nuclear weapons.

Photonics Mast: The modern replacement for the traditional optical periscope. The first will be installed in the USS *Virginia* (see below). The photonics mast uses electronic imaging sensors, sends the data via thin electrical or fiber-optic cables, and displays the output on large high-definition TV screens in the control room. The photonics mast is "non-hull-penetrating," an important advantage over older scopes with their long, straight, thick tubes which must be able to move up and down and rotate.

Piezo-rubber: A hull coating which uses rubber embedded with materials that expand and contract in response to varying electrical currents. This permits piezo-rubber tiles to be used to help suppress both a submarine's self-noise and echoes from enemy active sonar (see active out-of-phase emissions, above).

Pump-jet: A main propulsor for nuclear submarines which replaces the traditional screw propeller. A pump-jet is a system of stator and rotor turbine blades within a cowling. (The rotors are turned by the main propulsion shaft, the same way the screw propeller's shaft would be turned.) Good pump-jet designs are quieter and more efficient than screw propellers, producing less cavitation noise and less wake turbulence.

Radiac: Radiation indications and control. A device for measuring radioactivity, such as a Geiger counter. There are several kinds of radiac, depending on whether alpha, beta, or gamma radiation, or a combination, is being measured.

ROEs: Rules of engagement. Formal procedures and conditions for determining exactly when weapons (including "special weapons" such as nuclear devices) may be fired at an enemy.

SEAL: Sea, air, land. U.S. Navy Special Warfare commandos. (The equivalent in the Royal Navy is the SBS, Special Boat Squadron.)

7MC: A dedicated intercom line to the maneuvering department, where a nuclear submarine's speed is controlled by a combination of reactor control rod and main stream throttle settings.

Sonobuoy: A small active ("pinging") or passive (listening-only) sonar detector, usually dropped in patterns (clusters) from an airplane or a helicopter. The sonobuoys transmit their data to the aircraft by a radio link. The aircraft might have onboard equipment to analyze this data, or it might relay the data to a surface warship for detailed analysis. (The aircraft will also carry torpedoes or depth charges, to be able to attack any enemy submarines which its sonobuoys detect.) Some types of sonobuoy are able to operate down to a depth of sixteen thousand feet.

SOSUS: Sound Surveillance System. The network of undersea hydrophone complexes installed by the U.S. Navy and used during the Cold War to monitor Soviet submarine movements (among other things). Now SOSUS refers generically to fixed-installation hydrophone lines used to monitor activities on and under the sea. The Advanced Deployable System (ADS) is one example: disposable modularized listening gear designed for rapid emplacement in a forward operating area. After the Cold War, some SOSUS data has been declassified, proving of immense value for oceanographic and environmental research.

Thermocline: The region of the sea in which temperature gradually declines with depth. Typically the thermocline begins at a few hundred feet and extends down to a few thousand feet, where the bottom isothermal zone starts (see above).

TMA: Target motion analysis. The use of data on an enemy vessel's position over time relative to one's own ship, in order to derive a complete firing solution (see above). TMA by passive sonar alone, using only relative bearings to the target over time—and instant ranging data where available (see above)—is very important in undersea warfare.

Towed array: A long cable equipped with hydrophones (see above), trailed behind a submarine. Towed arrays can also be used by surface warships. The towed array has two advantages: Because it lies behind the submarine's stern, aft of self-noise from the propulsion plant, the towed array is able to listen in directions where the submarine's on-hull sonars are "blind." Also, because the towed array is very long (possibly as lengthy as a mile), it is able to detect very long wavelength (very low frequency) sounds—which smaller, on-hull hydrophone arrays may miss completely. Recently, *active* towed arrays have been introduced. These are able to "ping" as well as listen at very low frequencies, which has significant tactical advantages in some sonar and terrain conditions. (When not in use, the towed array is retracted by winches in the submarine's hull. Towed arrays often need to be retracted if the submarine is in close proximity to bottom terrain or surface shipping, or if the submarine intends to move at high speed.)

Virginia-class: The latest class of nuclear-propelled fast-attack submarines (SSNs) being constructed for the United States Navy, to follow the *Seawolf* class. The first, the USS *Virginia*, is due to be commissioned in 2004. (Post–Cold War, some SSNs have been named for states, since construction of *Ohio*-class Trident missile "boomers" has been halted.)

Wide-aperture array: A sonar system introduced with the USS *Seawolf* in the mid-1990s, distinct from and in addition to the bow sphere, towed arrays, and forward hull array of the Cold War's *Los Angeles*–class SSNs. Each submarine so equipped actually has two wide-aperture arrays, one along each side of the hull. Each array consists of three separate rectangular hydrophone complexes. Powerful signal-processing algorithms allow sophisticated analysis of incoming passive sonar data. This includes instant ranging (see above).